MACBETH

ILLUSTRATED BY
ROBERT DEAS

Amulet Books, New York

PUBLISHER'S NOTE: This is a work of fiction. Names, characters, places, and incidents are either the product of the author's imagination or are used fictitiously, and any resemblance to actual persons, living or dead, business establishments, events, or locales is entirely coincidental.

Library of Congress Cataloging-in-Publication Data

Appignanesi, Richard.
Macbeth / by William Shakespeare ; adapted by Richard Appignanesi ; illustrated by Robert Deas.
p. cm. — (Manga Shakespeare)
Summary: Retells, in comic book format, Shakespeare's play about a man who kills his king after hearing the prophesies of three witches.
ISBN 978-0-8109-7073-1
1. Graphic novels. [1. Graphic novels. 2. Shakespeare, William, 1564-1616—Adaptations.] I. Deas, Robert, ill. II. Shakespeare, William, 1564-1616. Macbeth. III. Title.

PZ7.7.A94Mac 2008
741.5'973—dc22
2008018765

Originally published in the U.K. by SelfMadeHero
(www.selfmadehero.com)

Illustrator: Robert Deas
Text Adaptor: Richard Appignanesi
Designer: Andy Huckle
Textual Consultant: Nick de Somogyi
Originating Publisher: Emma Hayley

Printed and bound in China
10 9 8 7 6 5 4 3 2

Amulet Books are available at special discounts when purchased in quantity for premiums and promotions as well as fundraising or educational use. Special editions can also be created to specification. For details, contact specialmarkets@abramsbooks.com or the address below.

ABRAMS
THE ART OF BOOKS SINCE 1949
115 West 18th Street
New York, NY 10011
www.abramsbooks.com

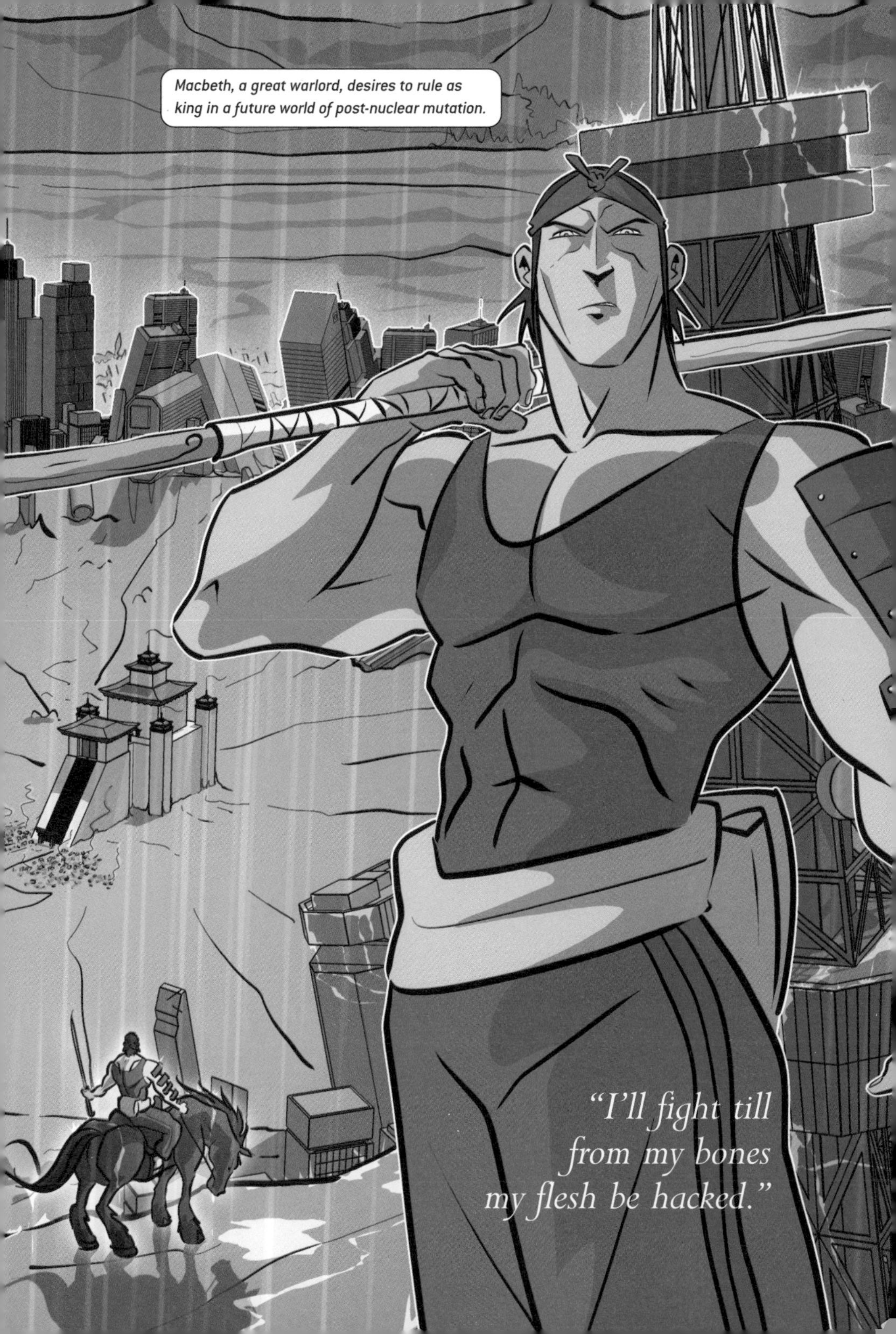
Macbeth, a great warlord, desires to rule as king in a future world of post-nuclear mutation.
"I'll fight till from my bones my flesh be hacked."

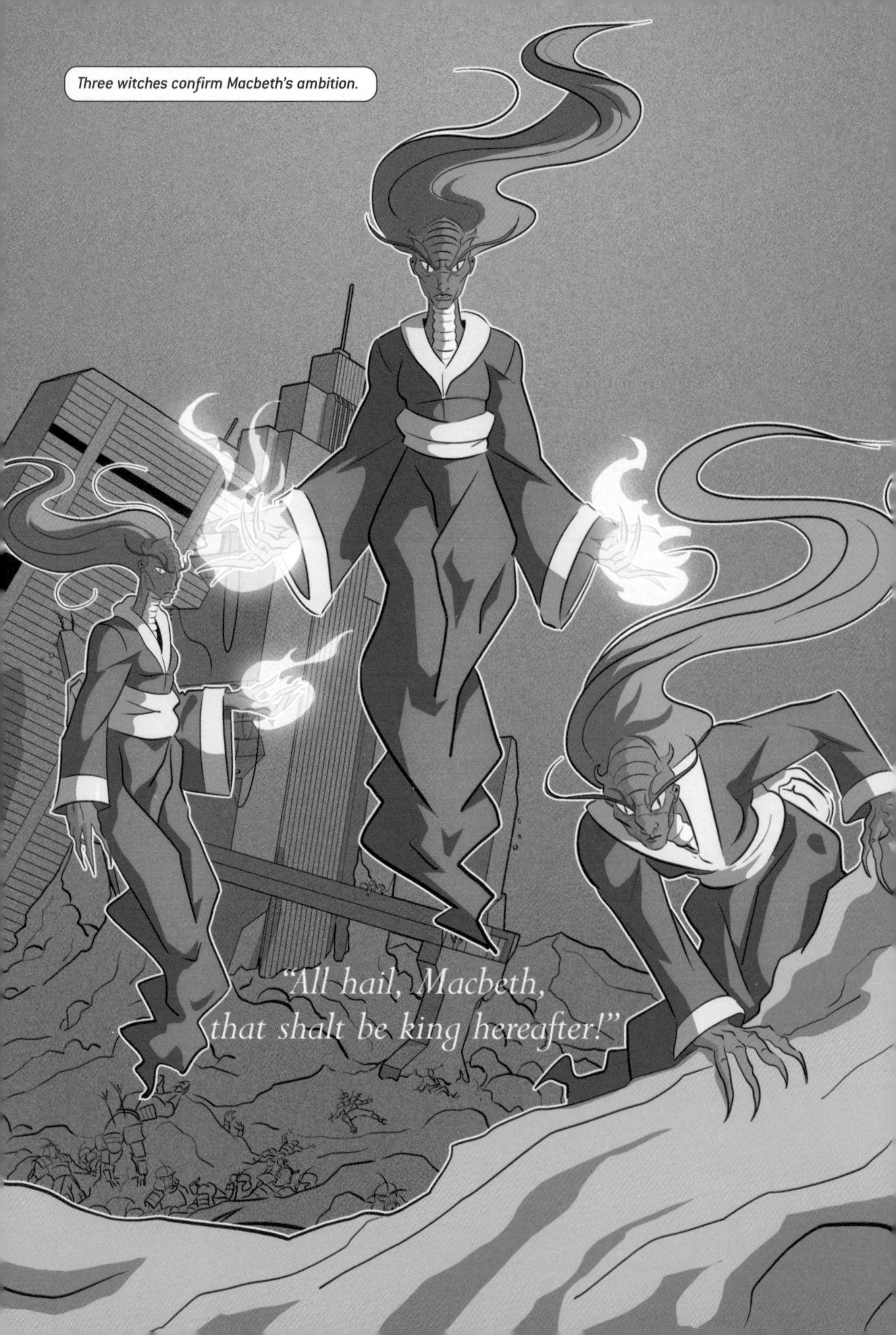
Three witches confirm Macbeth's ambition.
"All hail, Macbeth, that shalt be king hereafter!"

Macbeth and Lady Macbeth
"But screw your courage to the sticking-place and we'll not fail!"
"I dare do all that may become a man."

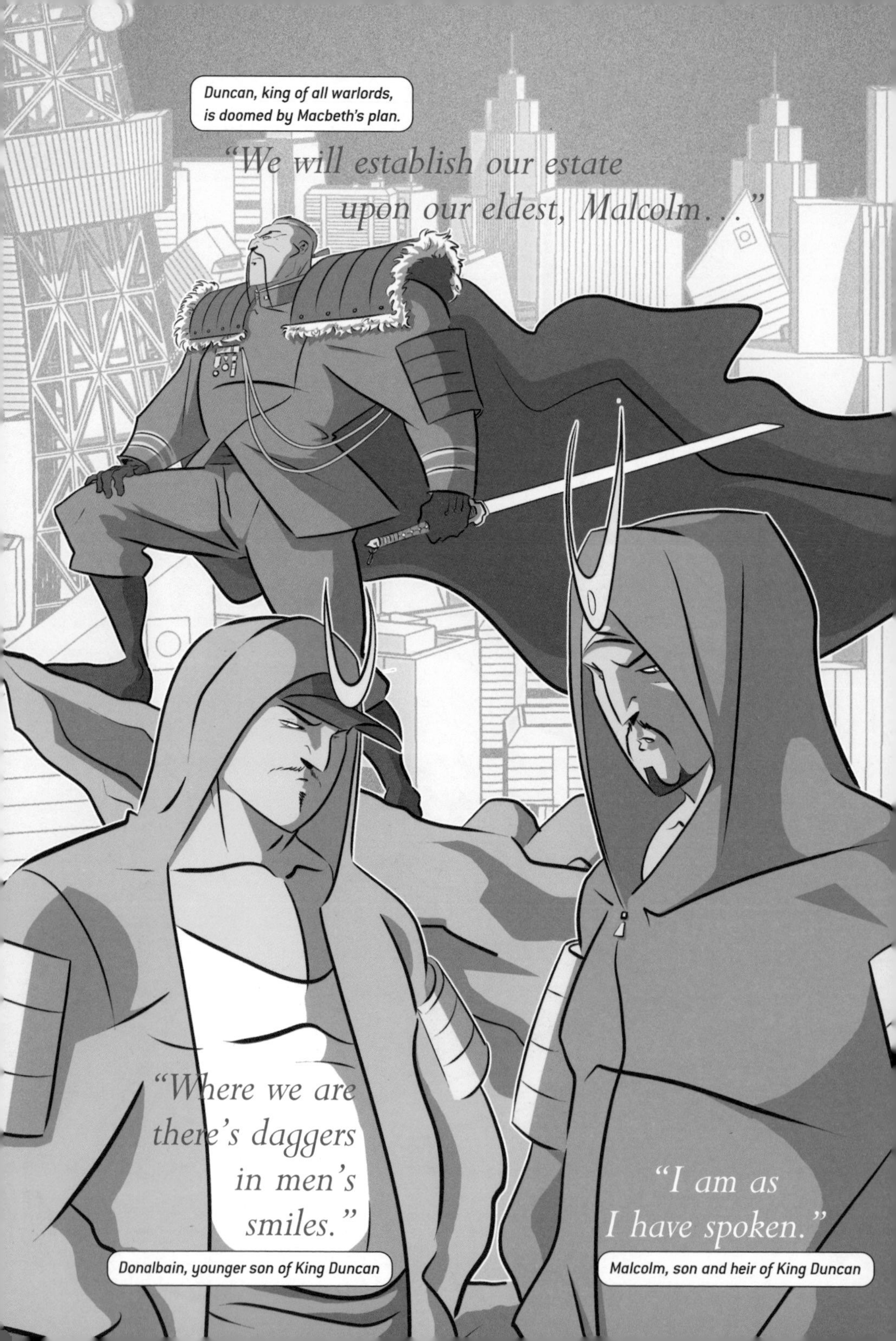
Duncan, king of all warlords, is doomed by Macbeth's plan.
"We will establish our estate upon our eldest, Malcolm. . ."
"Where we are there's daggers in men's smiles."
Donalbain, younger son of King Duncan
"I am as I have spoken."
Malcolm, son and heir of King Duncan

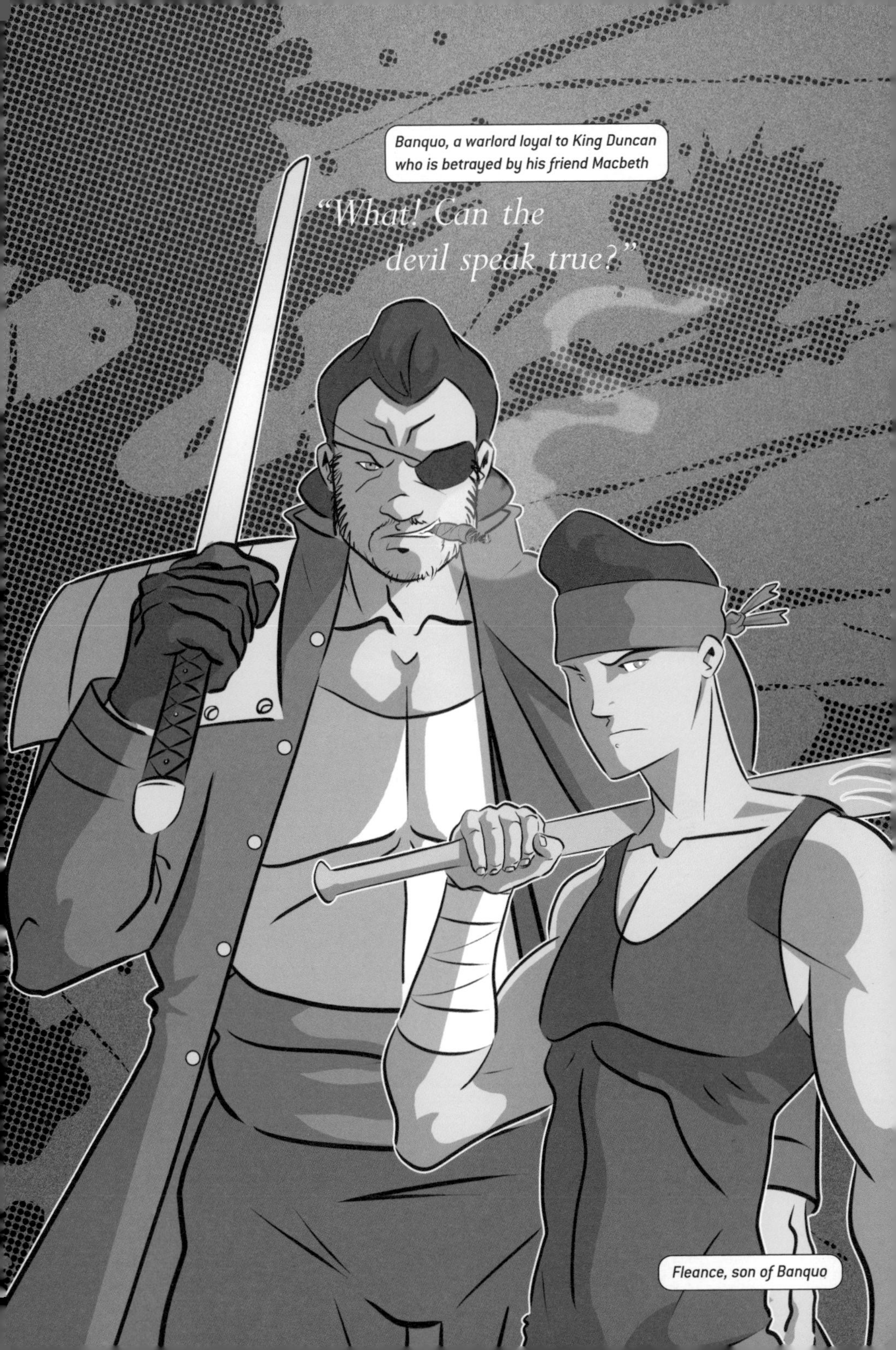
Banquo, a warlord loyal to King Duncan who is betrayed by his friend Macbeth
"What! Can the devil speak true?"
Fleance, son of Banquo

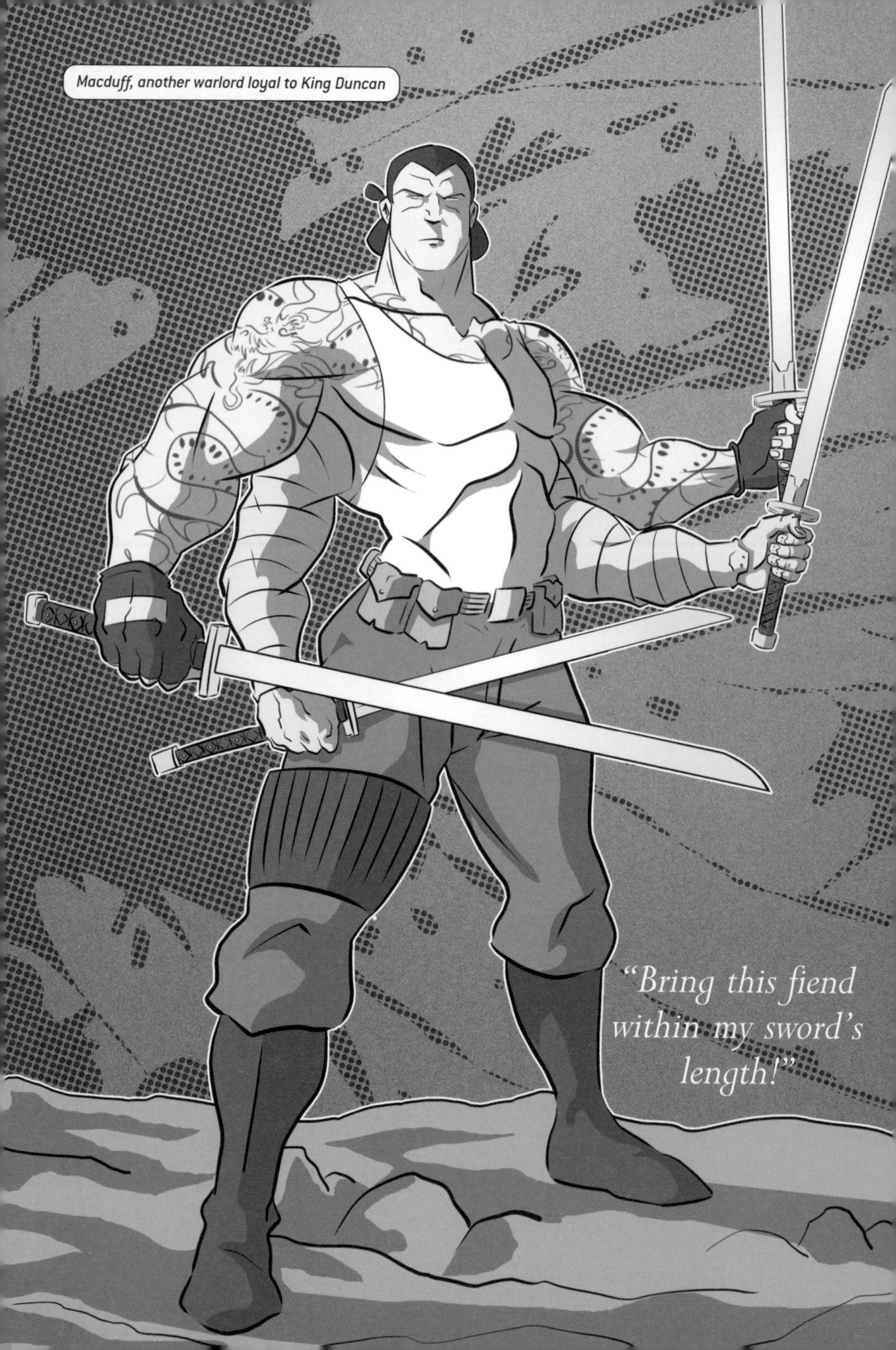
Macduff, another warlord loyal to King Duncan
"Bring this fiend within my sword's length!"

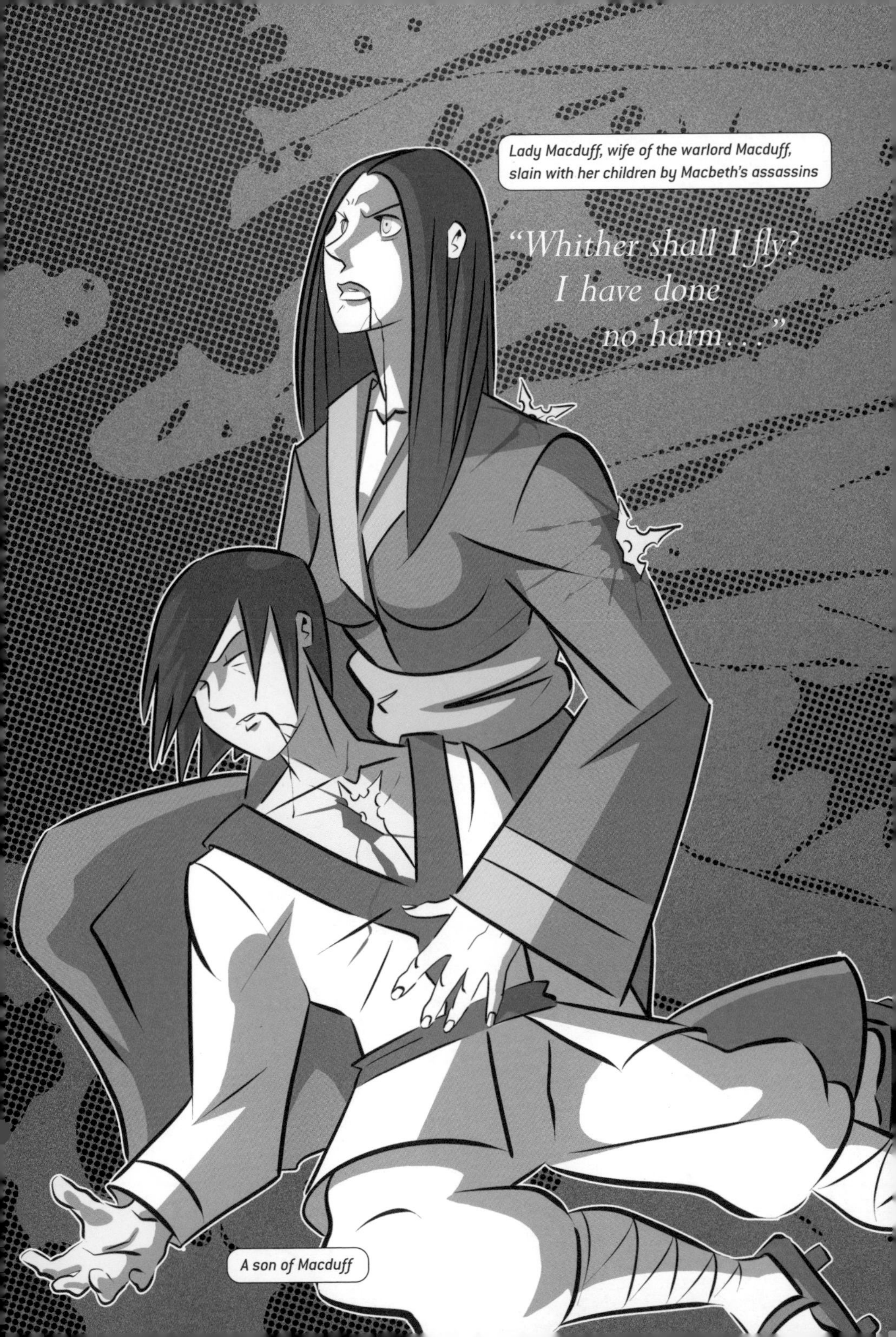
Lady Macduff, wife of the warlord Macduff, slain with her children by Macbeth's assassins
"Whither shall I fly? I have done no harm. . . ."
A son of Macduff

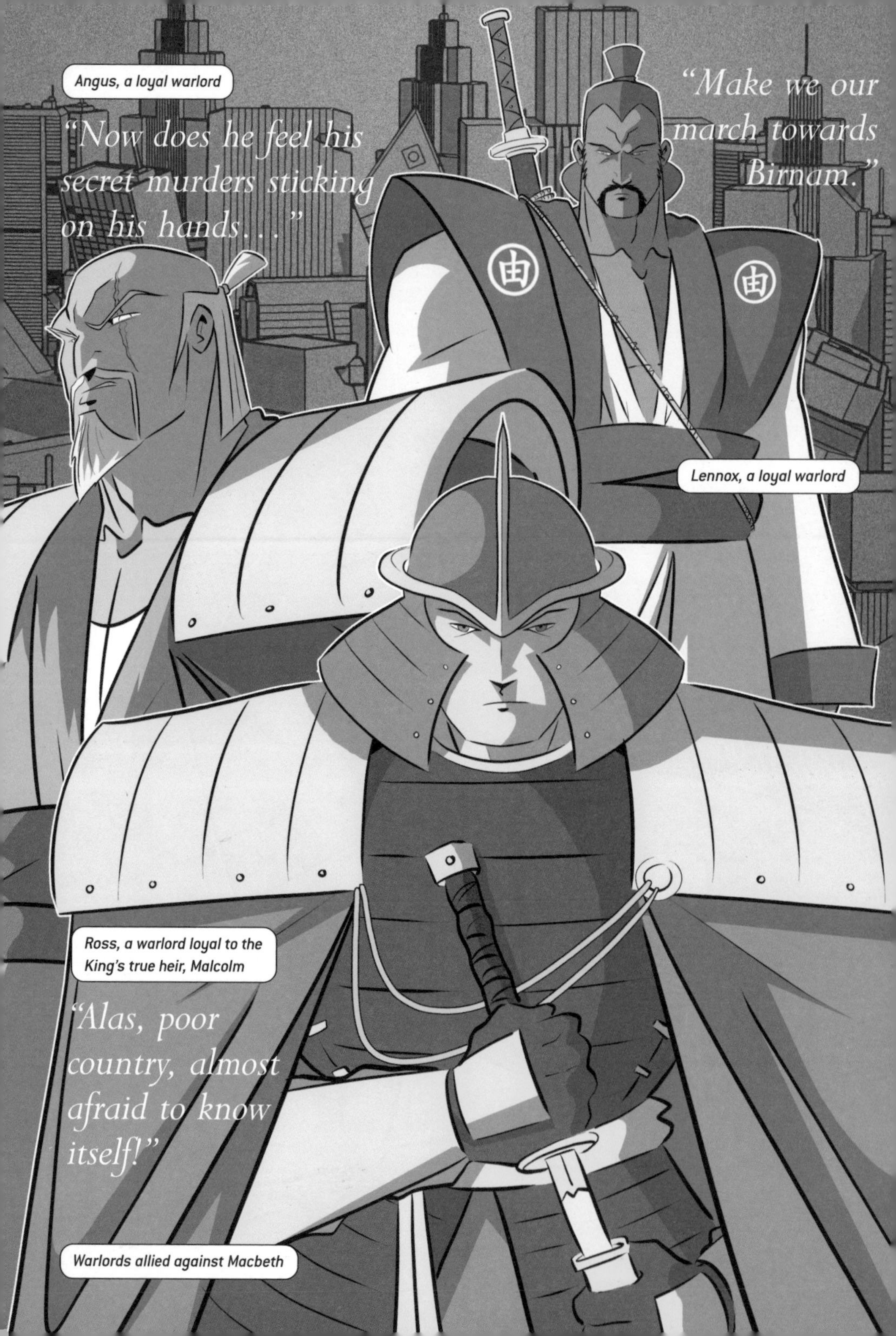
Angus, a loyal warlord
"Now does he feel his secret murders sticking on his hands. . . ."
"Make we our march towards Birnam."
Lennox, a loyal warlord
Ross, a warlord loyal to the King's true heir, Malcolm
"Alas, poor country, almost afraid to know itself!"
Warlords allied against Macbeth

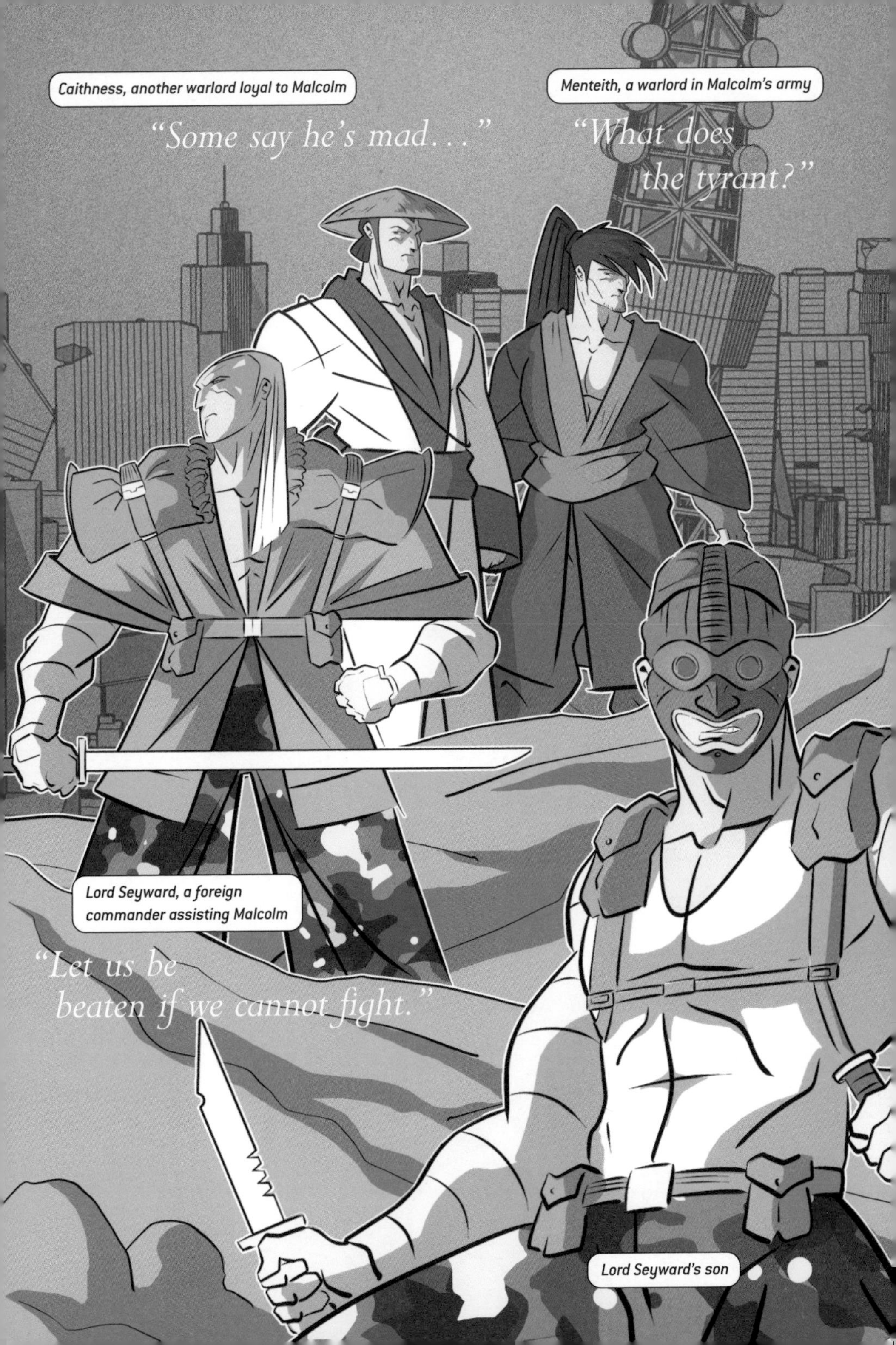
Caithness, another warlord loyal to Malcolm
"Some say he's mad…"
Menteith, a warlord in Malcolm's army
"What does the tyrant?"
Lord Seyward, a foreign commander assisting Malcolm
"Let us be beaten if we cannot fight."
Lord Seyward's son

WHEN SHALL WE THREE MEET AGAIN? IN THUNDER, LIGHTNING OR IN RAIN?
WHEN THE HURLYBURLY'S DONE, WHEN THE BATTLE'S LOST AND WON.

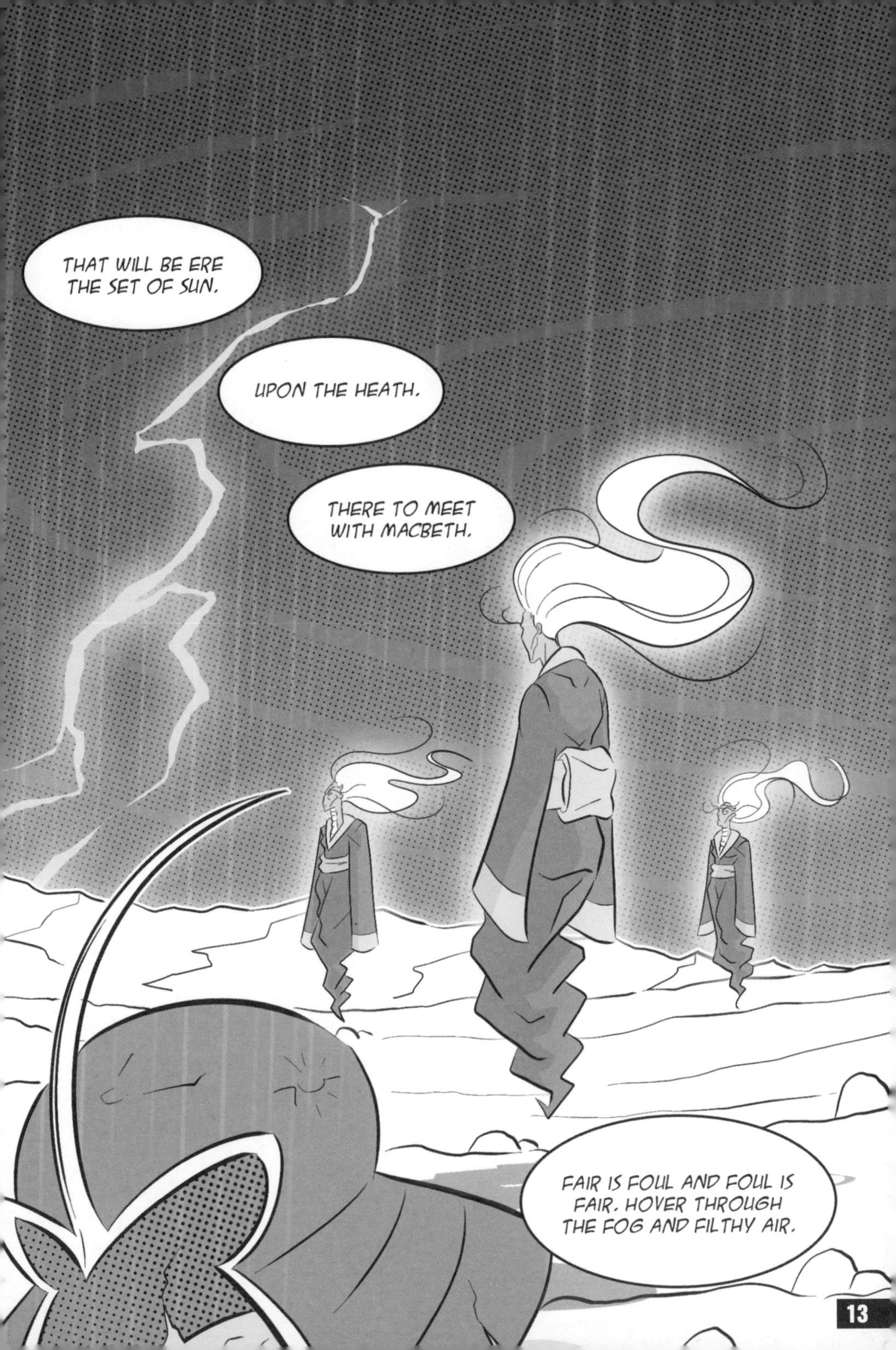
THAT WILL BE ERE THE SET OF SUN.
UPON THE HEATH.
THERE TO MEET WITH MACBETH.
FAIR IS FOUL AND FOUL IS FAIR. HOVER THROUGH THE FOG AND FILTHY AIR.

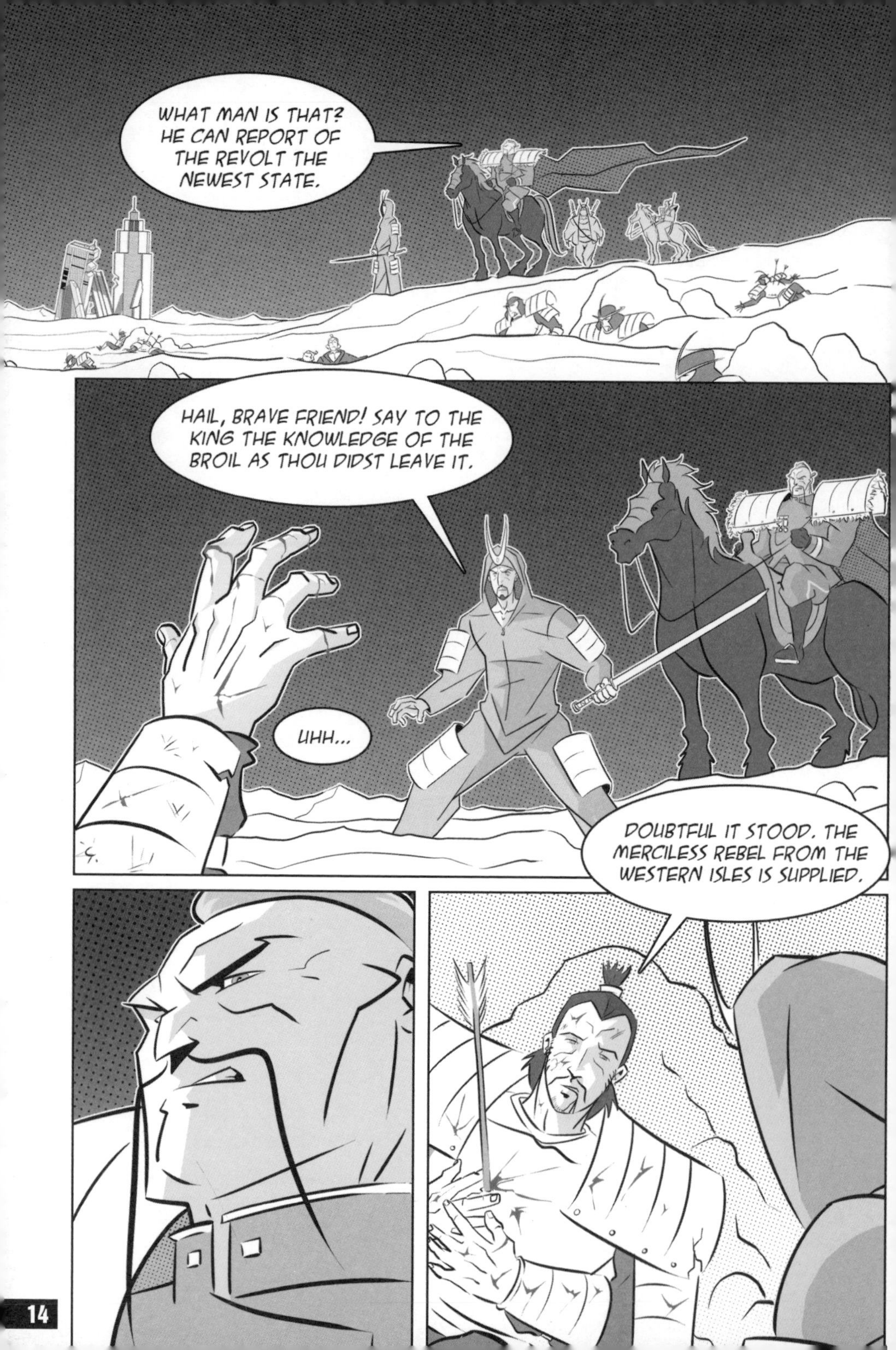
WHAT MAN IS THAT? HE CAN REPORT OF THE REVOLT THE NEWEST STATE.
HAIL, BRAVE FRIEND! SAY TO THE KING THE KNOWLEDGE OF THE BROIL AS THOU DIDST LEAVE IT.
UHH...
DOUBTFUL IT STOOD. THE MERCILESS REBEL FROM THE WESTERN ISLES IS SUPPLIED.

BUT ALL'S TOO WEAK, FOR BRAVE MACBETH WITH BRANDISHED STEEL CARVED OUT HIS PASSAGE TILL HE FACED THE SLAVE.

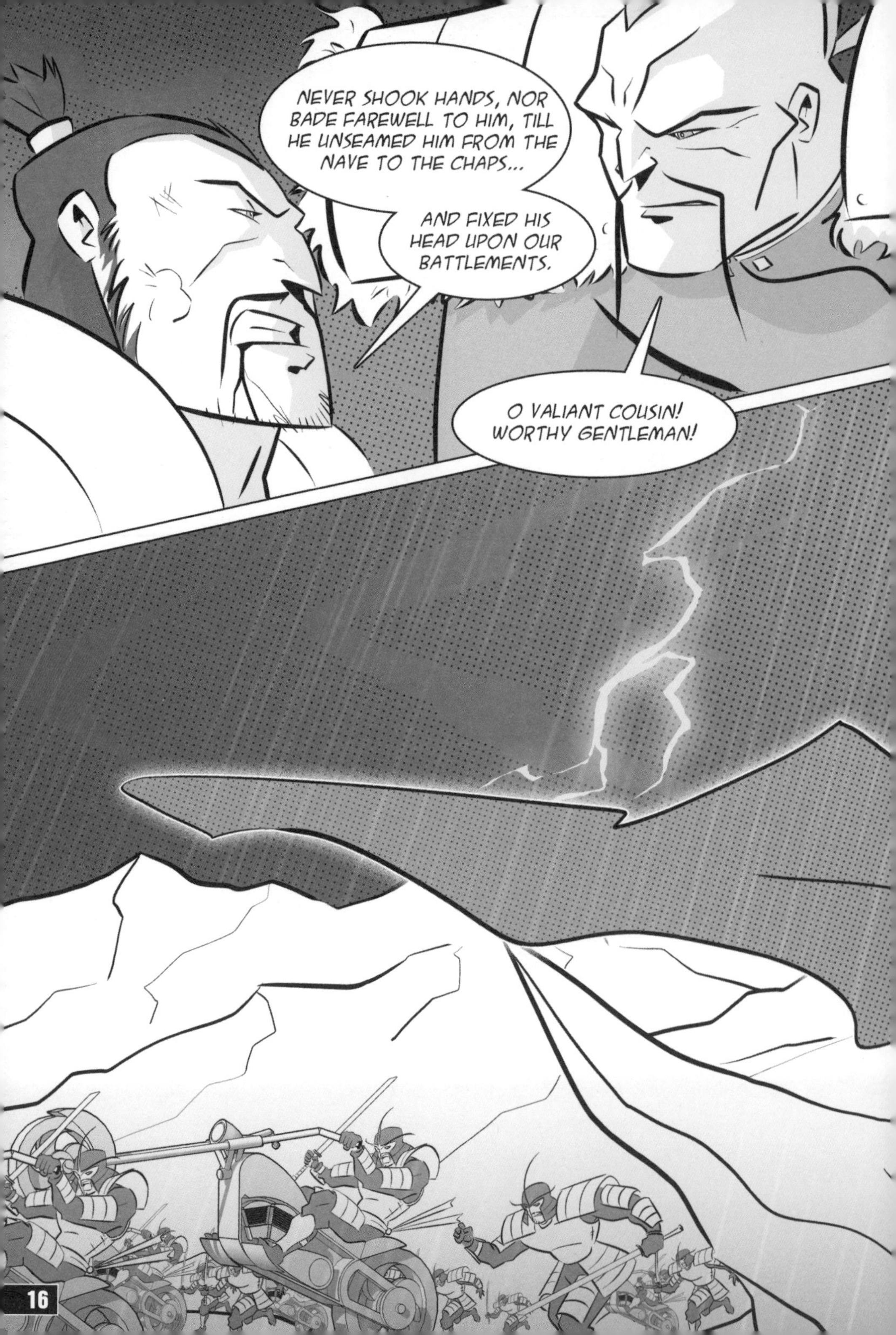
NEVER SHOOK HANDS, NOR BADE FAREWELL TO HIM, TILL HE UNSEAMED HIM FROM THE NAVE TO THE CHAPS...
AND FIXED HIS HEAD UPON OUR BATTLEMENTS.
O VALIANT COUSIN! WORTHY GENTLEMAN!

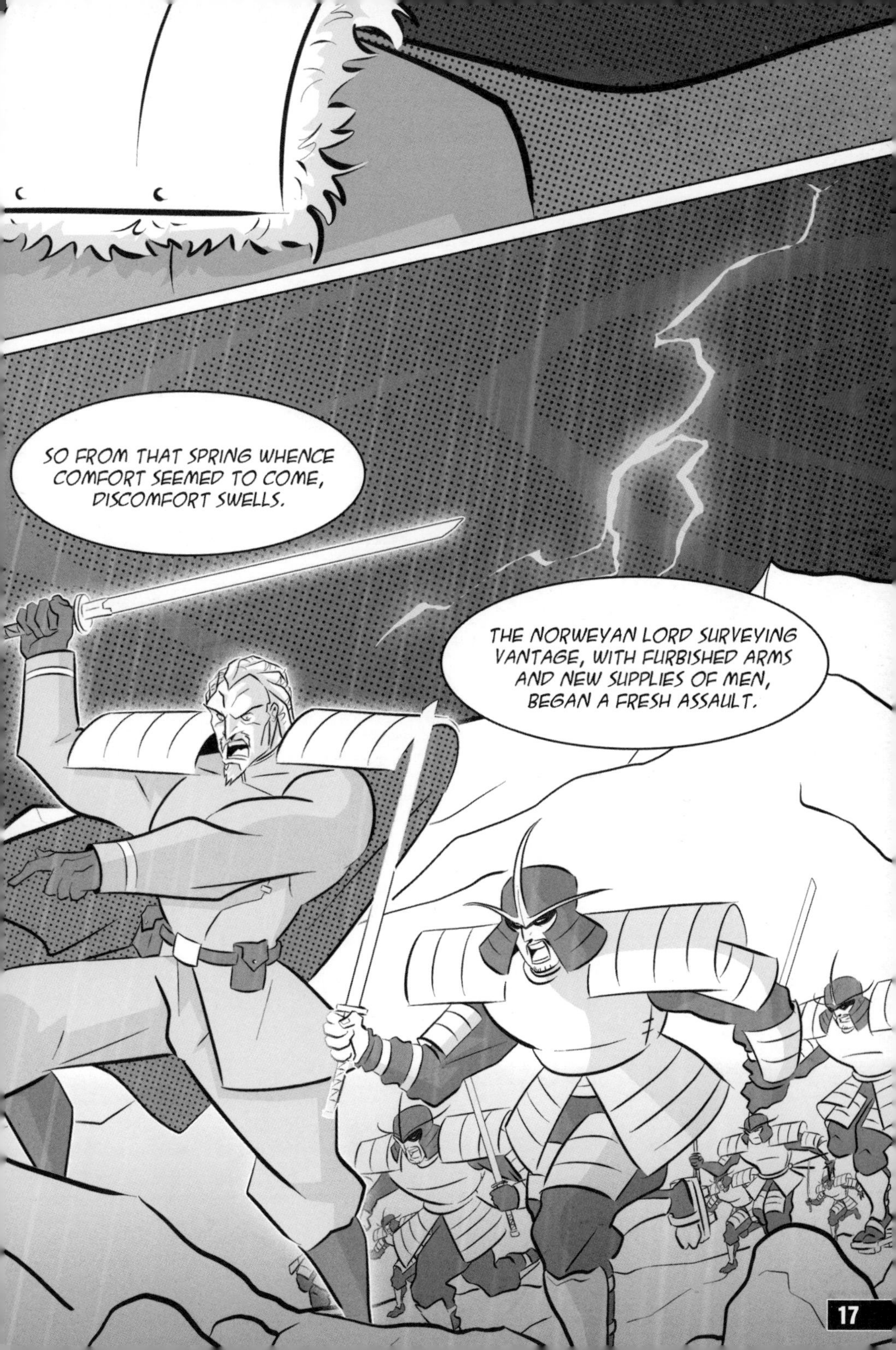
SO FROM THAT SPRING WHENCE COMFORT SEEMED TO COME, DISCOMFORT SWELLS.
THE NORWEYAN LORD SURVEYING VANTAGE, WITH FURBISHED ARMS AND NEW SUPPLIES OF MEN, BEGAN A FRESH ASSAULT.

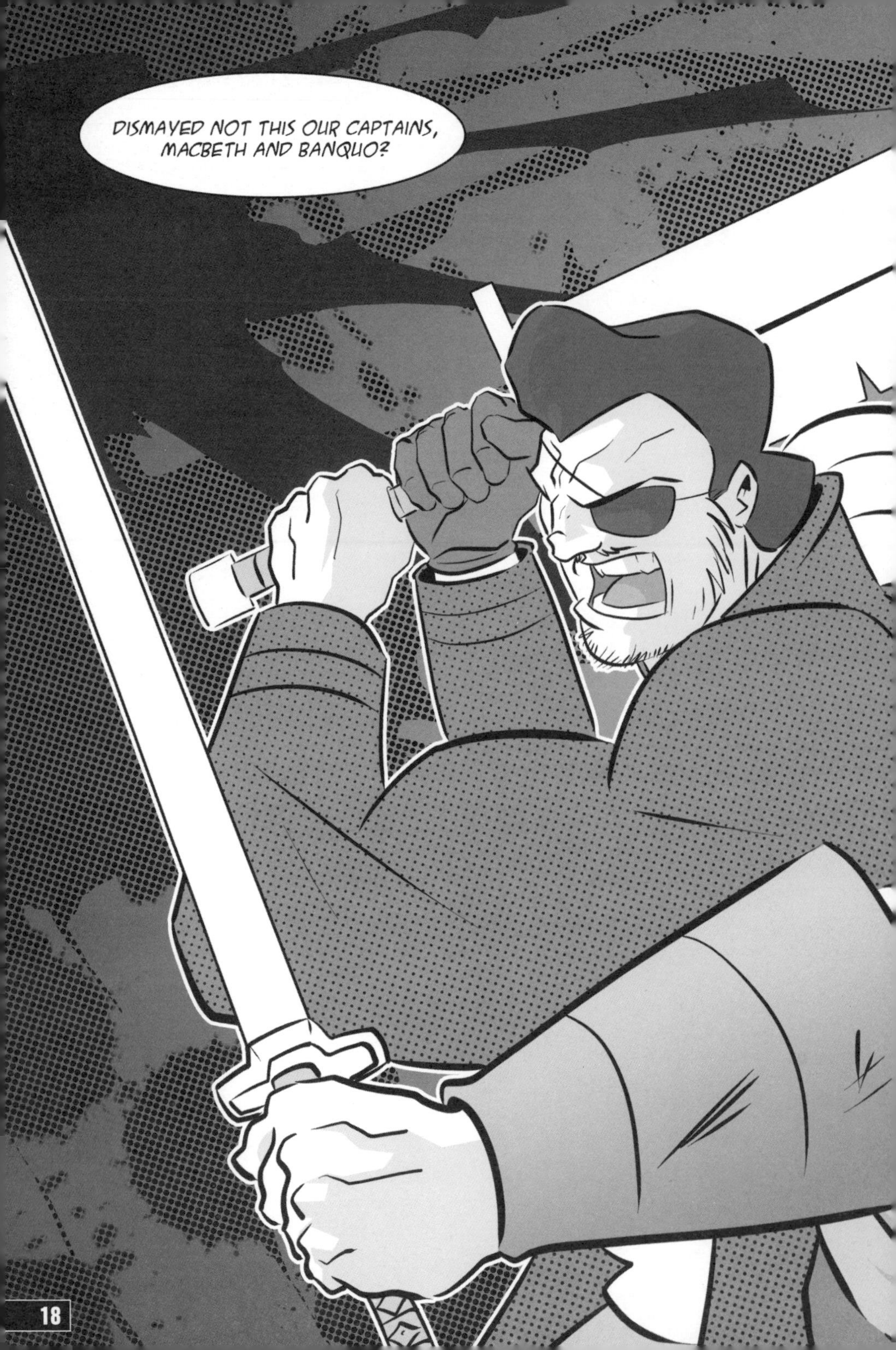
DISMAYED NOT THIS OUR CAPTAINS, MACBETH AND BANQUO?

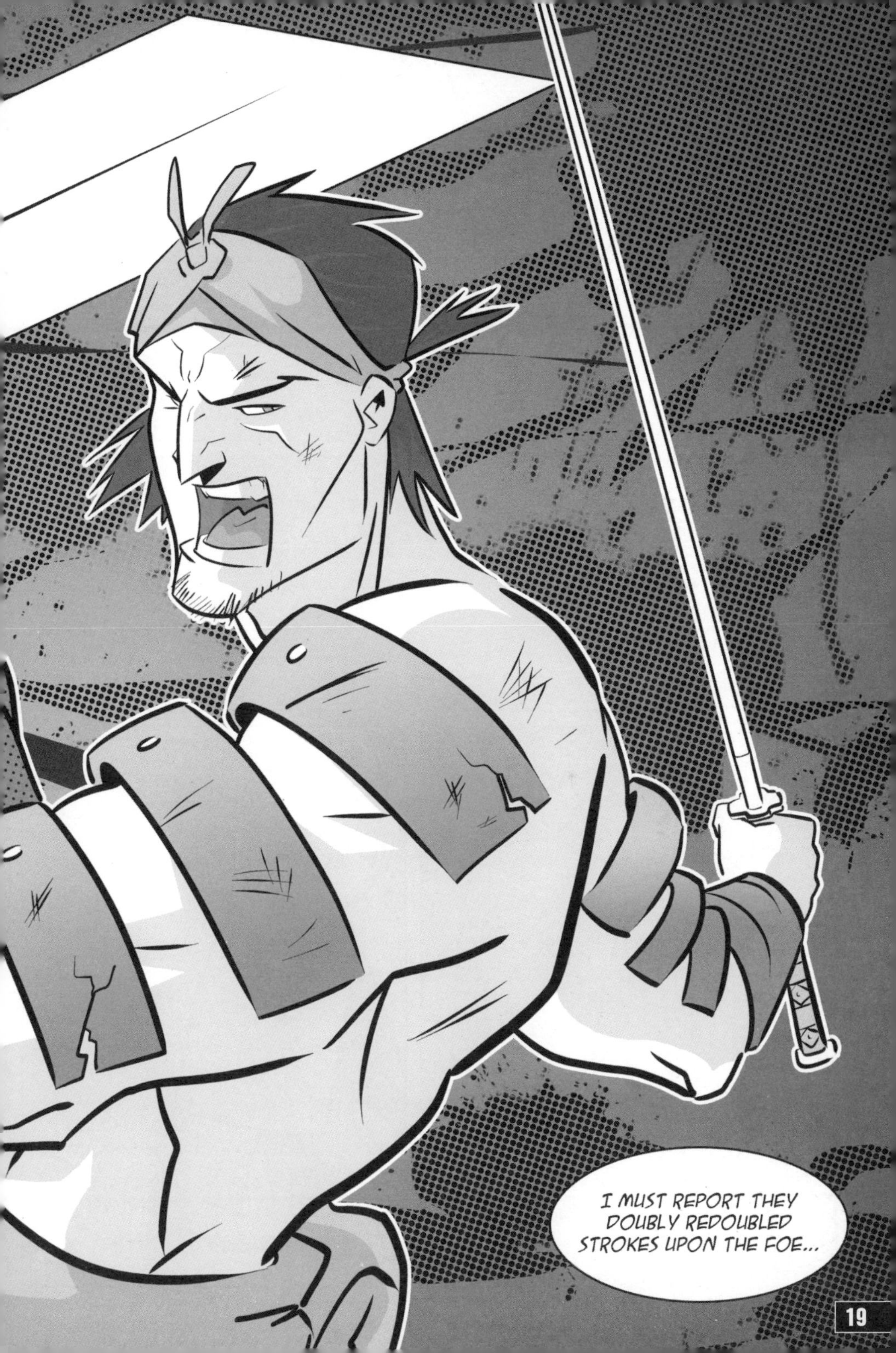
I MUST REPORT THEY DOUBLY REDOUBLED STROKES UPON THE FOE...

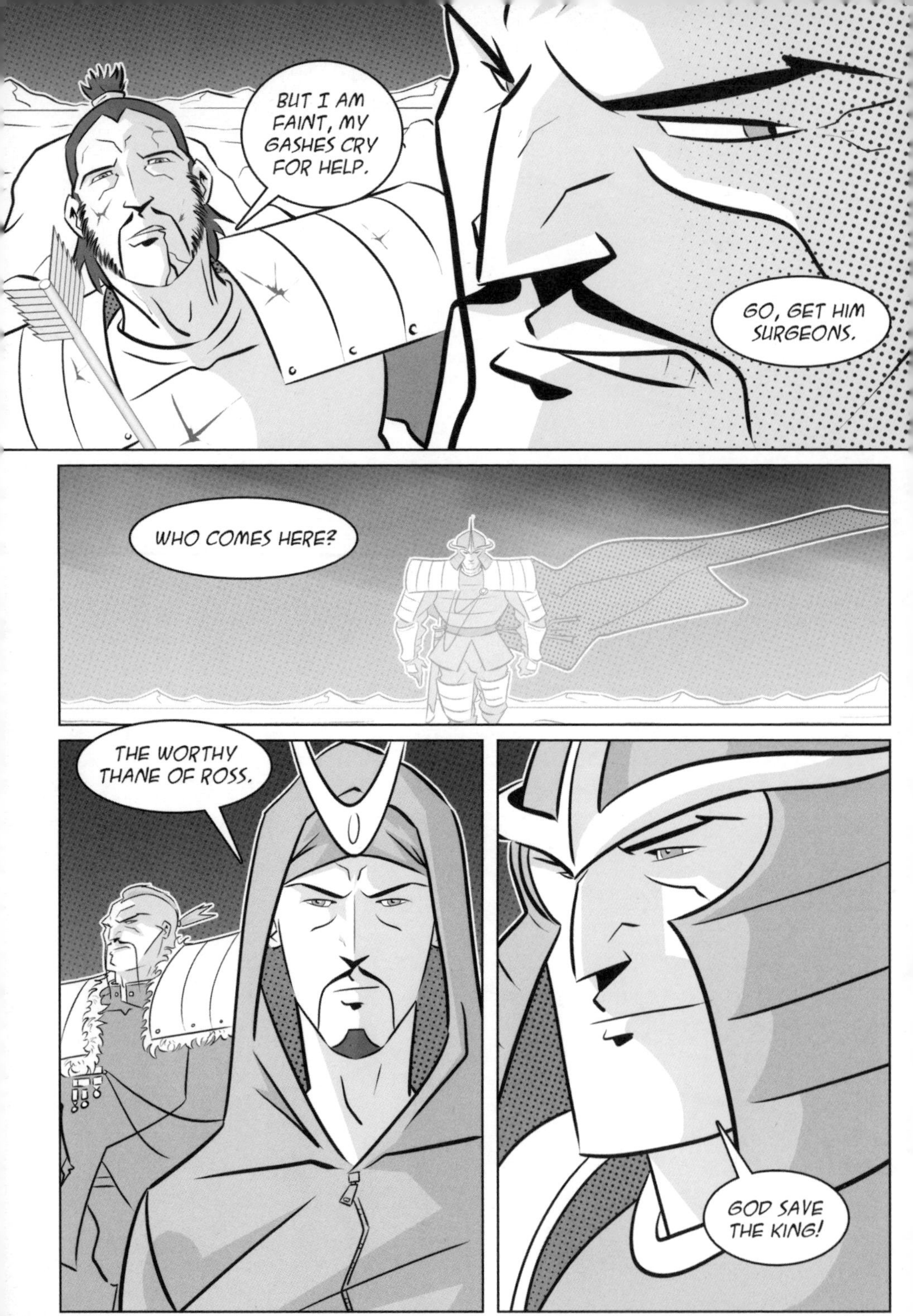
BUT I AM FAINT, MY GASHES CRY FOR HELP.
GO, GET HIM SURGEONS.
WHO COMES HERE?
THE WORTHY THANE OF ROSS.
GOD SAVE THE KING!

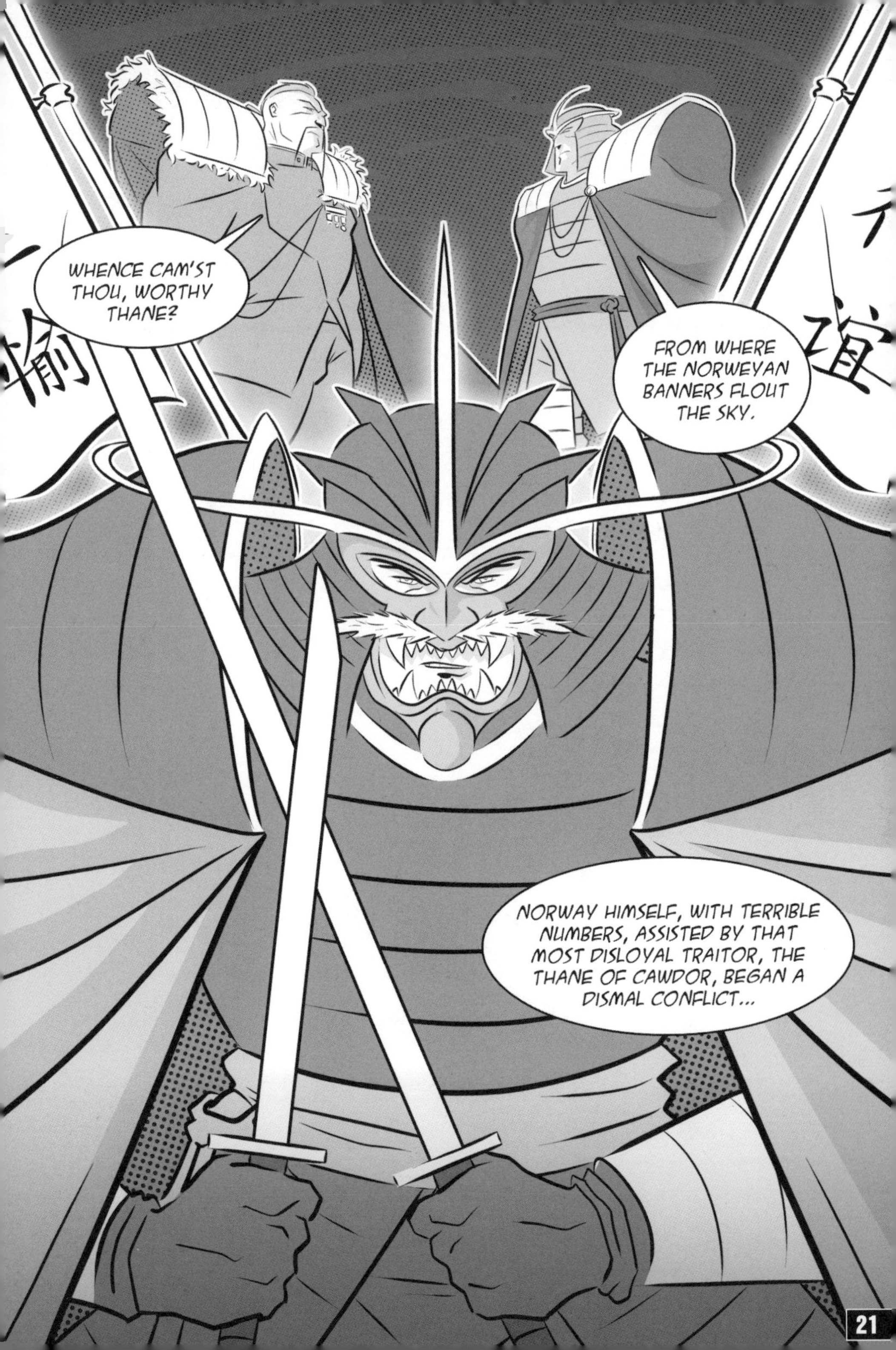
WHENCE CAM'ST THOU, WORTHY THANE?
FROM WHERE THE NORWEYAN BANNERS FLOUT THE SKY.
NORWAY HIMSELF, WITH TERRIBLE NUMBERS, ASSISTED BY THAT MOST DISLOYAL TRAITOR, THE THANE OF CAWDOR, BEGAN A DISMAL CONFLICT...

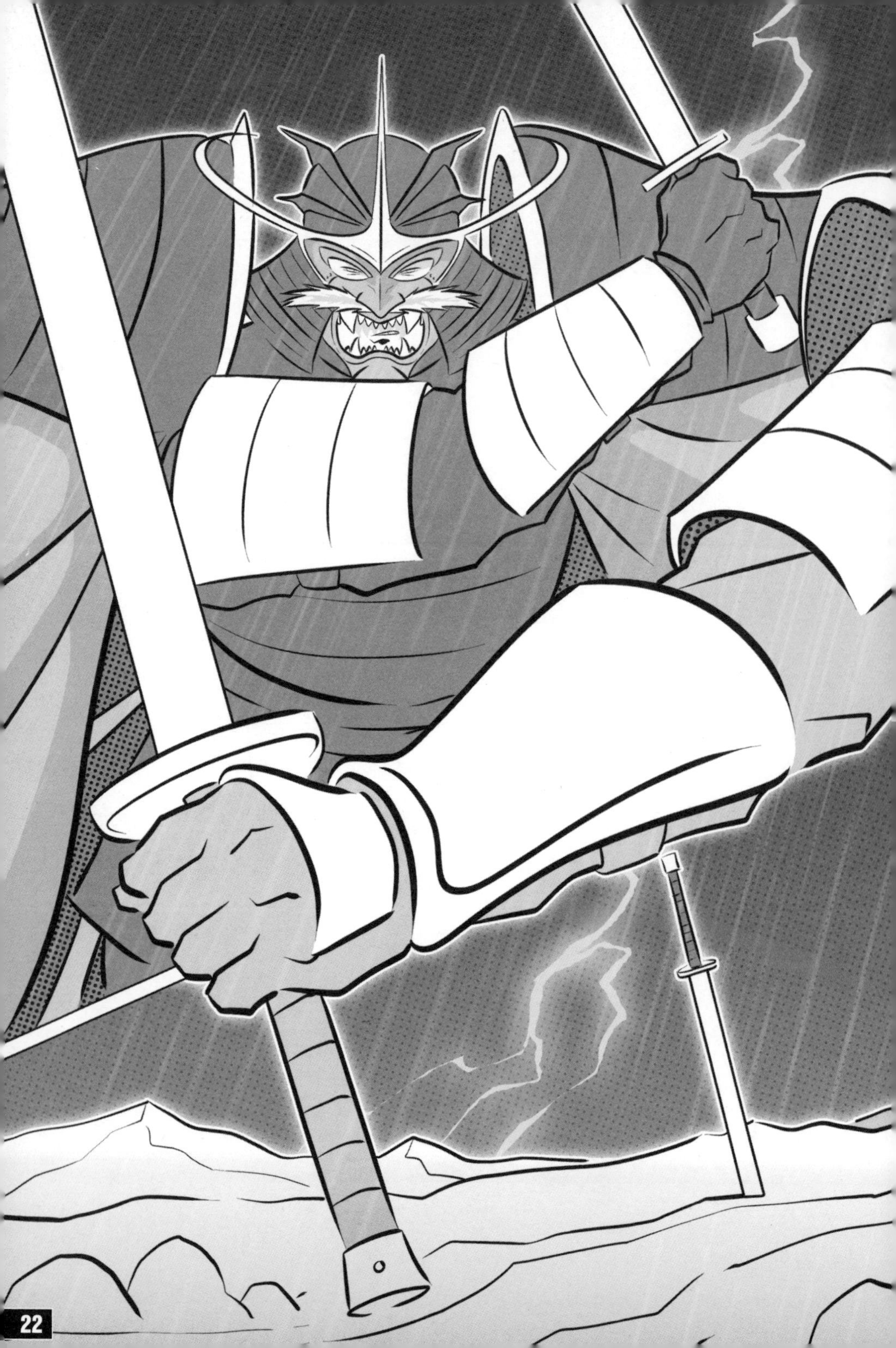

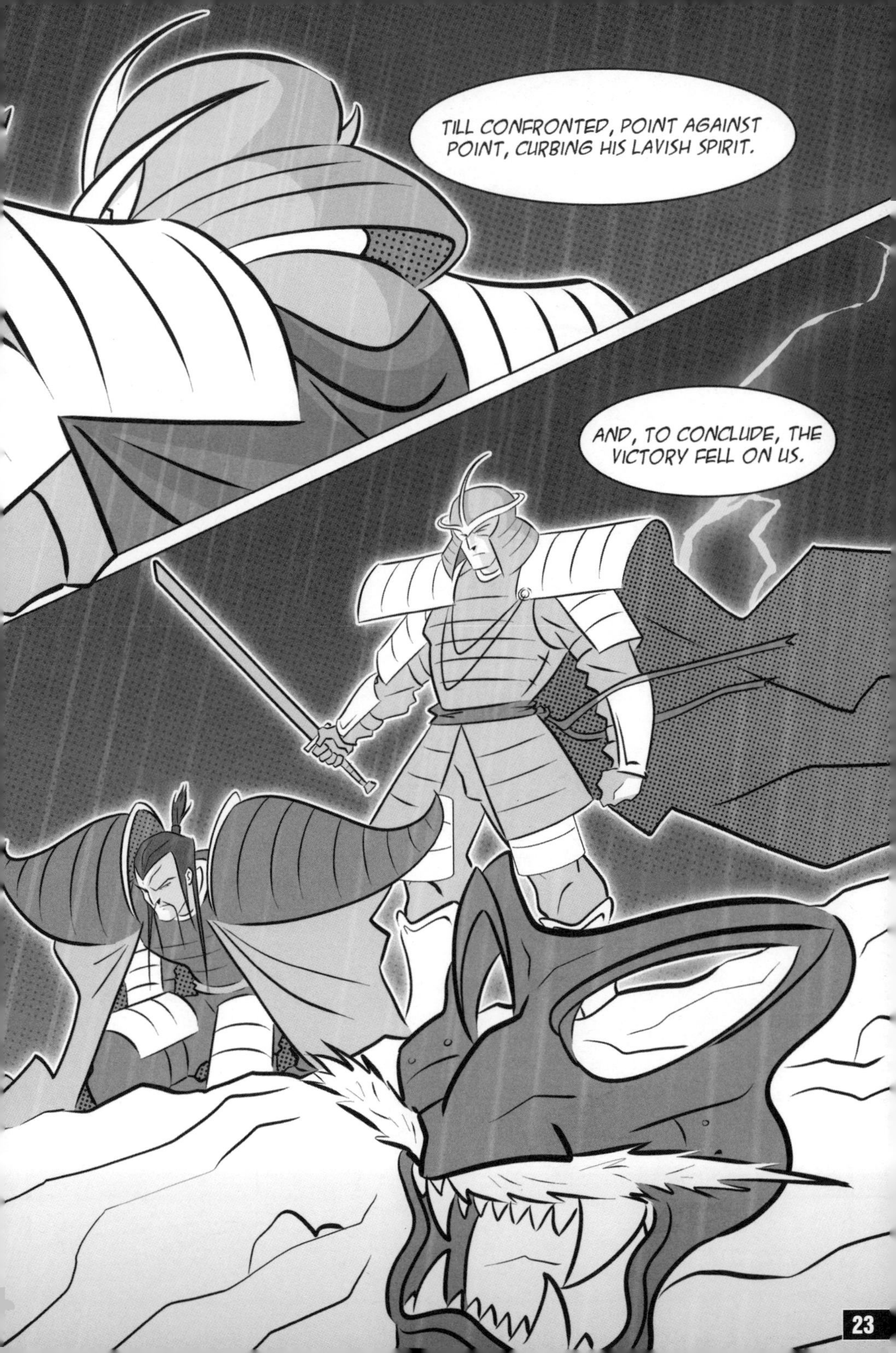
TILL CONFRONTED, POINT AGAINST POINT, CURBING HIS LAVISH SPIRIT.
AND, TO CONCLUDE, THE VICTORY FELL ON US.

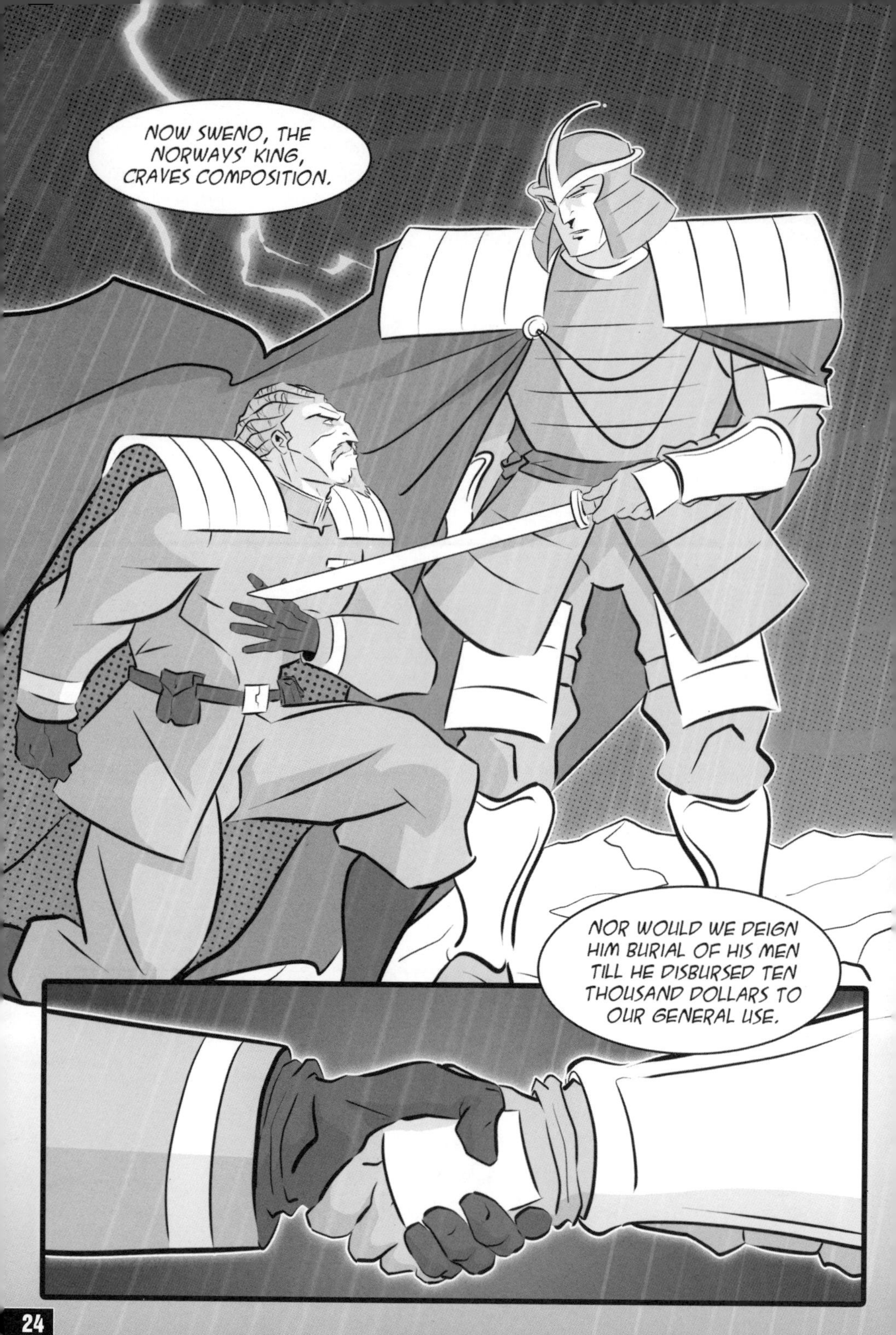
NOW SWENO, THE NORWAYS' KING, CRAVES COMPOSITION.
NOR WOULD WE DEIGN HIM BURIAL OF HIS MEN TILL HE DISBURSED TEN THOUSAND DOLLARS TO OUR GENERAL USE.

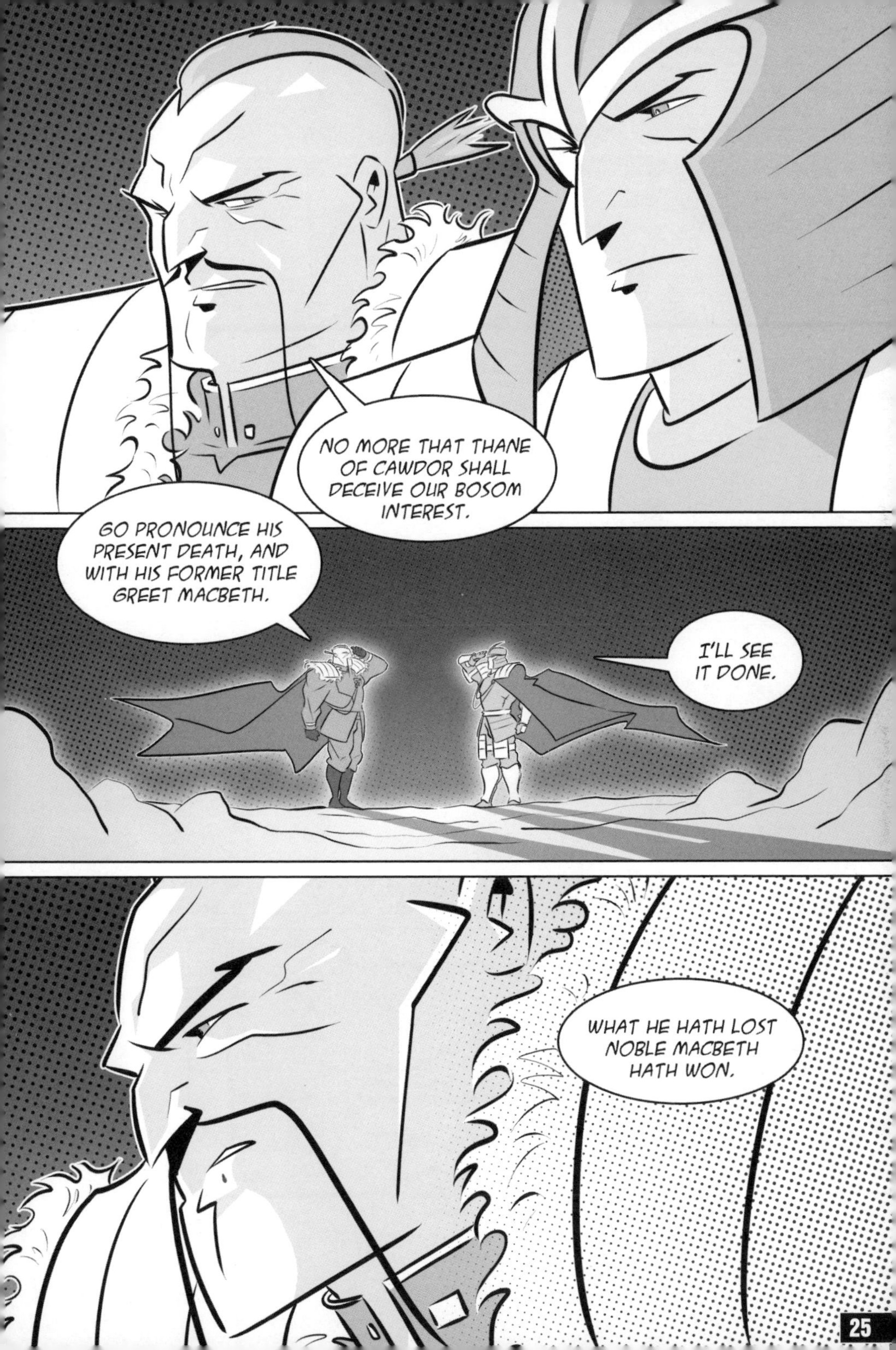
NO MORE THAT THANE OF CAWDOR SHALL DECEIVE OUR BOSOM INTEREST.
GO PRONOUNCE HIS PRESENT DEATH, AND WITH HIS FORMER TITLE GREET MACBETH.
I'LL SEE IT DONE.
WHAT HE HATH LOST NOBLE MACBETH HATH WON.

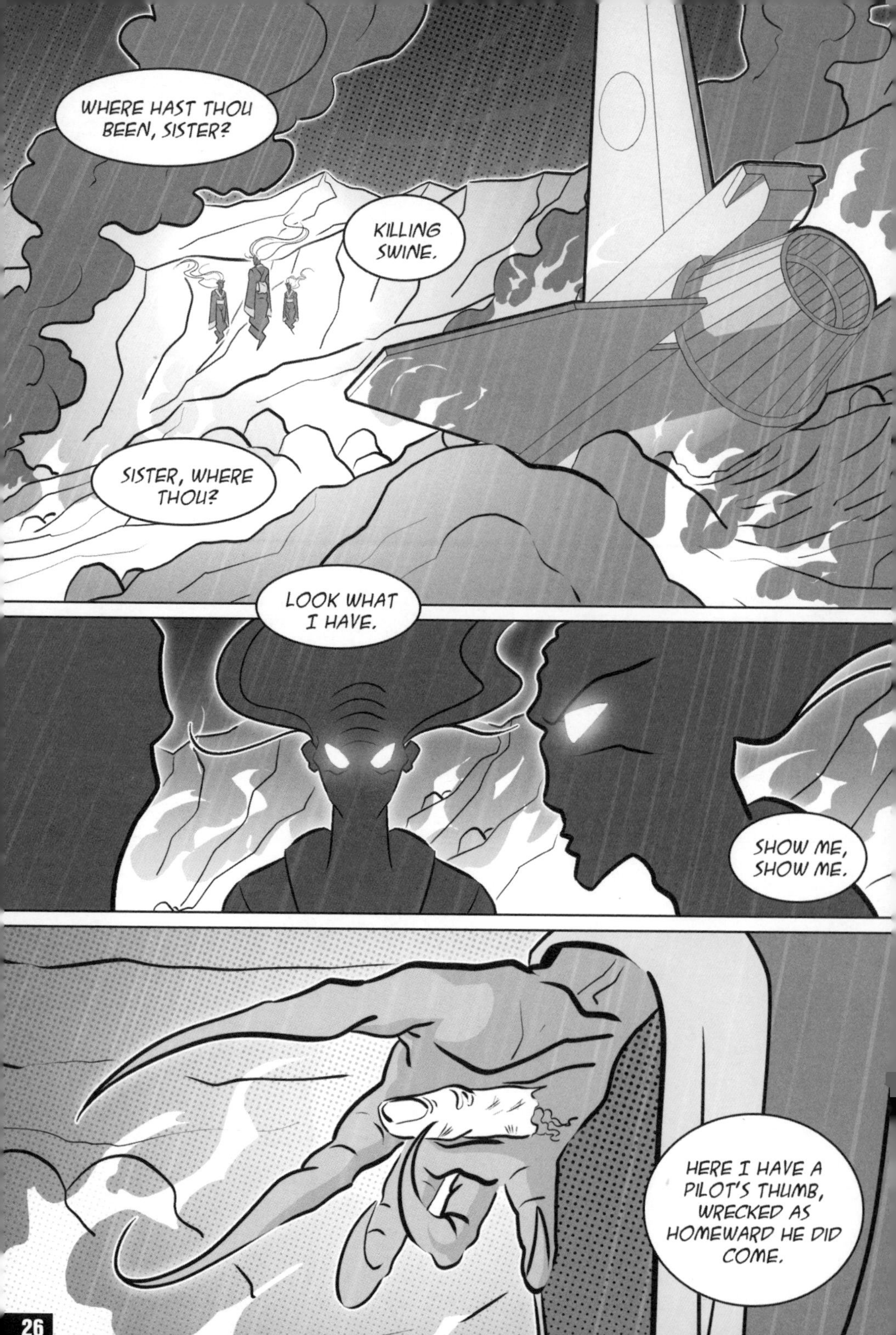
WHERE HAST THOU BEEN, SISTER?
KILLING SWINE.
SISTER, WHERE THOU?
LOOK WHAT I HAVE.
SHOW ME, SHOW ME.
HERE I HAVE A PILOT'S THUMB, WRECKED AS HOMEWARD HE DID COME.

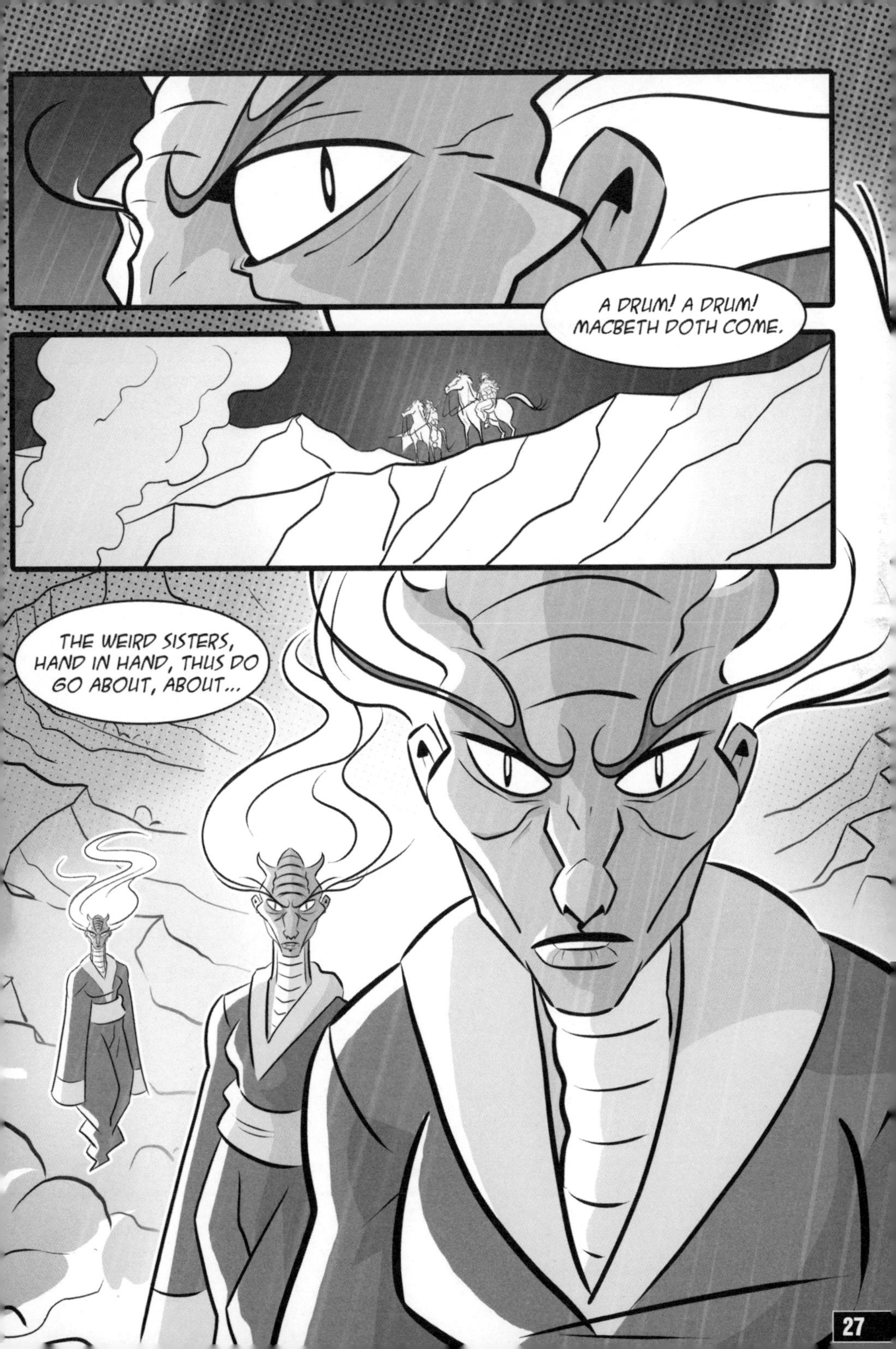
A DRUM! A DRUM! MACBETH DOTH COME.
THE WEIRD SISTERS, HAND IN HAND, THUS DO GO ABOUT, ABOUT...

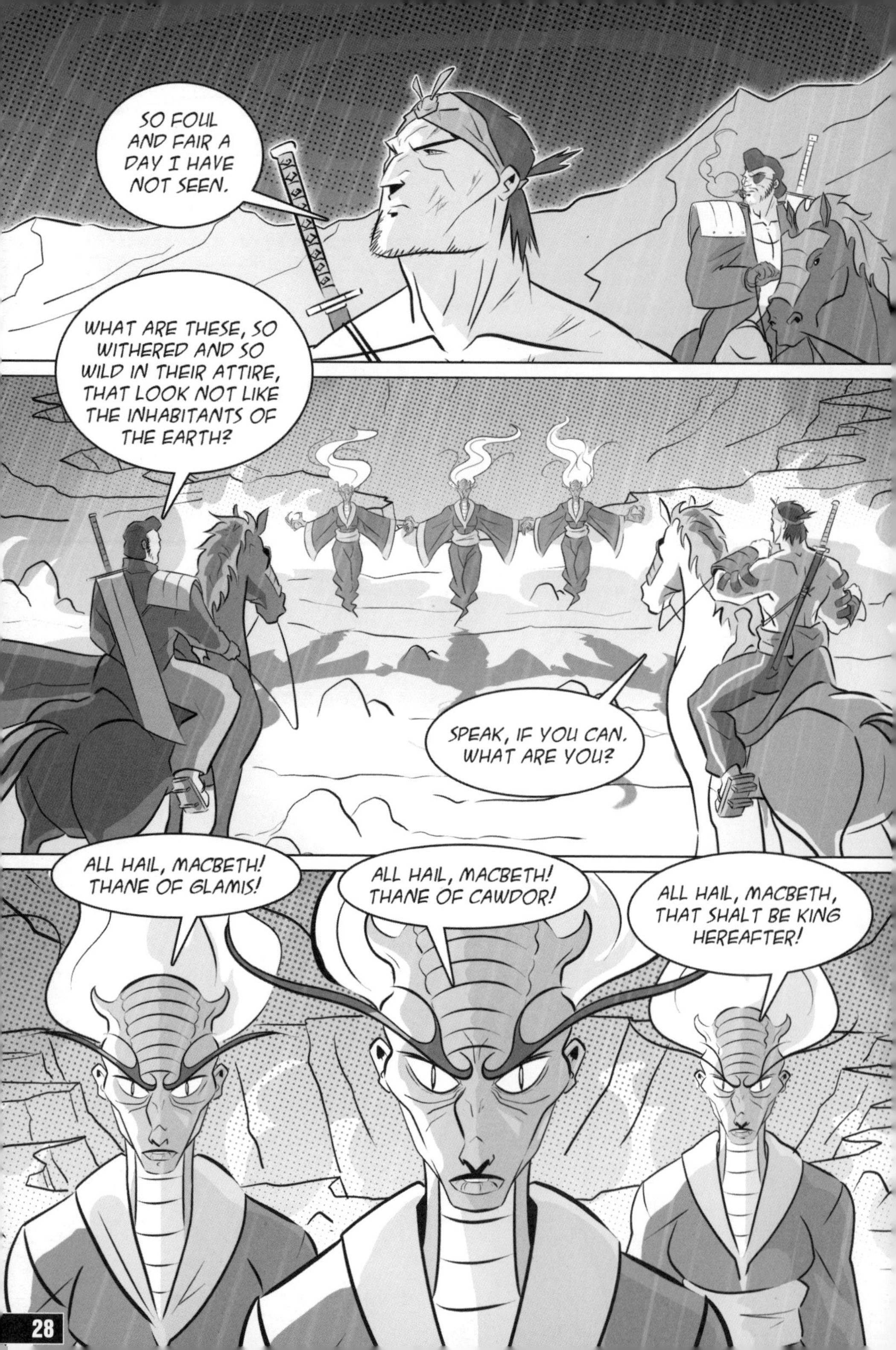
SO FOUL AND FAIR A DAY I HAVE NOT SEEN.
WHAT ARE THESE, SO WITHERED AND SO WILD IN THEIR ATTIRE, THAT LOOK NOT LIKE THE INHABITANTS OF THE EARTH?
SPEAK, IF YOU CAN. WHAT ARE YOU?
ALL HAIL, MACBETH! THANE OF GLAMIS!
ALL HAIL, MACBETH! THANE OF CAWDOR!
ALL HAIL, MACBETH, THAT SHALT BE KING HEREAFTER!

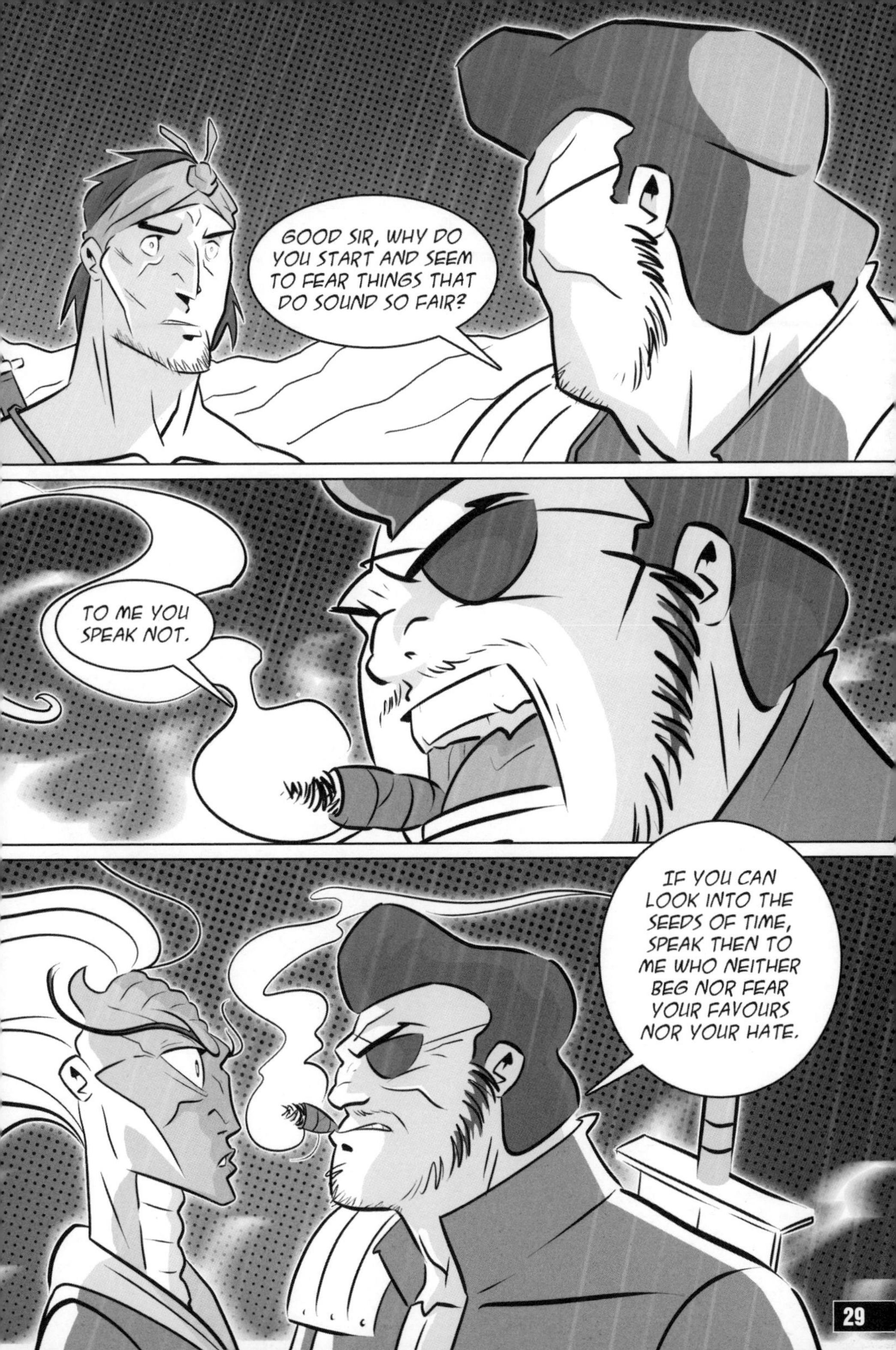
GOOD SIR, WHY DO YOU START AND SEEM TO FEAR THINGS THAT DO SOUND SO FAIR?
TO ME YOU SPEAK NOT.
IF YOU CAN LOOK INTO THE SEEDS OF TIME, SPEAK THEN TO ME WHO NEITHER BEG NOR FEAR YOUR FAVOURS NOR YOUR HATE.

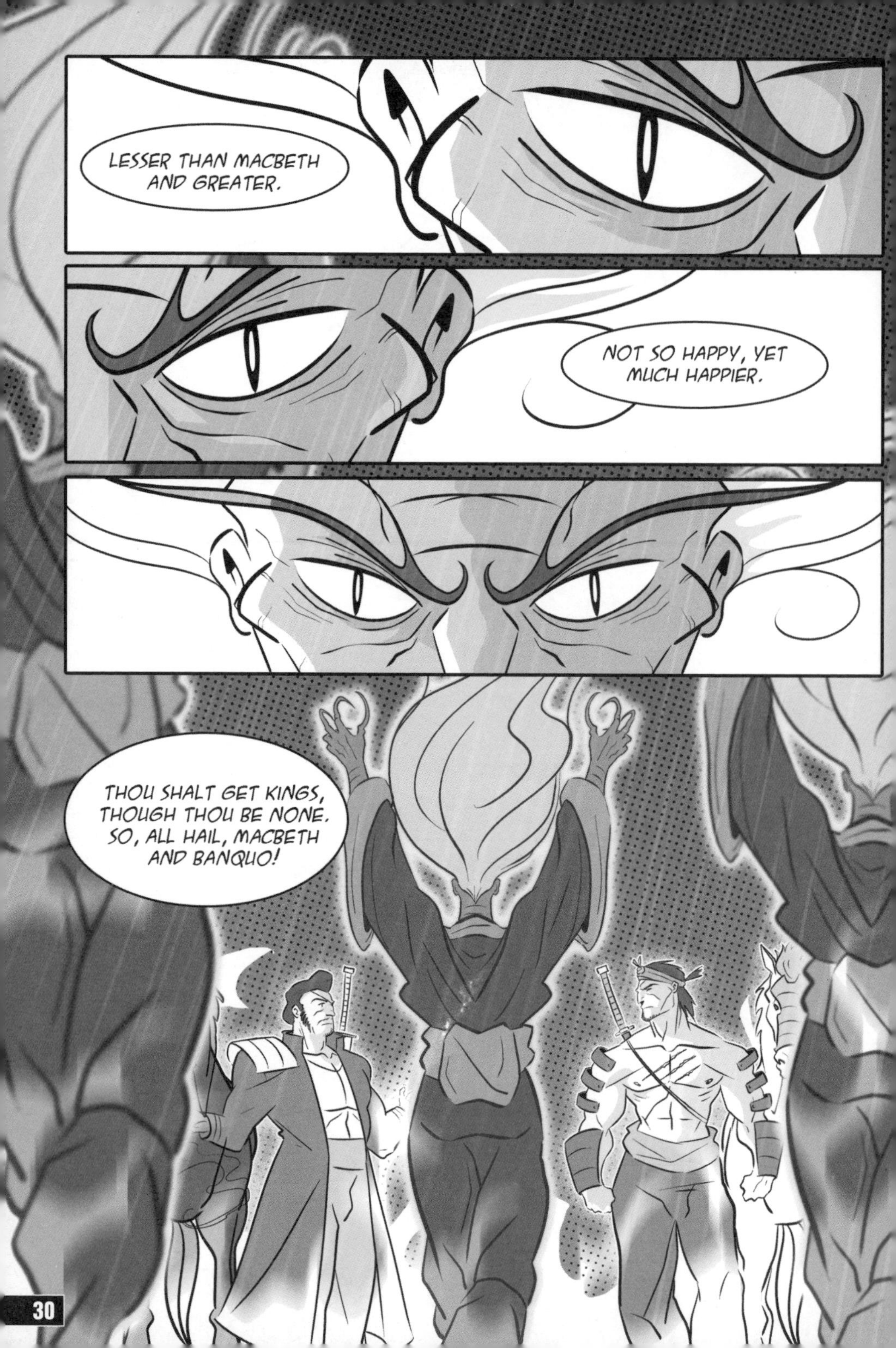
LESSER THAN MACBETH AND GREATER.
NOT SO HAPPY, YET MUCH HAPPIER.
THOU SHALT GET KINGS, THOUGH THOU BE NONE. SO, ALL HAIL, MACBETH AND BANQUO!

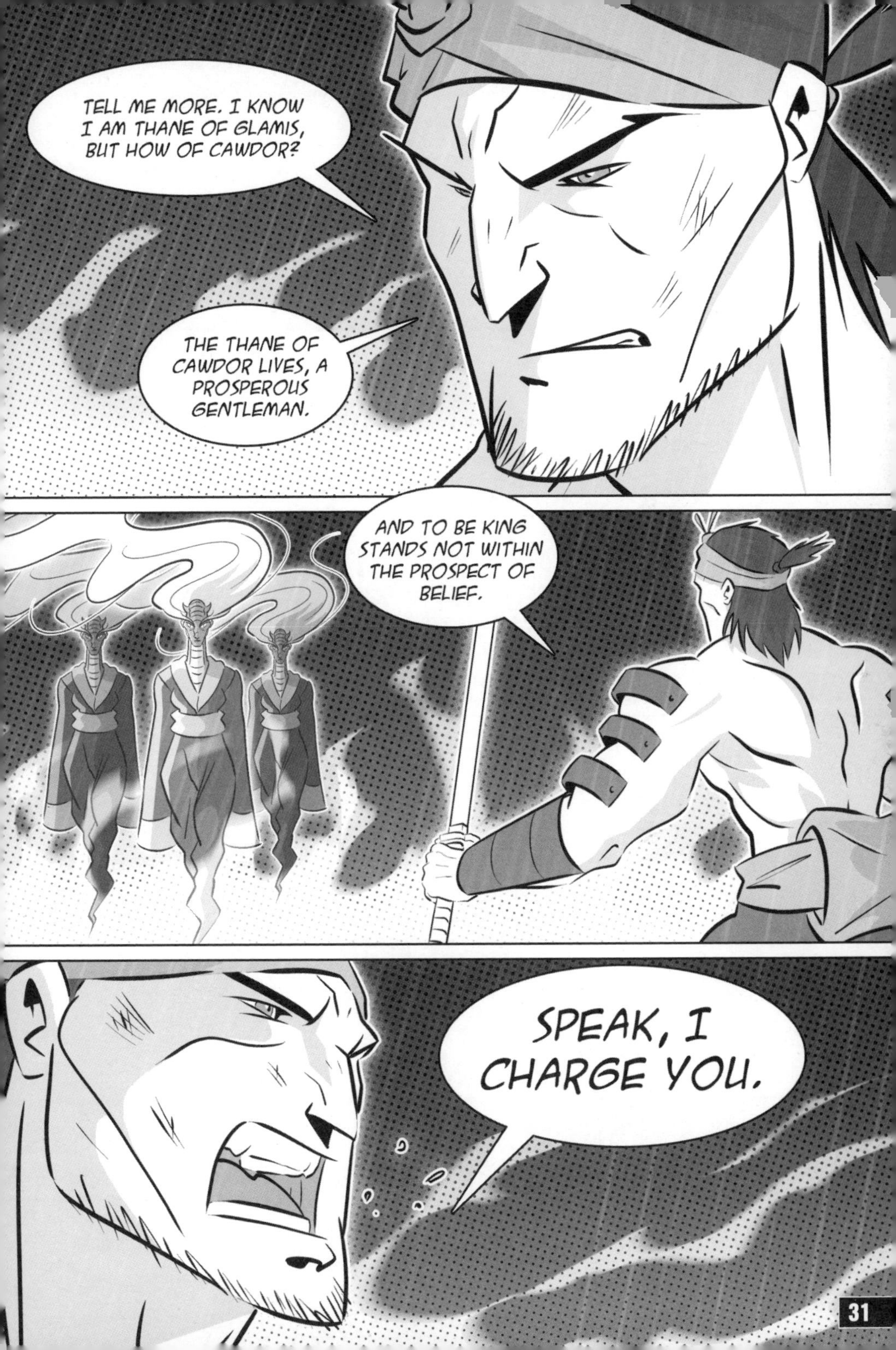
TELL ME MORE. I KNOW I AM THANE OF GLAMIS, BUT HOW OF CAWDOR?
THE THANE OF CAWDOR LIVES, A PROSPEROUS GENTLEMAN.
AND TO BE KING STANDS NOT WITHIN THE PROSPECT OF BELIEF.
SPEAK, I CHARGE YOU.

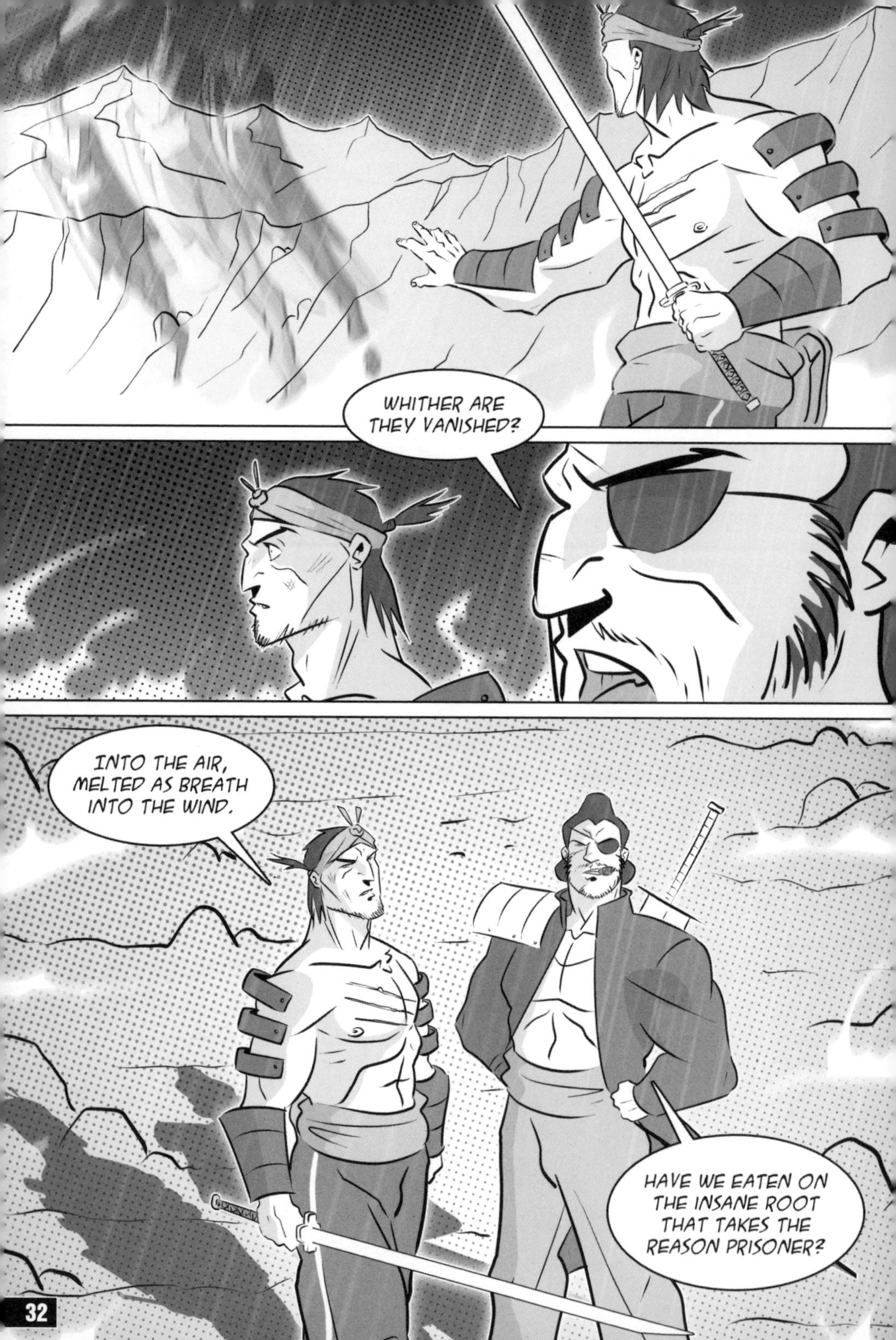
WHITHER ARE THEY VANISHED?
INTO THE AIR, MELTED AS BREATH INTO THE WIND.
HAVE WE EATEN ON THE INSANE ROOT THAT TAKES THE REASON PRISONER?

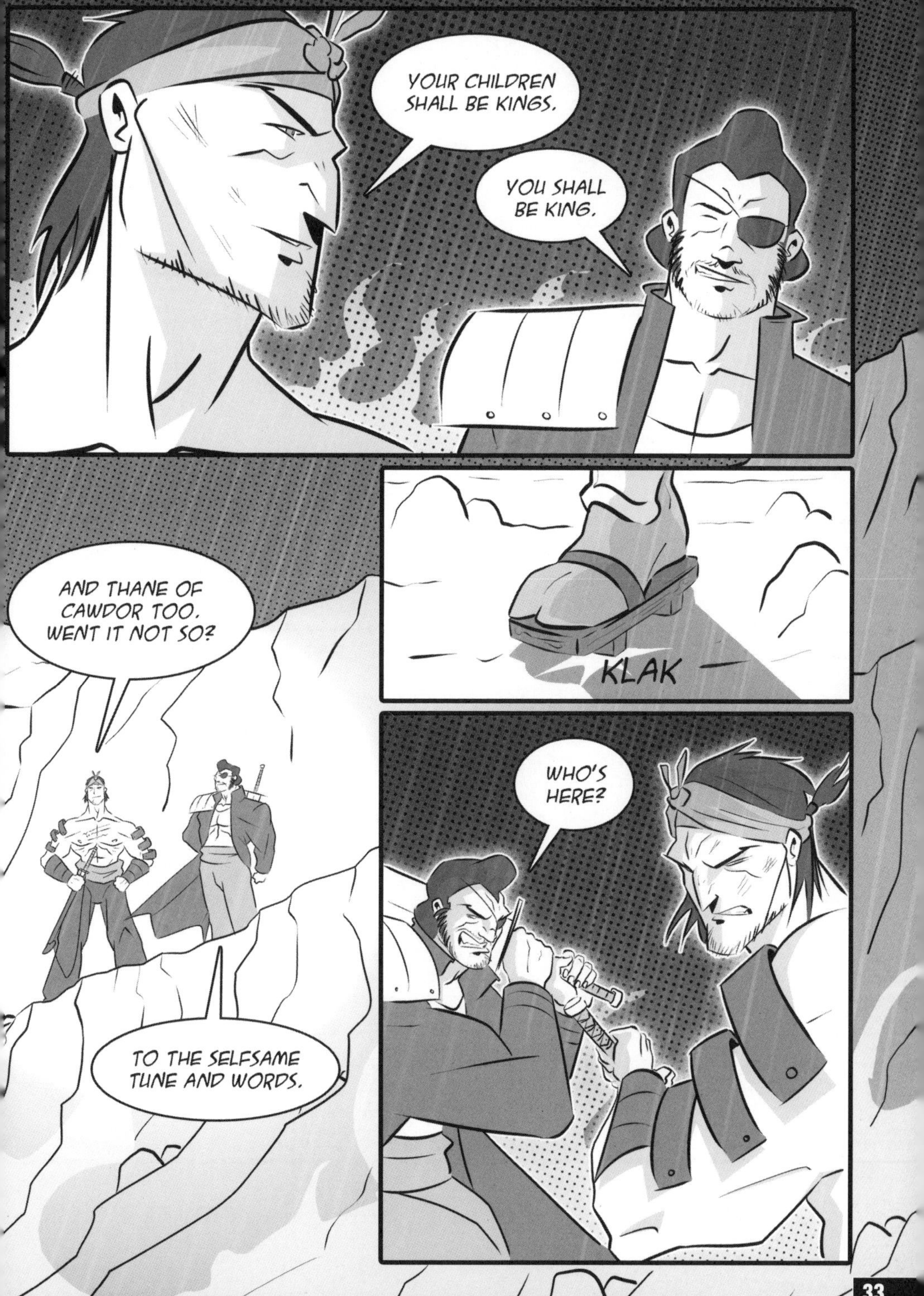
YOUR CHILDREN SHALL BE KINGS.
YOU SHALL BE KING.
AND THANE OF CAWDOR TOO. WENT IT NOT SO?
TO THE SELFSAME TUNE AND WORDS.
KLAK
WHO'S HERE?

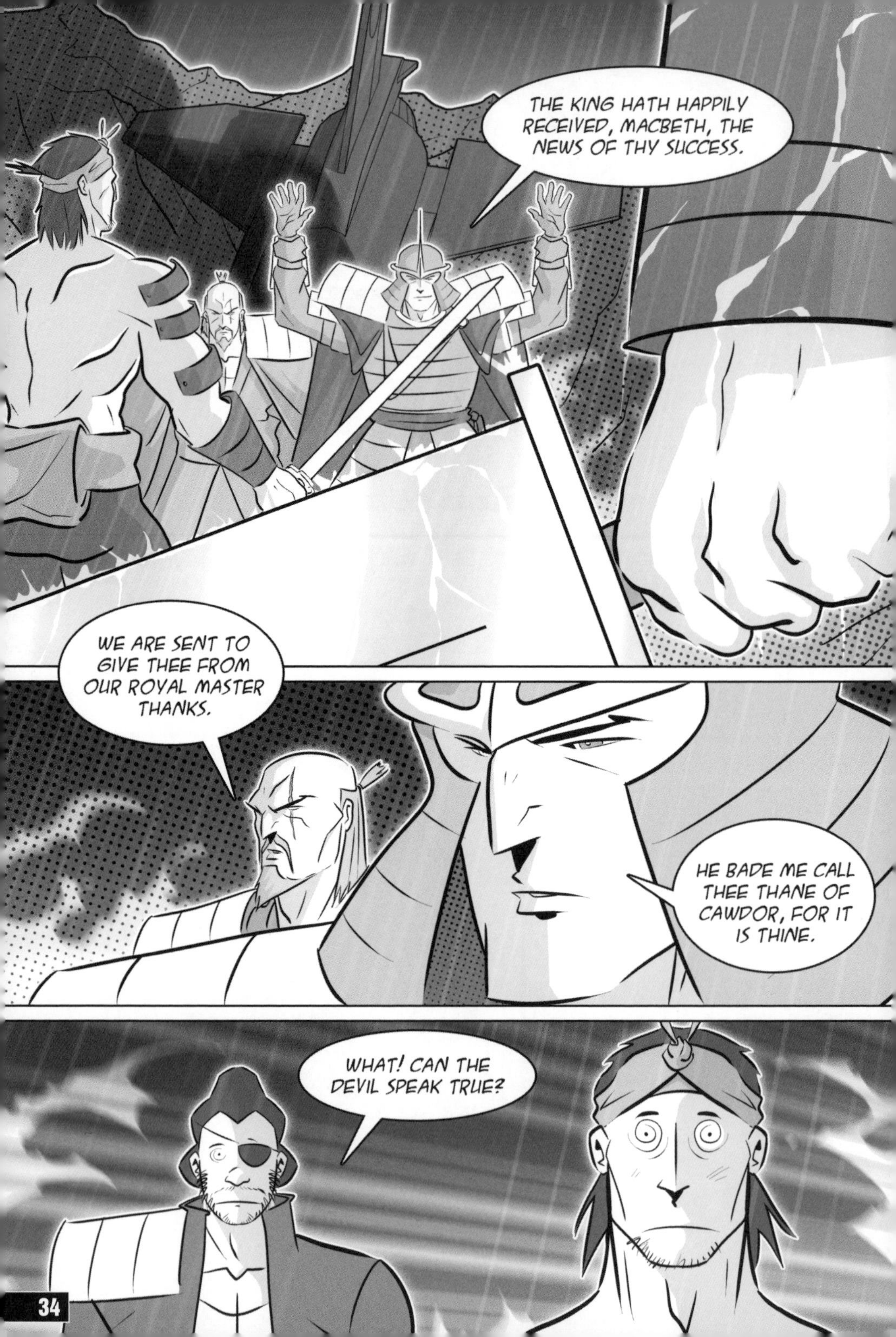
THE KING HATH HAPPILY RECEIVED, MACBETH, THE NEWS OF THY SUCCESS.
WE ARE SENT TO GIVE THEE FROM OUR ROYAL MASTER THANKS.
HE BADE ME CALL THEE THANE OF CAWDOR, FOR IT IS THINE.
WHAT! CAN THE DEVIL SPEAK TRUE?

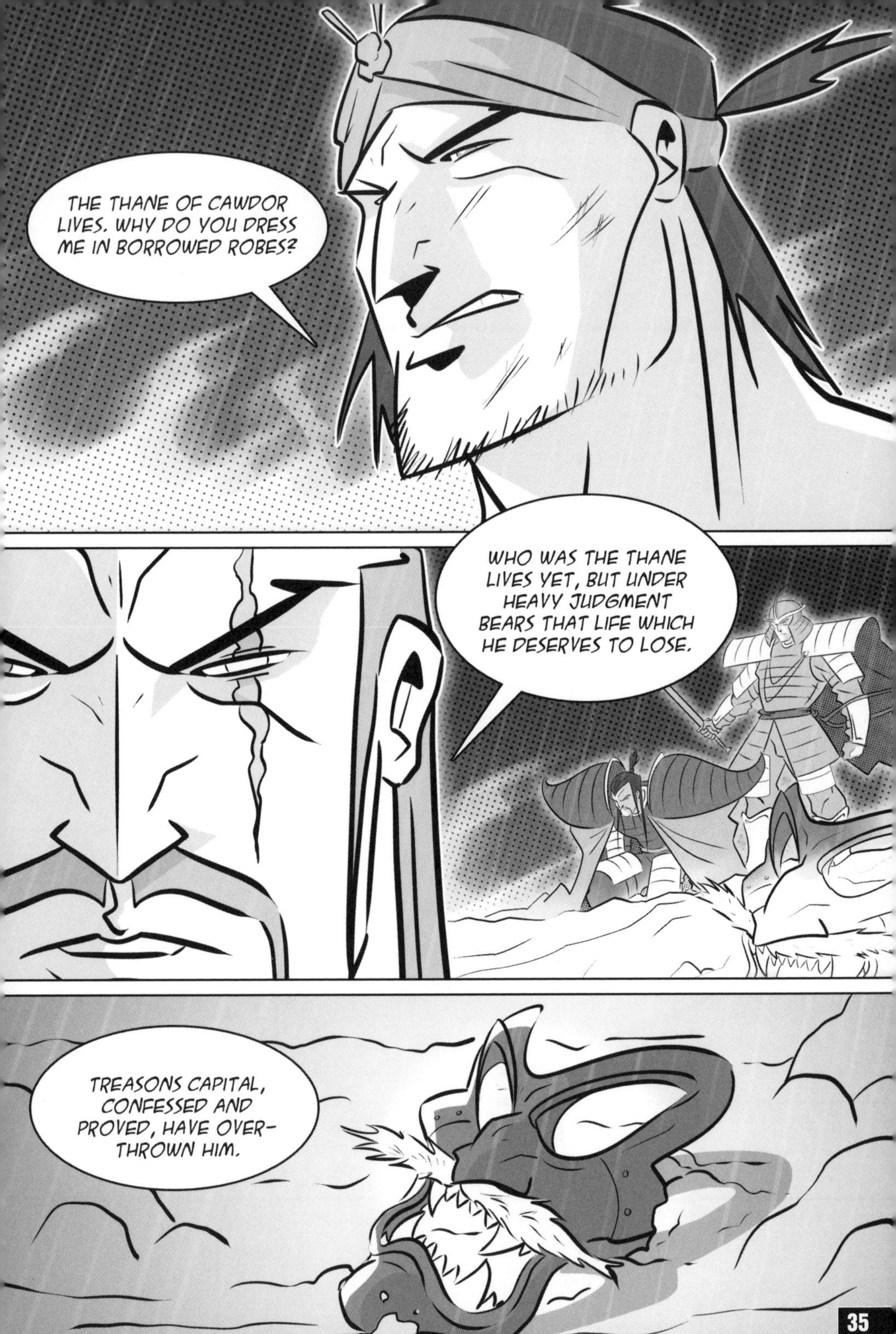
THE THANE OF CAWDOR LIVES. WHY DO YOU DRESS ME IN BORROWED ROBES?
WHO WAS THE THANE LIVES YET, BUT UNDER HEAVY JUDGMENT BEARS THAT LIFE WHICH HE DESERVES TO LOSE.
TREASONS CAPITAL, CONFESSED AND PROVED, HAVE OVER-THROWN HIM.

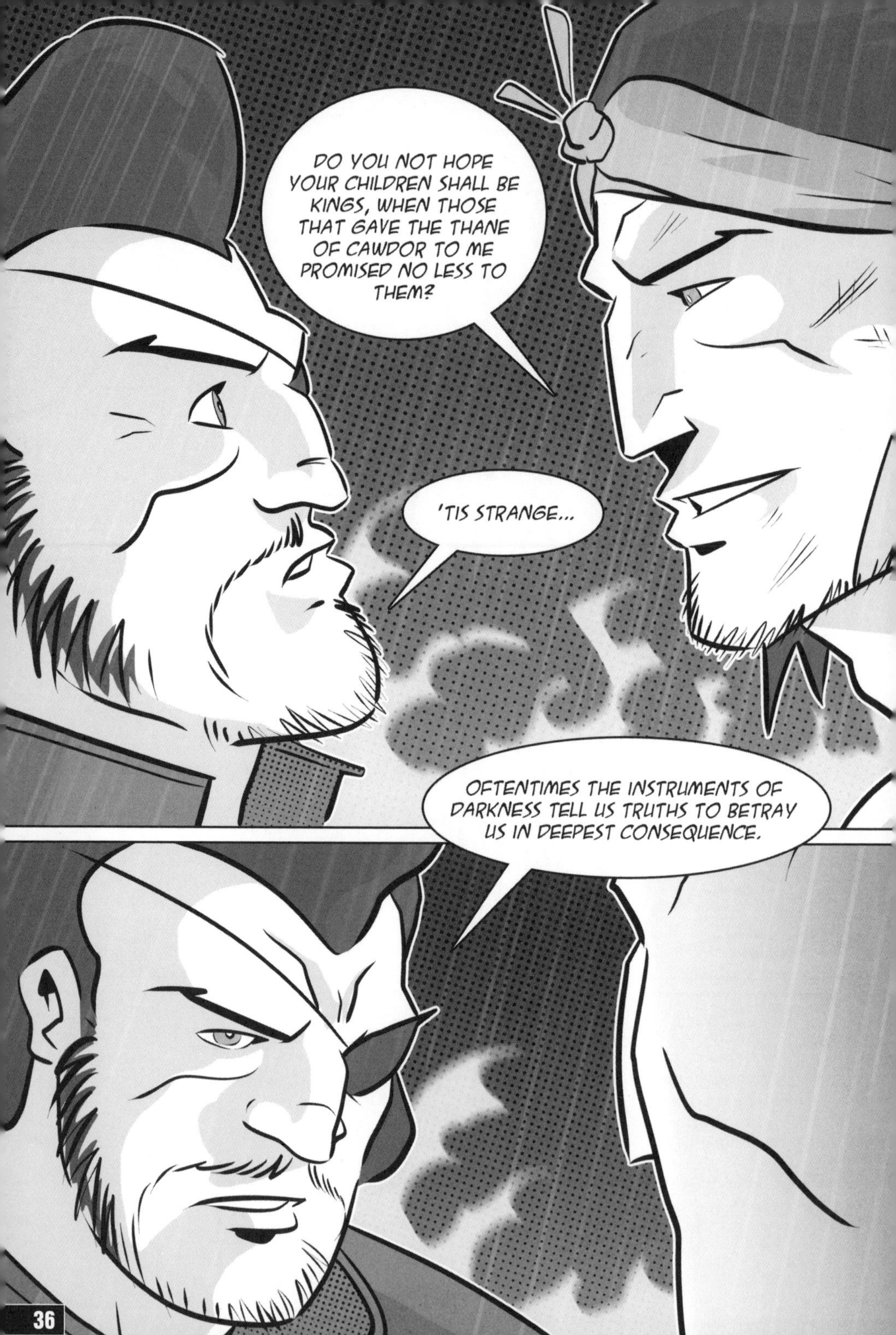
DO YOU NOT HOPE YOUR CHILDREN SHALL BE KINGS, WHEN THOSE THAT GAVE THE THANE OF CAWDOR TO ME PROMISED NO LESS TO THEM?
'TIS STRANGE...
OFTENTIMES THE INSTRUMENTS OF DARKNESS TELL US TRUTHS TO BETRAY US IN DEEPEST CONSEQUENCE.

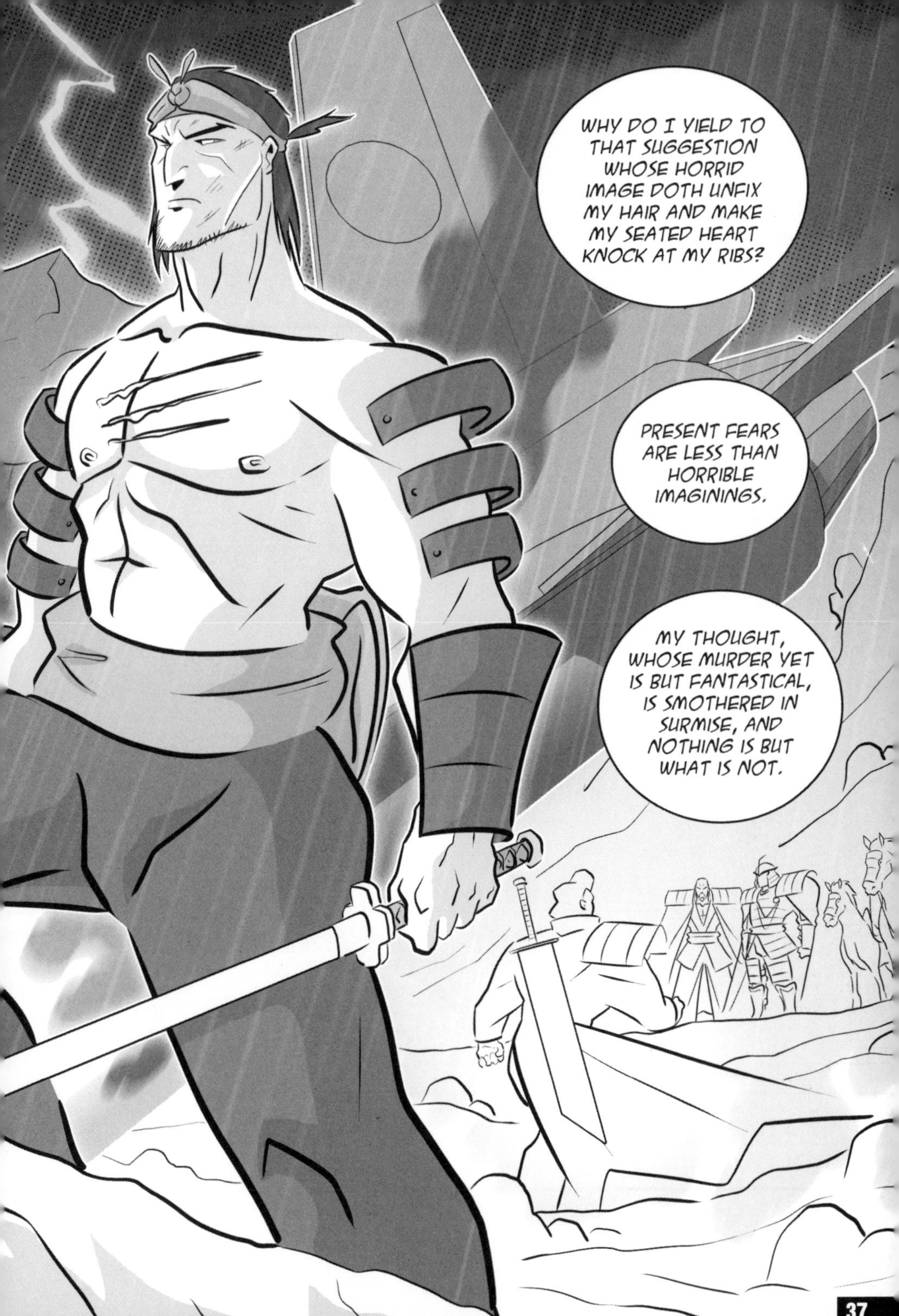
WHY DO I YIELD TO THAT SUGGESTION WHOSE HORRID IMAGE DOTH UNFIX MY HAIR AND MAKE MY SEATED HEART KNOCK AT MY RIBS?
PRESENT FEARS ARE LESS THAN HORRIBLE IMAGININGS.
MY THOUGHT, WHOSE MURDER YET IS BUT FANTASTICAL, IS SMOTHERED IN SURMISE, AND NOTHING IS BUT WHAT IS NOT.

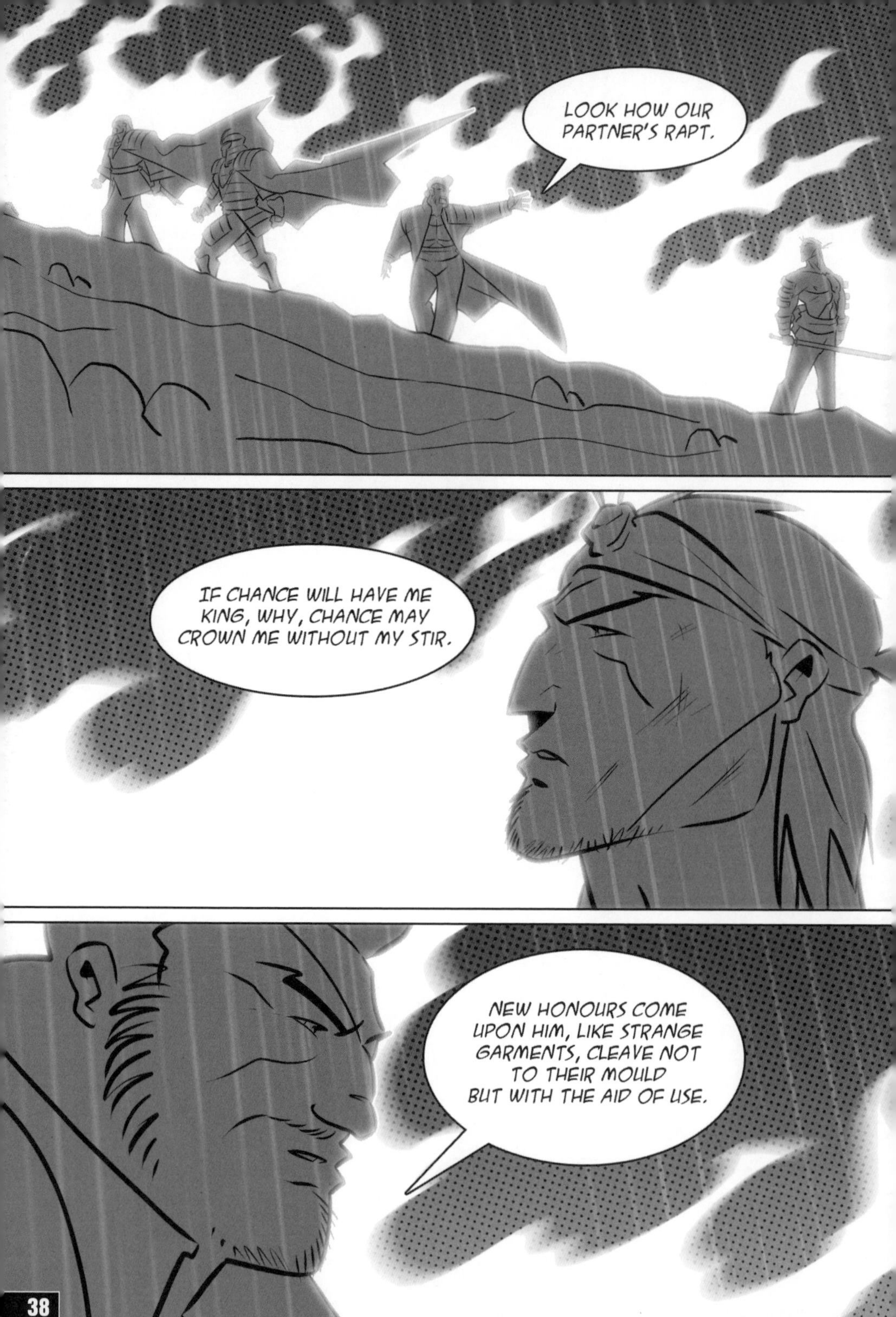
LOOK HOW OUR PARTNER'S RAPT.
IF CHANCE WILL HAVE ME KING, WHY, CHANCE MAY CROWN ME WITHOUT MY STIR.
NEW HONOURS COME UPON HIM, LIKE STRANGE GARMENTS, CLEAVE NOT TO THEIR MOULD BUT WITH THE AID OF USE.

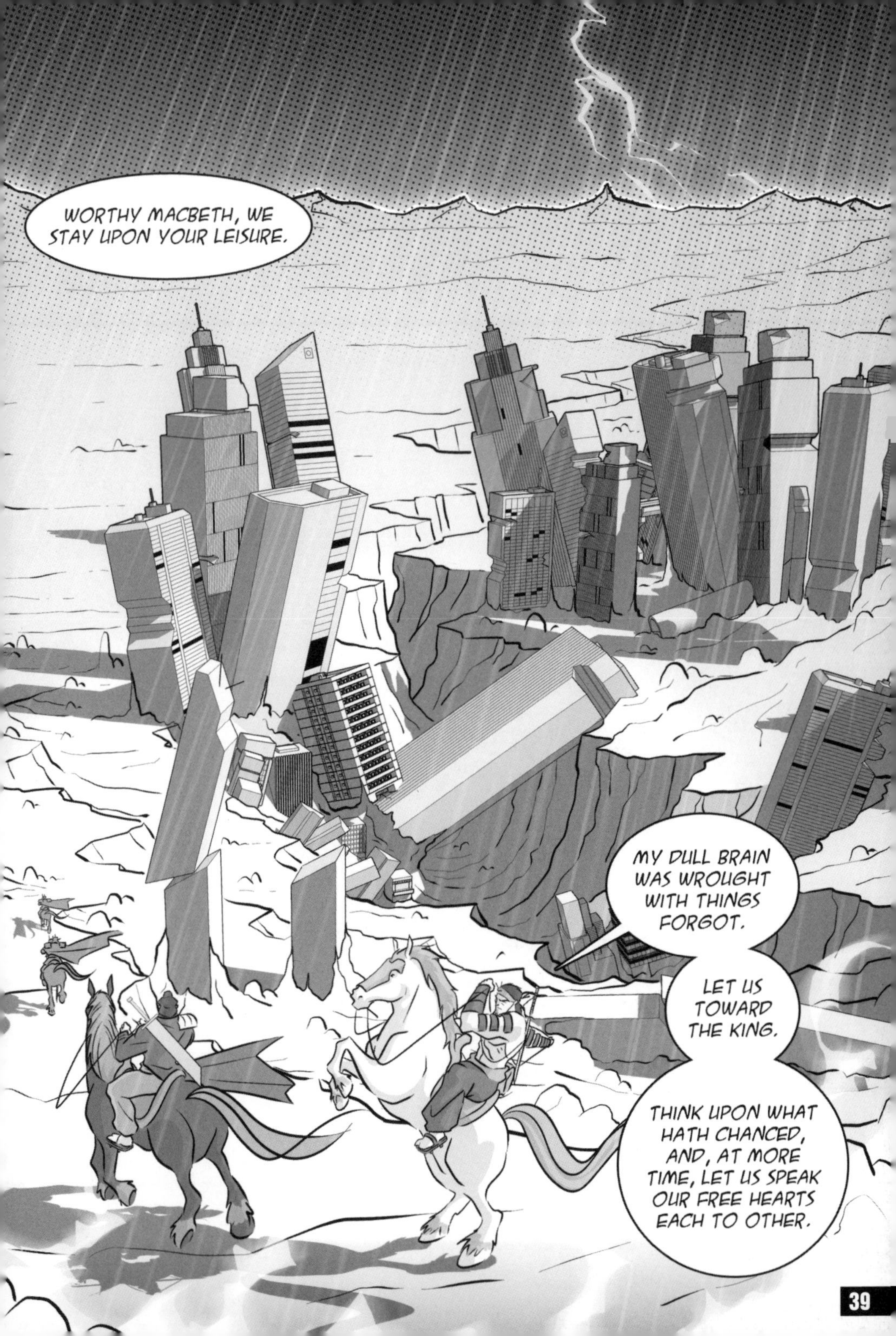
WORTHY MACBETH, WE STAY UPON YOUR LEISURE.
MY DULL BRAIN WAS WROUGHT WITH THINGS FORGOT.
LET US TOWARD THE KING.
THINK UPON WHAT HATH CHANCED, AND, AT MORE TIME, LET US SPEAK OUR FREE HEARTS EACH TO OTHER.

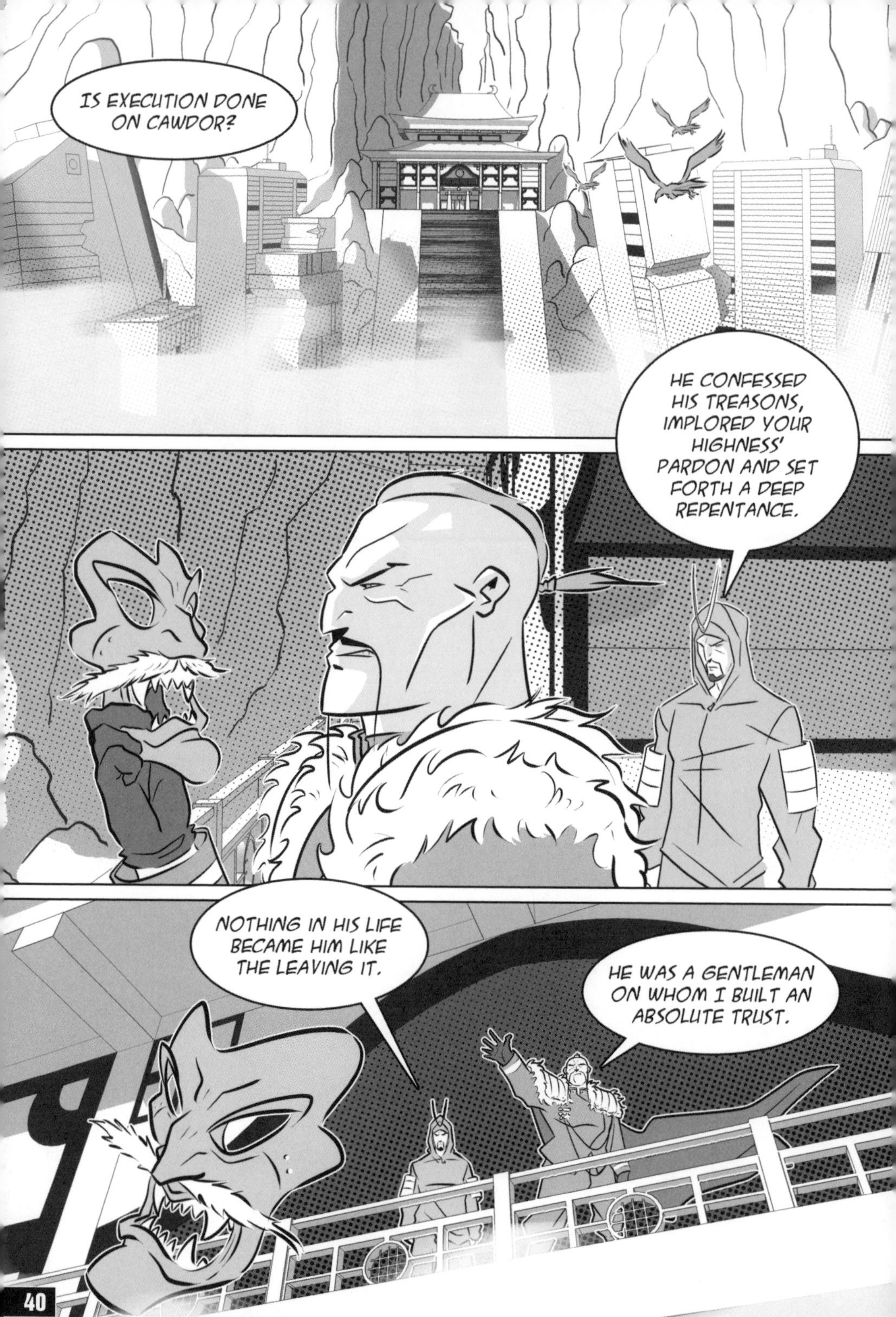
IS EXECUTION DONE ON CAWDOR?
HE CONFESSED HIS TREASONS, IMPLORED YOUR HIGHNESS' PARDON AND SET FORTH A DEEP REPENTANCE.
NOTHING IN HIS LIFE BECAME HIM LIKE THE LEAVING IT.
HE WAS A GENTLEMAN ON WHOM I BUILT AN ABSOLUTE TRUST.

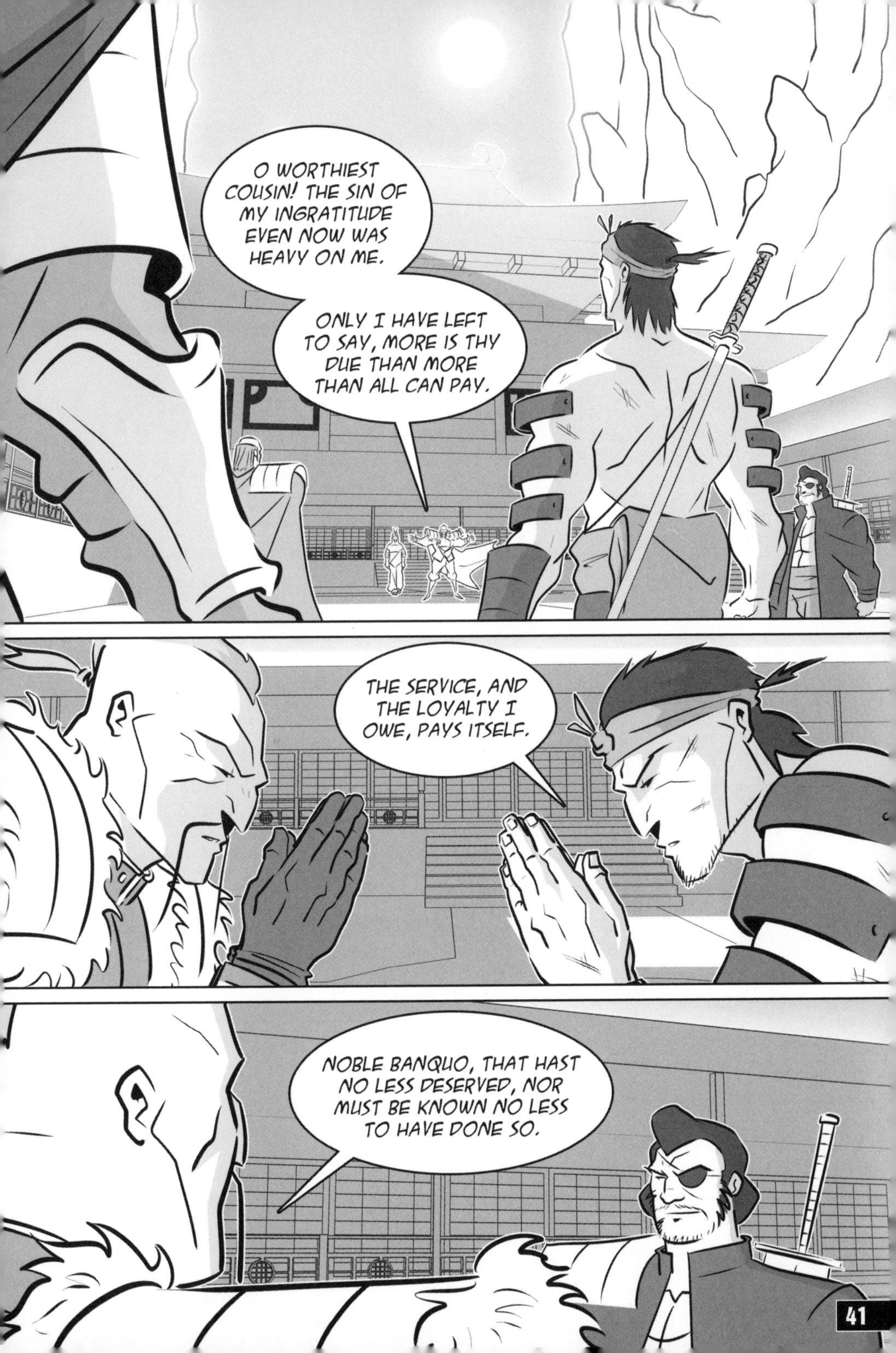
O WORTHIEST COUSIN! THE SIN OF MY INGRATITUDE EVEN NOW WAS HEAVY ON ME.
ONLY I HAVE LEFT TO SAY, MORE IS THY DUE THAN MORE THAN ALL CAN PAY.
THE SERVICE, AND THE LOYALTY I OWE, PAYS ITSELF.
NOBLE BANQUO, THAT HAST NO LESS DESERVED, NOR MUST BE KNOWN NO LESS TO HAVE DONE SO.

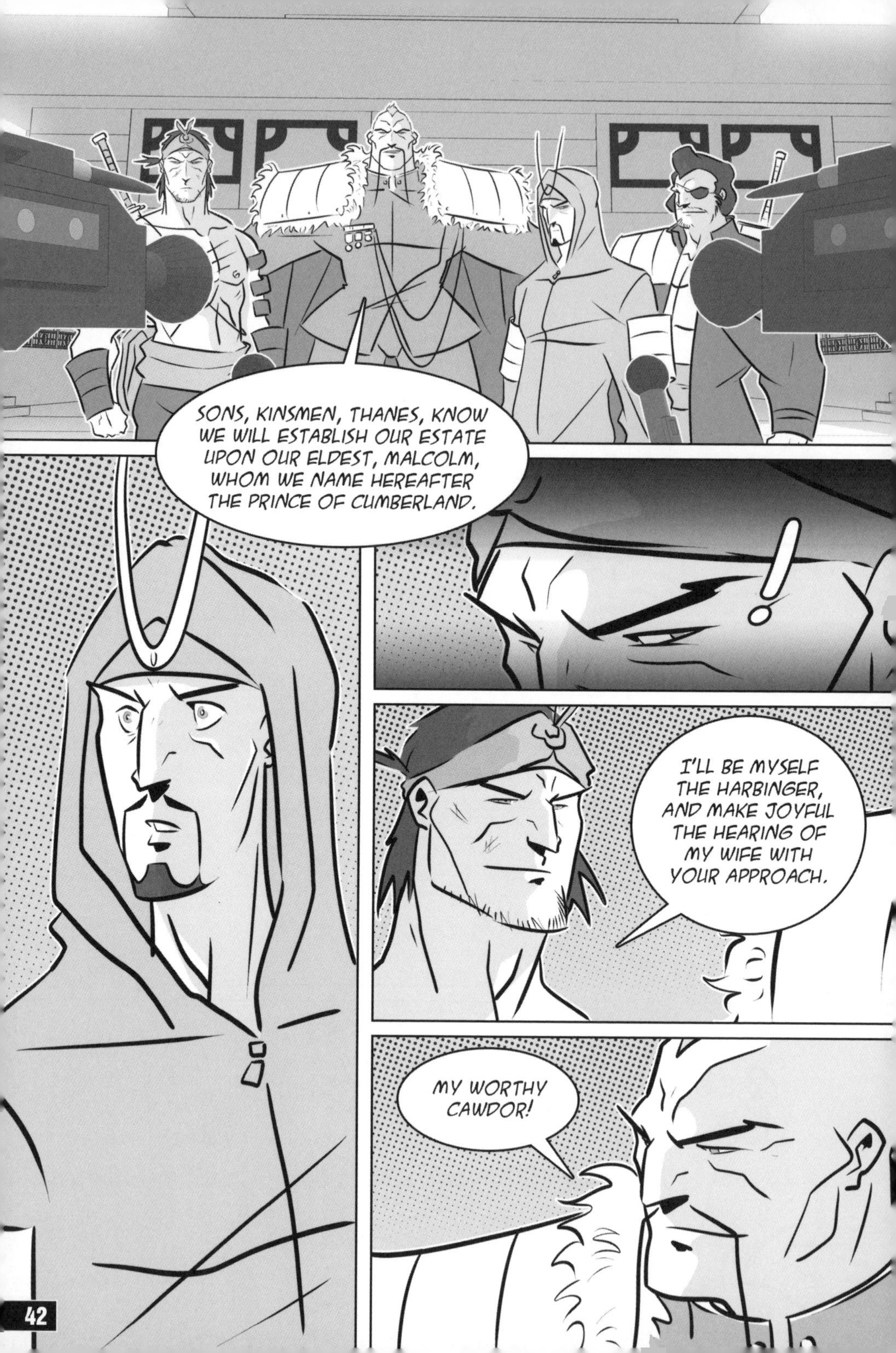
SONS, KINSMEN, THANES, KNOW WE WILL ESTABLISH OUR ESTATE UPON OUR ELDEST, MALCOLM, WHOM WE NAME HEREAFTER THE PRINCE OF CUMBERLAND.
!
I'LL BE MYSELF THE HARBINGER, AND MAKE JOYFUL THE HEARING OF MY WIFE WITH YOUR APPROACH.
MY WORTHY CAWDOR!

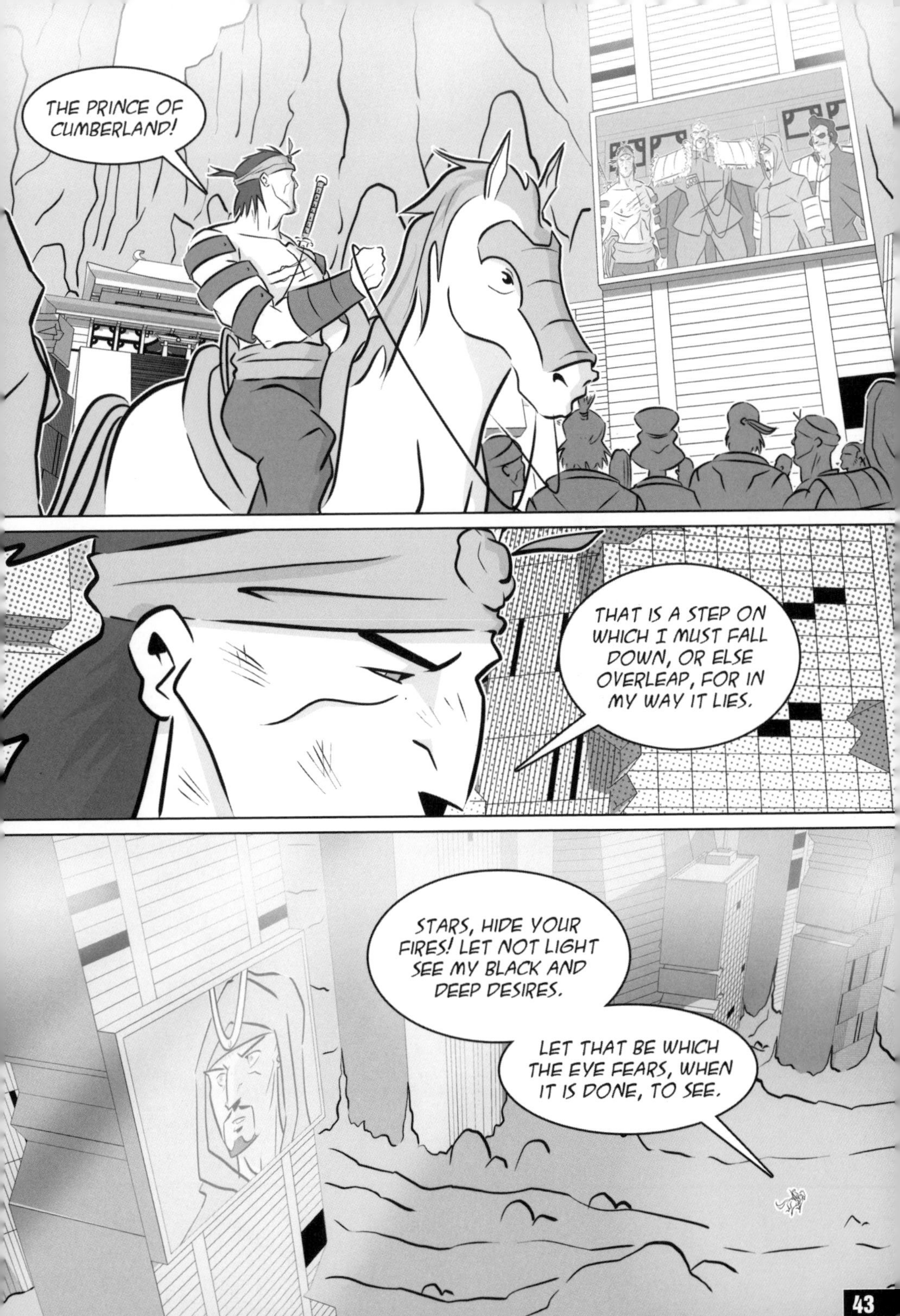
THE PRINCE OF CUMBERLAND!
THAT IS A STEP ON WHICH I MUST FALL DOWN, OR ELSE OVERLEAP, FOR IN MY WAY IT LIES.
STARS, HIDE YOUR FIRES! LET NOT LIGHT SEE MY BLACK AND DEEP DESIRES.
LET THAT BE WHICH THE EYE FEARS, WHEN IT IS DONE, TO SEE.

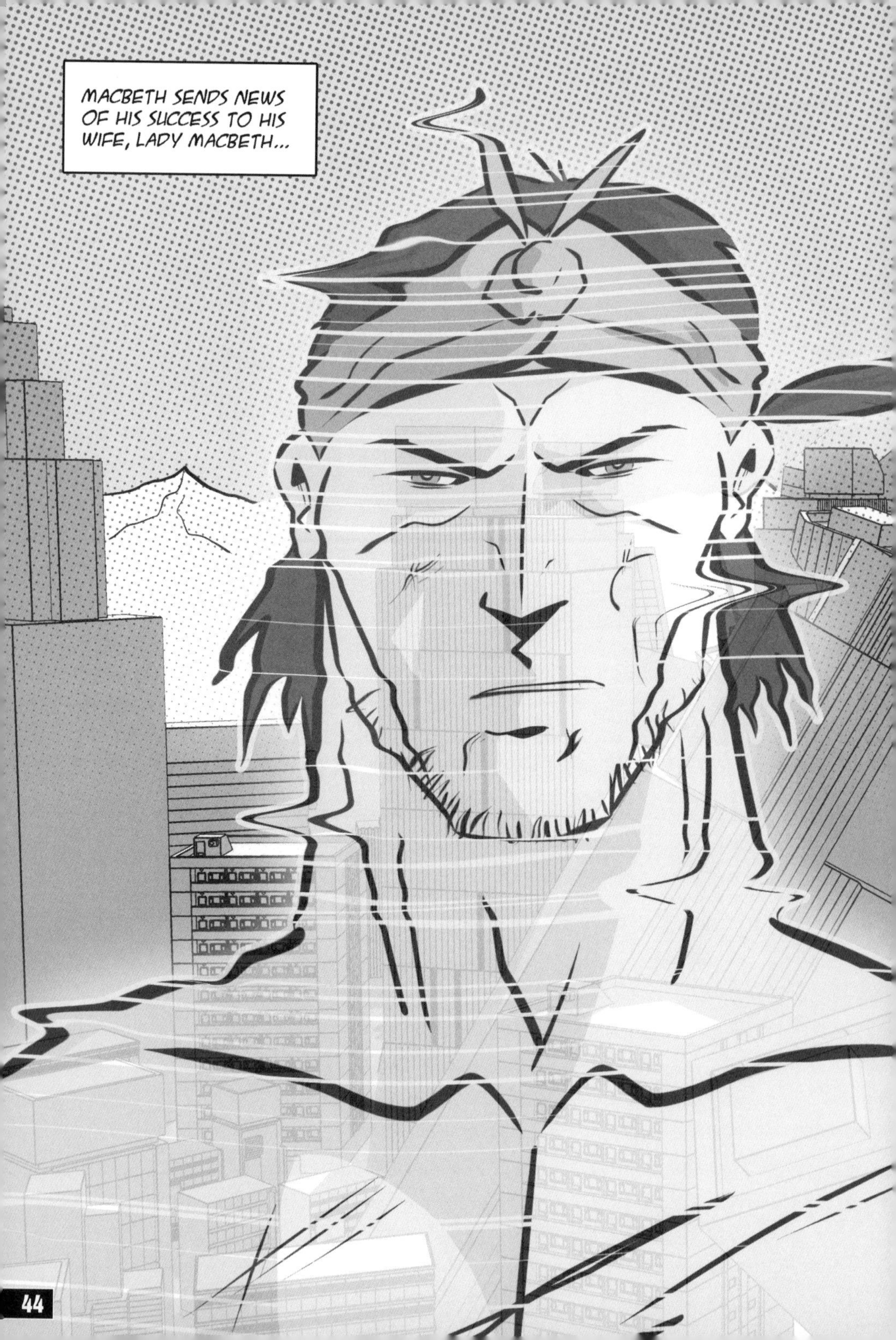
MACBETH SENDS NEWS OF HIS SUCCESS TO HIS WIFE, LADY MACBETH...

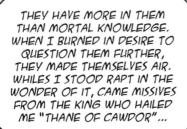

THEY HAVE MORE IN THEM THAN MORTAL KNOWLEDGE. WHEN I BURNED IN DESIRE TO QUESTION THEM FURTHER, THEY MADE THEMSELVES AIR. WHILES I STOOD RAPT IN THE WONDER OF IT, CAME MISSIVES FROM THE KING WHO HAILED ME "THANE OF CAWDOR"...

... BY WHICH TITLE, BEFORE, THESE WEIRD SISTERS SALUTED ME, AND REFERRED ME TO THE COMING ON OF TIME WITH "HAIL, KING THAT SHALT BE!" THIS HAVE I THOUGHT GOOD TO DELIVER THEE, MY DEAREST PARTNER OF GREATNESS.

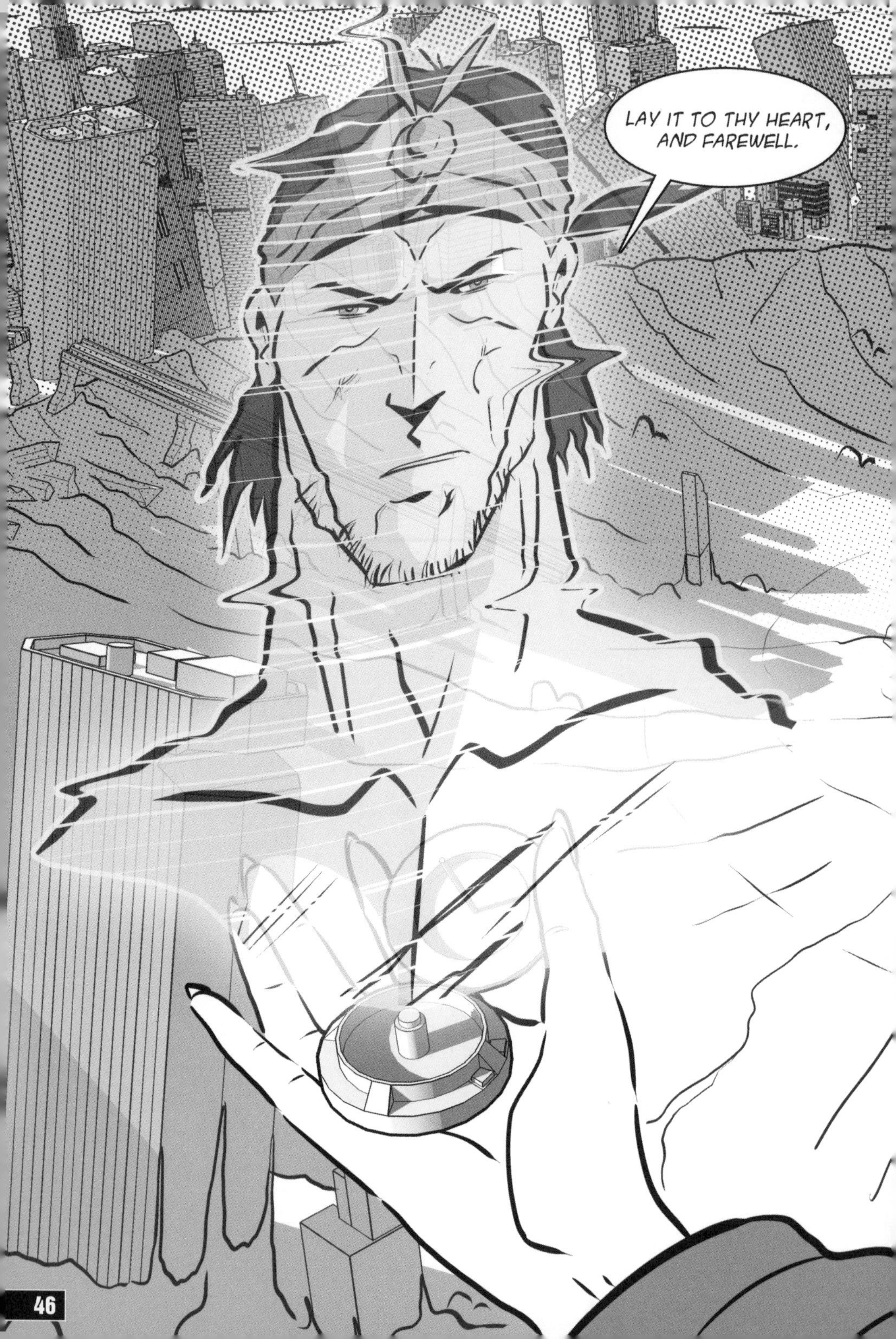
LAY IT TO THY HEART, AND FAREWELL.

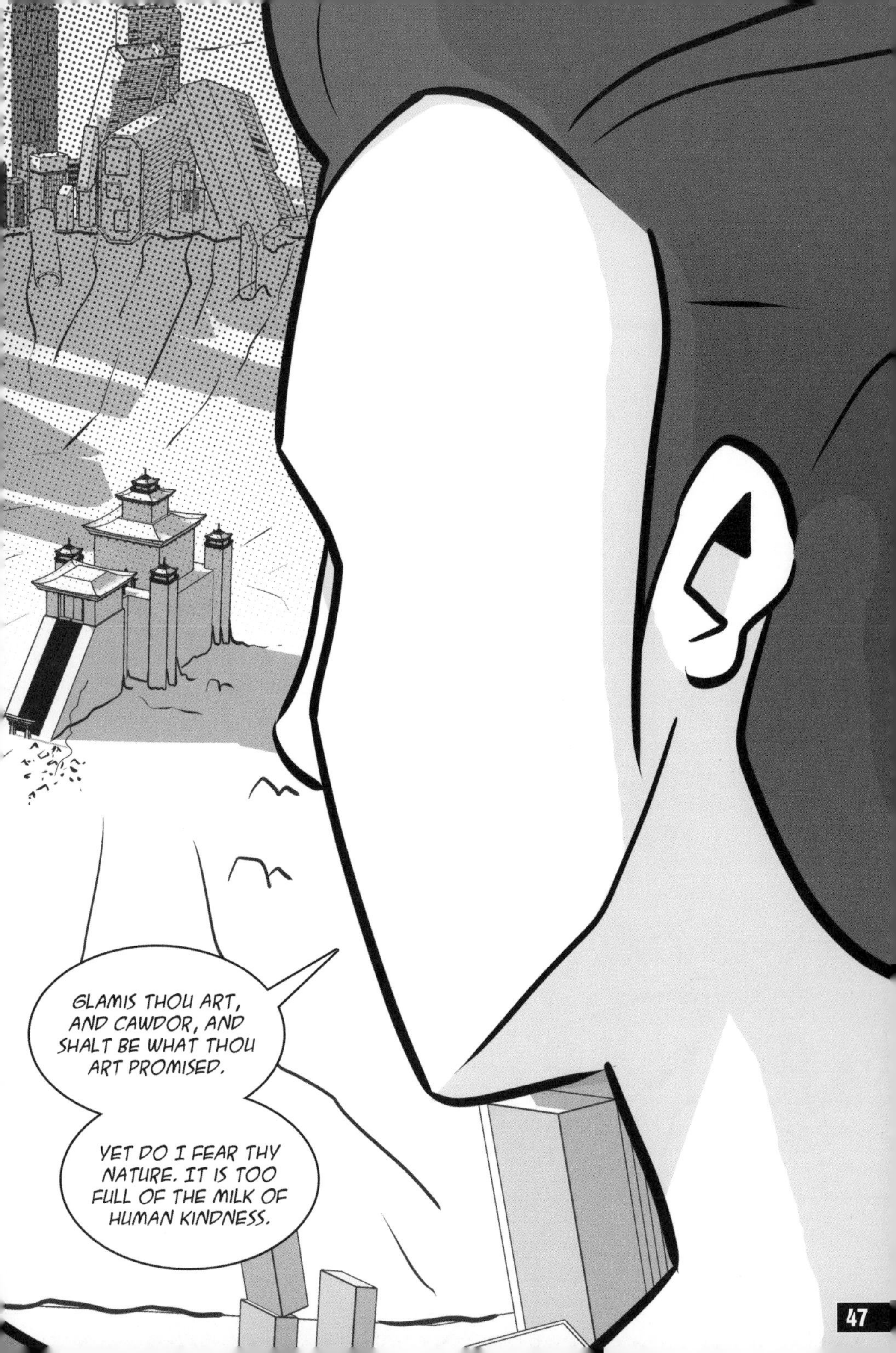
GLAMIS THOU ART, AND CAWDOR, AND SHALT BE WHAT THOU ART PROMISED.
YET DO I FEAR THY NATURE. IT IS TOO FULL OF THE MILK OF HUMAN KINDNESS.

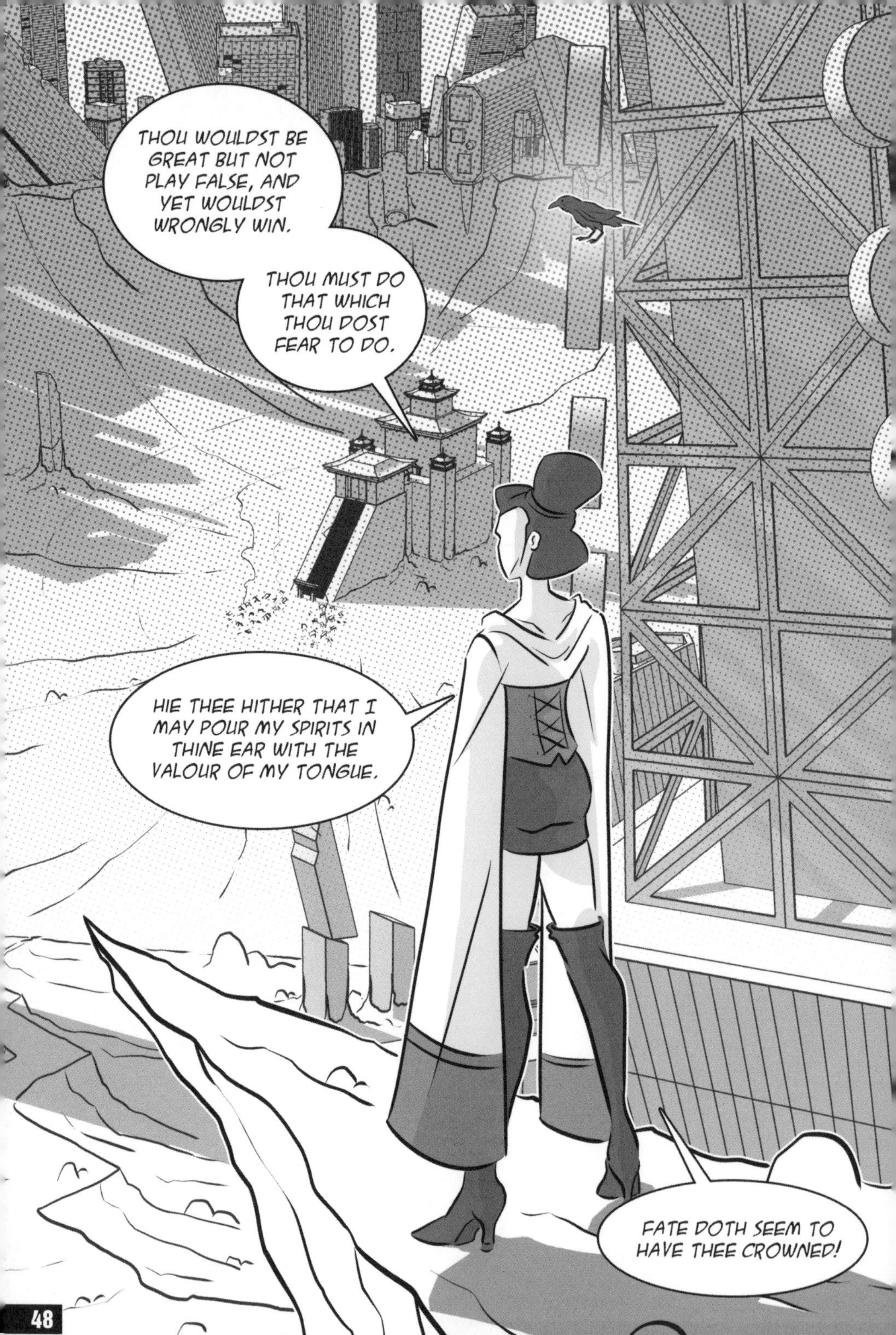
THOU WOULDST BE GREAT BUT NOT PLAY FALSE, AND YET WOULDST WRONGLY WIN.
THOU MUST DO THAT WHICH THOU DOST FEAR TO DO.
HIE THEE HITHER THAT I MAY POUR MY SPIRITS IN THINE EAR WITH THE VALOUR OF MY TONGUE.
FATE DOTH SEEM TO HAVE THEE CROWNED!

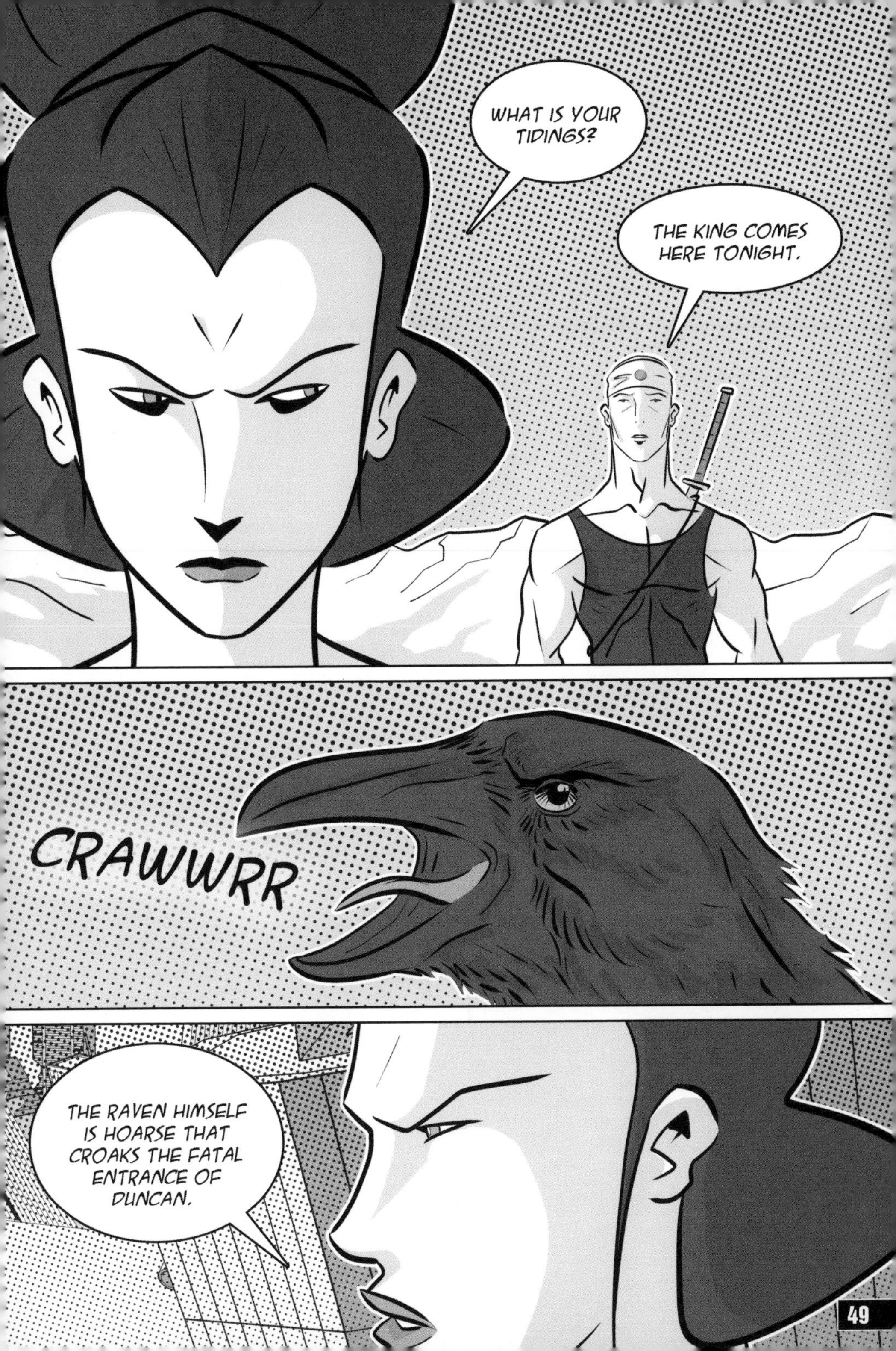
WHAT IS YOUR TIDINGS?
THE KING COMES HERE TONIGHT.
CRAWWRR
THE RAVEN HIMSELF IS HOARSE THAT CROAKS THE FATAL ENTRANCE OF DUNCAN.

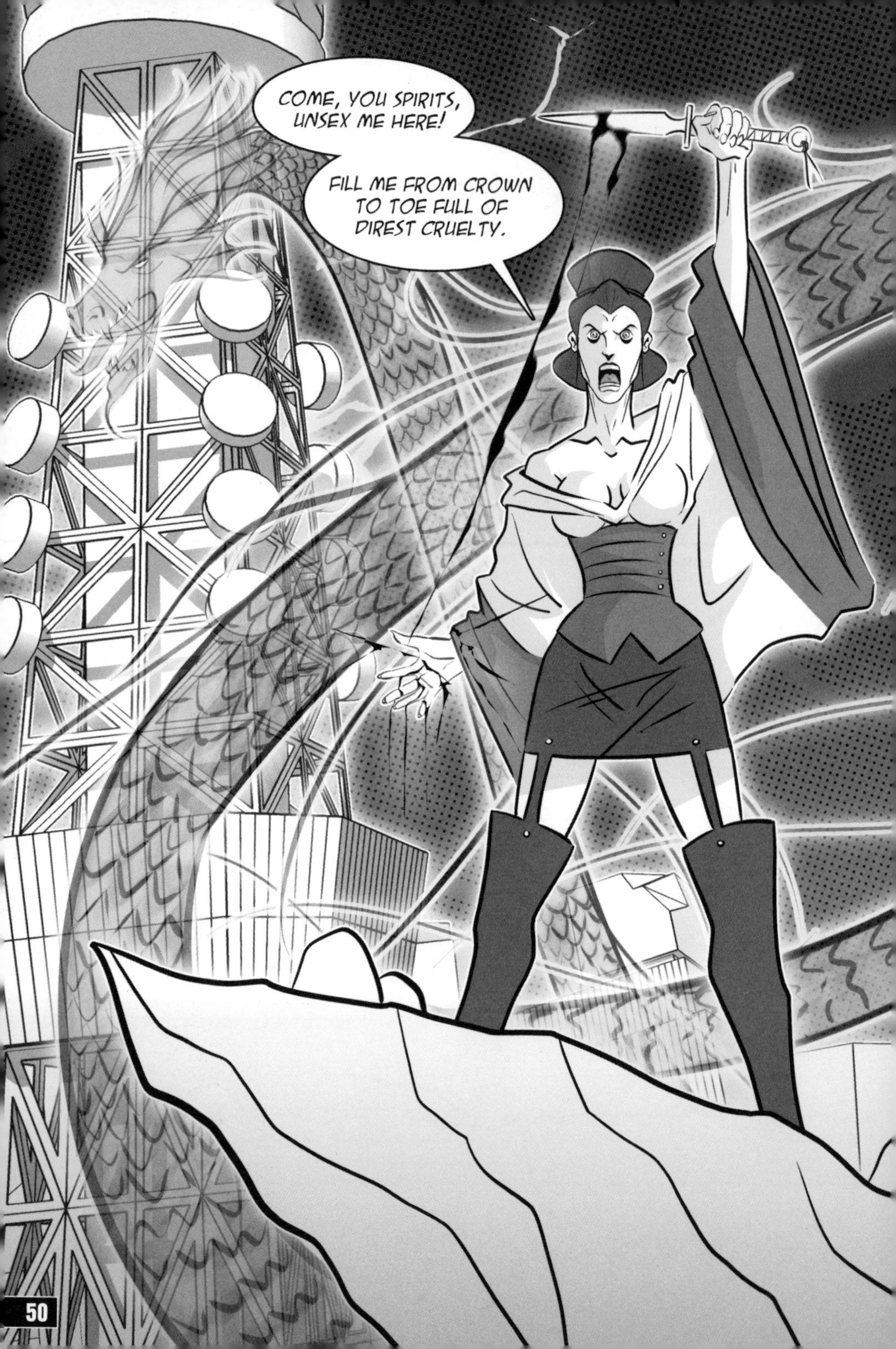
COME, YOU SPIRITS, UNSEX ME HERE!
FILL ME FROM CROWN TO TOE FULL OF DIREST CRUELTY.

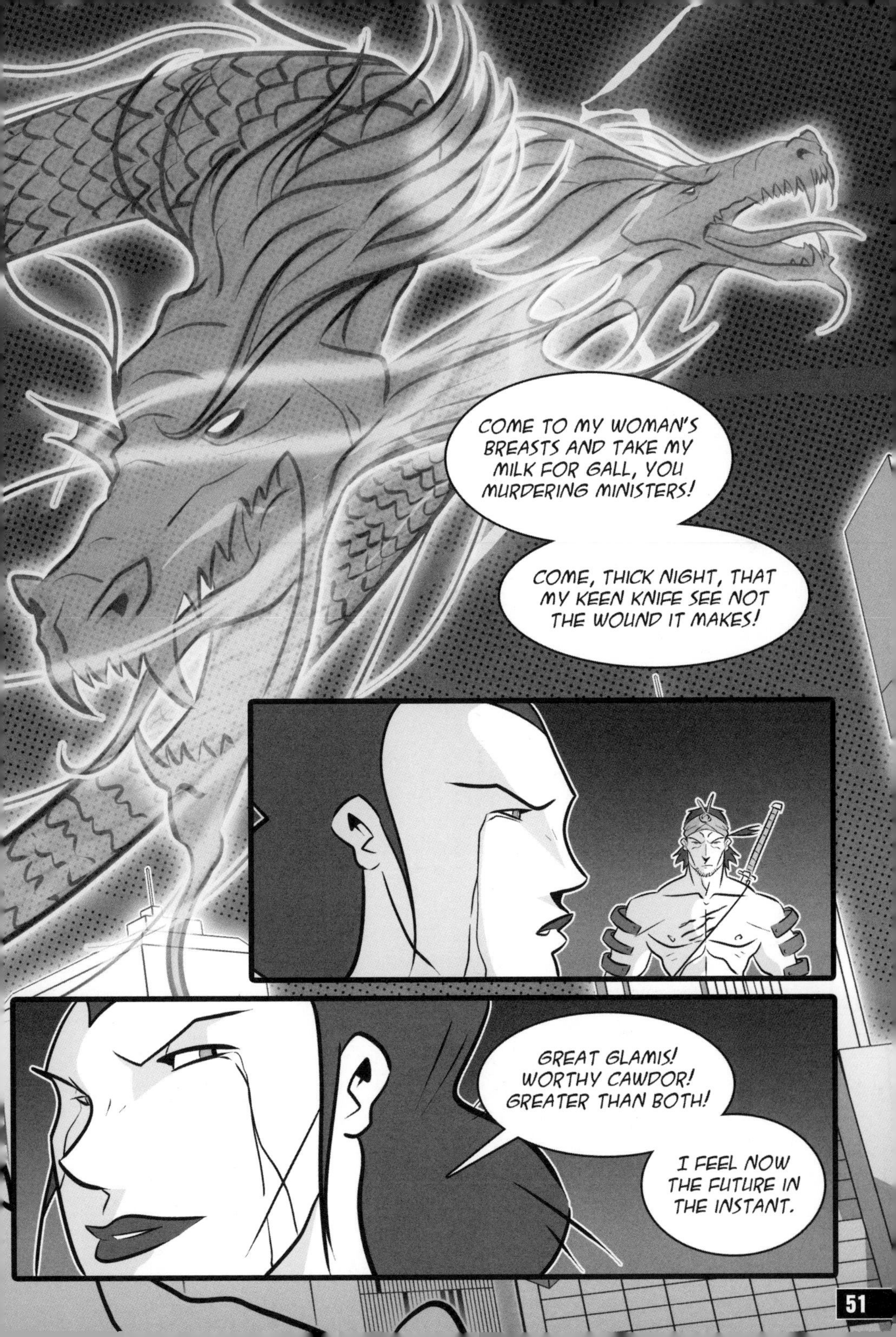
COME TO MY WOMAN'S BREASTS AND TAKE MY MILK FOR GALL, YOU MURDERING MINISTERS!
COME, THICK NIGHT, THAT MY KEEN KNIFE SEE NOT THE WOUND IT MAKES!
GREAT GLAMIS! WORTHY CAWDOR! GREATER THAN BOTH!
I FEEL NOW THE FUTURE IN THE INSTANT.

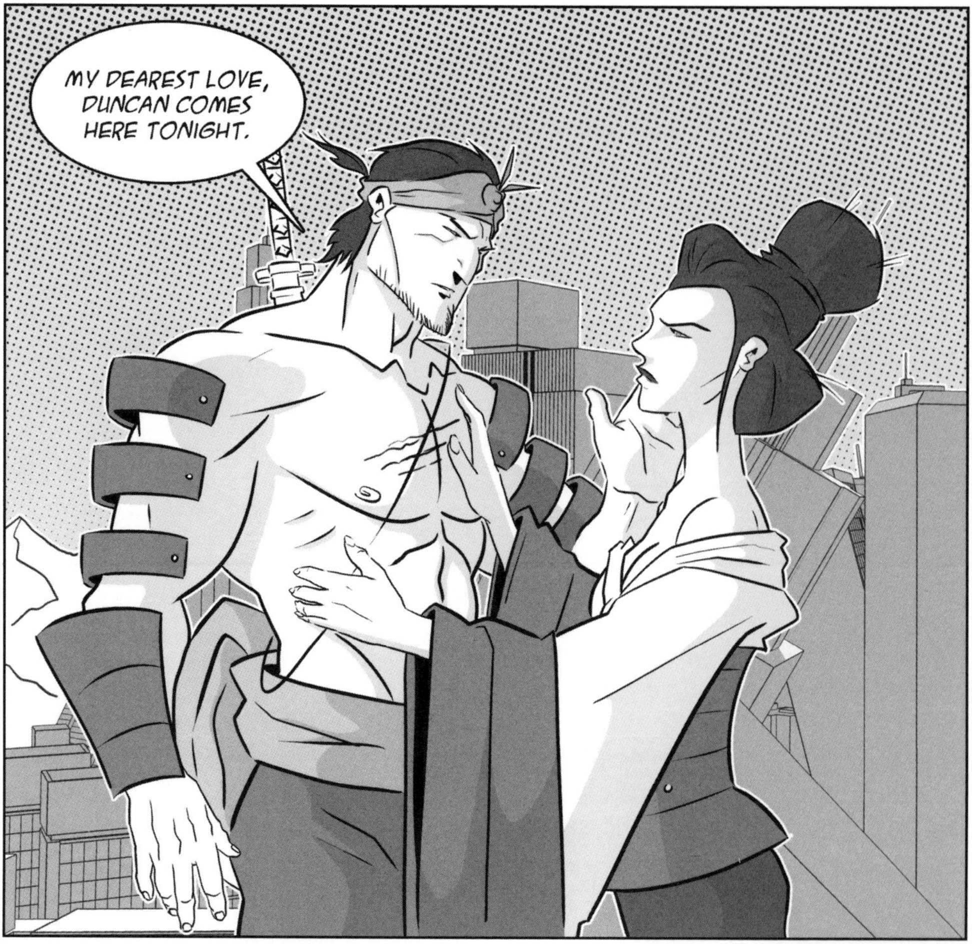
MY DEAREST LOVE, DUNCAN COMES HERE TONIGHT.

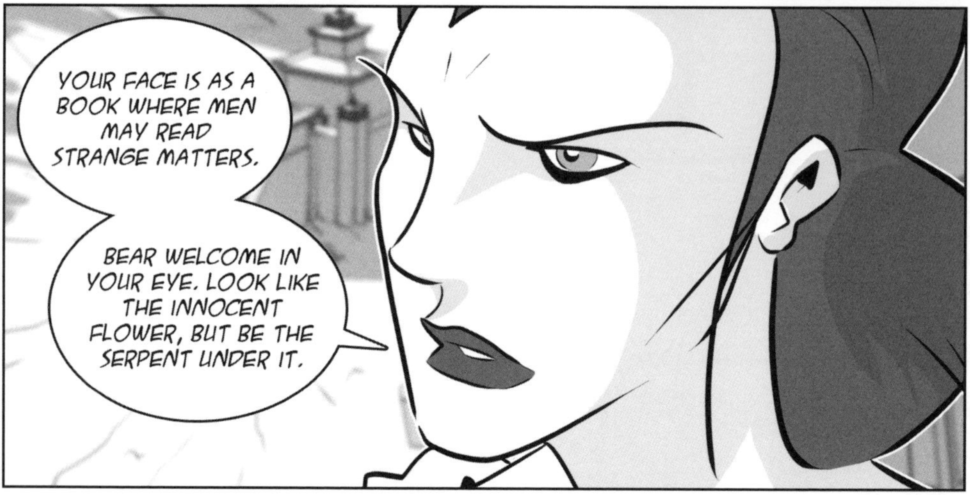
YOUR FACE IS AS A BOOK WHERE MEN MAY READ STRANGE MATTERS.
BEAR WELCOME IN YOUR EYE. LOOK LIKE THE INNOCENT FLOWER, BUT BE THE SERPENT UNDER IT.

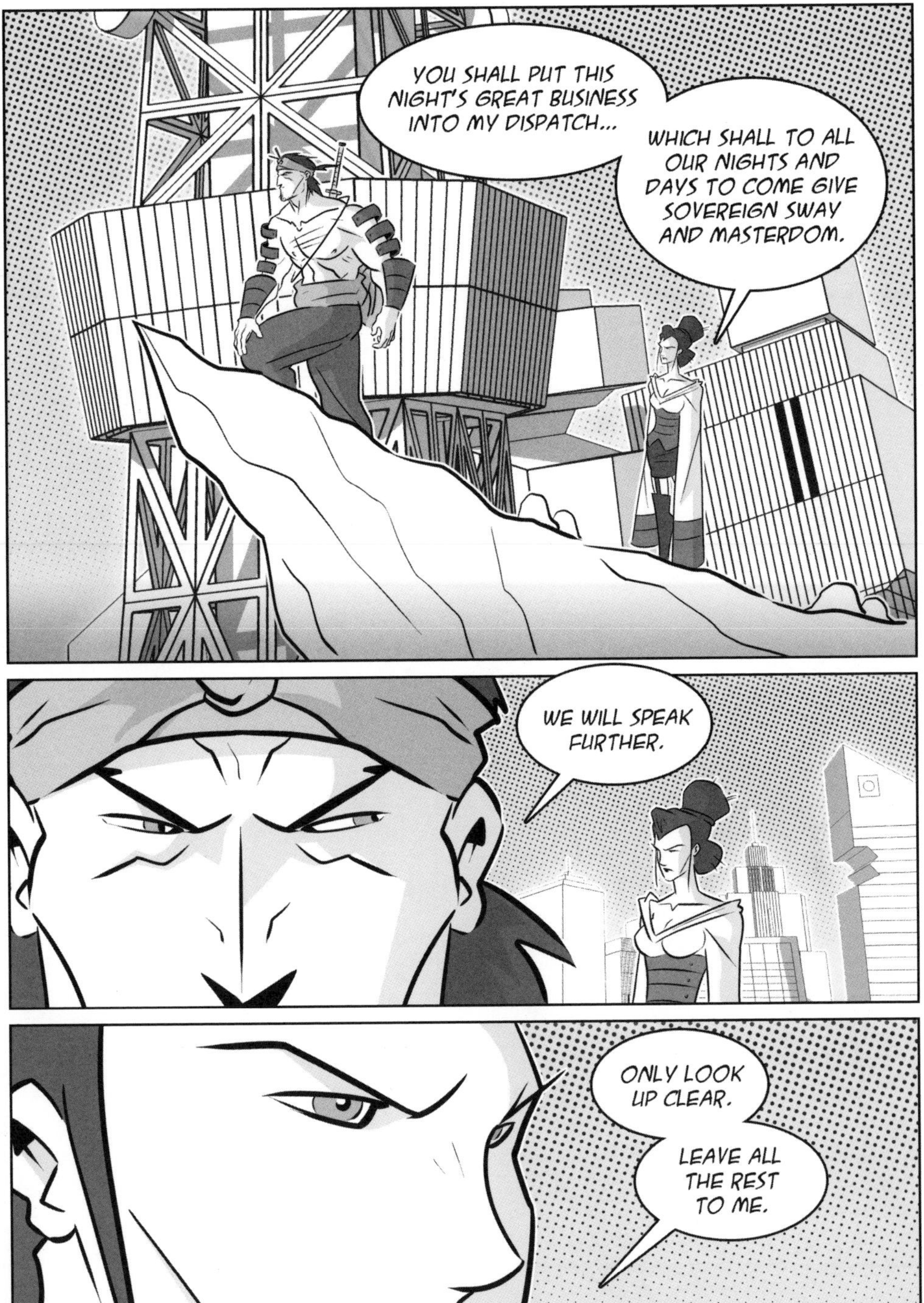
YOU SHALL PUT THIS NIGHT'S GREAT BUSINESS INTO MY DISPATCH...
WHICH SHALL TO ALL OUR NIGHTS AND DAYS TO COME GIVE SOVEREIGN SWAY AND MASTERDOM.
WE WILL SPEAK FURTHER.
ONLY LOOK UP CLEAR.
LEAVE ALL THE REST TO ME.

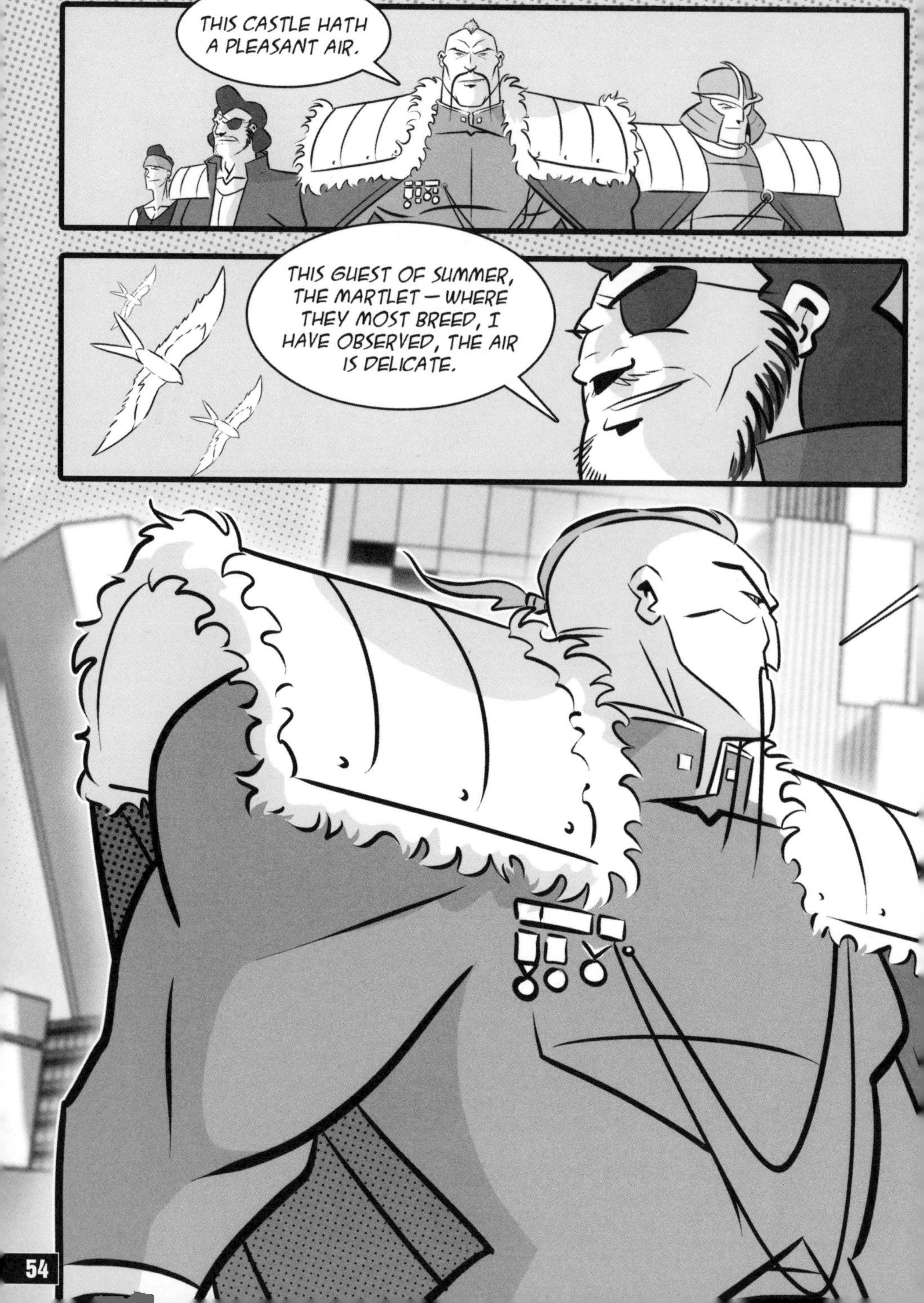
THIS CASTLE HATH A PLEASANT AIR.
THIS GUEST OF SUMMER, THE MARTLET — WHERE THEY MOST BREED, I HAVE OBSERVED, THE AIR IS DELICATE.

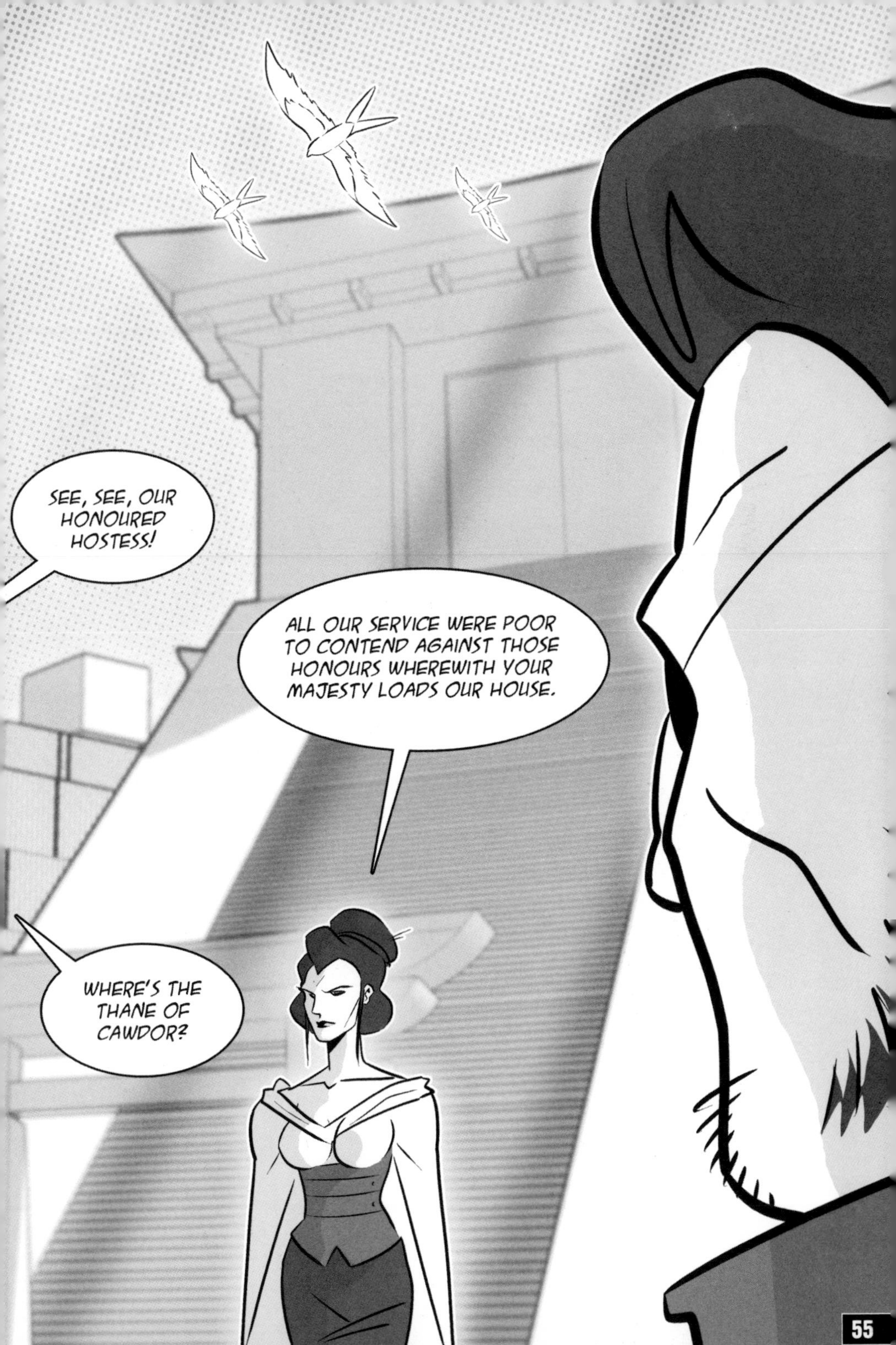
SEE, SEE, OUR HONOURED HOSTESS!
ALL OUR SERVICE WERE POOR TO CONTEND AGAINST THOSE HONOURS WHEREWITH YOUR MAJESTY LOADS OUR HOUSE.
WHERE'S THE THANE OF CAWDOR?

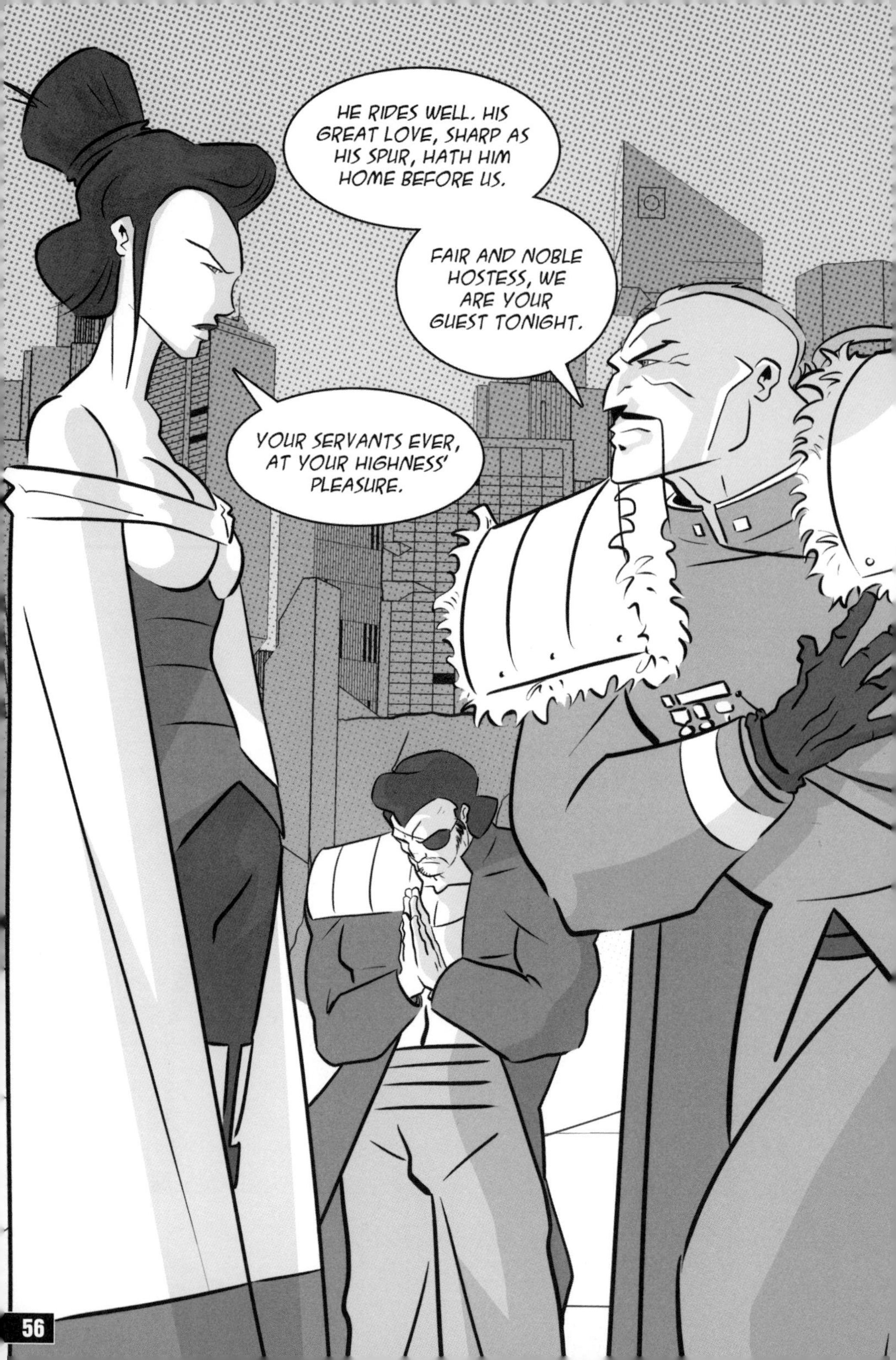
HE RIDES WELL. HIS GREAT LOVE, SHARP AS HIS SPUR, HATH HIM HOME BEFORE US.
FAIR AND NOBLE HOSTESS, WE ARE YOUR GUEST TONIGHT.
YOUR SERVANTS EVER, AT YOUR HIGHNESS' PLEASURE.

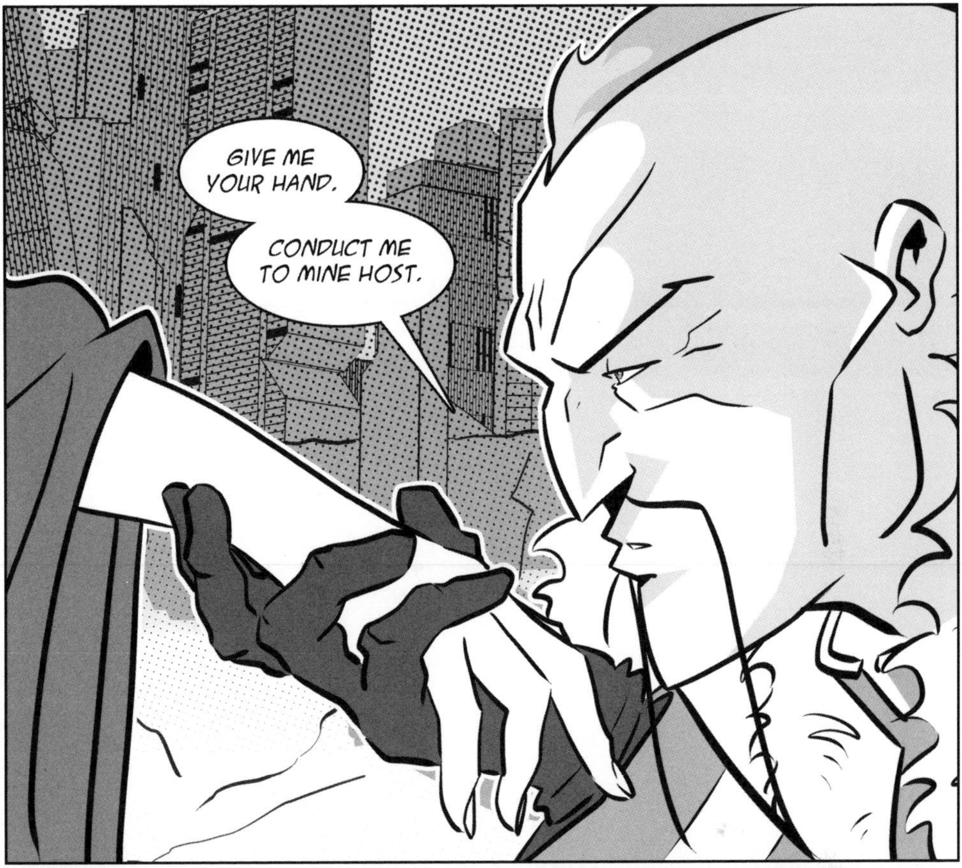
GIVE ME YOUR HAND.
CONDUCT ME TO MINE HOST.

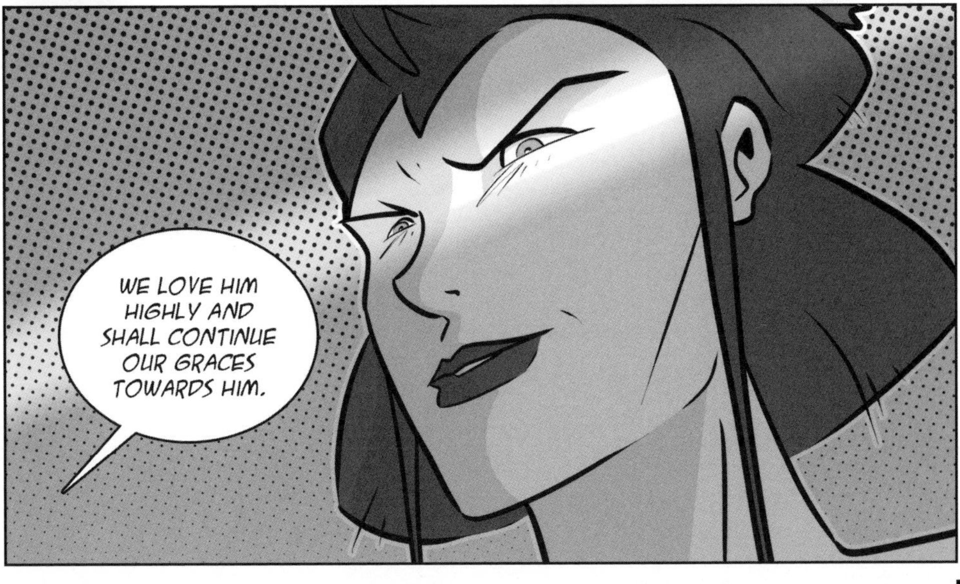
WE LOVE HIM HIGHLY AND SHALL CONTINUE OUR GRACES TOWARDS HIM.

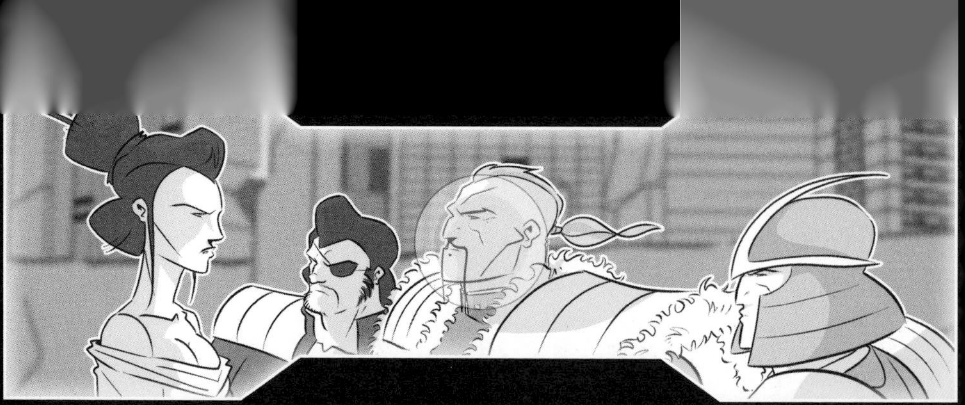
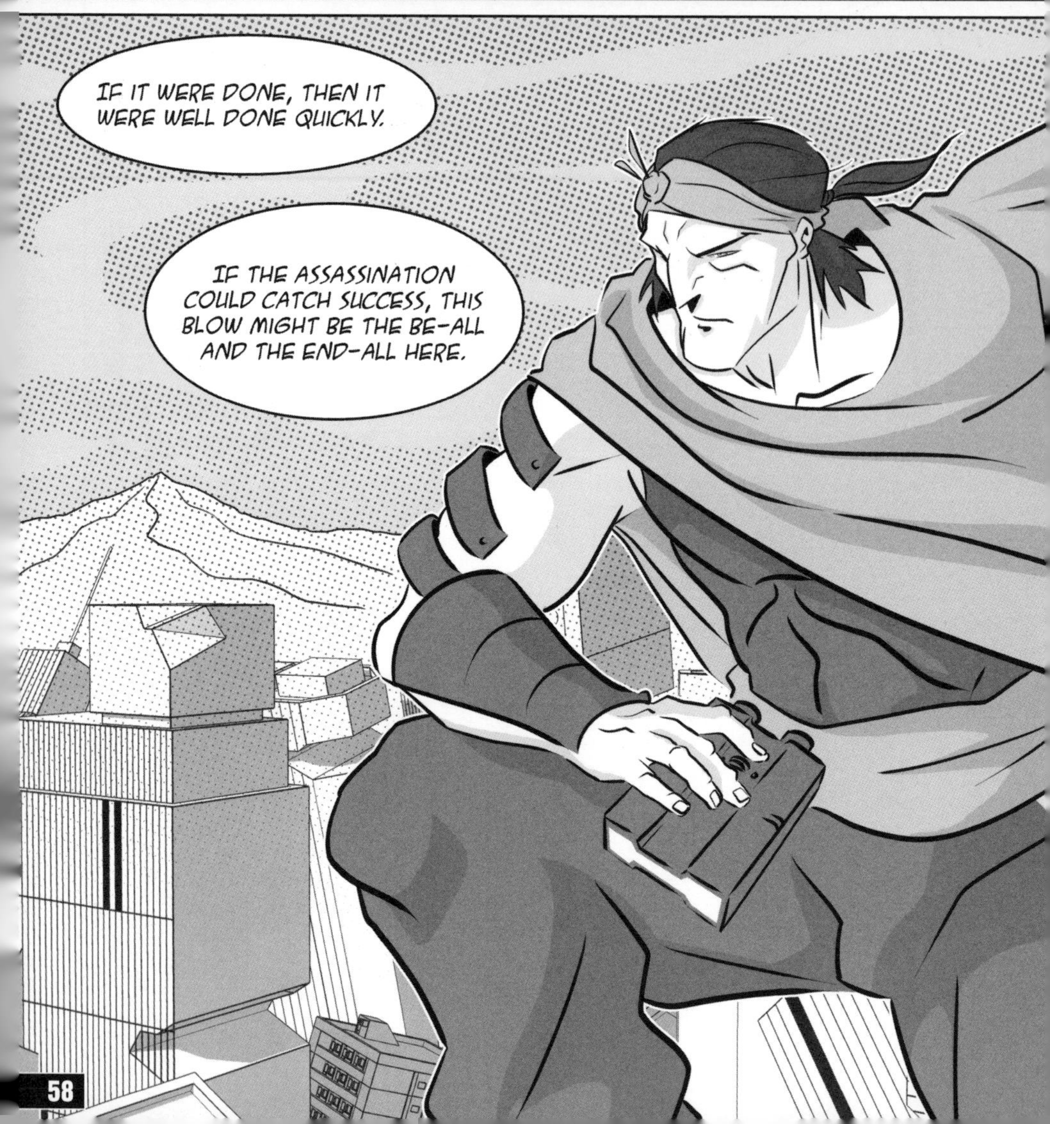
IF IT WERE DONE, THEN IT WERE WELL DONE QUICKLY.
IF THE ASSASSINATION COULD CATCH SUCCESS, THIS BLOW MIGHT BE THE BE-ALL AND THE END-ALL HERE.

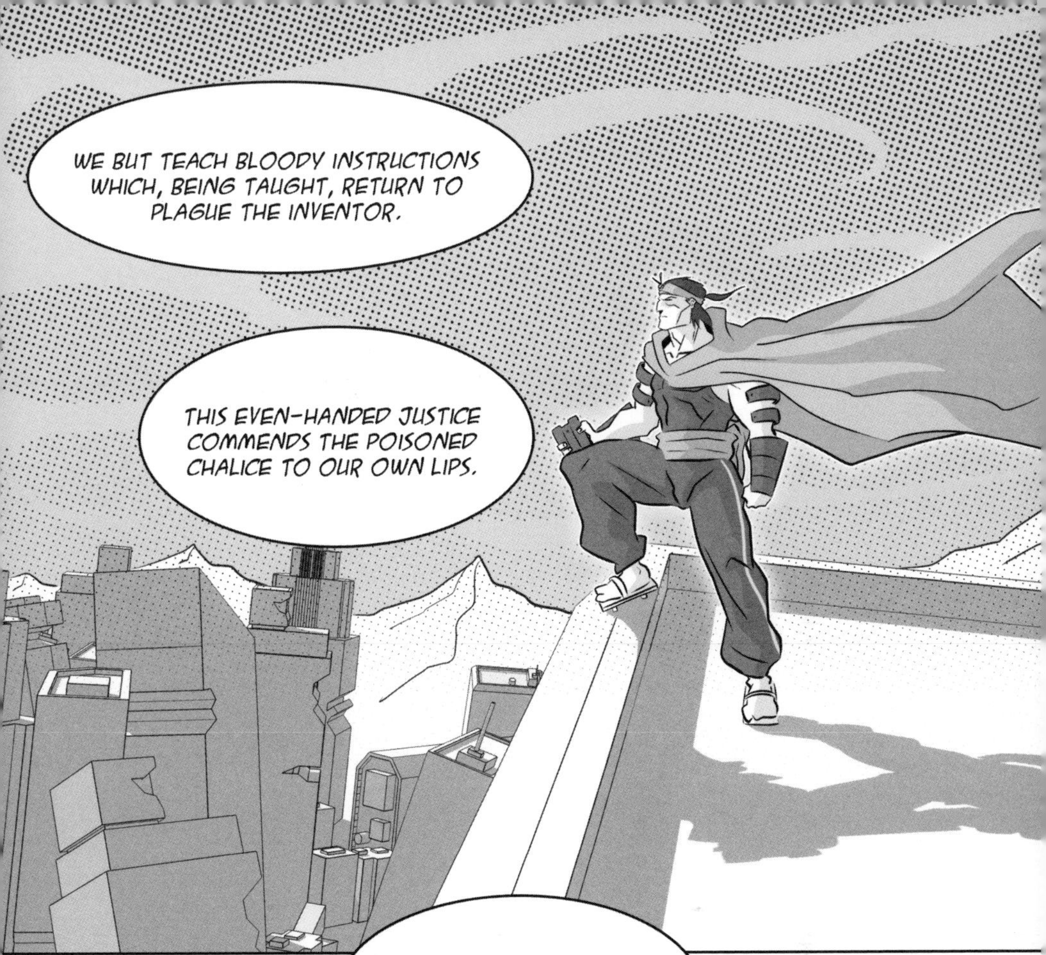
WE BUT TEACH BLOODY INSTRUCTIONS WHICH, BEING TAUGHT, RETURN TO PLAGUE THE INVENTOR.
THIS EVEN-HANDED JUSTICE COMMENDS THE POISONED CHALICE TO OUR OWN LIPS.
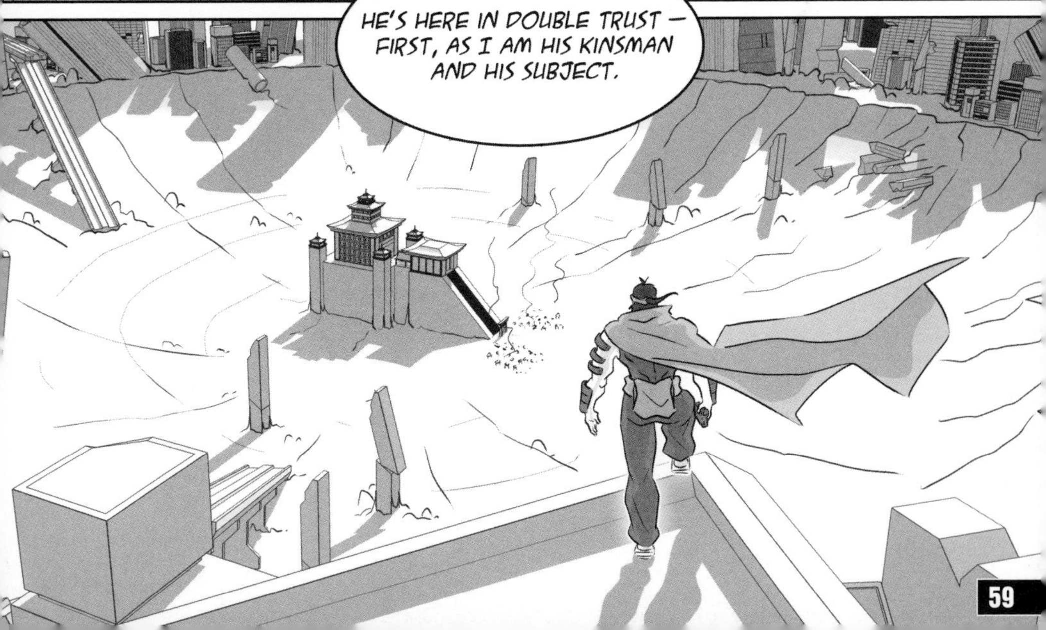
HE'S HERE IN DOUBLE TRUST — FIRST, AS I AM HIS KINSMAN AND HIS SUBJECT.

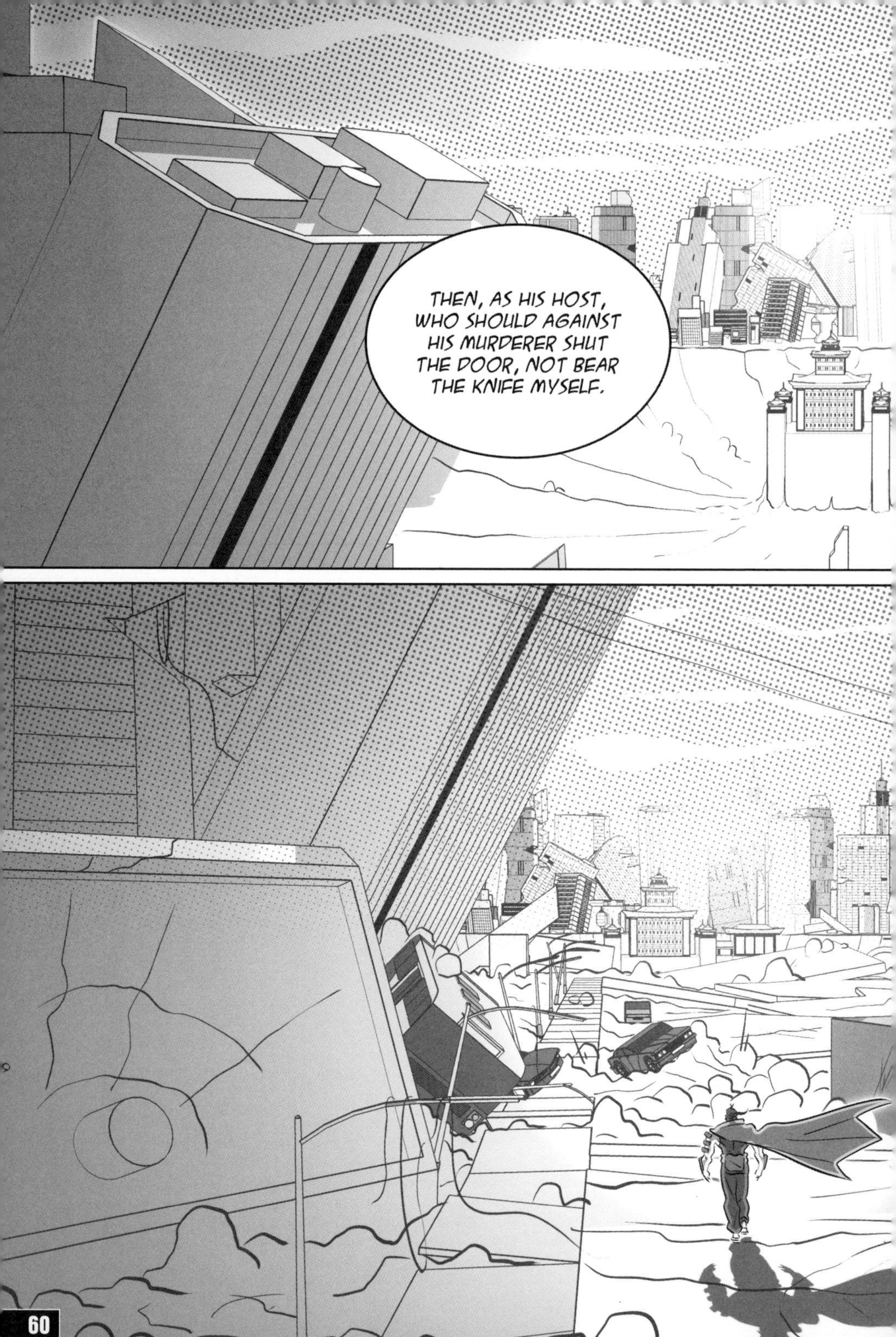
THEN, AS HIS HOST, WHO SHOULD AGAINST HIS MURDERER SHUT THE DOOR, NOT BEAR THE KNIFE MYSELF.

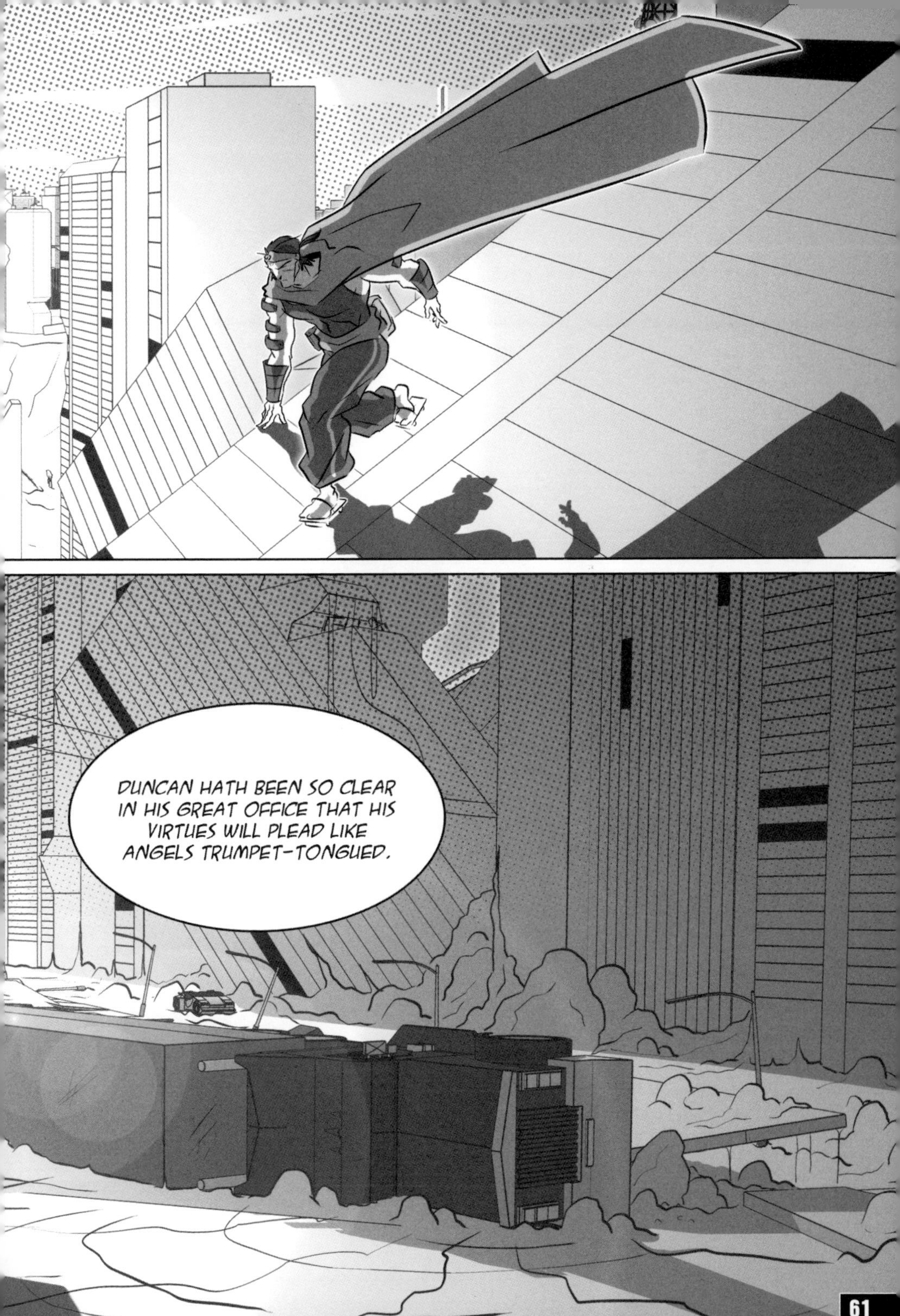
DUNCAN HATH BEEN SO CLEAR IN HIS GREAT OFFICE THAT HIS VIRTUES WILL PLEAD LIKE ANGELS TRUMPET-TONGUED.

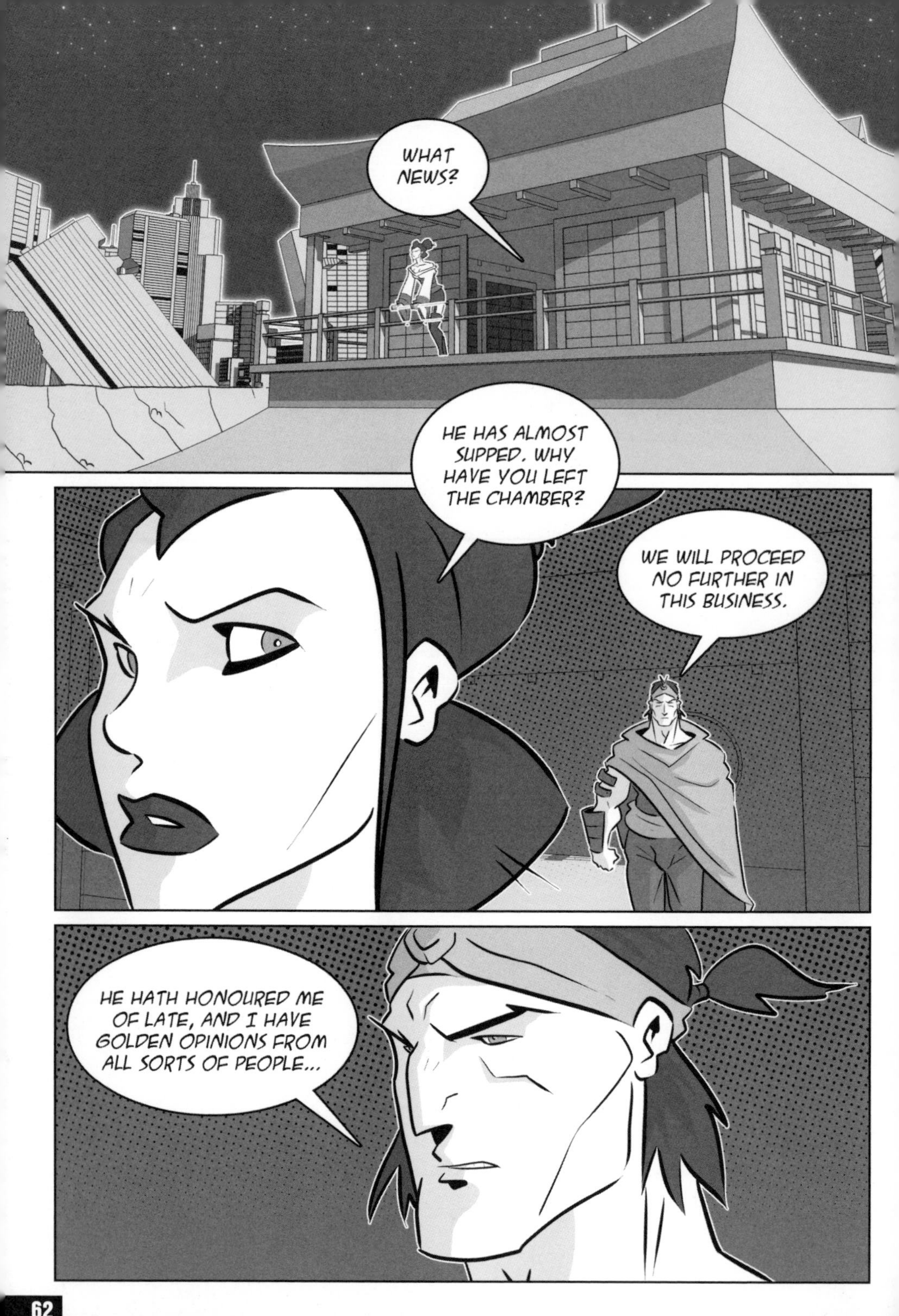
WHAT NEWS?
HE HAS ALMOST SUPPED. WHY HAVE YOU LEFT THE CHAMBER?
WE WILL PROCEED NO FURTHER IN THIS BUSINESS.
HE HATH HONOURED ME OF LATE, AND I HAVE GOLDEN OPINIONS FROM ALL SORTS OF PEOPLE...

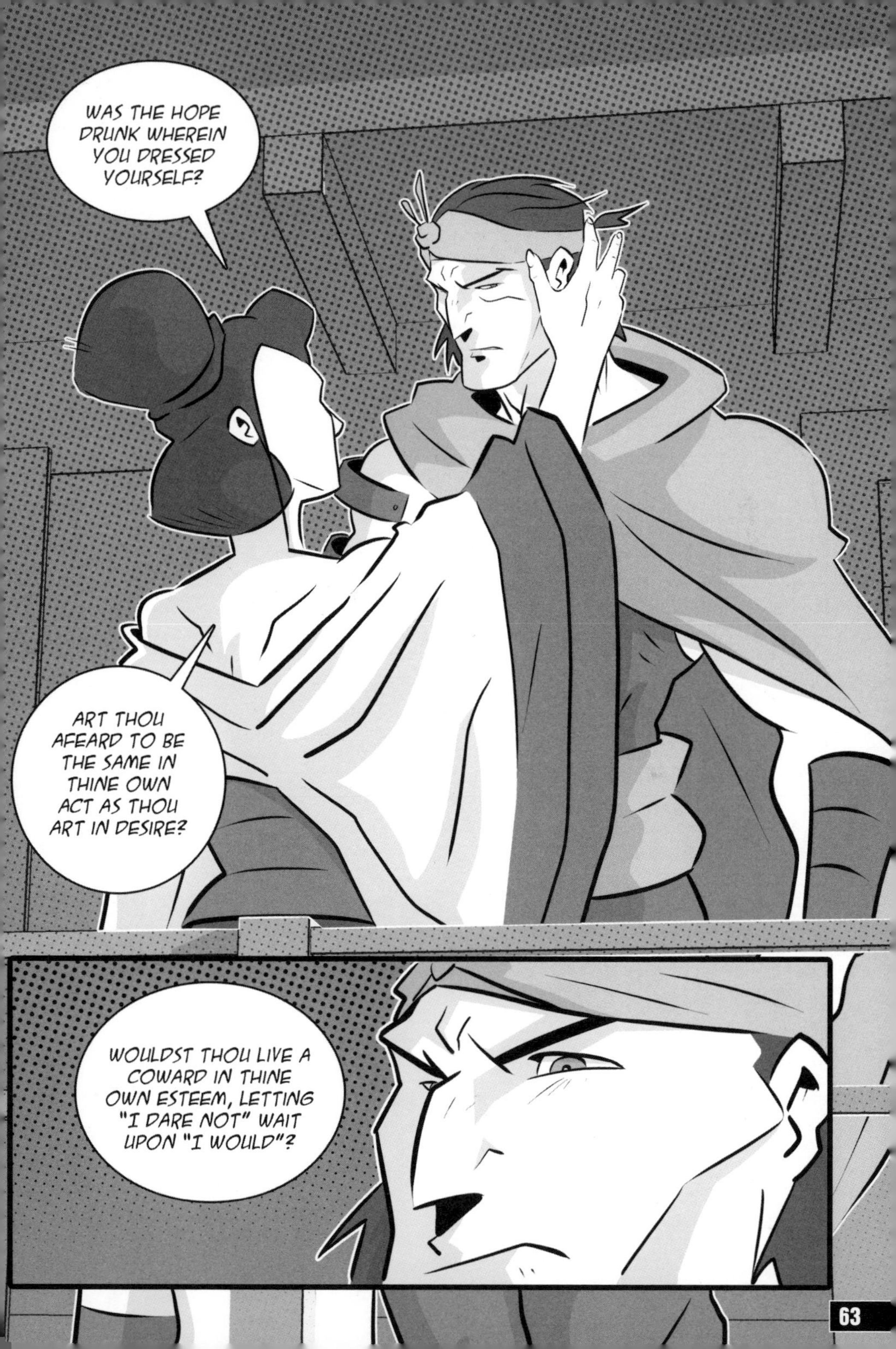
WAS THE HOPE DRUNK WHEREIN YOU DRESSED YOURSELF?
ART THOU AFEARD TO BE THE SAME IN THINE OWN ACT AS THOU ART IN DESIRE?
WOULDST THOU LIVE A COWARD IN THINE OWN ESTEEM, LETTING "I DARE NOT" WAIT UPON "I WOULD"?

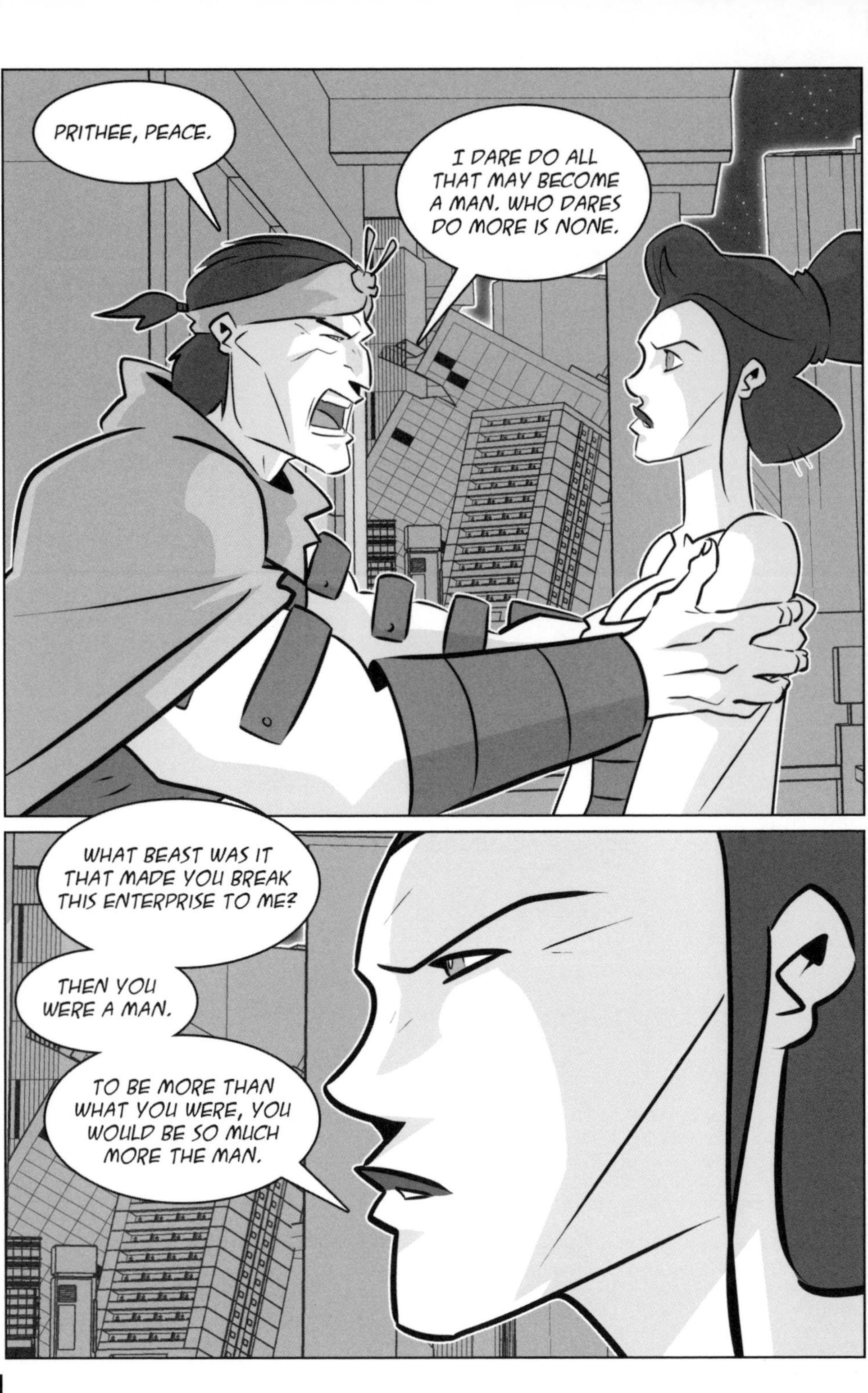
PRITHEE, PEACE.
I DARE DO ALL THAT MAY BECOME A MAN. WHO DARES DO MORE IS NONE.
WHAT BEAST WAS IT THAT MADE YOU BREAK THIS ENTERPRISE TO ME?
THEN YOU WERE A MAN.
TO BE MORE THAN WHAT YOU WERE, YOU WOULD BE SO MUCH MORE THE MAN.

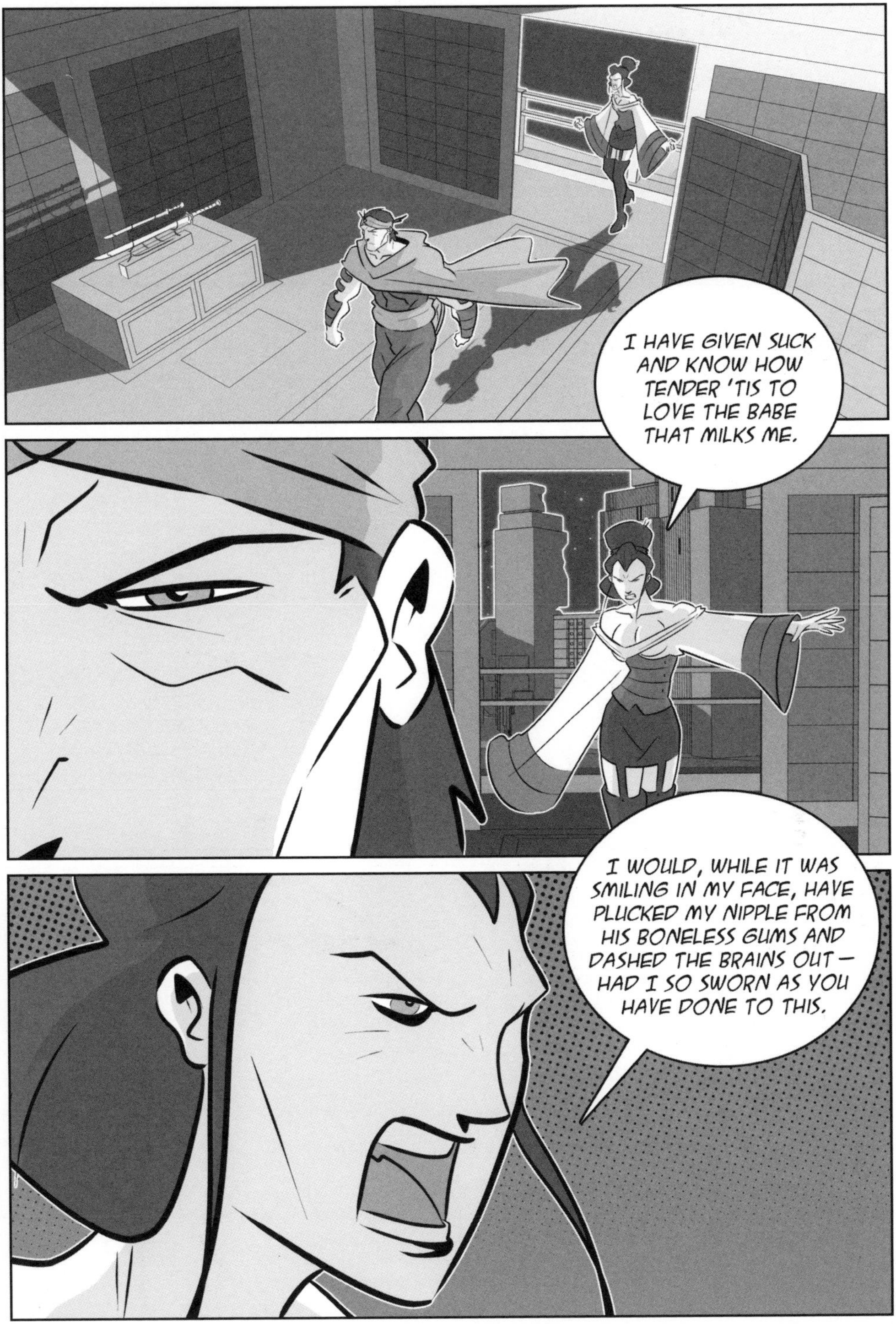
I HAVE GIVEN SUCK AND KNOW HOW TENDER 'TIS TO LOVE THE BABE THAT MILKS ME.
I WOULD, WHILE IT WAS SMILING IN MY FACE, HAVE PLUCKED MY NIPPLE FROM HIS BONELESS GUMS AND DASHED THE BRAINS OUT— HAD I SO SWORN AS YOU HAVE DONE TO THIS.

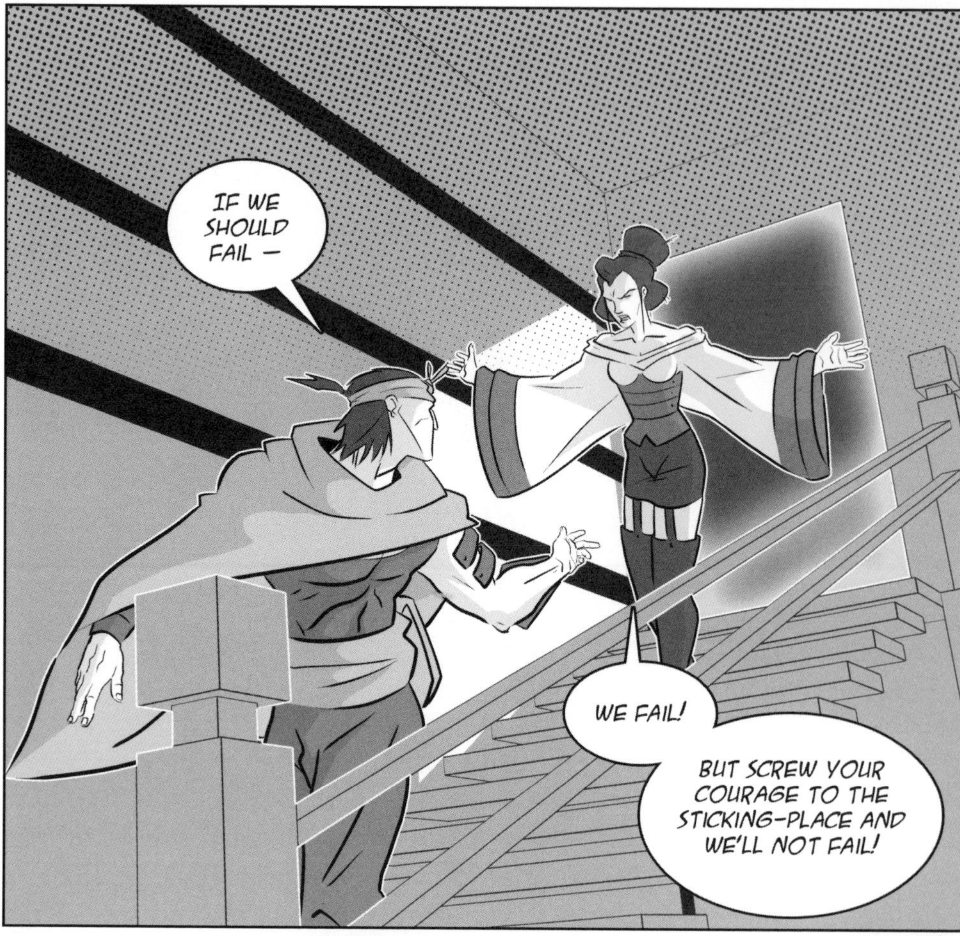
IF WE SHOULD FAIL —
WE FAIL!
BUT SCREW YOUR COURAGE TO THE STICKING-PLACE AND WE'LL NOT FAIL!

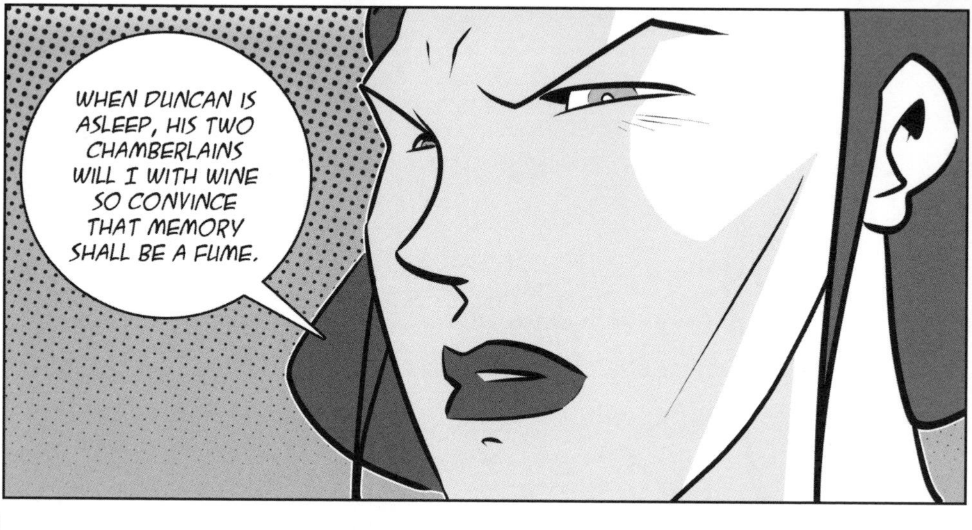
WHEN DUNCAN IS ASLEEP, HIS TWO CHAMBERLAINS WILL I WITH WINE SO CONVINCE THAT MEMORY SHALL BE A FUME.

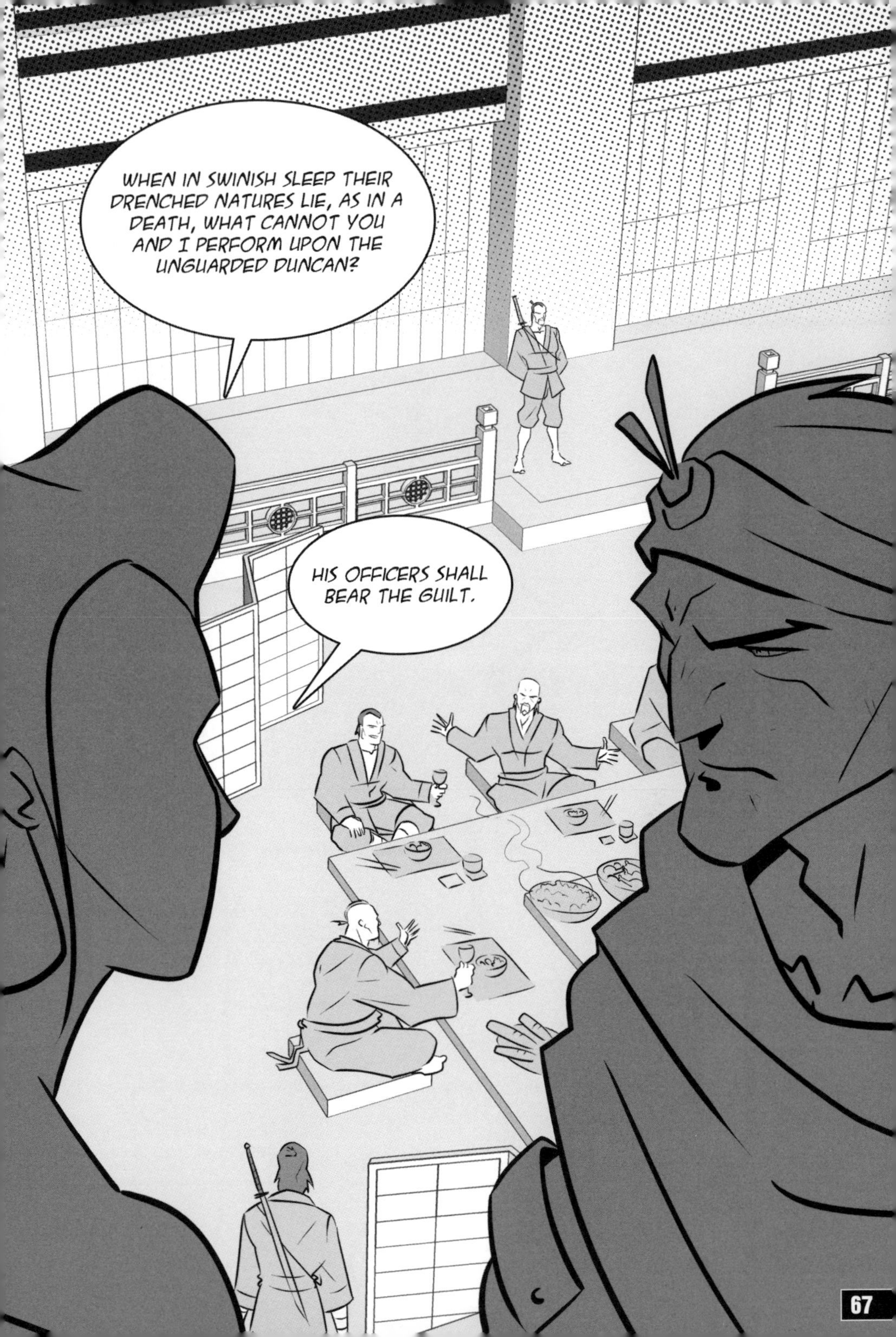
WHEN IN SWINISH SLEEP THEIR DRENCHED NATURES LIE, AS IN A DEATH, WHAT CANNOT YOU AND I PERFORM UPON THE UNGUARDED DUNCAN?
HIS OFFICERS SHALL BEAR THE GUILT.

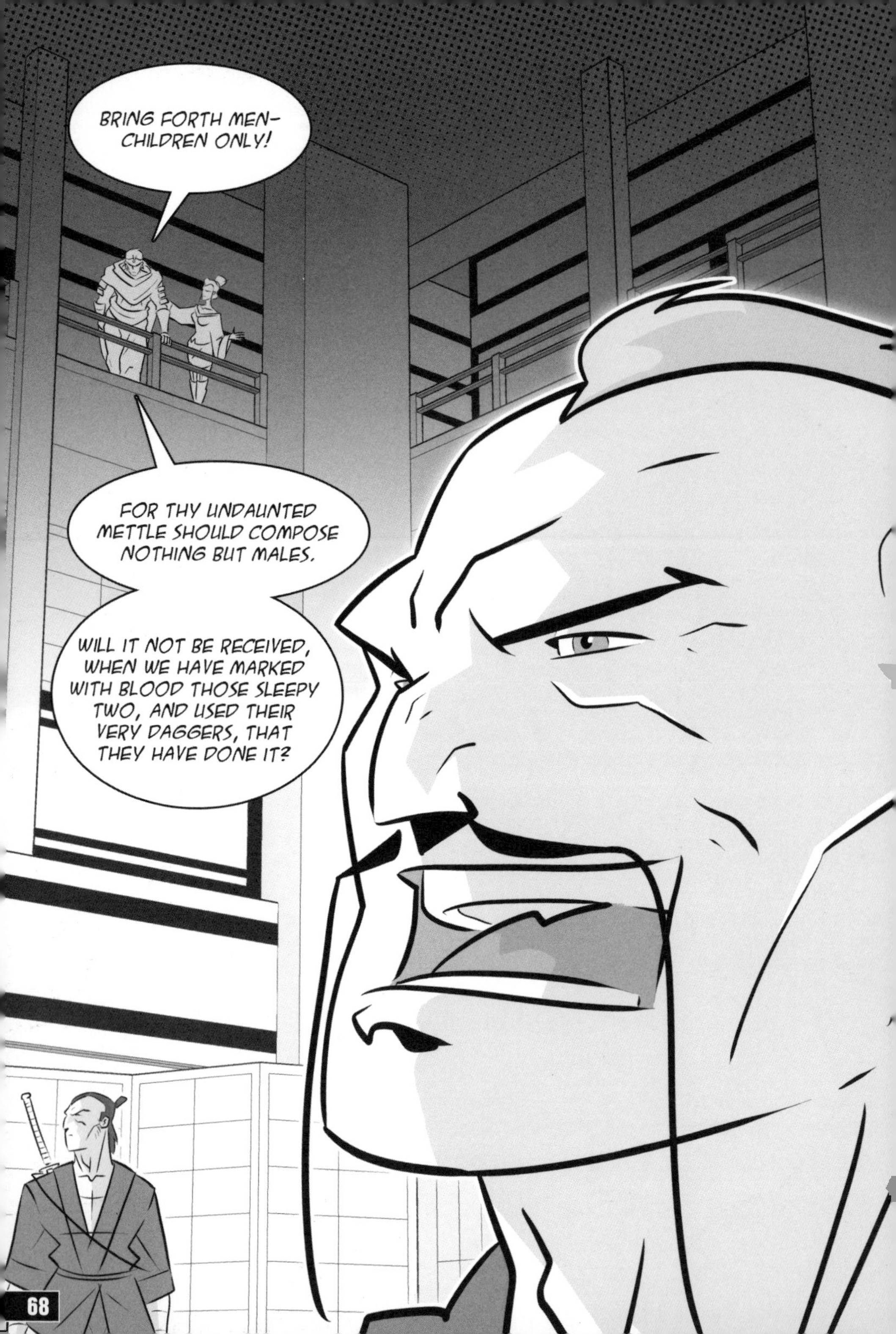
BRING FORTH MEN-CHILDREN ONLY!
FOR THY UNDAUNTED METTLE SHOULD COMPOSE NOTHING BUT MALES.
WILL IT NOT BE RECEIVED, WHEN WE HAVE MARKED WITH BLOOD THOSE SLEEPY TWO, AND USED THEIR VERY DAGGERS, THAT THEY HAVE DONE IT?

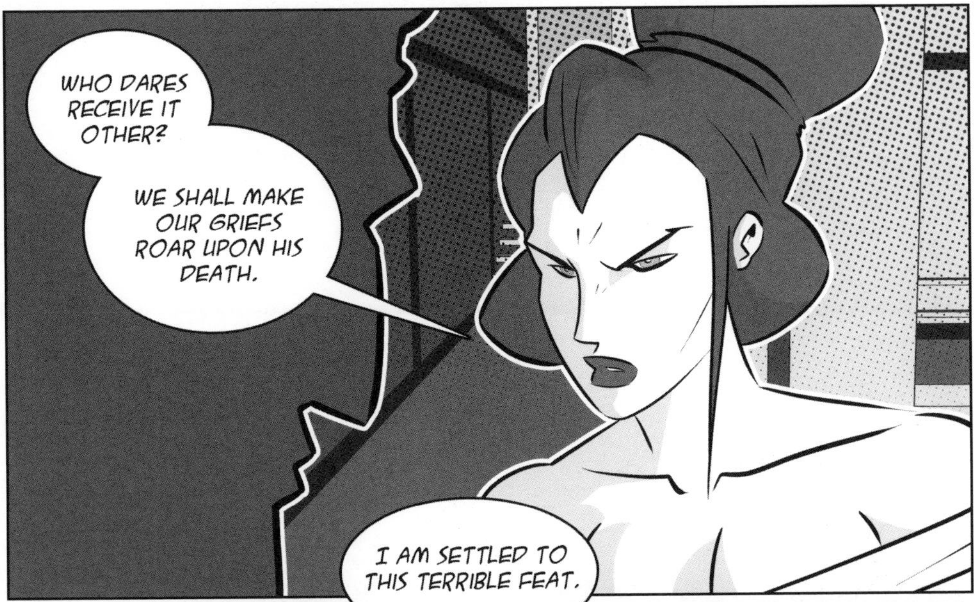
WHO DARES RECEIVE IT OTHER?
WE SHALL MAKE OUR GRIEFS ROAR UPON HIS DEATH.
I AM SETTLED TO THIS TERRIBLE FEAT.
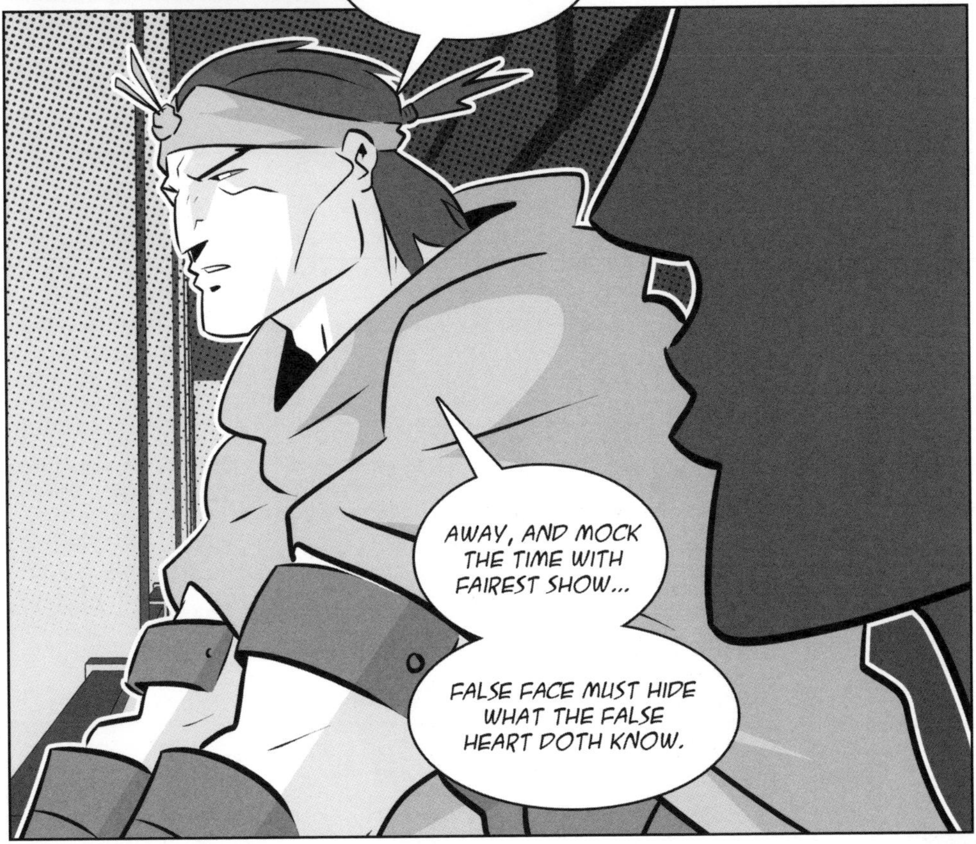
AWAY, AND MOCK THE TIME WITH FAIREST SHOW...
FALSE FACE MUST HIDE WHAT THE FALSE HEART DOTH KNOW.

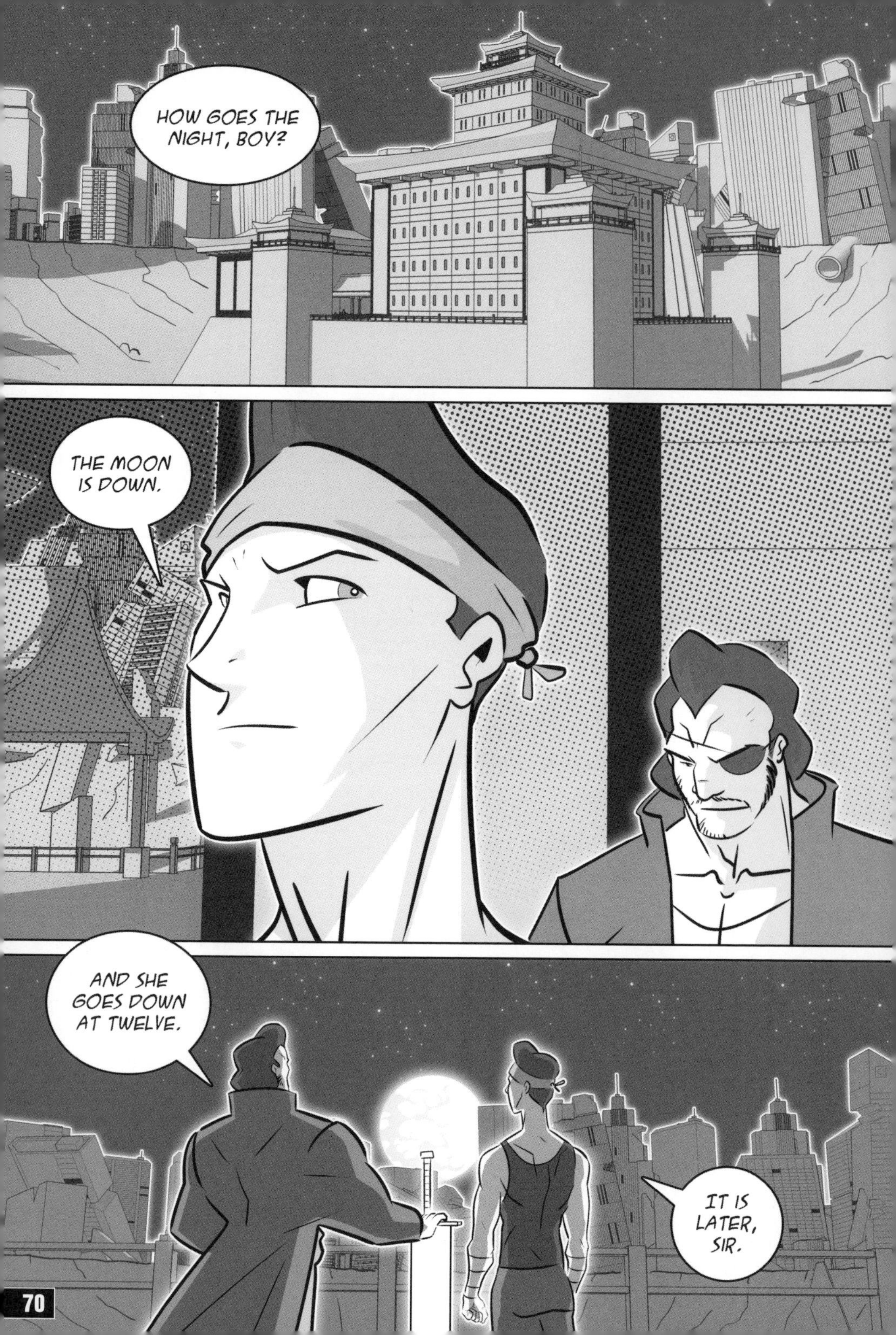
HOW GOES THE NIGHT, BOY?
THE MOON IS DOWN.
AND SHE GOES DOWN AT TWELVE.
IT IS LATER, SIR.

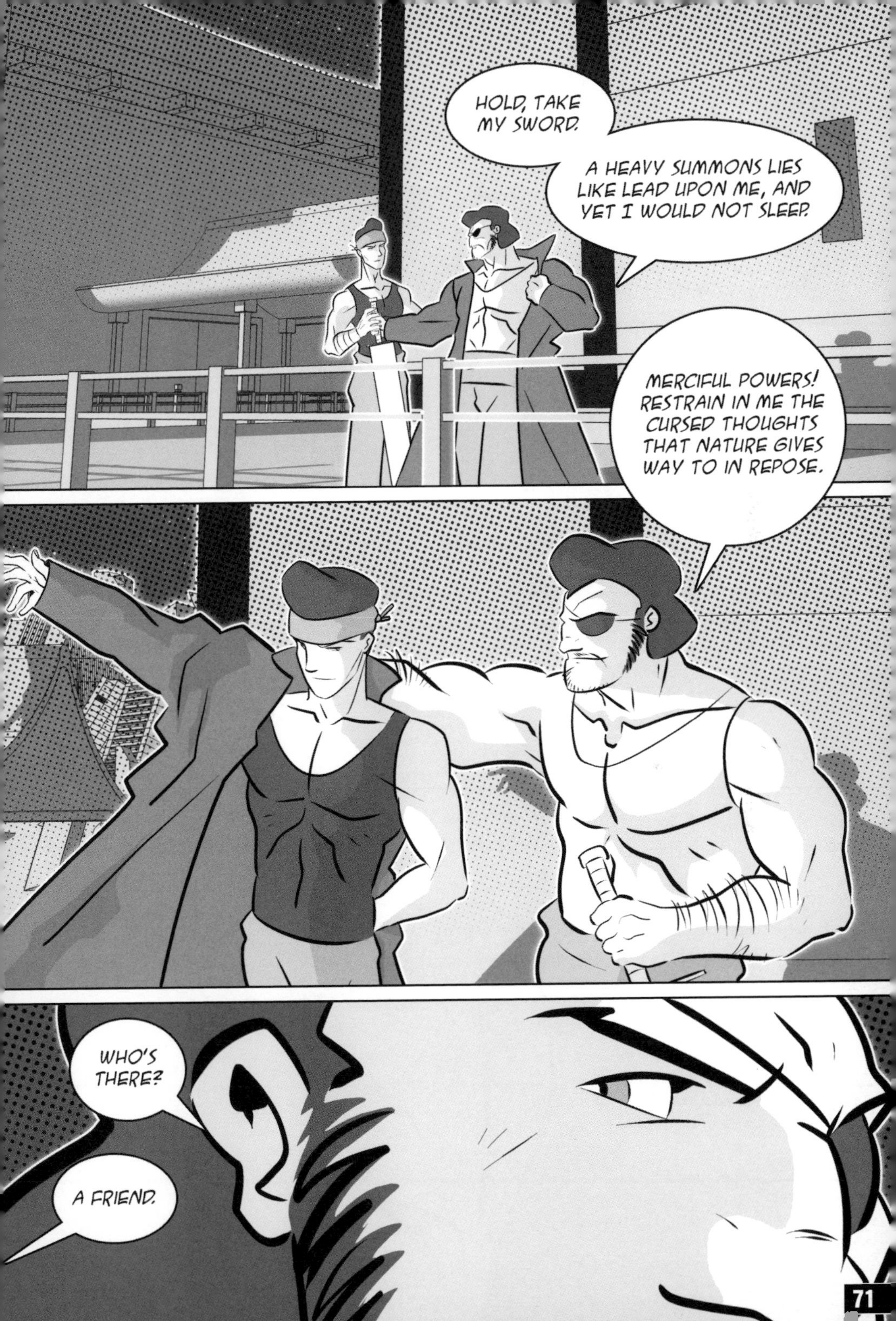
HOLD, TAKE MY SWORD.
A HEAVY SUMMONS LIES LIKE LEAD UPON ME, AND YET I WOULD NOT SLEEP.
MERCIFUL POWERS! RESTRAIN IN ME THE CURSED THOUGHTS THAT NATURE GIVES WAY TO IN REPOSE.
WHO'S THERE?
A FRIEND.

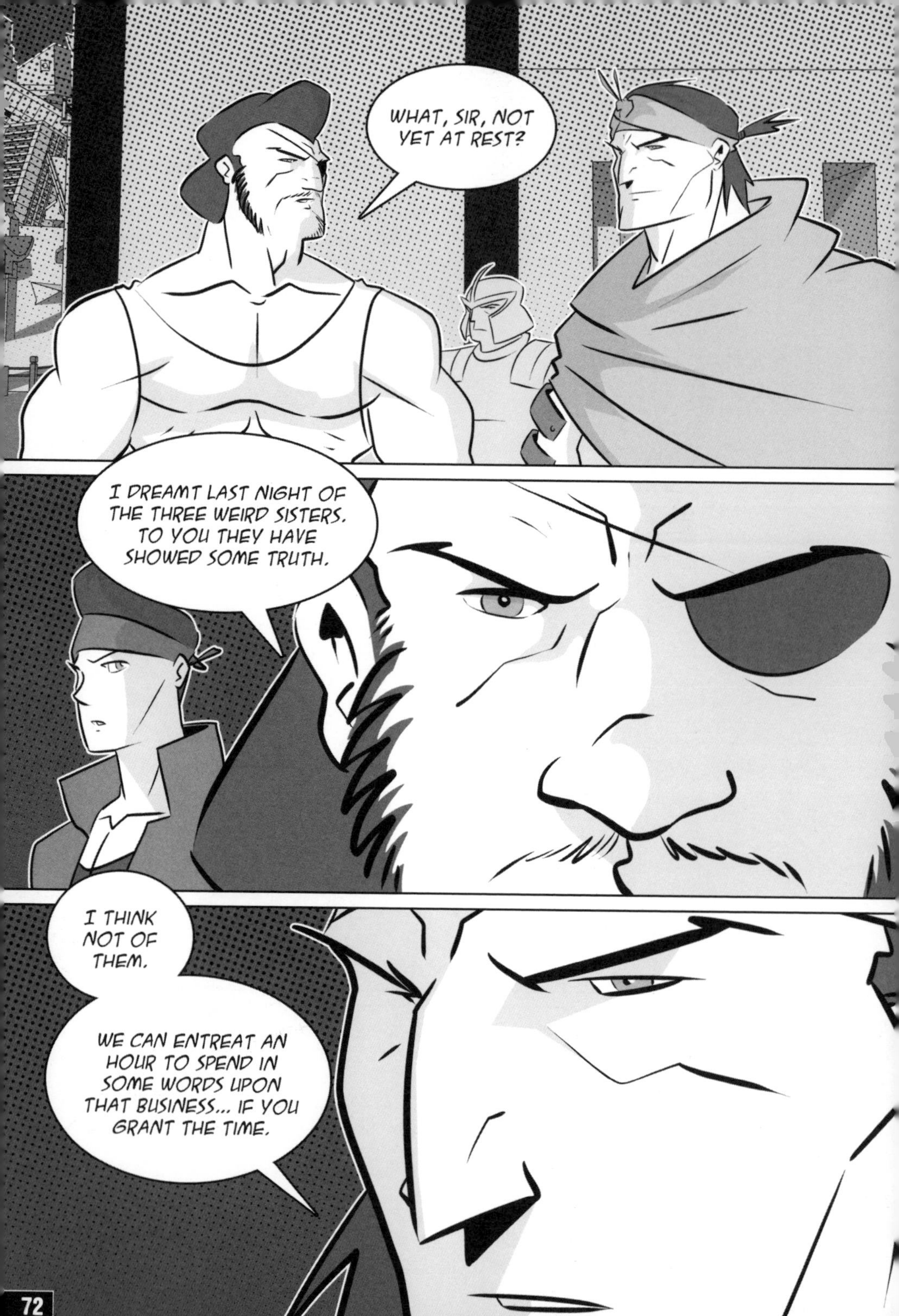
WHAT, SIR, NOT YET AT REST?
I DREAMT LAST NIGHT OF THE THREE WEIRD SISTERS. TO YOU THEY HAVE SHOWED SOME TRUTH.
I THINK NOT OF THEM.
WE CAN ENTREAT AN HOUR TO SPEND IN SOME WORDS UPON THAT BUSINESS... IF YOU GRANT THE TIME.

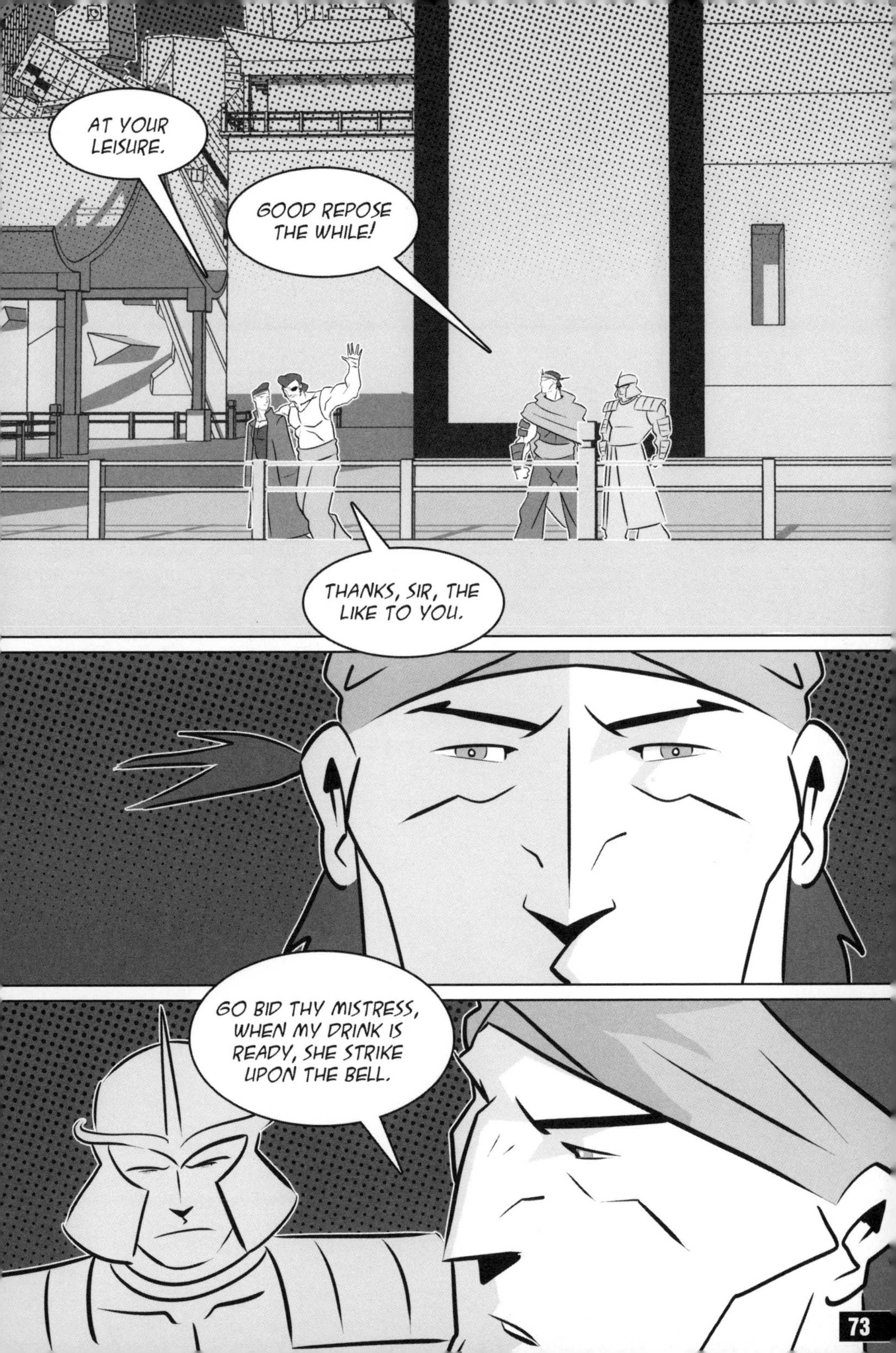
AT YOUR LEISURE.
GOOD REPOSE THE WHILE!
THANKS, SIR, THE LIKE TO YOU.
GO BID THY MISTRESS, WHEN MY DRINK IS READY, SHE STRIKE UPON THE BELL.

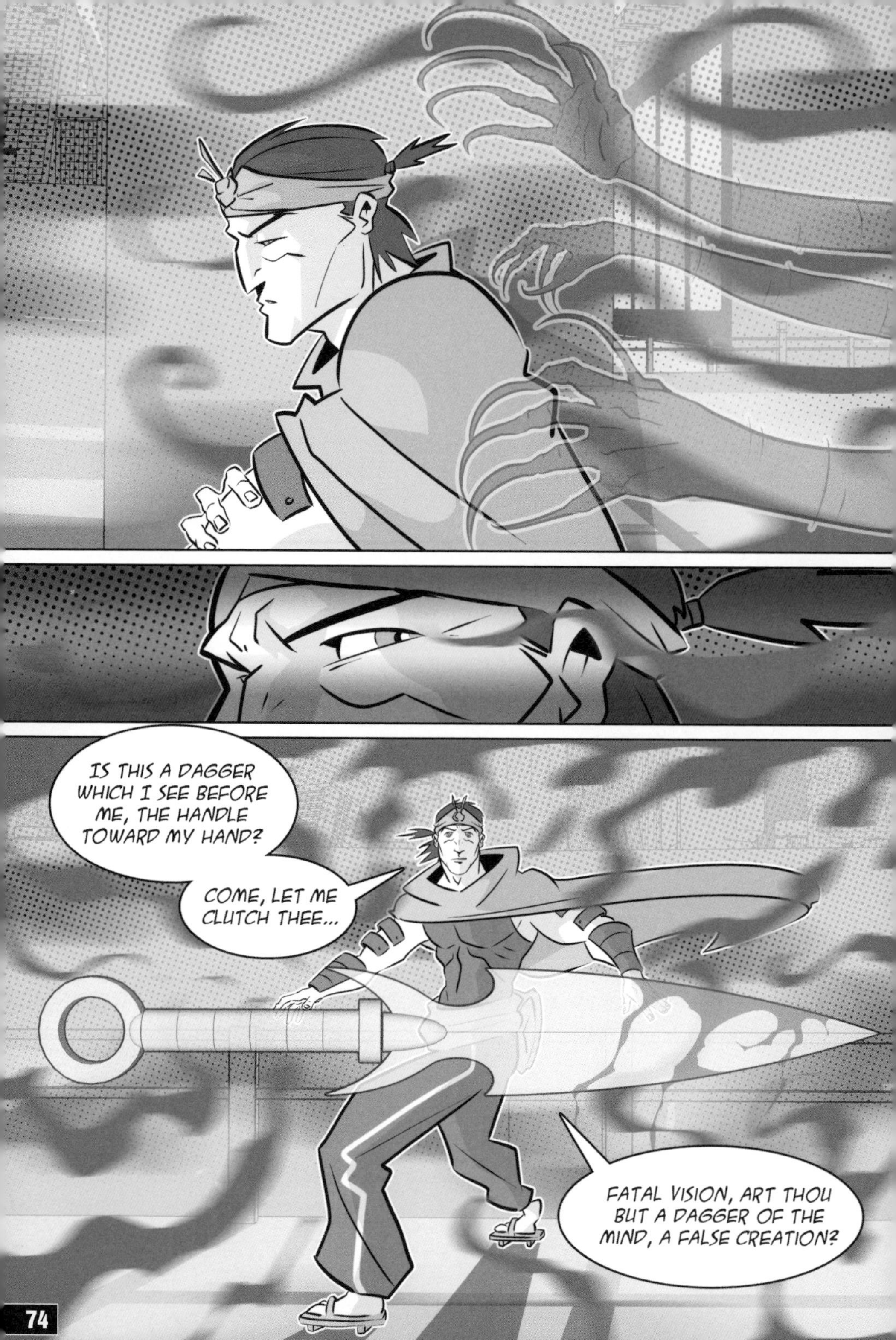
IS THIS A DAGGER WHICH I SEE BEFORE ME, THE HANDLE TOWARD MY HAND?
COME, LET ME CLUTCH THEE...
FATAL VISION, ART THOU BUT A DAGGER OF THE MIND, A FALSE CREATION?

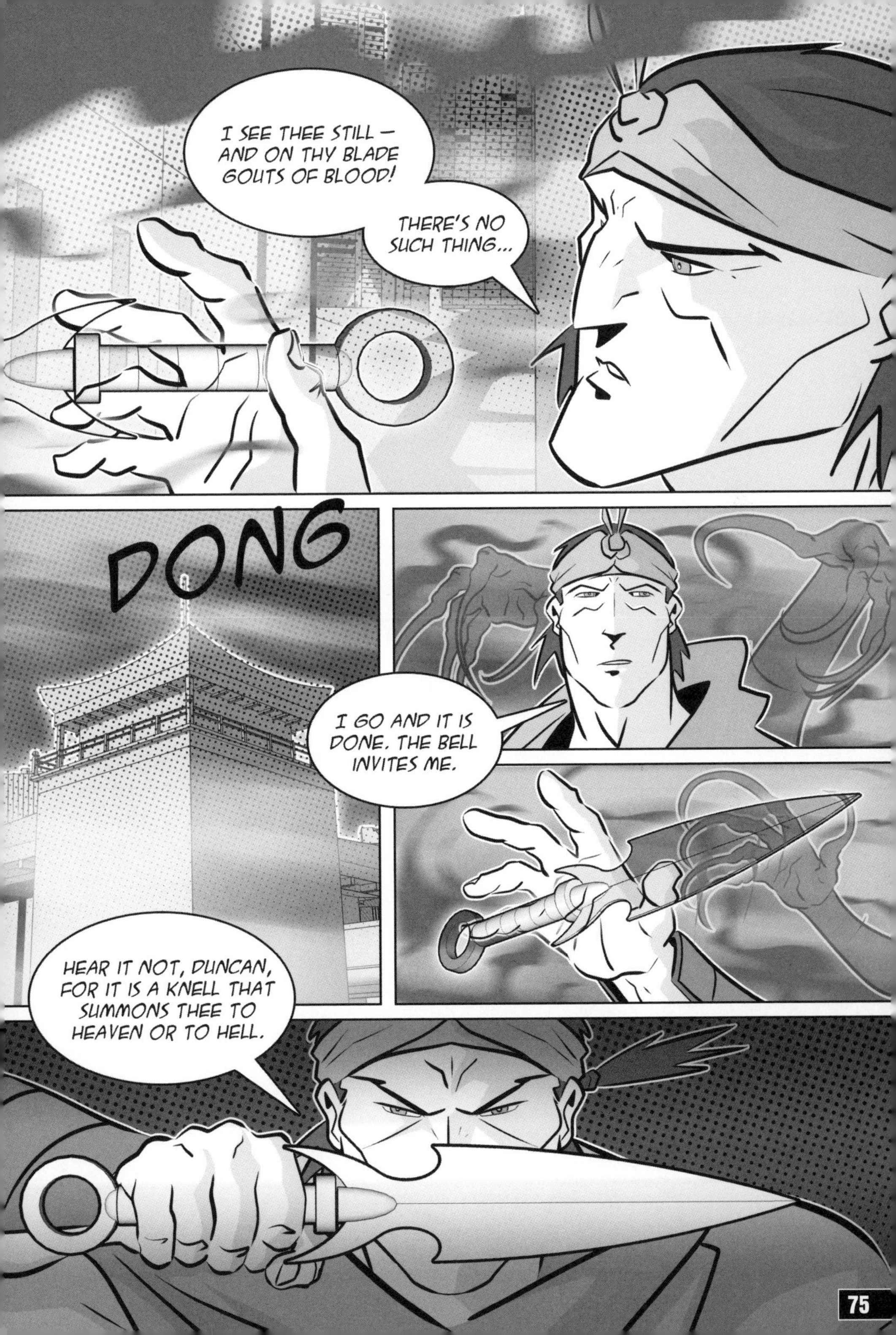
I SEE THEE STILL — AND ON THY BLADE GOUTS OF BLOOD!
THERE'S NO SUCH THING...
DONG
I GO AND IT IS DONE. THE BELL INVITES ME.
HEAR IT NOT, DUNCAN, FOR IT IS A KNELL THAT SUMMONS THEE TO HEAVEN OR TO HELL.

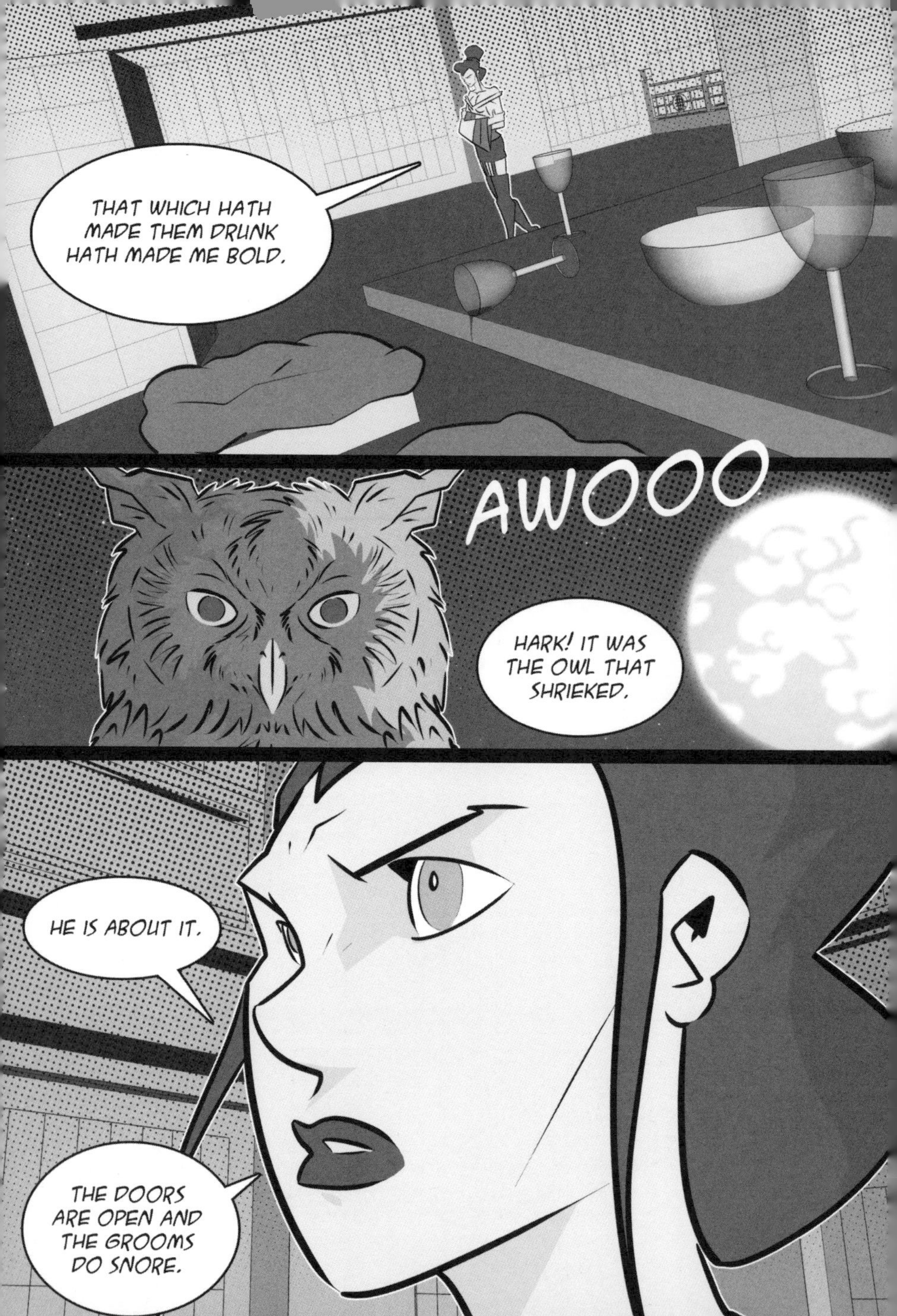
THAT WHICH HATH MADE THEM DRUNK HATH MADE ME BOLD.
AWOOO
HARK! IT WAS THE OWL THAT SHRIEKED.
HE IS ABOUT IT.
THE DOORS ARE OPEN AND THE GROOMS DO SNORE.

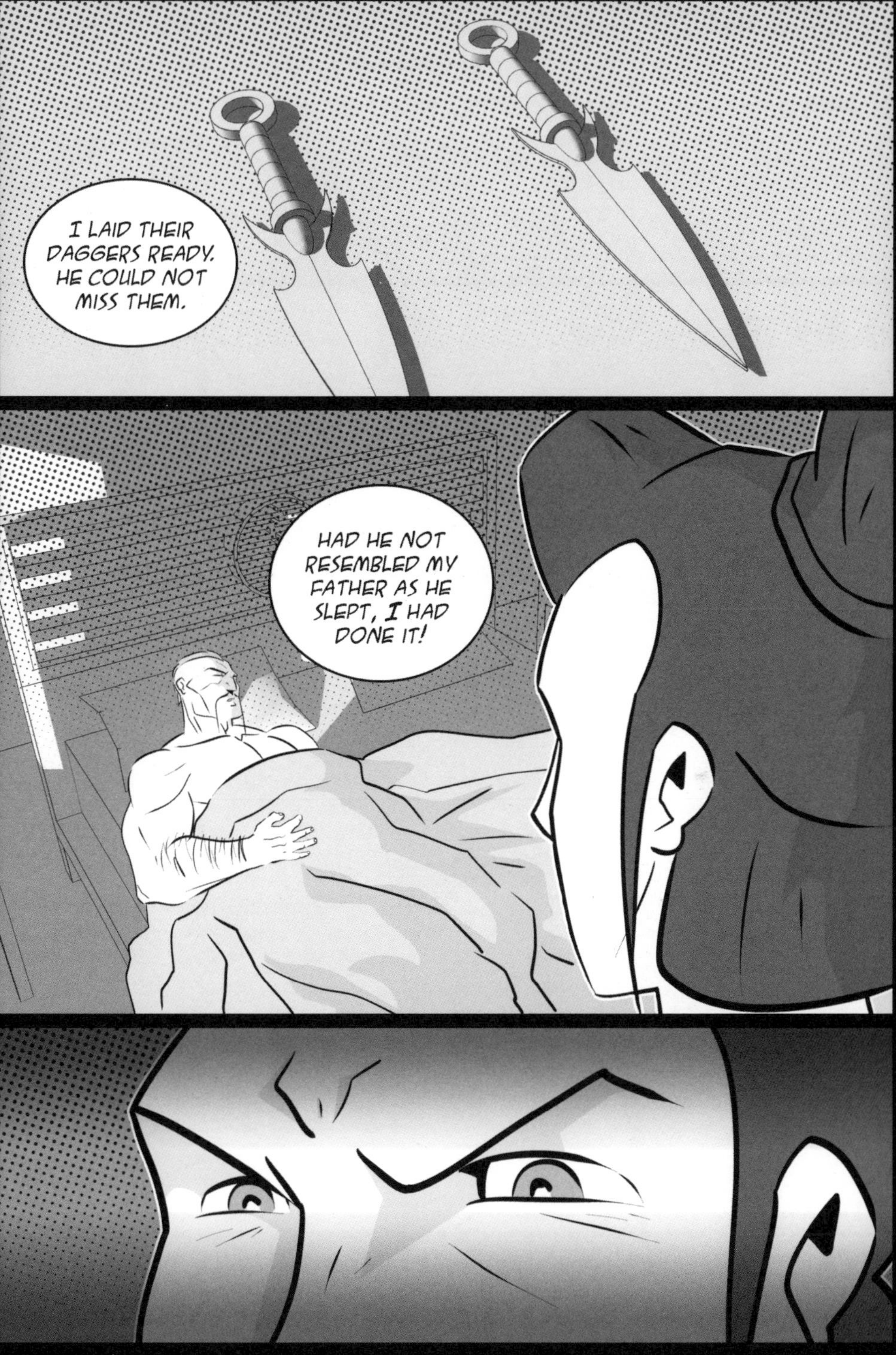
I LAID THEIR DAGGERS READY. HE COULD NOT MISS THEM.
HAD HE NOT RESEMBLED MY FATHER AS HE SLEPT, I HAD DONE IT!

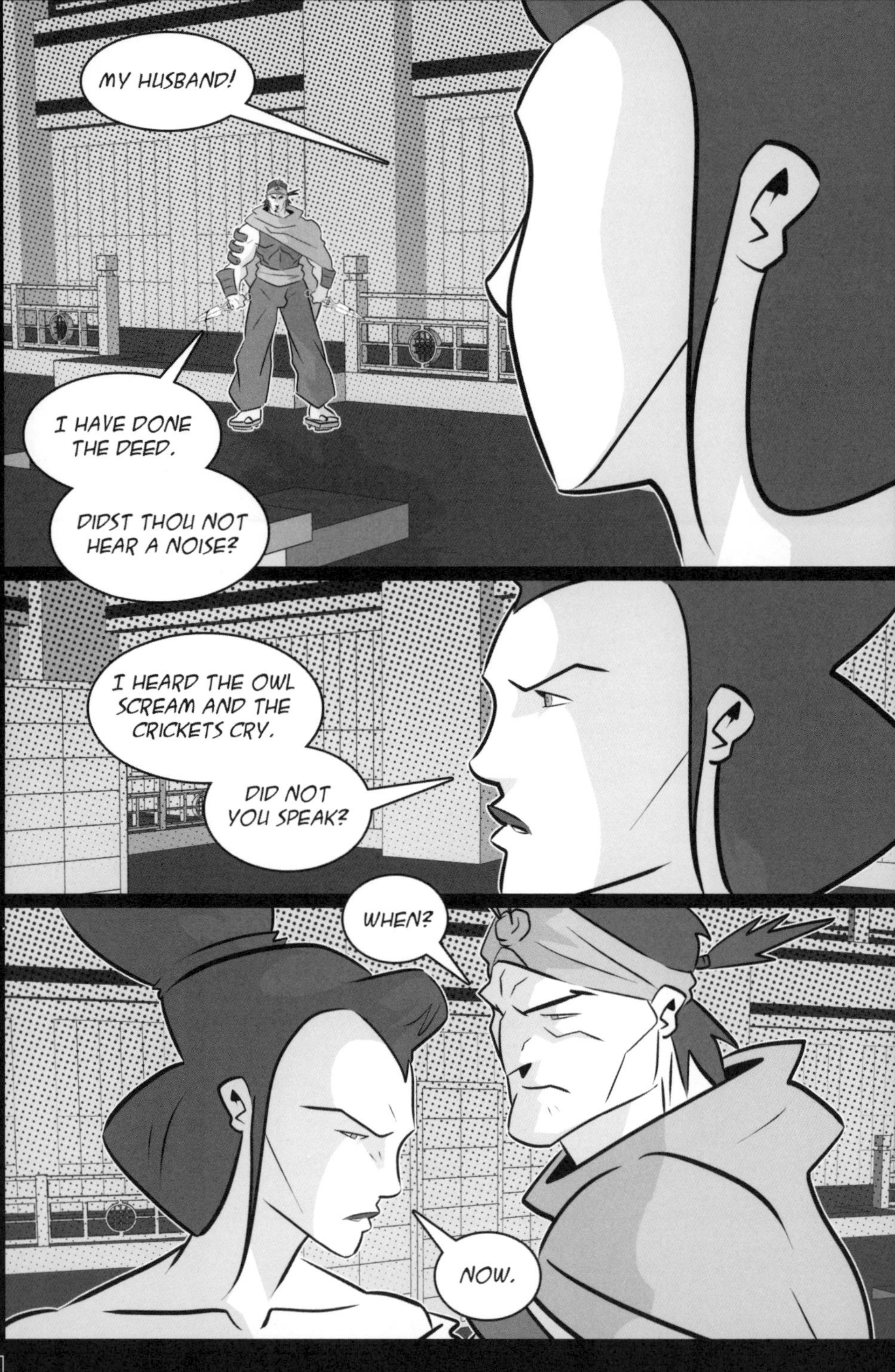
MY HUSBAND!
I HAVE DONE THE DEED.
DIDST THOU NOT HEAR A NOISE?
I HEARD THE OWL SCREAM AND THE CRICKETS CRY.
DID NOT YOU SPEAK?
WHEN?
NOW.

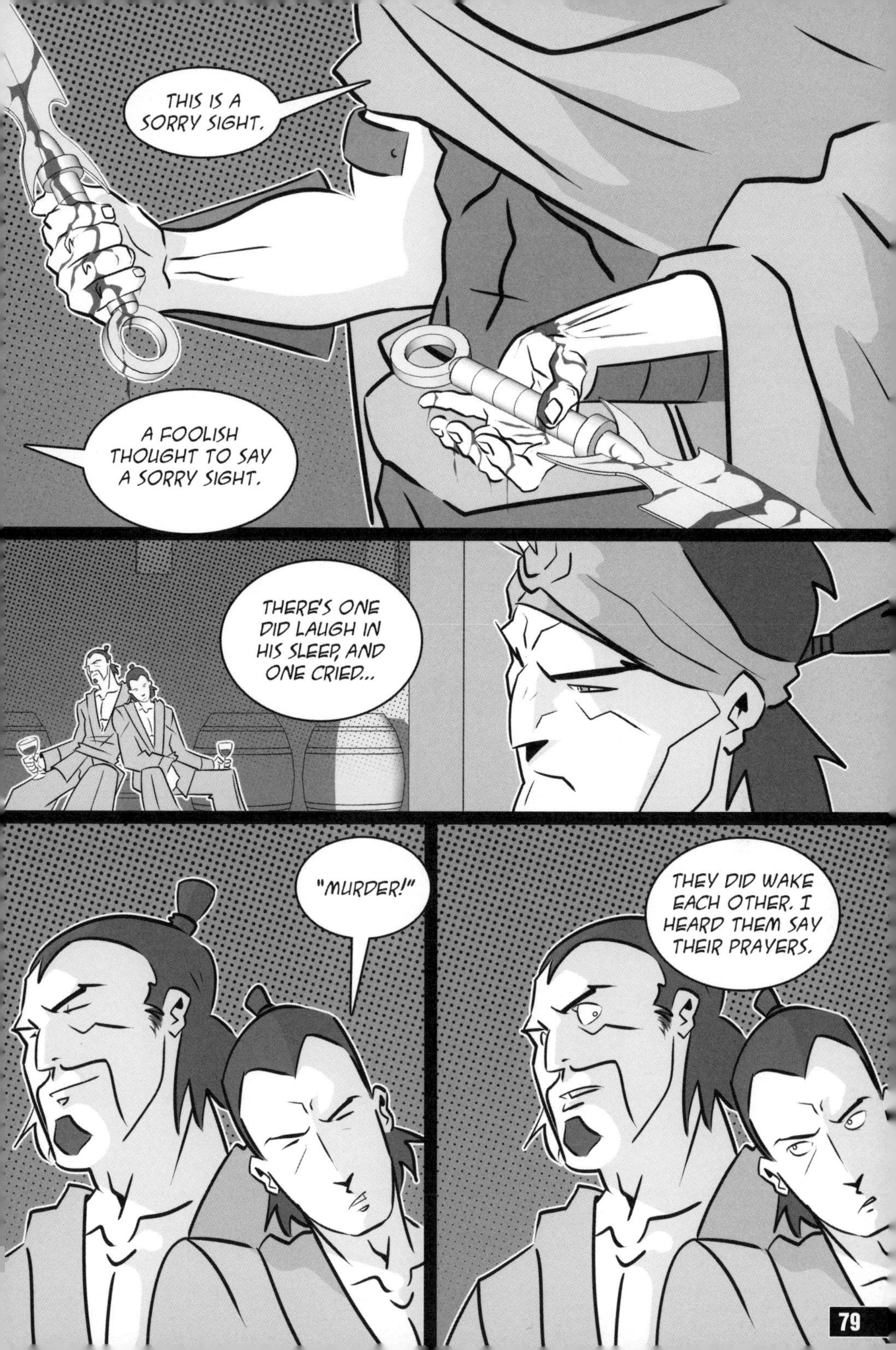
THIS IS A SORRY SIGHT.
A FOOLISH THOUGHT TO SAY A SORRY SIGHT.
THERE'S ONE DID LAUGH IN HIS SLEEP, AND ONE CRIED...
"MURDER!"
THEY DID WAKE EACH OTHER. I HEARD THEM SAY THEIR PRAYERS.

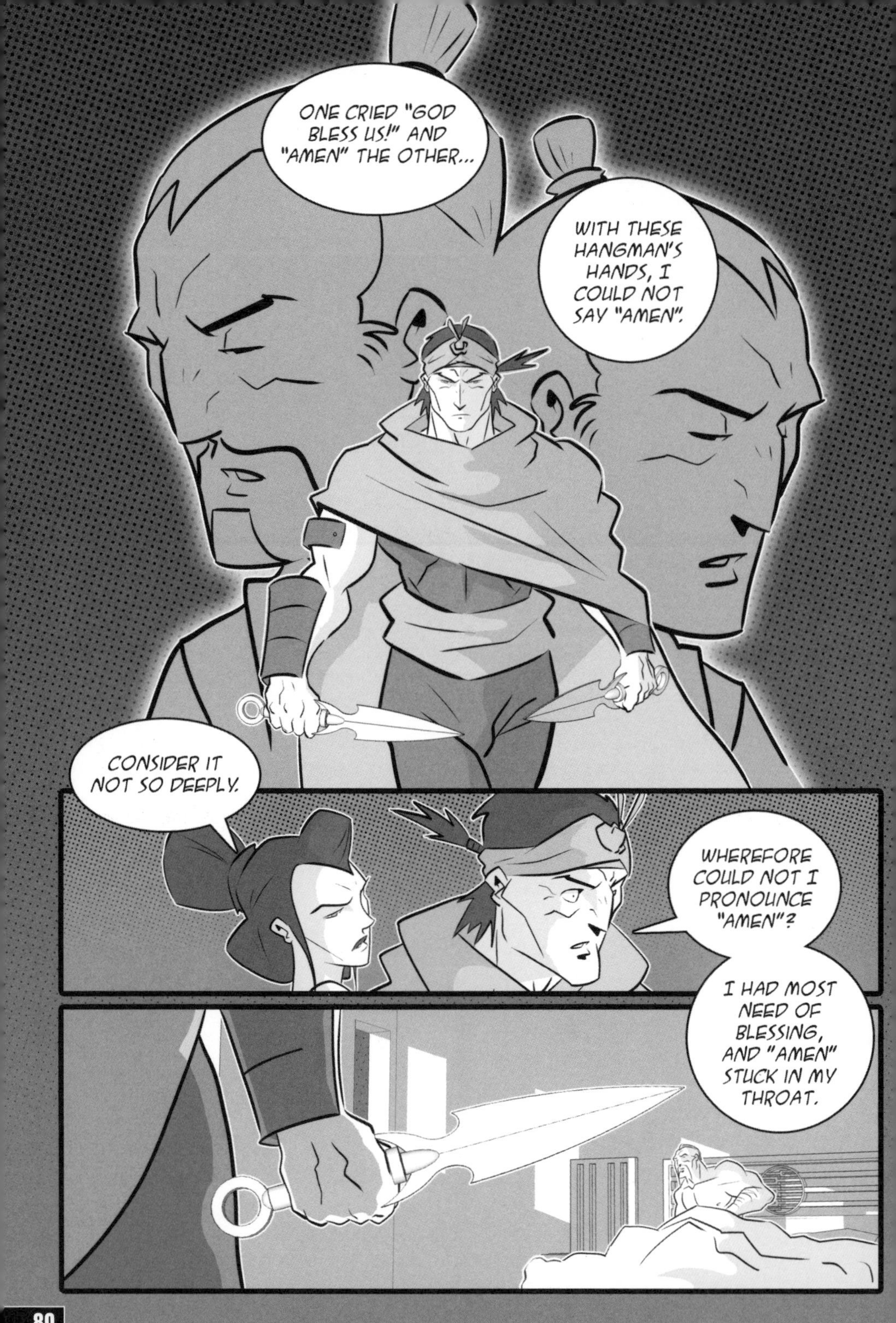
ONE CRIED "GOD BLESS US!" AND "AMEN" THE OTHER...
WITH THESE HANGMAN'S HANDS, I COULD NOT SAY "AMEN".
CONSIDER IT NOT SO DEEPLY.
WHEREFORE COULD NOT I PRONOUNCE "AMEN"?
I HAD MOST NEED OF BLESSING, AND "AMEN" STUCK IN MY THROAT.

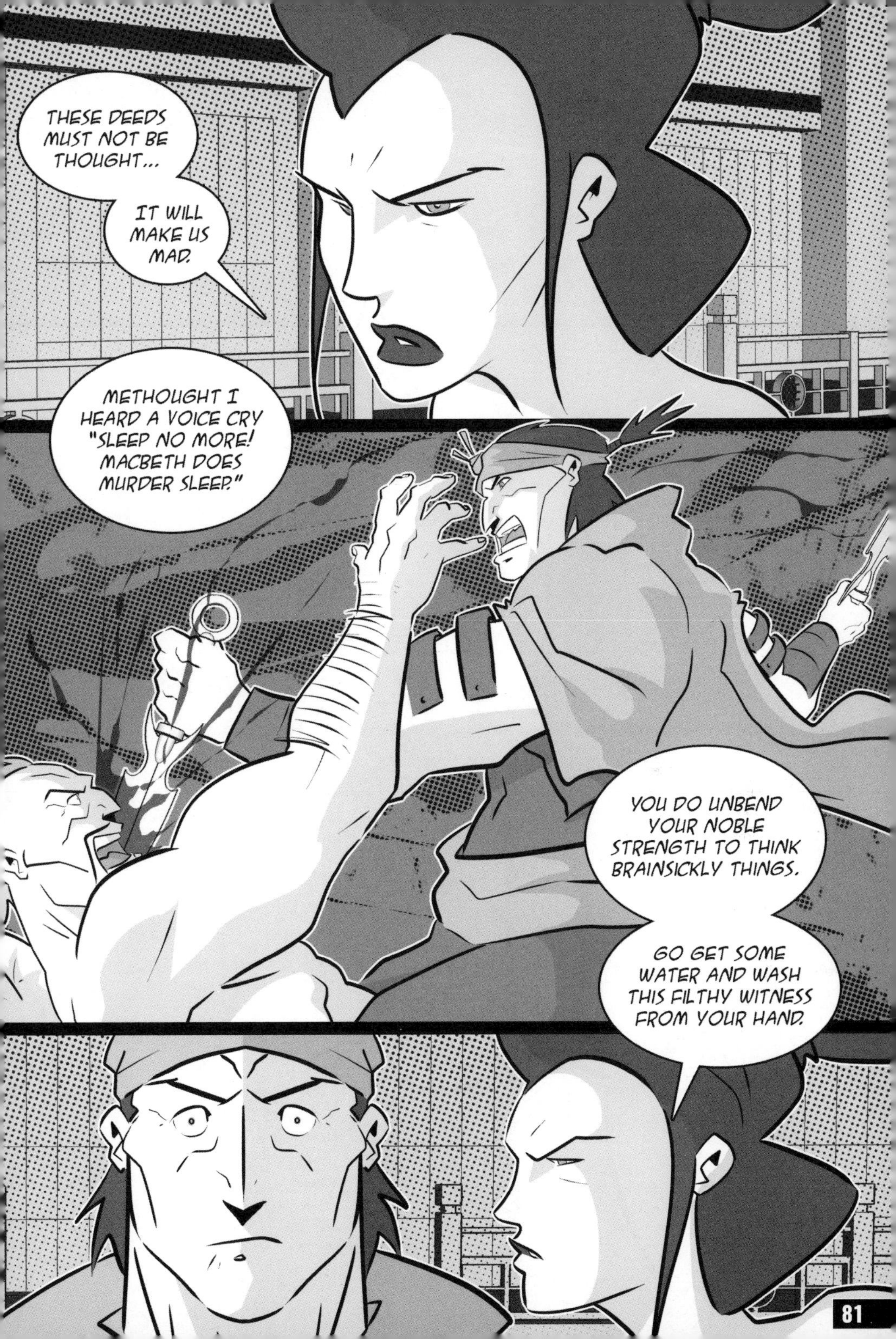
THESE DEEDS MUST NOT BE THOUGHT...
IT WILL MAKE US MAD.
METHOUGHT I HEARD A VOICE CRY "SLEEP NO MORE! MACBETH DOES MURDER SLEEP."
YOU DO UNBEND YOUR NOBLE STRENGTH TO THINK BRAINSICKLY THINGS.
GO GET SOME WATER AND WASH THIS FILTHY WITNESS FROM YOUR HAND.

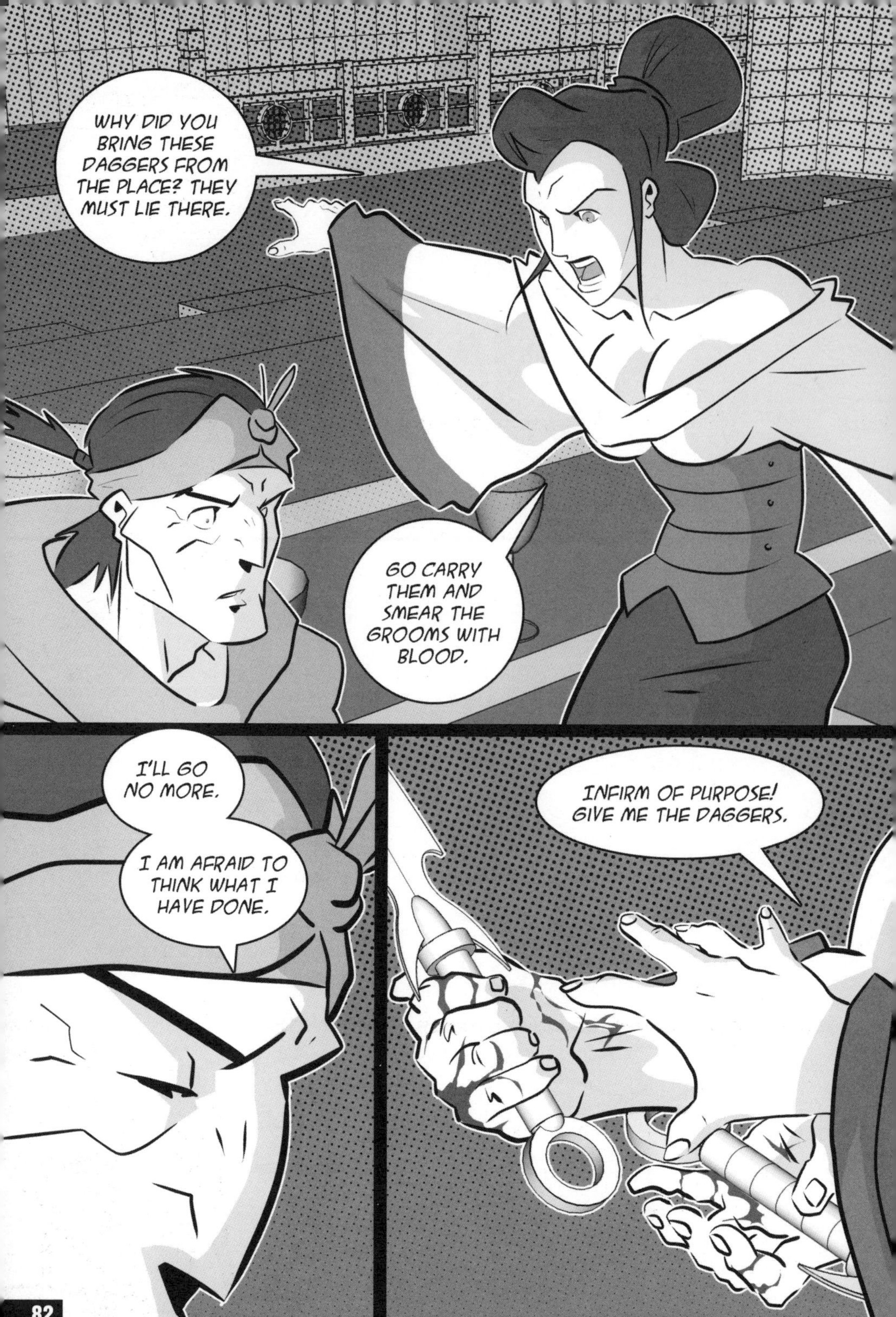

WHY DID YOU BRING THESE DAGGERS FROM THE PLACE? THEY MUST LIE THERE.
GO CARRY THEM AND SMEAR THE GROOMS WITH BLOOD.
I'LL GO NO MORE.
I AM AFRAID TO THINK WHAT I HAVE DONE.
INFIRM OF PURPOSE! GIVE ME THE DAGGERS.

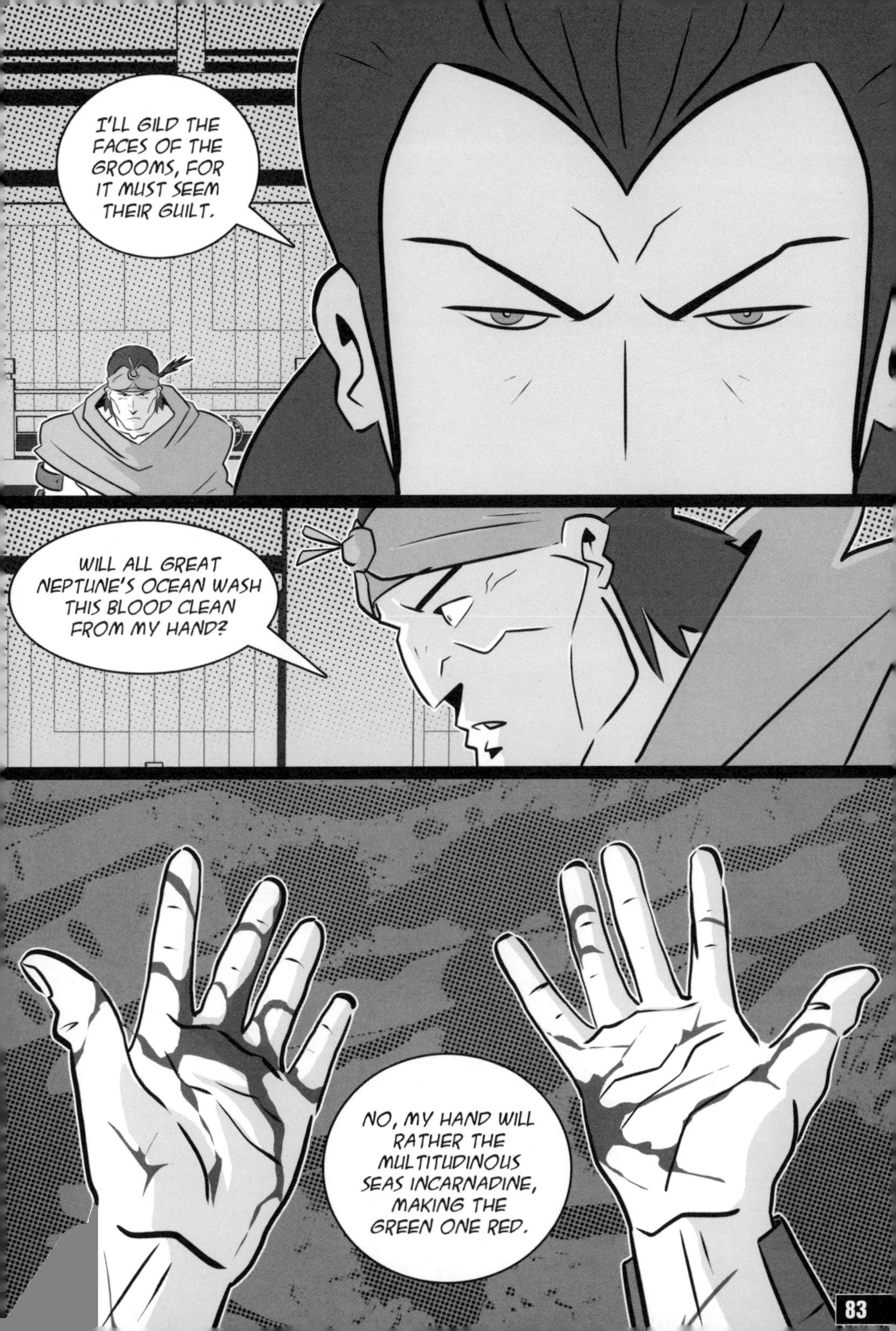
I'LL GILD THE FACES OF THE GROOMS, FOR IT MUST SEEM THEIR GUILT.
WILL ALL GREAT NEPTUNE'S OCEAN WASH THIS BLOOD CLEAN FROM MY HAND?
NO, MY HAND WILL RATHER THE MULTITUDINOUS SEAS INCARNADINE, MAKING THE GREEN ONE RED.

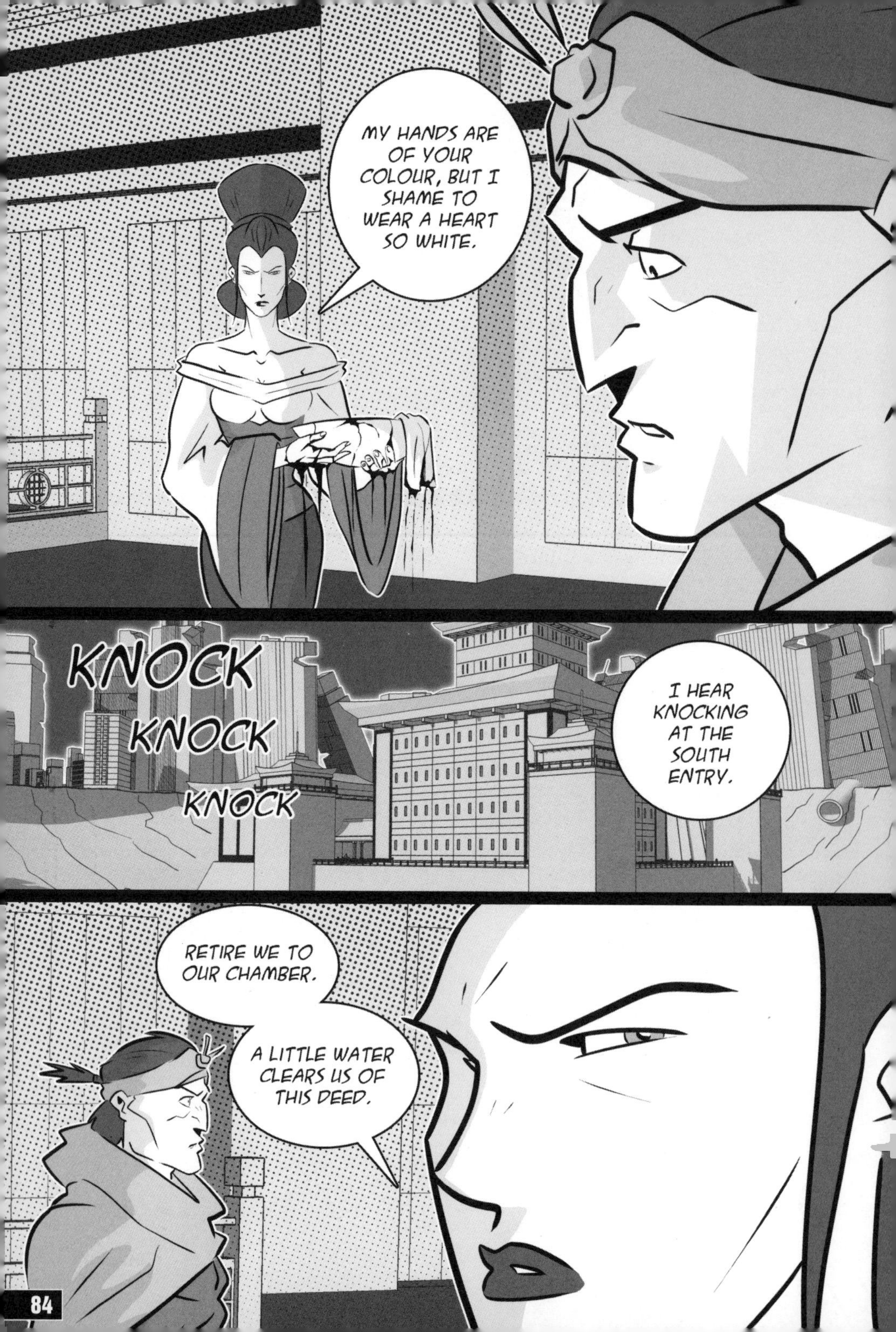
MY HANDS ARE OF YOUR COLOUR, BUT I SHAME TO WEAR A HEART SO WHITE.
KNOCK
KNOCK
KNOCK
I HEAR KNOCKING AT THE SOUTH ENTRY.
RETIRE WE TO OUR CHAMBER.
A LITTLE WATER CLEARS US OF THIS DEED.

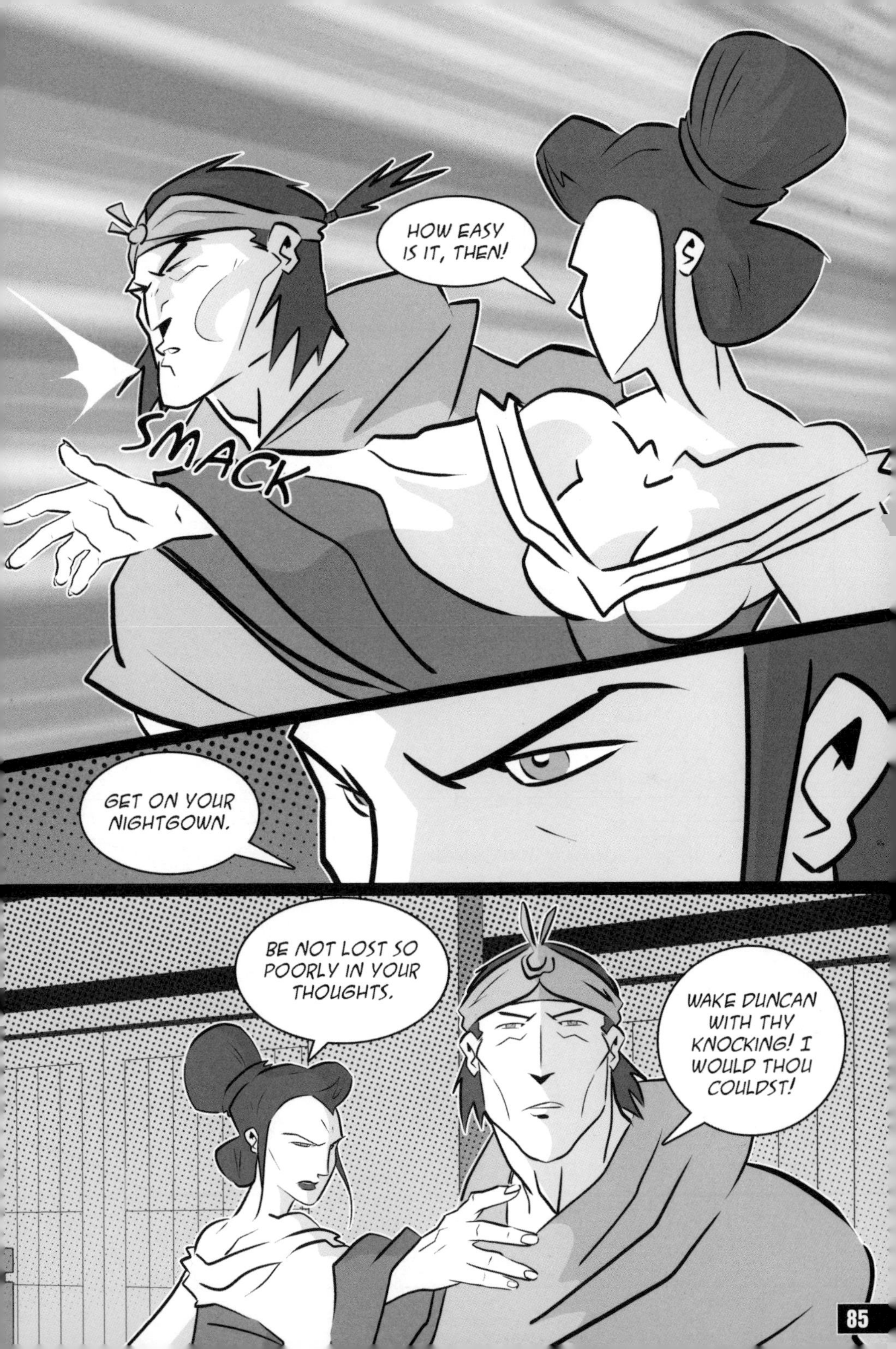
HOW EASY IS IT, THEN!
SMACK
GET ON YOUR NIGHTGOWN.
BE NOT LOST SO POORLY IN YOUR THOUGHTS.
WAKE DUNCAN WITH THY KNOCKING! I WOULD THOU COULDST!

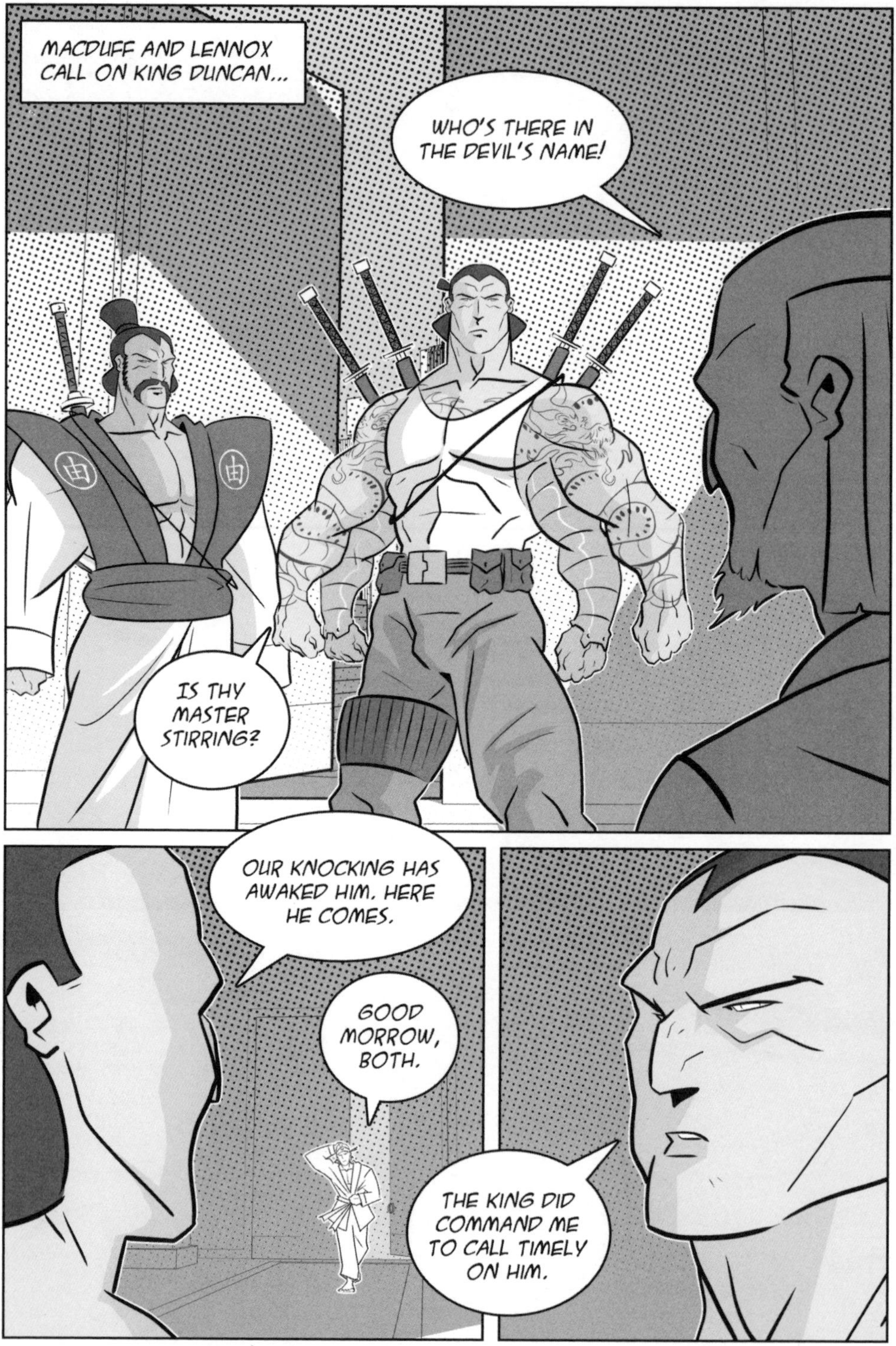
MACDUFF AND LENNOX CALL ON KING DUNCAN...
WHO'S THERE IN THE DEVIL'S NAME!
IS THY MASTER STIRRING?
OUR KNOCKING HAS AWAKED HIM. HERE HE COMES.
GOOD MORROW, BOTH.
THE KING DID COMMAND ME TO CALL TIMELY ON HIM.

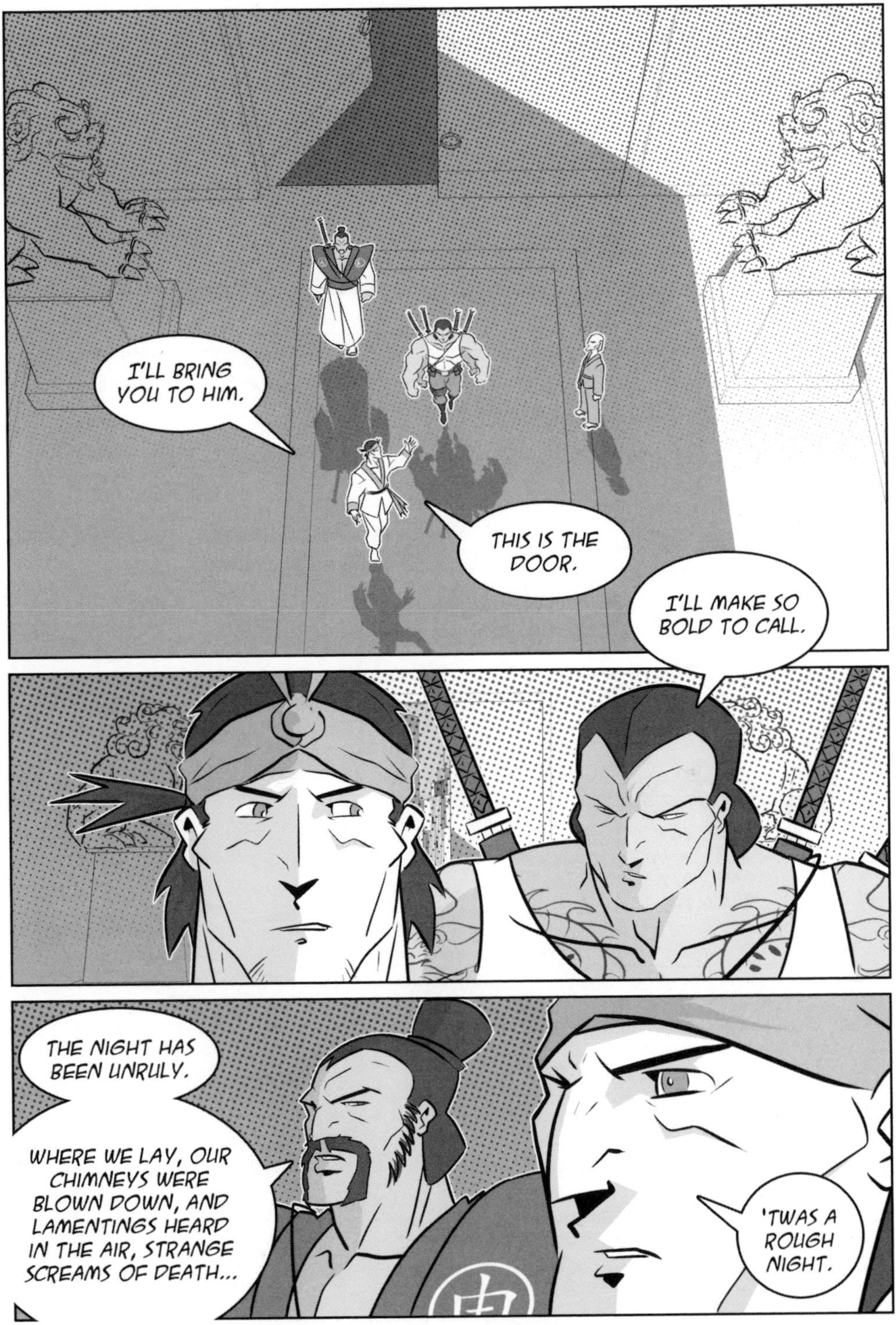
I'LL BRING YOU TO HIM.
THIS IS THE DOOR.
I'LL MAKE SO BOLD TO CALL.
THE NIGHT HAS BEEN UNRULY.
WHERE WE LAY, OUR CHIMNEYS WERE BLOWN DOWN, AND LAMENTINGS HEARD IN THE AIR, STRANGE SCREAMS OF DEATH...
'TWAS A ROUGH NIGHT.

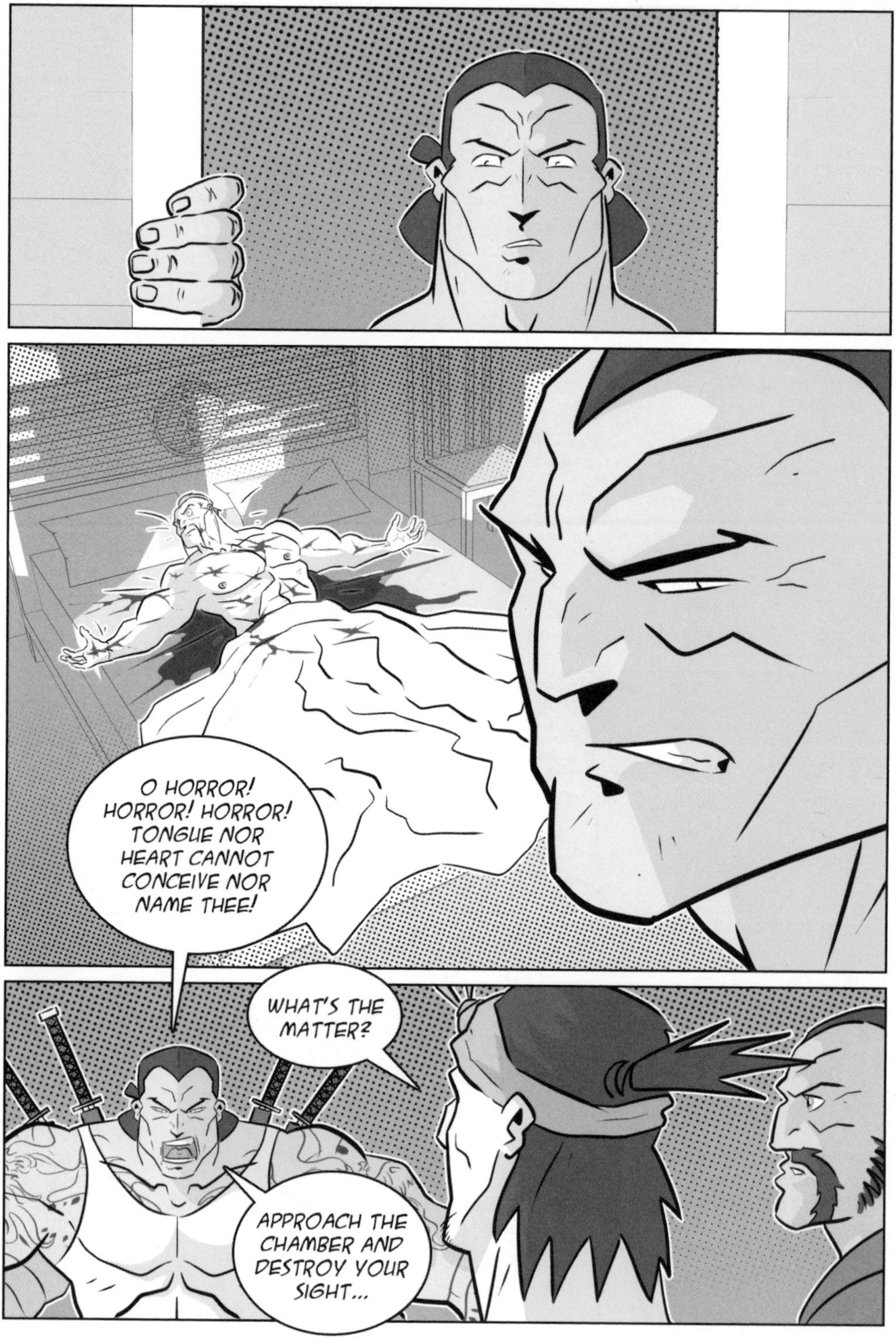
O HORROR! HORROR! HORROR! TONGUE NOR HEART CANNOT CONCEIVE NOR NAME THEE!
WHAT'S THE MATTER?
APPROACH THE CHAMBER AND DESTROY YOUR SIGHT...

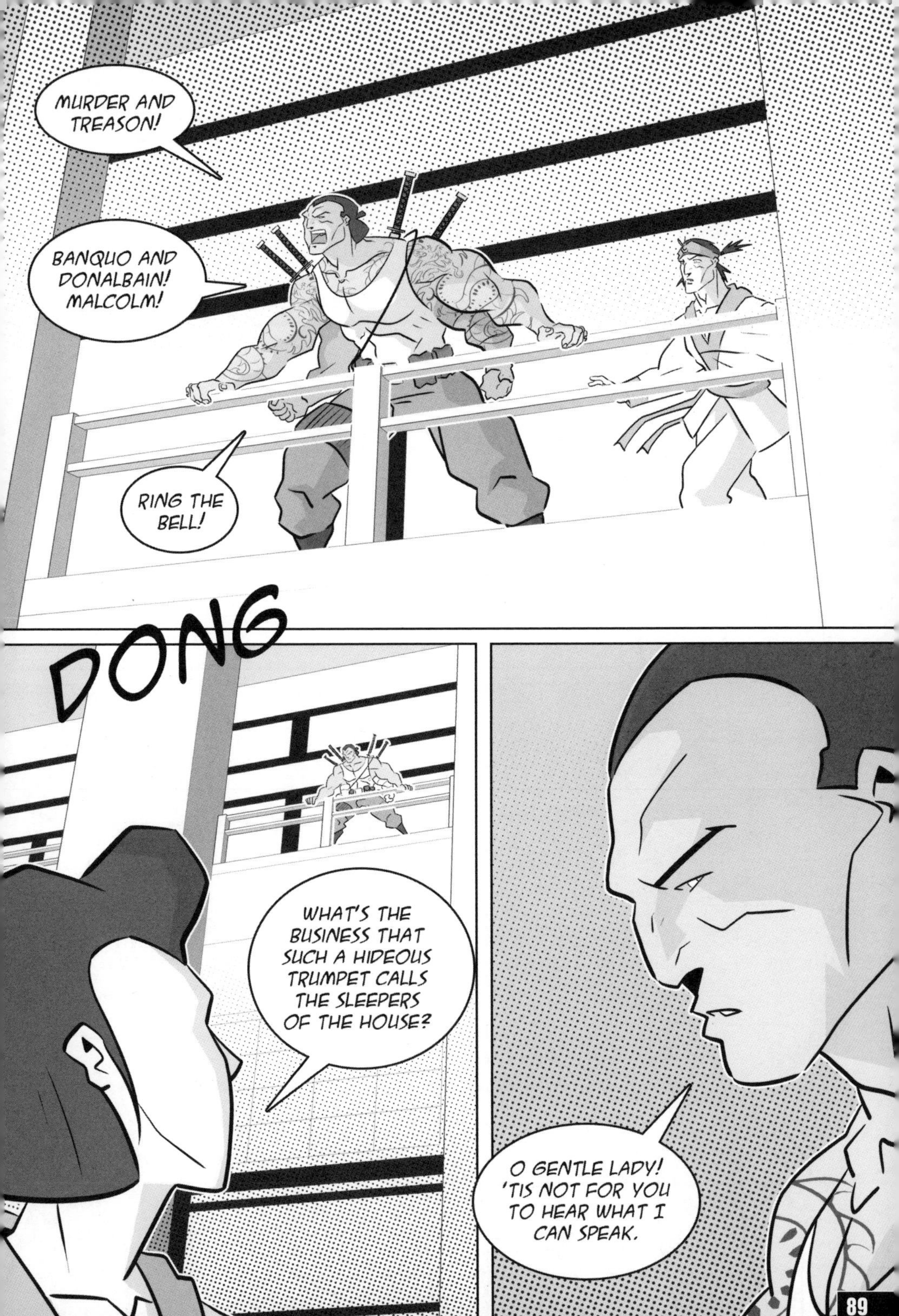
MURDER AND TREASON!
BANQUO AND DONALBAIN! MALCOLM!
RING THE BELL!
DONG
WHAT'S THE BUSINESS THAT SUCH A HIDEOUS TRUMPET CALLS THE SLEEPERS OF THE HOUSE?
O GENTLE LADY! 'TIS NOT FOR YOU TO HEAR WHAT I CAN SPEAK.

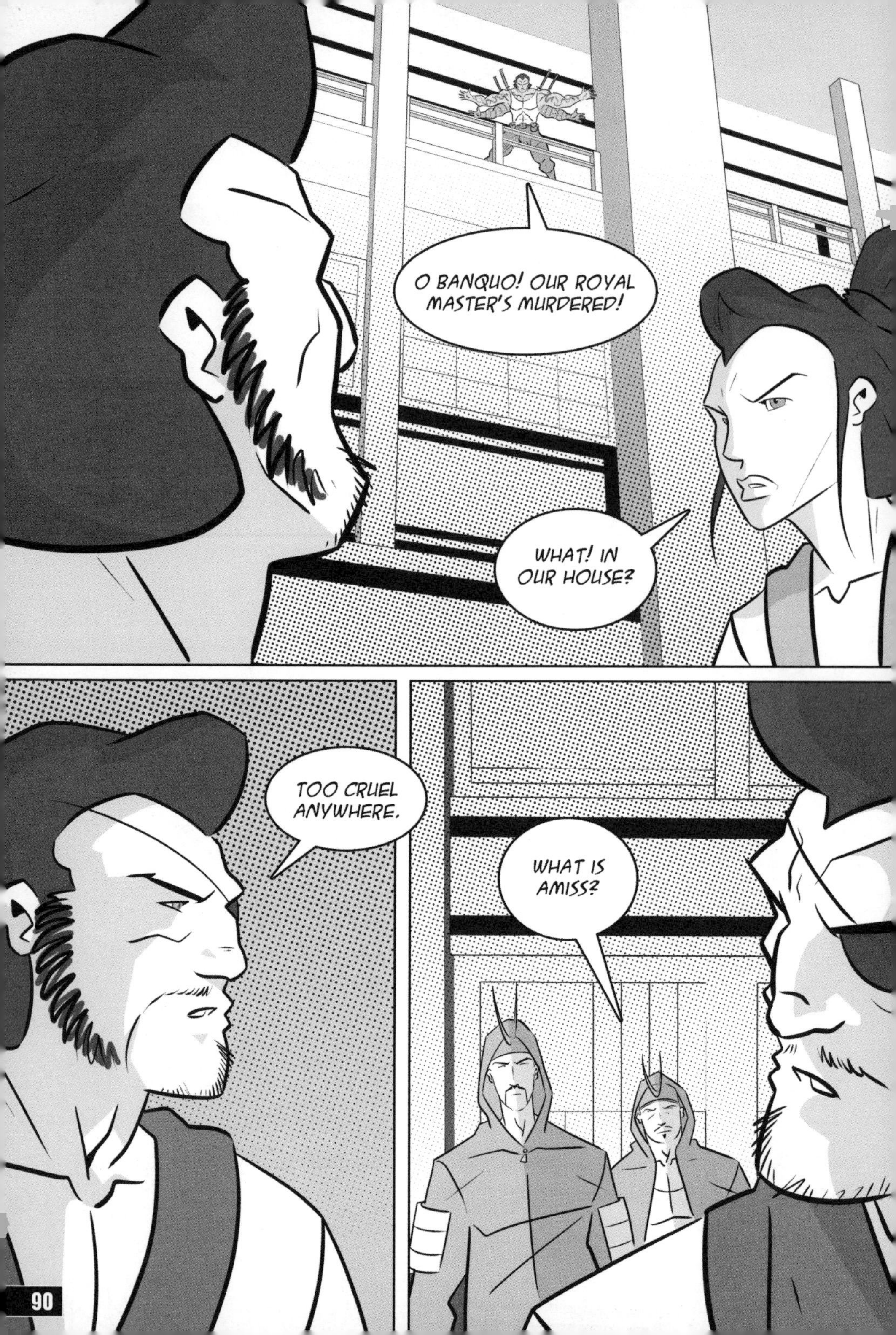
O BANQUO! OUR ROYAL MASTER'S MURDERED!
WHAT! IN OUR HOUSE?
TOO CRUEL ANYWHERE.
WHAT IS AMISS?

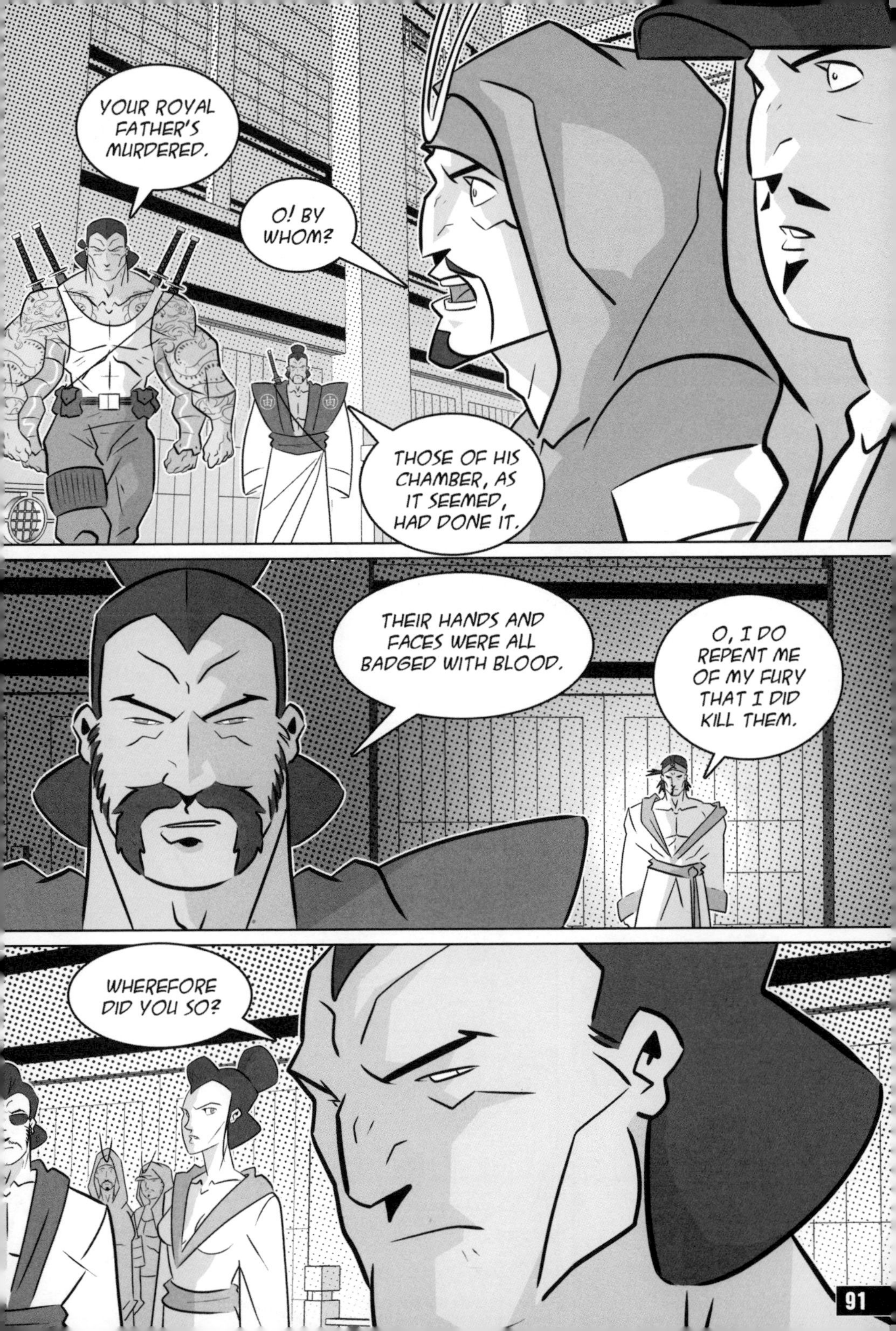
YOUR ROYAL FATHER'S MURDERED.
O! BY WHOM?
THOSE OF HIS CHAMBER, AS IT SEEMED, HAD DONE IT.
THEIR HANDS AND FACES WERE ALL BADGED WITH BLOOD.
O, I DO REPENT ME OF MY FURY THAT I DID KILL THEM.
WHEREFORE DID YOU SO?

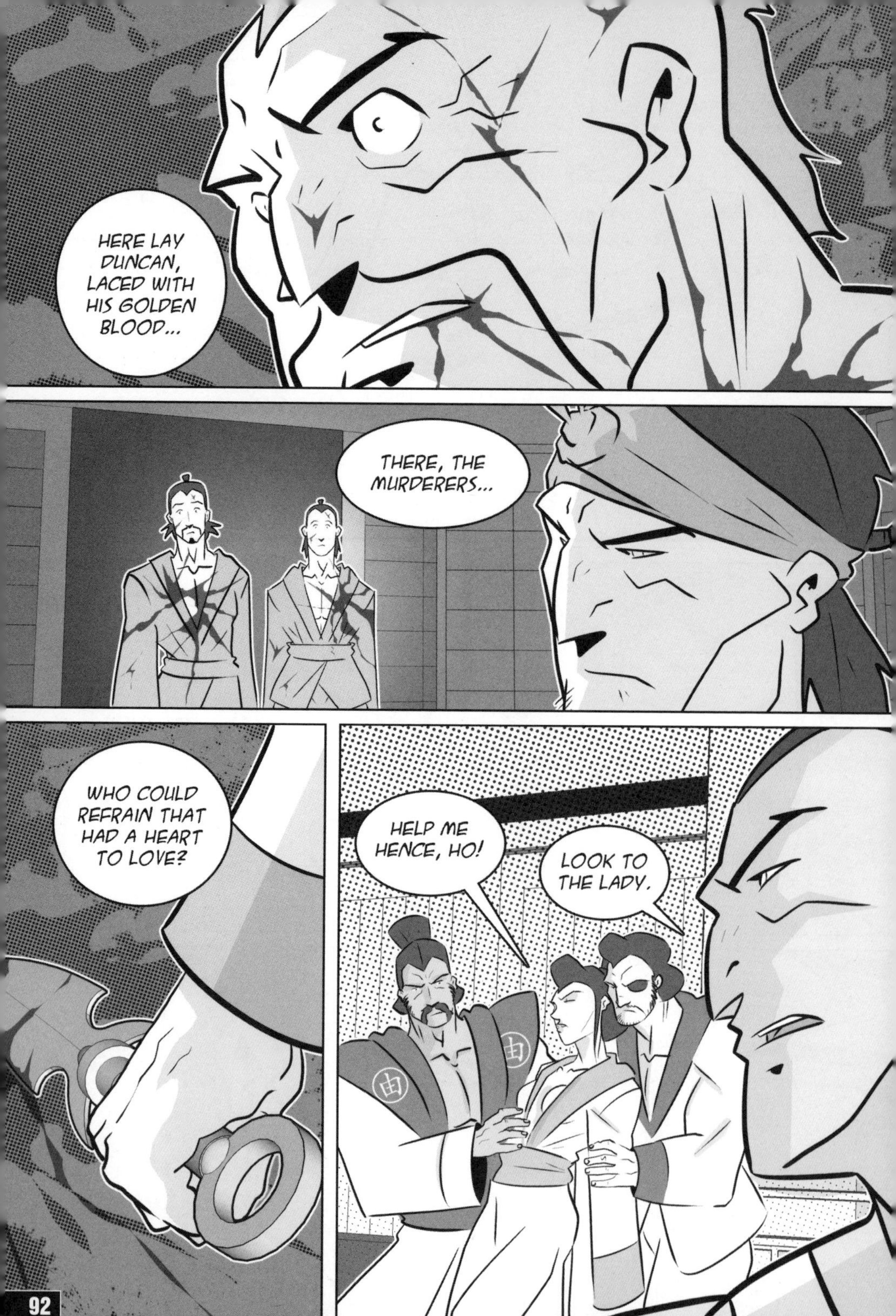
HERE LAY DUNCAN, LACED WITH HIS GOLDEN BLOOD...
THERE, THE MURDERERS...
WHO COULD REFRAIN THAT HAD A HEART TO LOVE?
HELP ME HENCE, HO!
LOOK TO THE LADY.

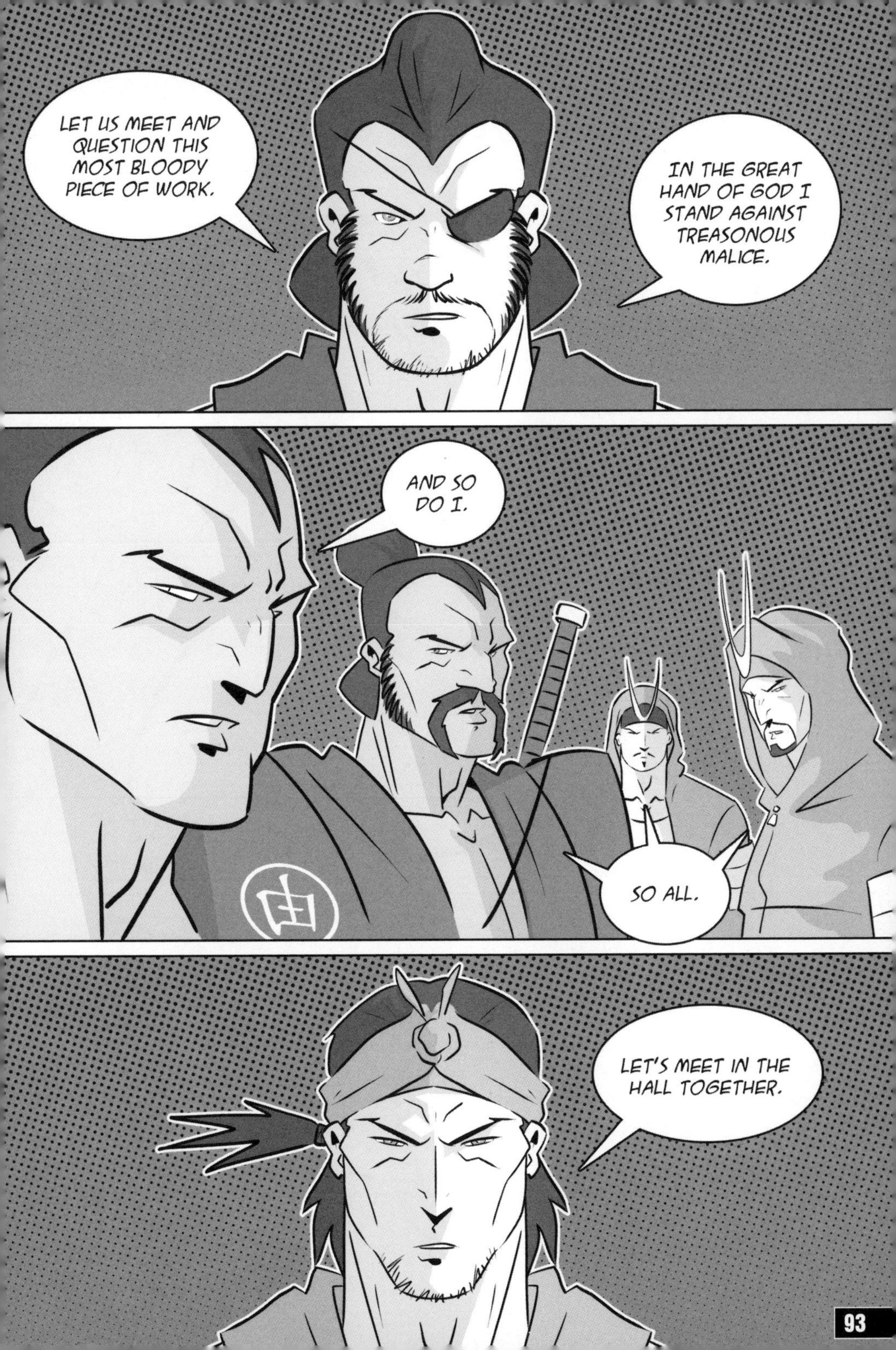
LET US MEET AND QUESTION THIS MOST BLOODY PIECE OF WORK.
IN THE GREAT HAND OF GOD I STAND AGAINST TREASONOUS MALICE.
AND SO DO I.
SO ALL.
LET'S MEET IN THE HALL TOGETHER.

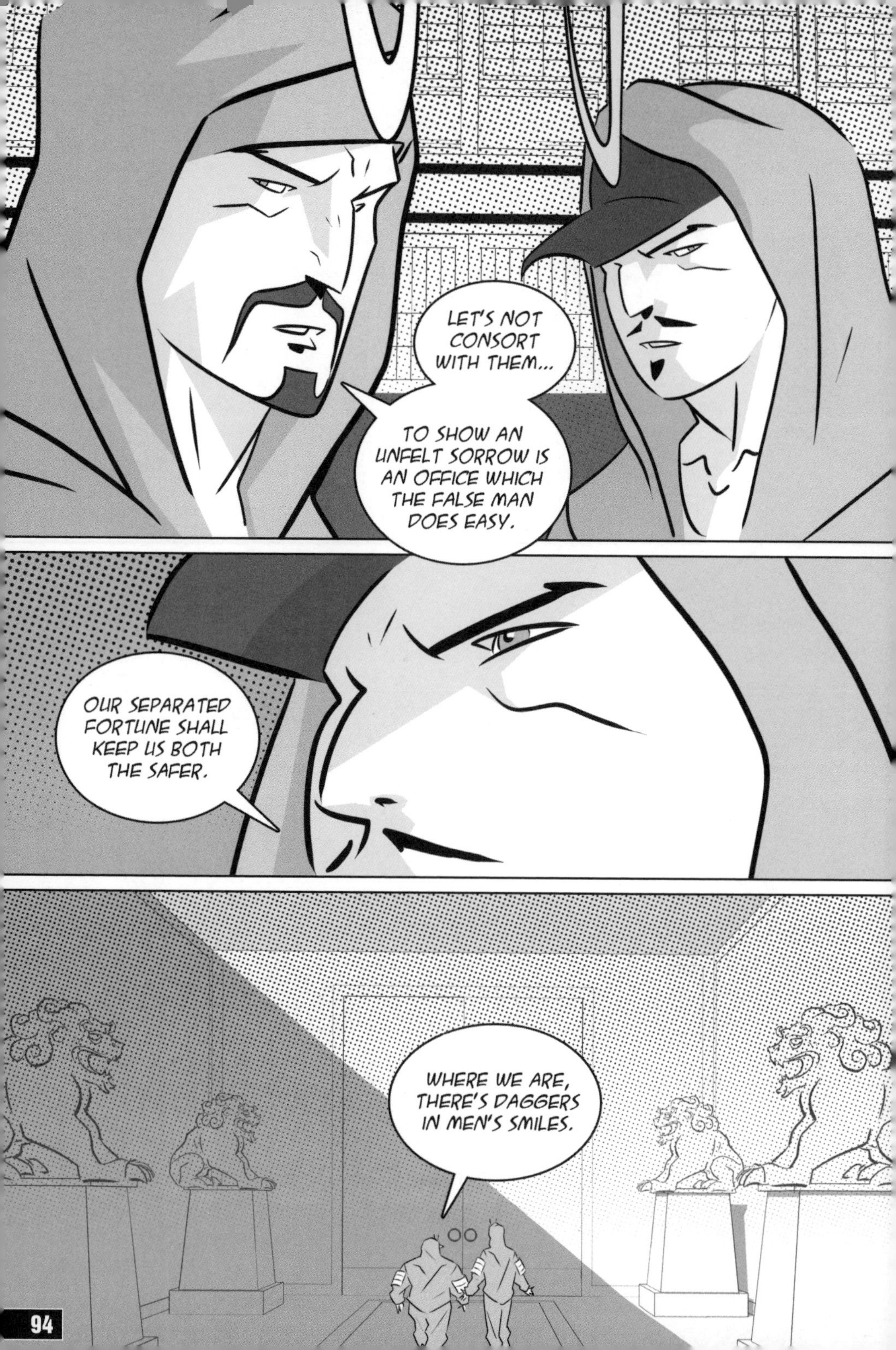
LET'S NOT CONSORT WITH THEM...
TO SHOW AN UNFELT SORROW IS AN OFFICE WHICH THE FALSE MAN DOES EASY.
OUR SEPARATED FORTUNE SHALL KEEP US BOTH THE SAFER.
WHERE WE ARE, THERE'S DAGGERS IN MEN'S SMILES.

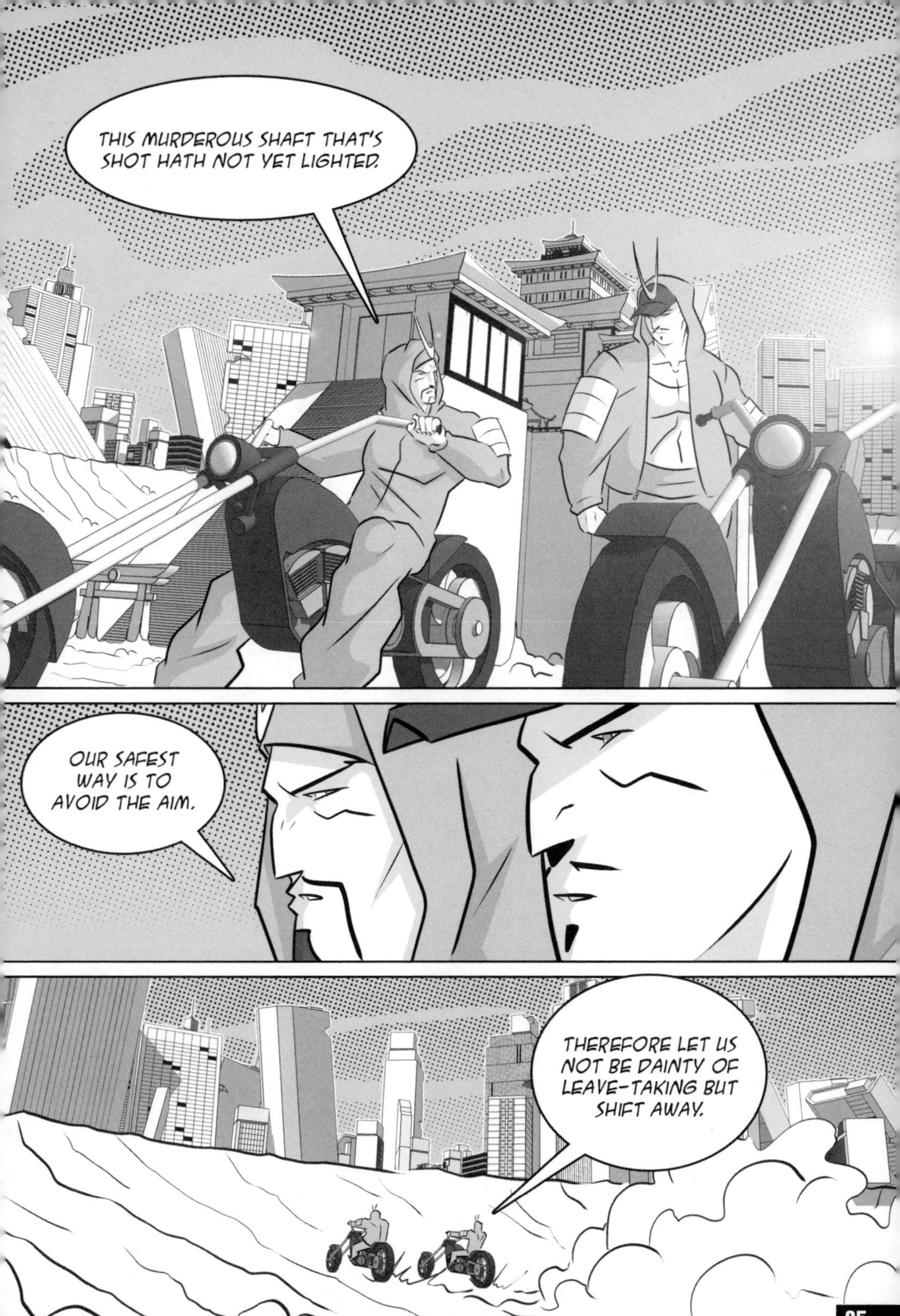
THIS MURDEROUS SHAFT THAT'S SHOT HATH NOT YET LIGHTED.
OUR SAFEST WAY IS TO AVOID THE AIM.
THEREFORE LET US NOT BE DAINTY OF LEAVE-TAKING BUT SHIFT AWAY.

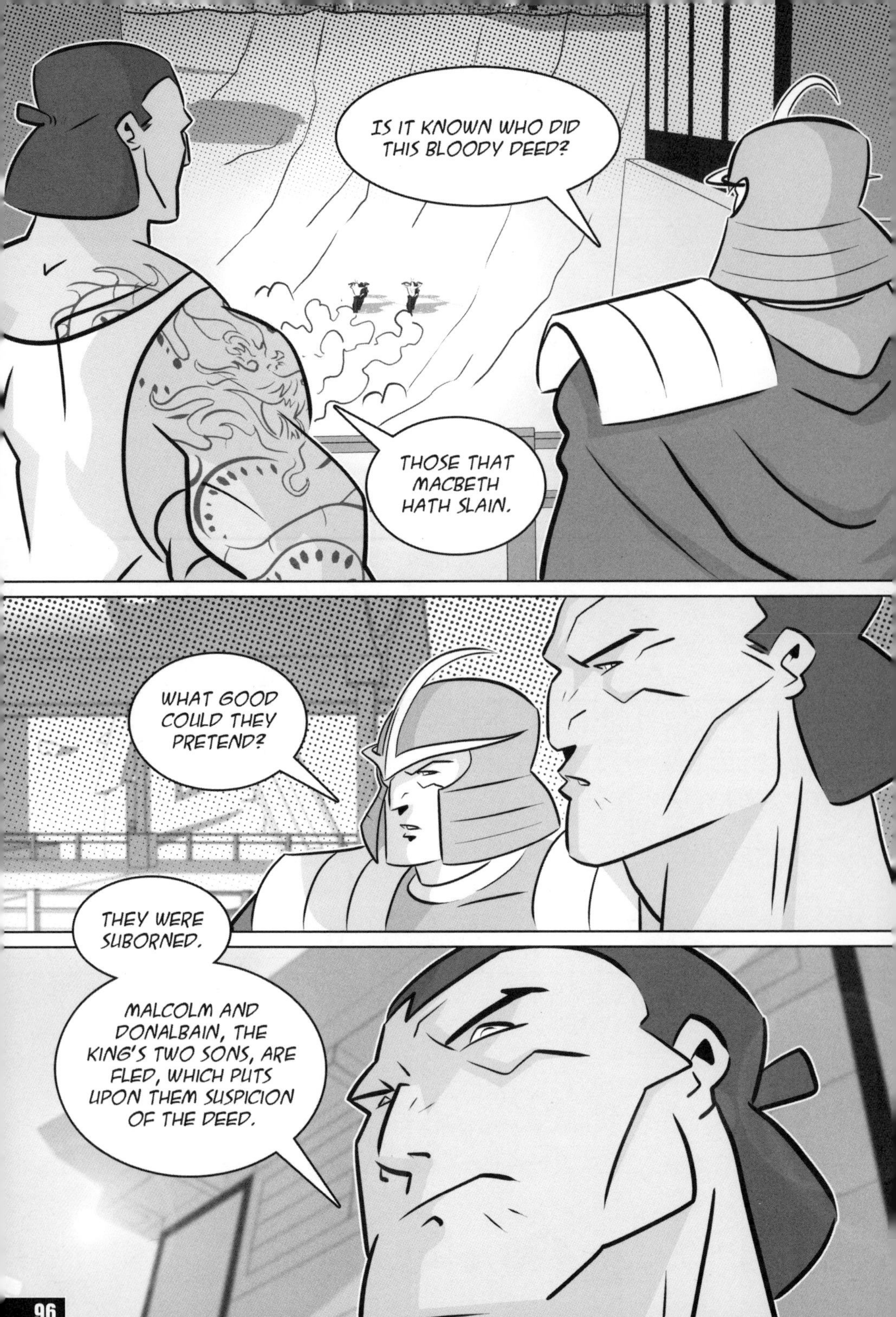
IS IT KNOWN WHO DID THIS BLOODY DEED?
THOSE THAT MACBETH HATH SLAIN.
WHAT GOOD COULD THEY PRETEND?
THEY WERE SUBORNED.
MALCOLM AND DONALBAIN, THE KING'S TWO SONS, ARE FLED, WHICH PUTS UPON THEM SUSPICION OF THE DEED.

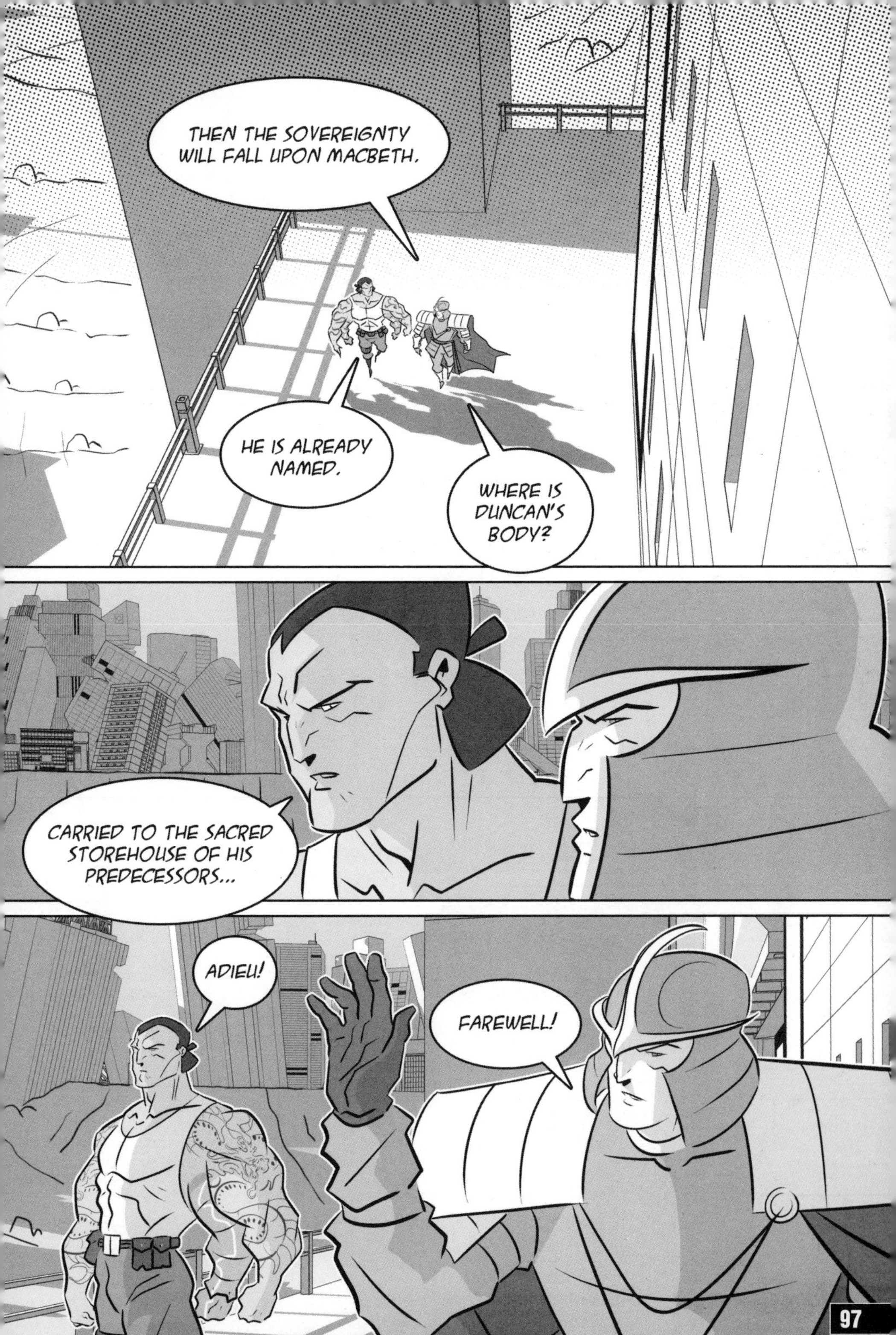
THEN THE SOVEREIGNTY WILL FALL UPON MACBETH.
HE IS ALREADY NAMED.
WHERE IS DUNCAN'S BODY?
CARRIED TO THE SACRED STOREHOUSE OF HIS PREDECESSORS...
ADIEU!
FAREWELL!

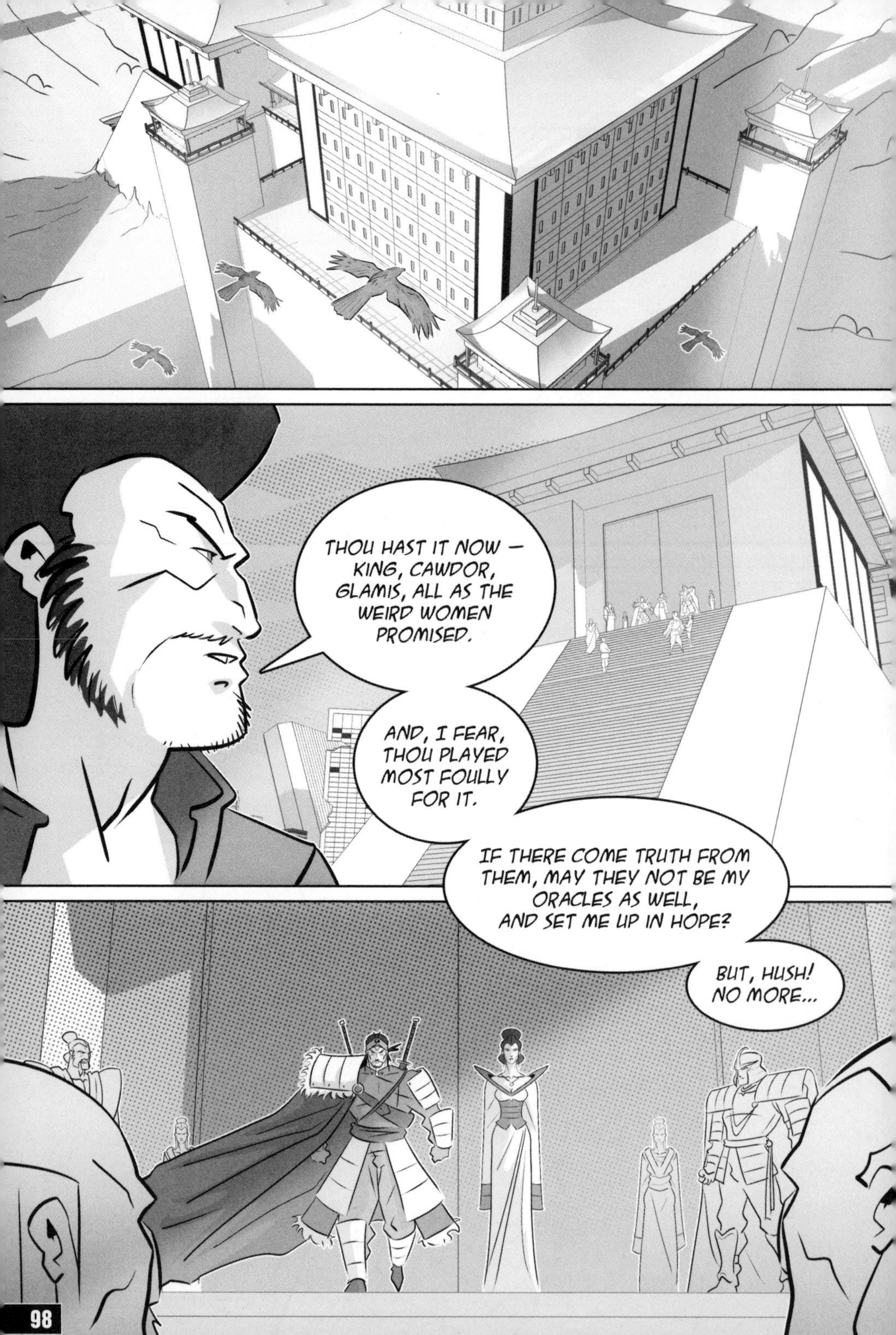
THOU HAST IT NOW — KING, CAWDOR, GLAMIS, ALL AS THE WEIRD WOMEN PROMISED.
AND, I FEAR, THOU PLAYED MOST FOULLY FOR IT.
IF THERE COME TRUTH FROM THEM, MAY THEY NOT BE MY ORACLES AS WELL, AND SET ME UP IN HOPE?
BUT, HUSH! NO MORE...

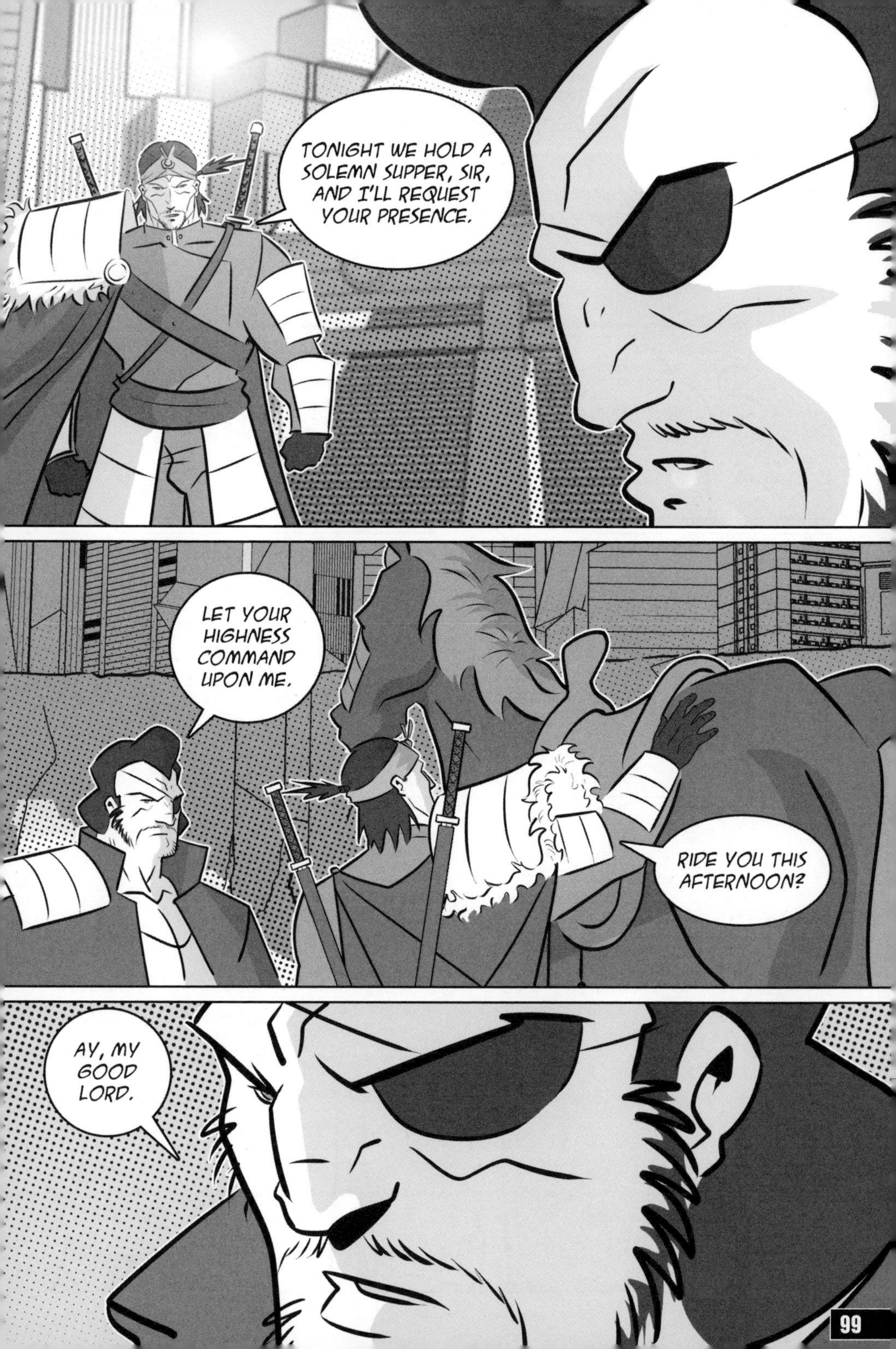
TONIGHT WE HOLD A SOLEMN SUPPER, SIR, AND I'LL REQUEST YOUR PRESENCE.
LET YOUR HIGHNESS COMMAND UPON ME.
RIDE YOU THIS AFTERNOON?
AY, MY GOOD LORD.

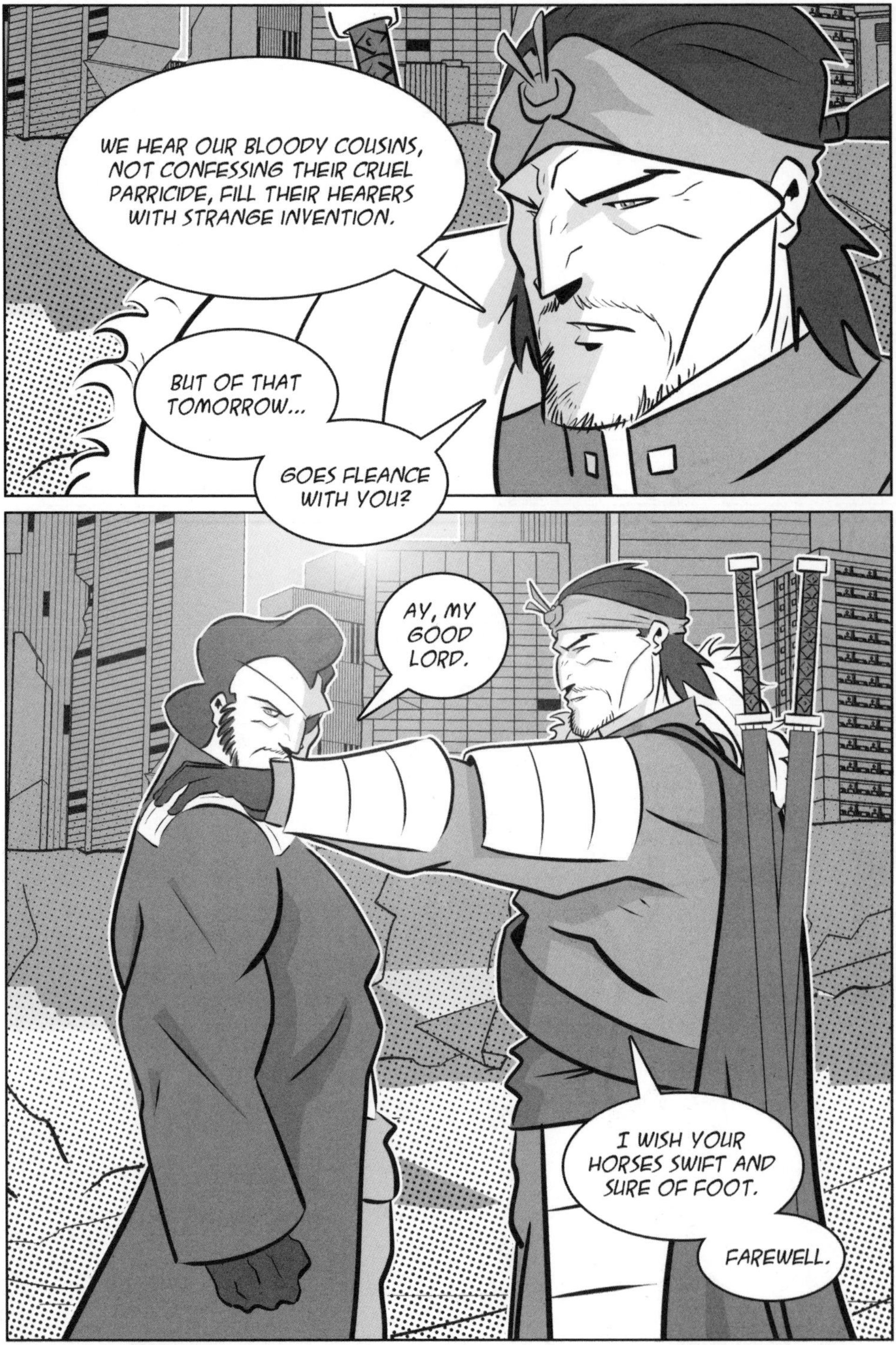
WE HEAR OUR BLOODY COUSINS, NOT CONFESSING THEIR CRUEL PARRICIDE, FILL THEIR HEARERS WITH STRANGE INVENTION.
BUT OF THAT TOMORROW...
GOES FLEANCE WITH YOU?
AY, MY GOOD LORD.
I WISH YOUR HORSES SWIFT AND SURE OF FOOT.
FAREWELL.

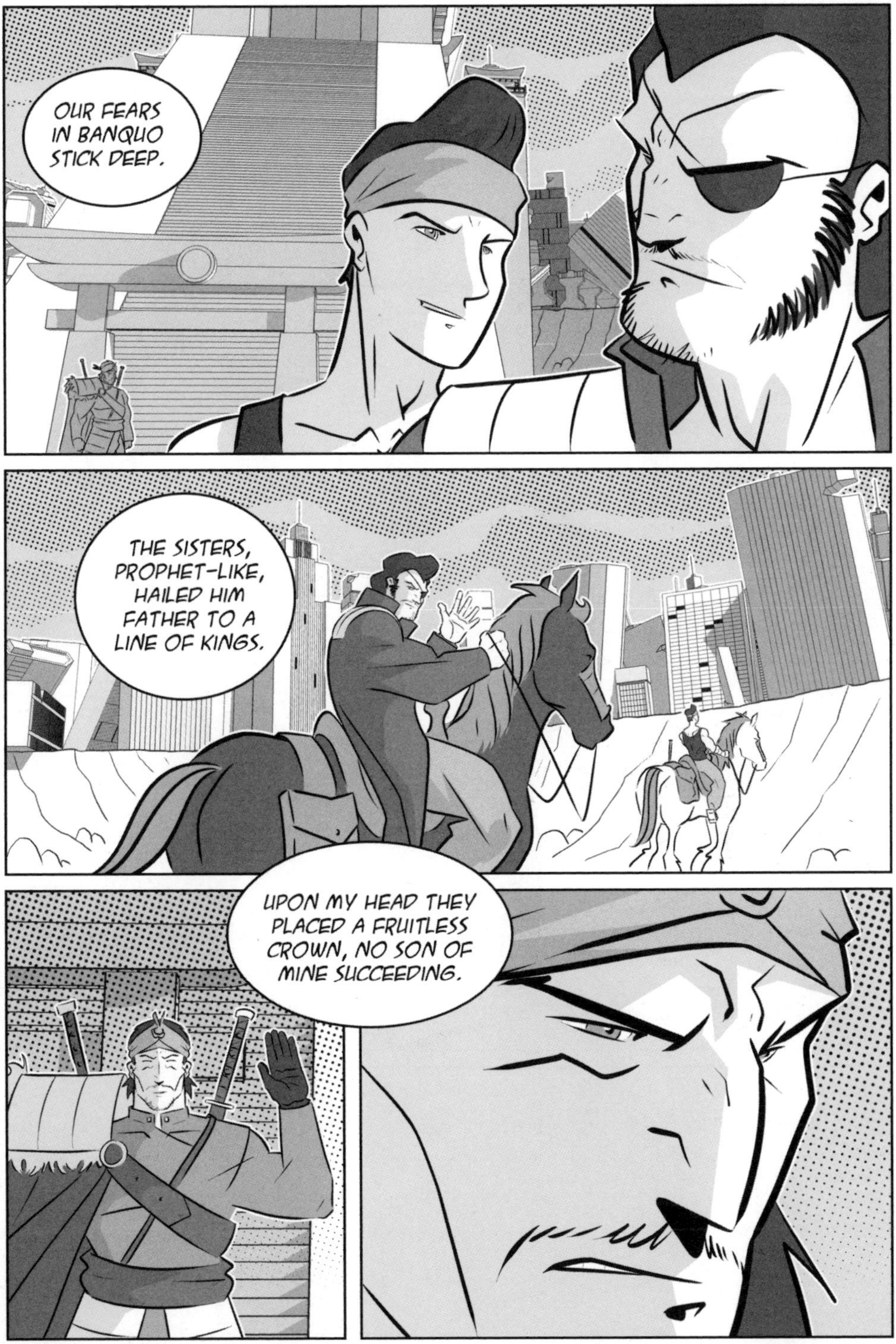
OUR FEARS IN BANQUO STICK DEEP.
THE SISTERS, PROPHET-LIKE, HAILED HIM FATHER TO A LINE OF KINGS.
UPON MY HEAD THEY PLACED A FRUITLESS CROWN, NO SON OF MINE SUCCEEDING.

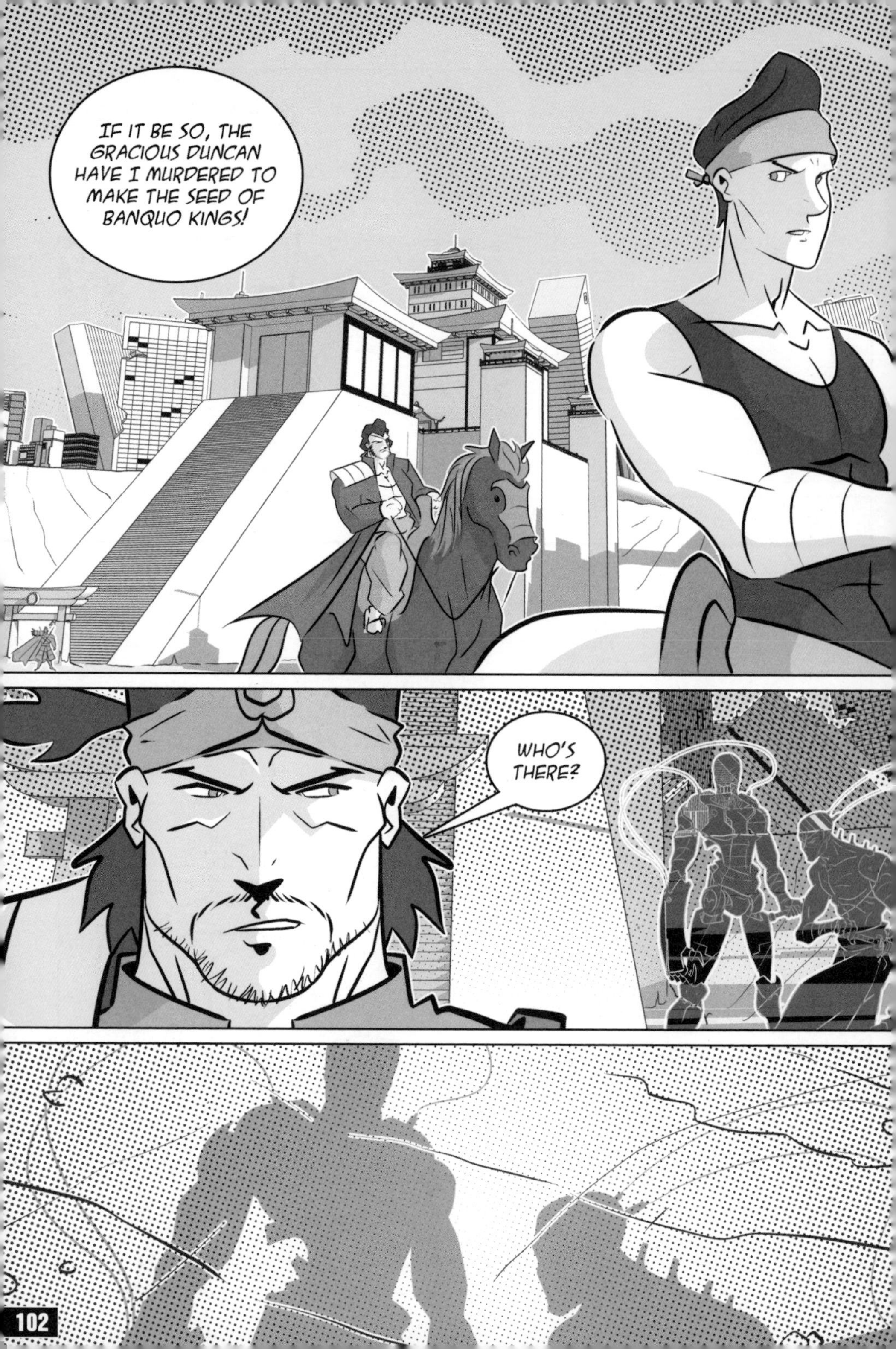
IF IT BE SO, THE GRACIOUS DUNCAN HAVE I MURDERED TO MAKE THE SEED OF BANQUO KINGS!
WHO'S THERE?

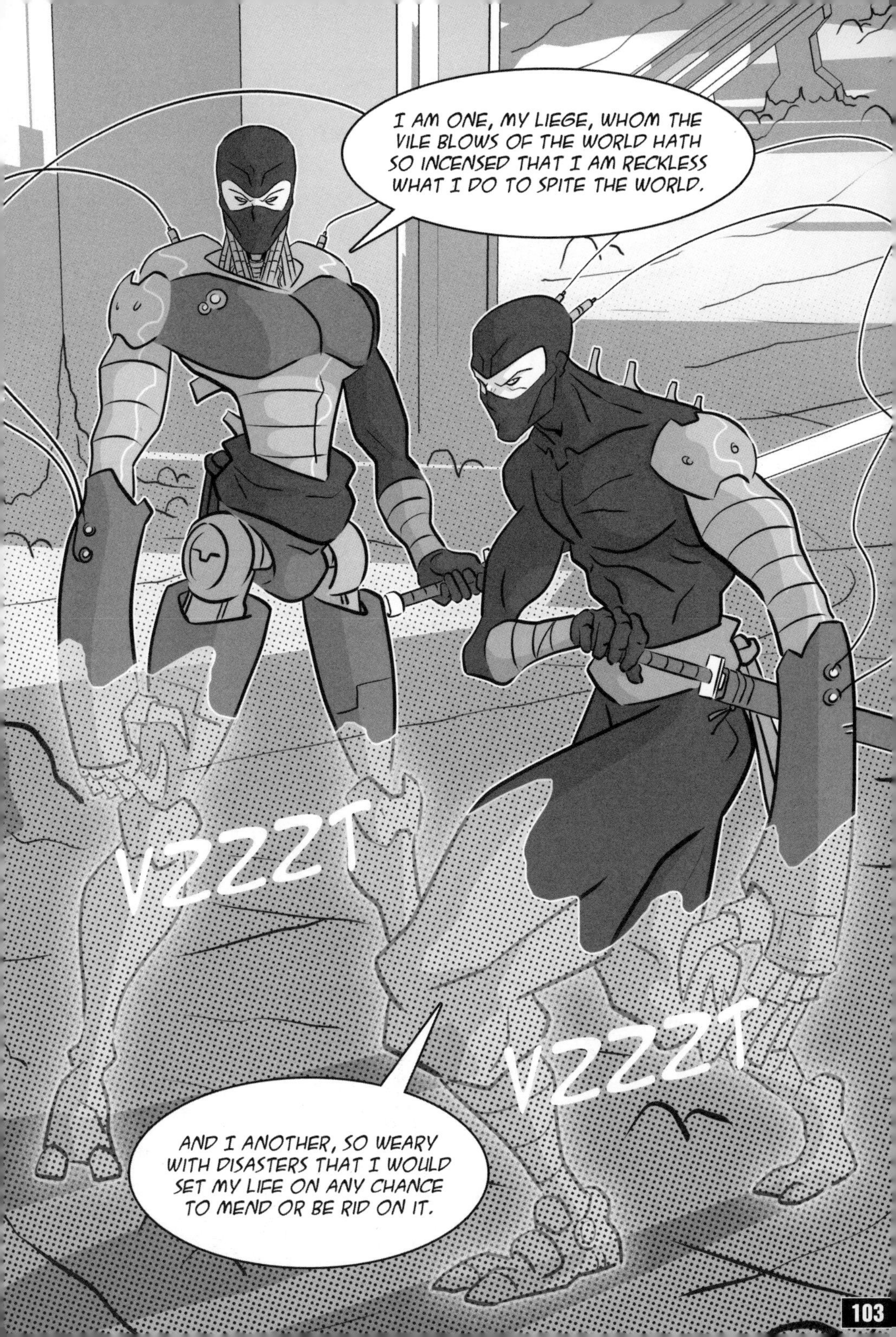
I AM ONE, MY LIEGE, WHOM THE VILE BLOWS OF THE WORLD HATH SO INCENSED THAT I AM RECKLESS WHAT I DO TO SPITE THE WORLD.
VZZZT
VZZZT
AND I ANOTHER, SO WEARY WITH DISASTERS THAT I WOULD SET MY LIFE ON ANY CHANCE TO MEND OR BE RID ON IT.

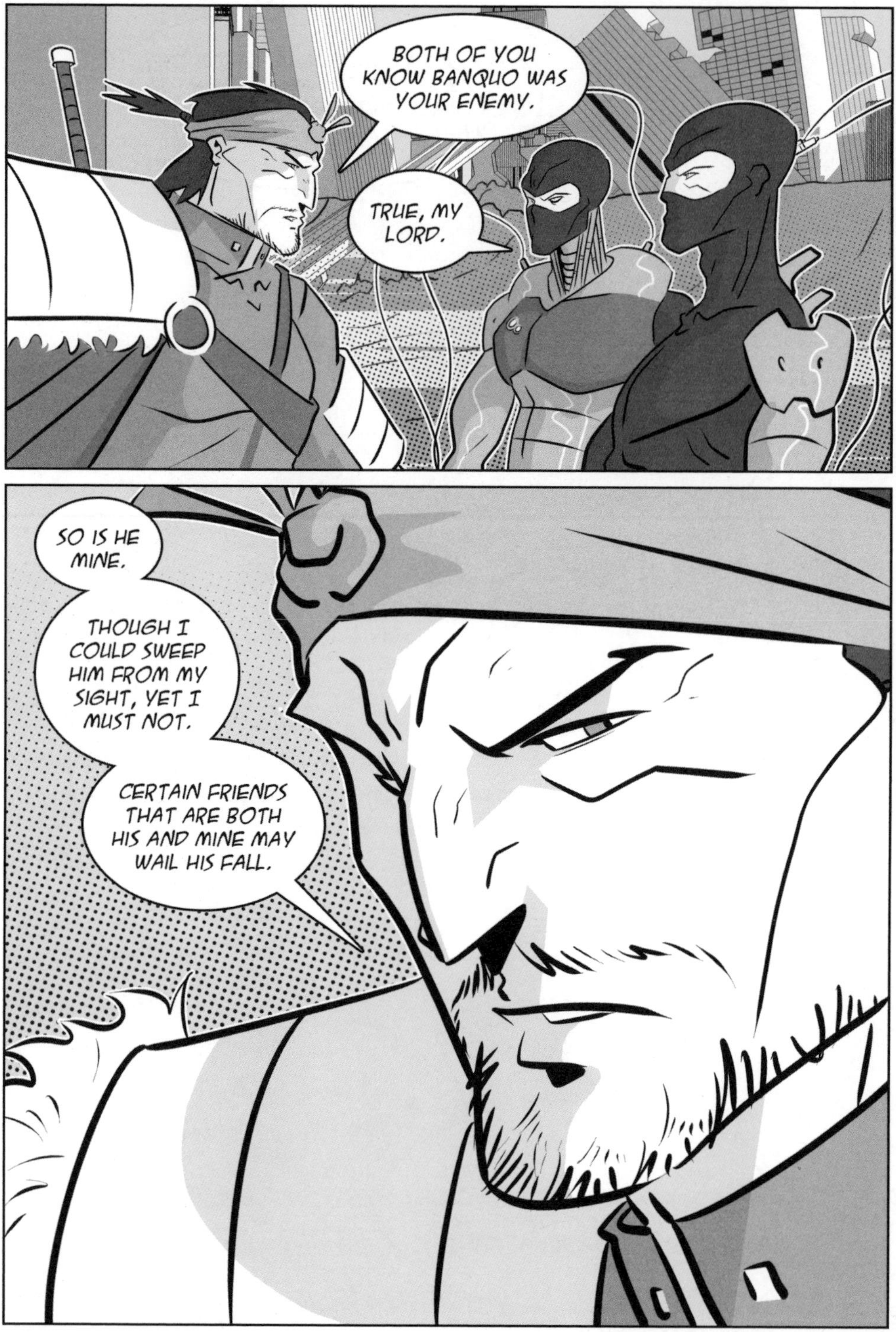
BOTH OF YOU KNOW BANQUO WAS YOUR ENEMY.
TRUE, MY LORD.
SO IS HE MINE.
THOUGH I COULD SWEEP HIM FROM MY SIGHT, YET I MUST NOT.
CERTAIN FRIENDS THAT ARE BOTH HIS AND MINE MAY WAIL HIS FALL.

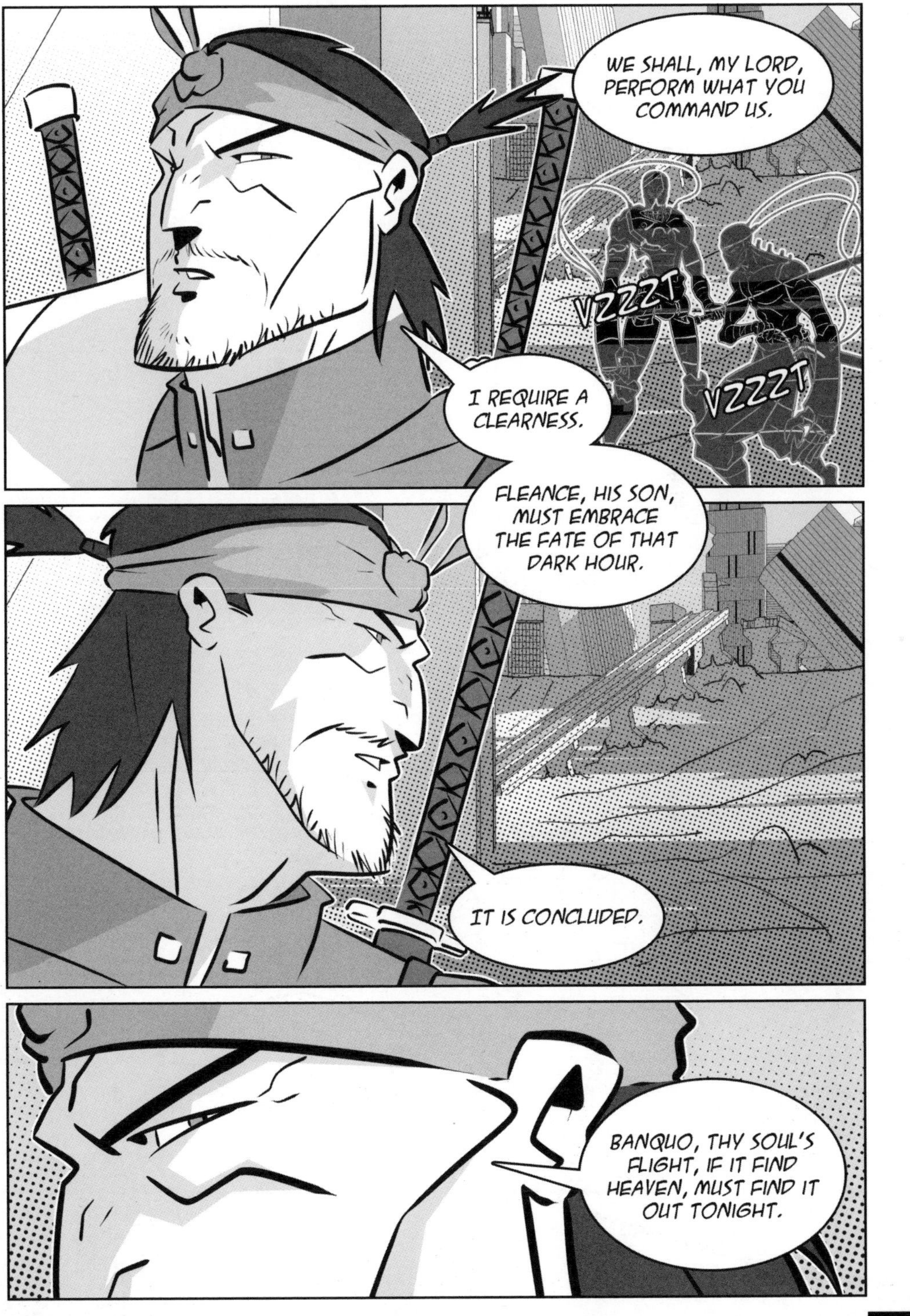
WE SHALL, MY LORD, PERFORM WHAT YOU COMMAND US.
VZZZT
VZZZT
I REQUIRE A CLEARNESS.
FLEANCE, HIS SON, MUST EMBRACE THE FATE OF THAT DARK HOUR.
IT IS CONCLUDED.
BANQUO, THY SOUL'S FLIGHT, IF IT FIND HEAVEN, MUST FIND IT OUT TONIGHT.

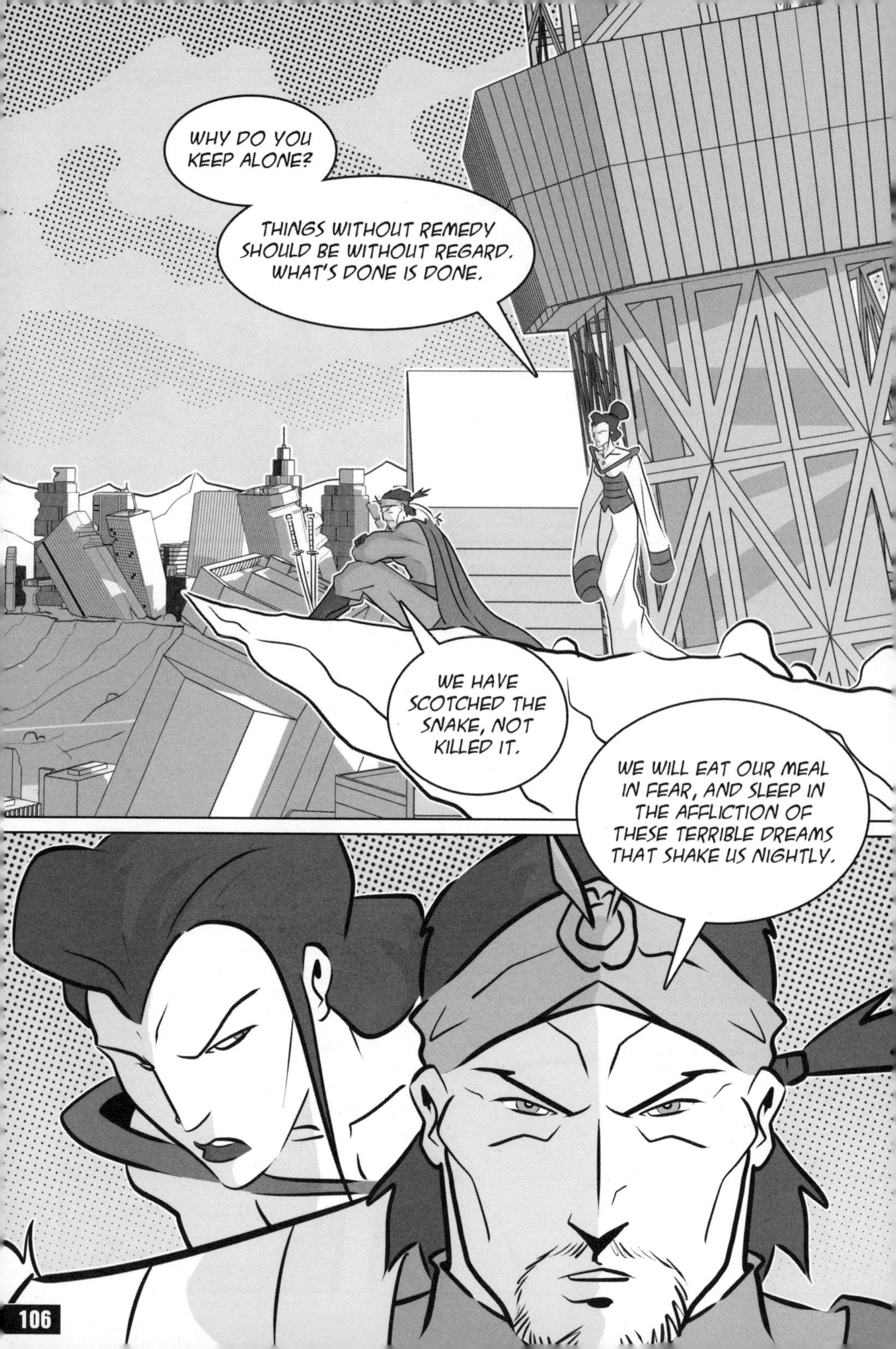
WHY DO YOU KEEP ALONE?
THINGS WITHOUT REMEDY SHOULD BE WITHOUT REGARD. WHAT'S DONE IS DONE.
WE HAVE SCOTCHED THE SNAKE, NOT KILLED IT.
WE WILL EAT OUR MEAL IN FEAR, AND SLEEP IN THE AFFLICTION OF THESE TERRIBLE DREAMS THAT SHAKE US NIGHTLY.

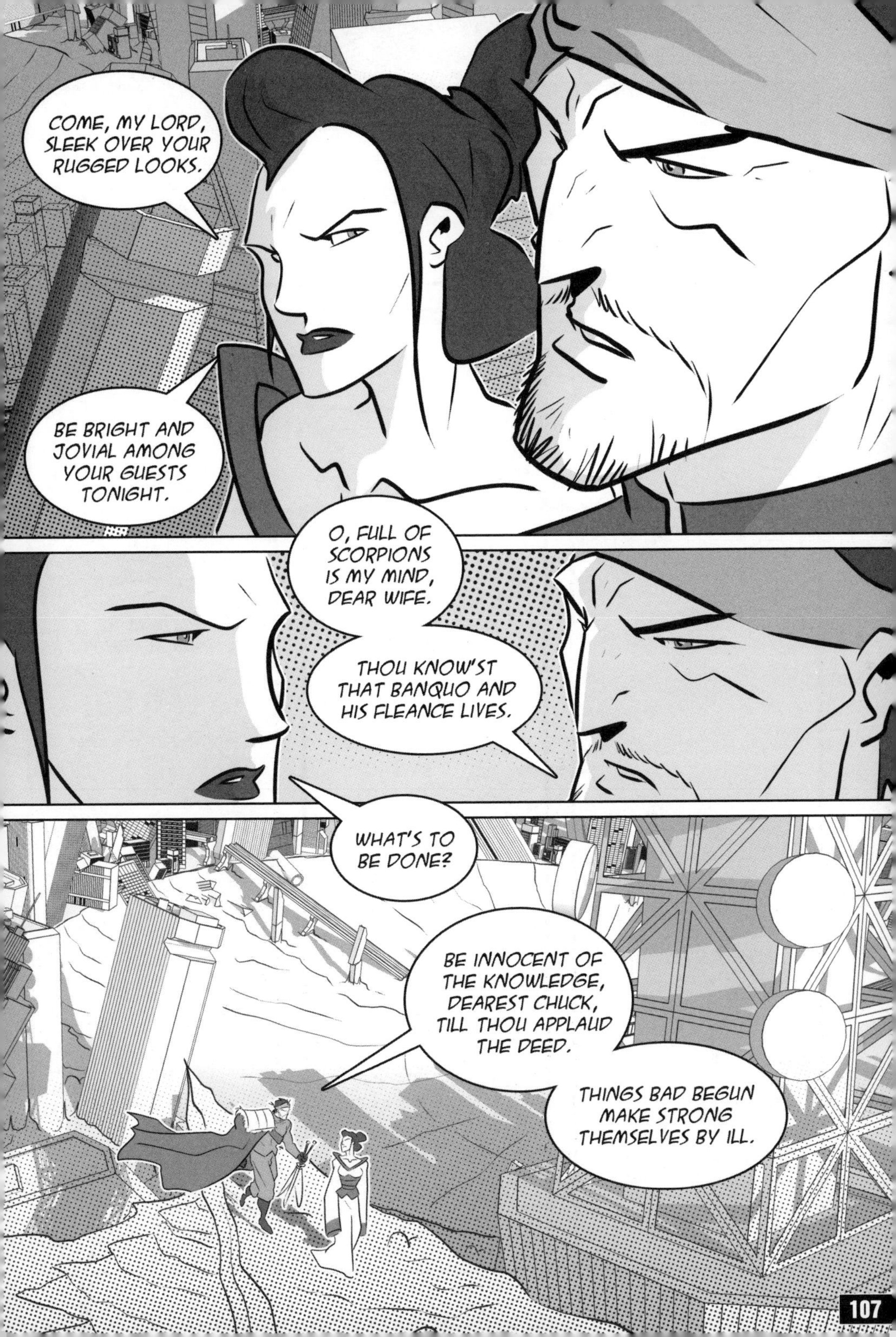
COME, MY LORD, SLEEK OVER YOUR RUGGED LOOKS.
BE BRIGHT AND JOVIAL AMONG YOUR GUESTS TONIGHT.
O, FULL OF SCORPIONS IS MY MIND, DEAR WIFE.
THOU KNOW'ST THAT BANQUO AND HIS FLEANCE LIVES.
WHAT'S TO BE DONE?
BE INNOCENT OF THE KNOWLEDGE, DEAREST CHUCK, TILL THOU APPLAUD THE DEED.
THINGS BAD BEGUN MAKE STRONG THEMSELVES BY ILL.

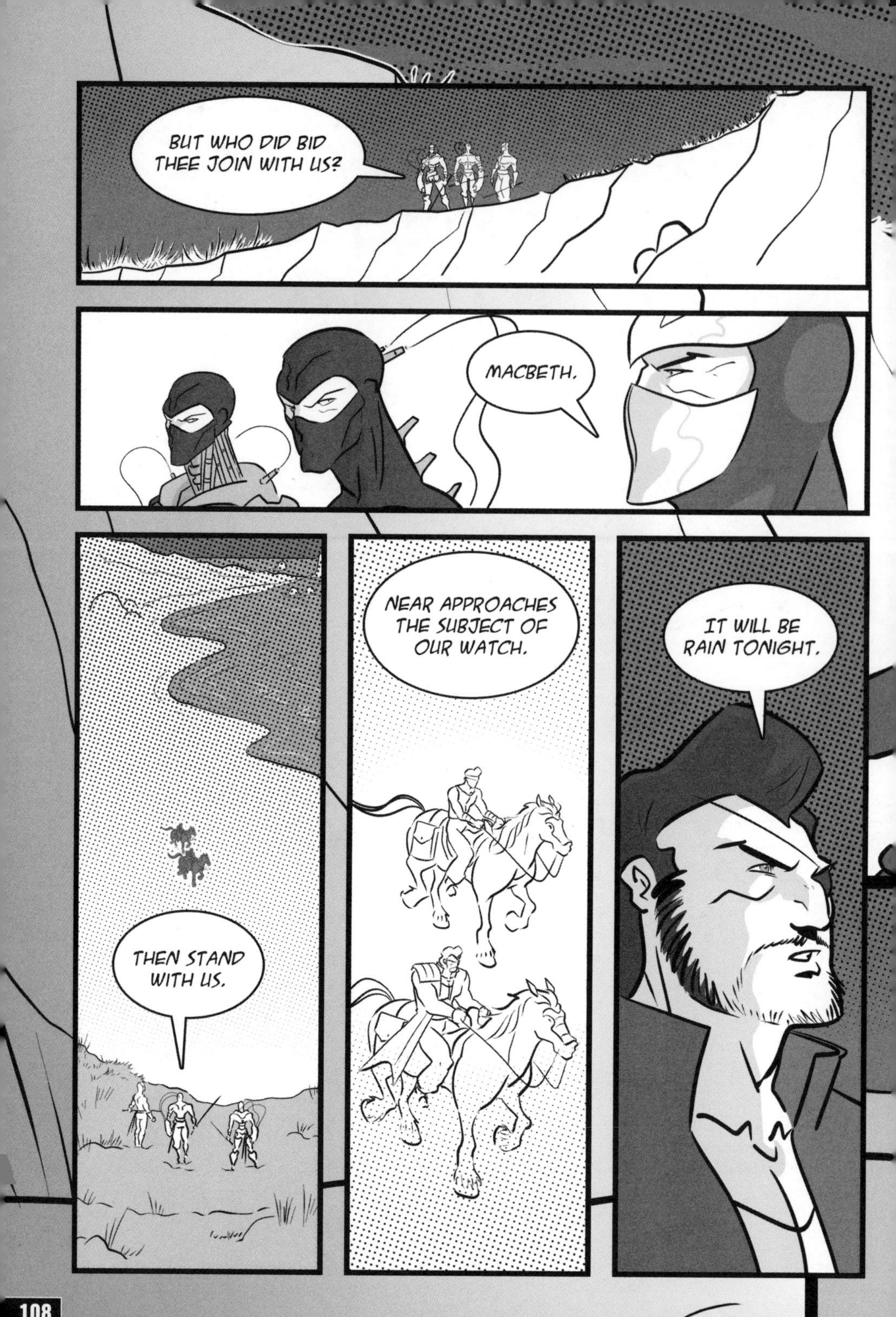
BUT WHO DID BID THEE JOIN WITH US?
MACBETH.
THEN STAND WITH US.
NEAR APPROACHES THE SUBJECT OF OUR WATCH.
IT WILL BE RAIN TONIGHT.

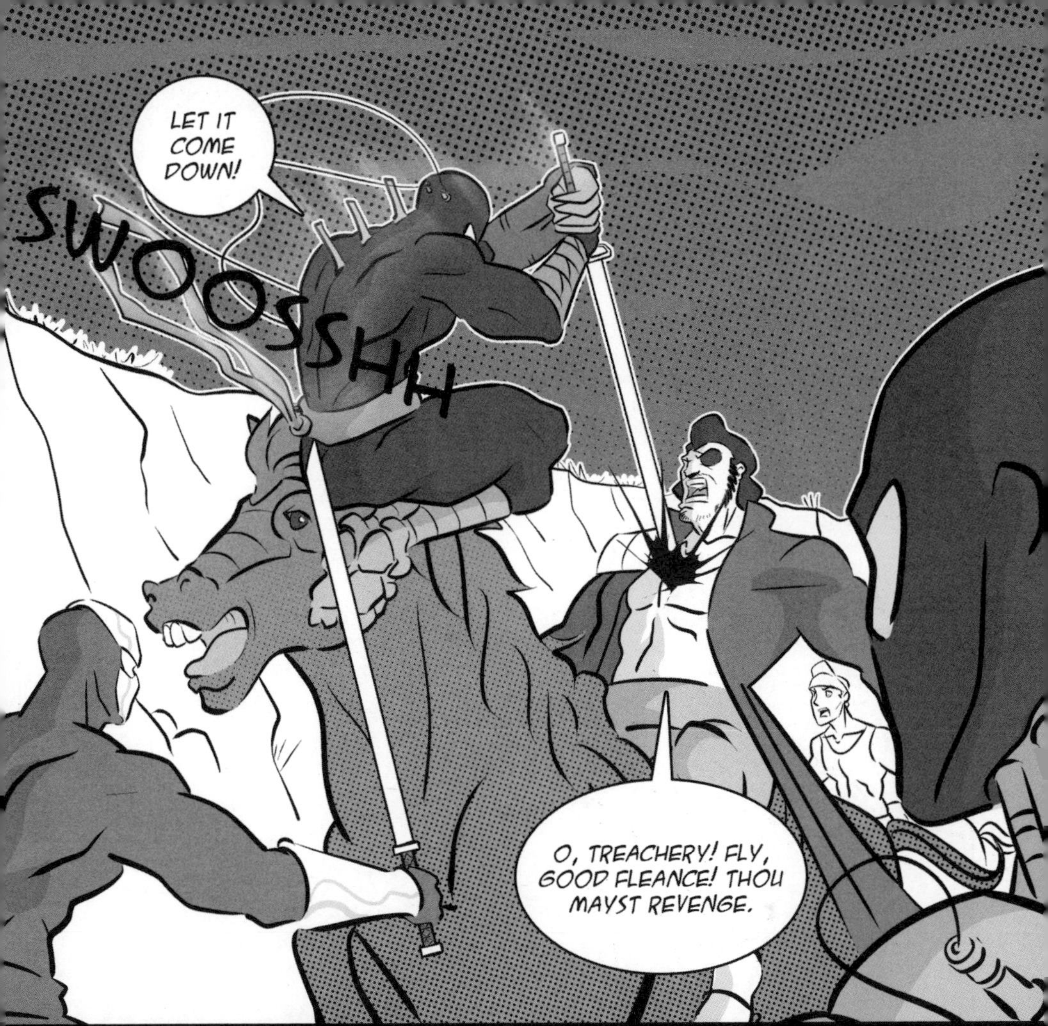
LET IT COME DOWN!
SWOOSSHH
O, TREACHERY! FLY, GOOD FLEANCE! THOU MAYST REVENGE.

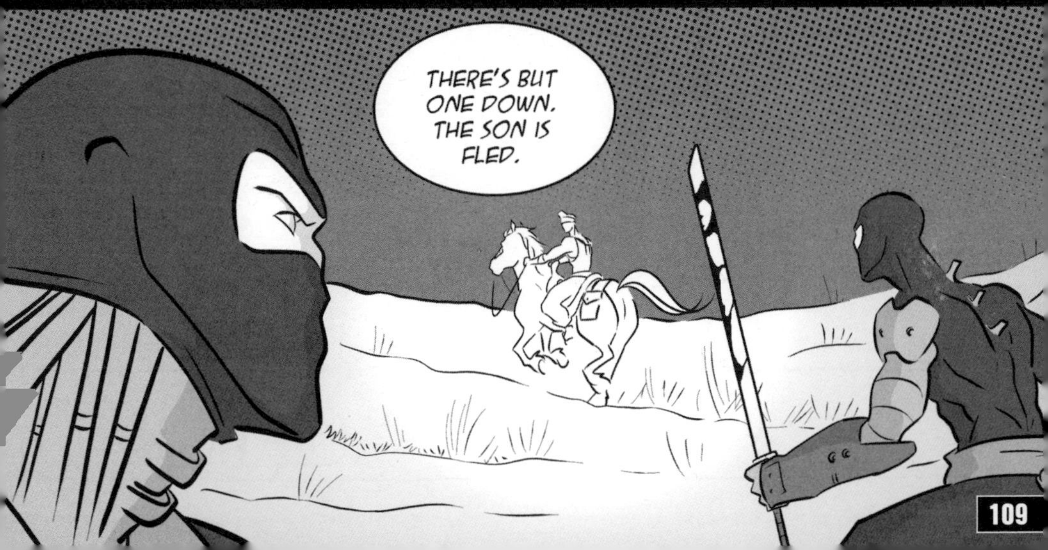
THERE'S BUT ONE DOWN. THE SON IS FLED.

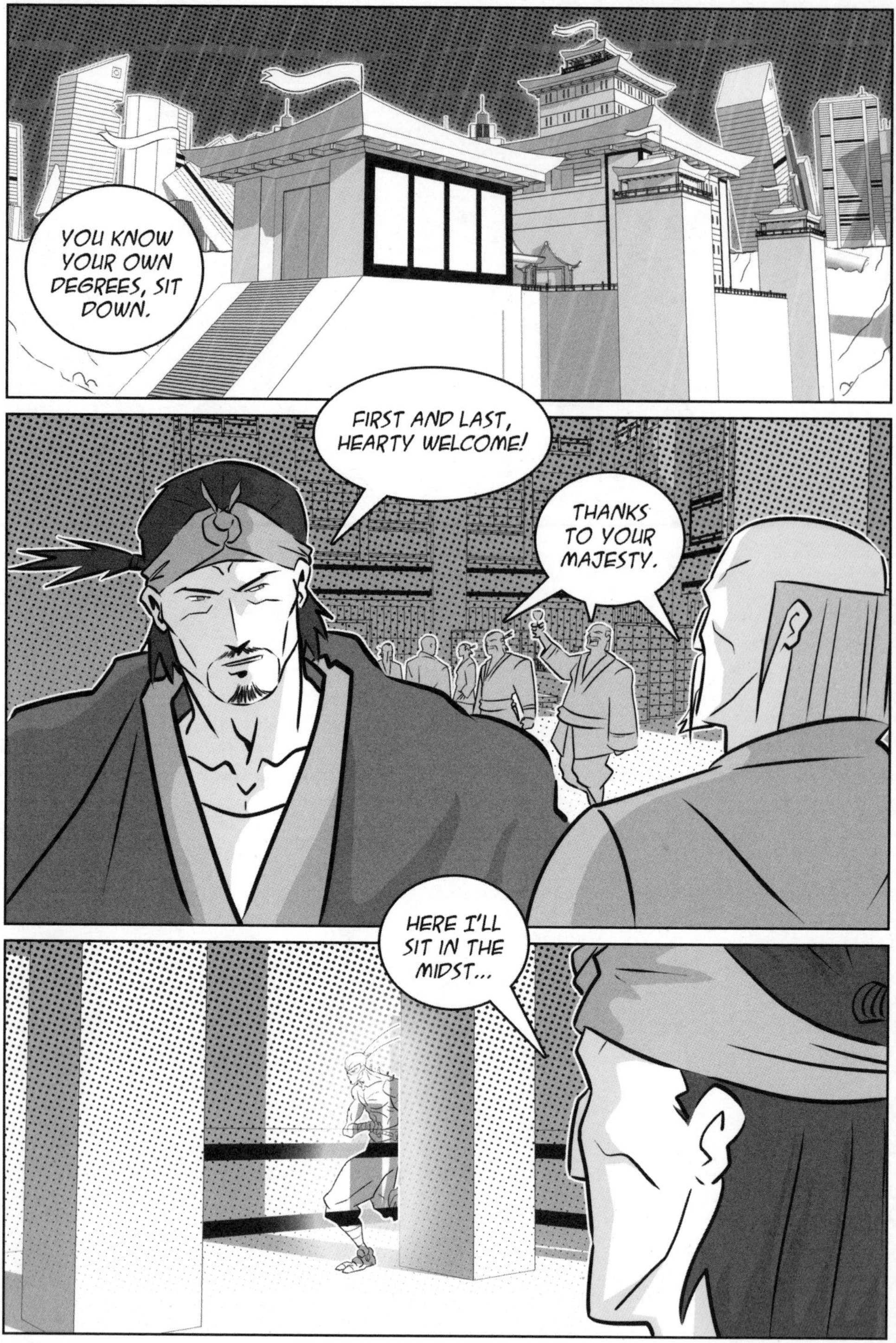
YOU KNOW YOUR OWN DEGREES, SIT DOWN.
FIRST AND LAST, HEARTY WELCOME!
THANKS TO YOUR MAJESTY.
HERE I'LL SIT IN THE MIDST...

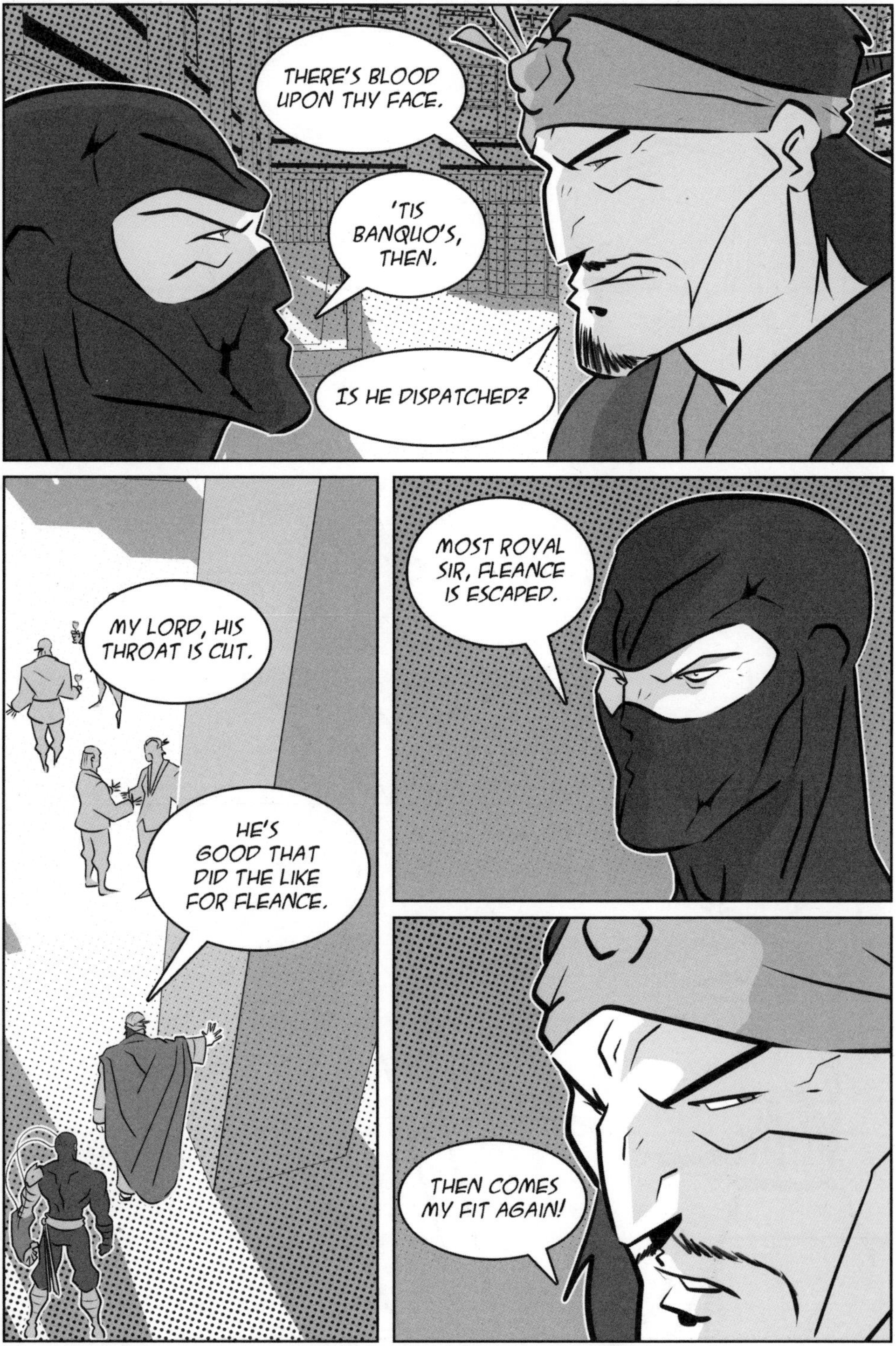
THERE'S BLOOD UPON THY FACE.
'TIS BANQUO'S, THEN.
IS HE DISPATCHED?
MY LORD, HIS THROAT IS CUT.
HE'S GOOD THAT DID THE LIKE FOR FLEANCE.
MOST ROYAL SIR, FLEANCE IS ESCAPED.
THEN COMES MY FIT AGAIN!

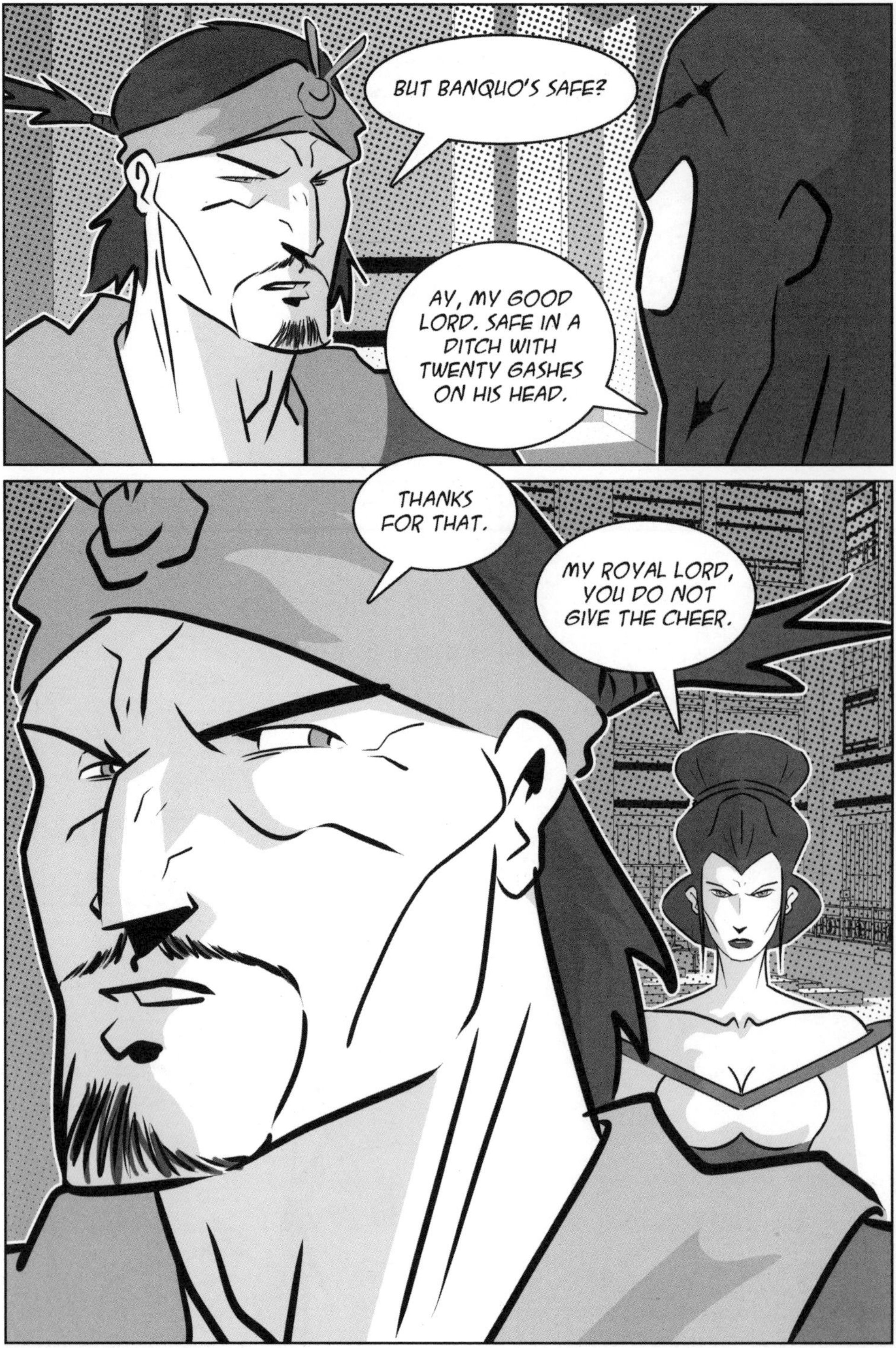
BUT BANQUO'S SAFE?
AY, MY GOOD LORD. SAFE IN A DITCH WITH TWENTY GASHES ON HIS HEAD.
THANKS FOR THAT.
MY ROYAL LORD, YOU DO NOT GIVE THE CHEER.

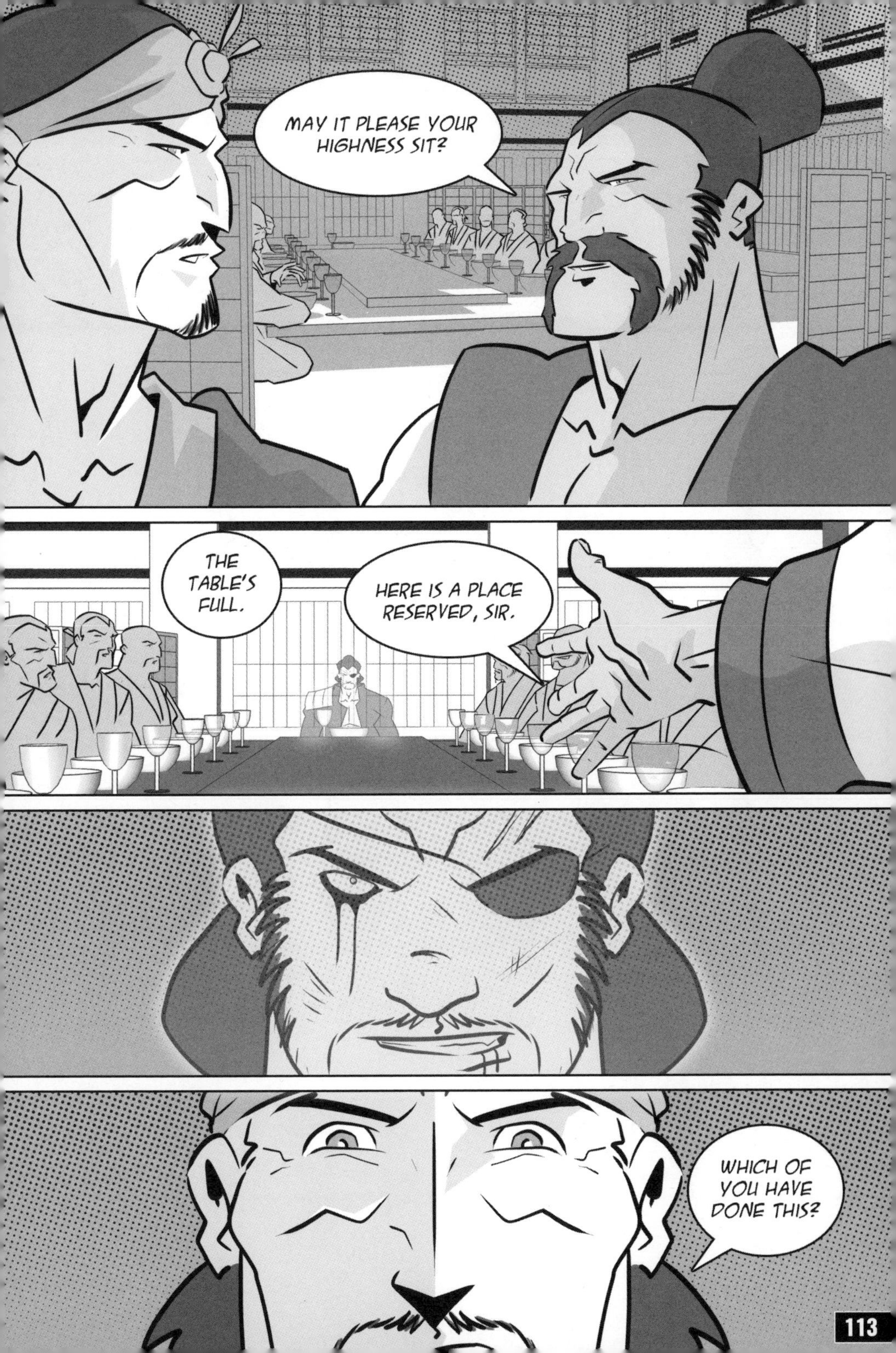
MAY IT PLEASE YOUR HIGHNESS SIT?
THE TABLE'S FULL.
HERE IS A PLACE RESERVED, SIR.
WHICH OF YOU HAVE DONE THIS?

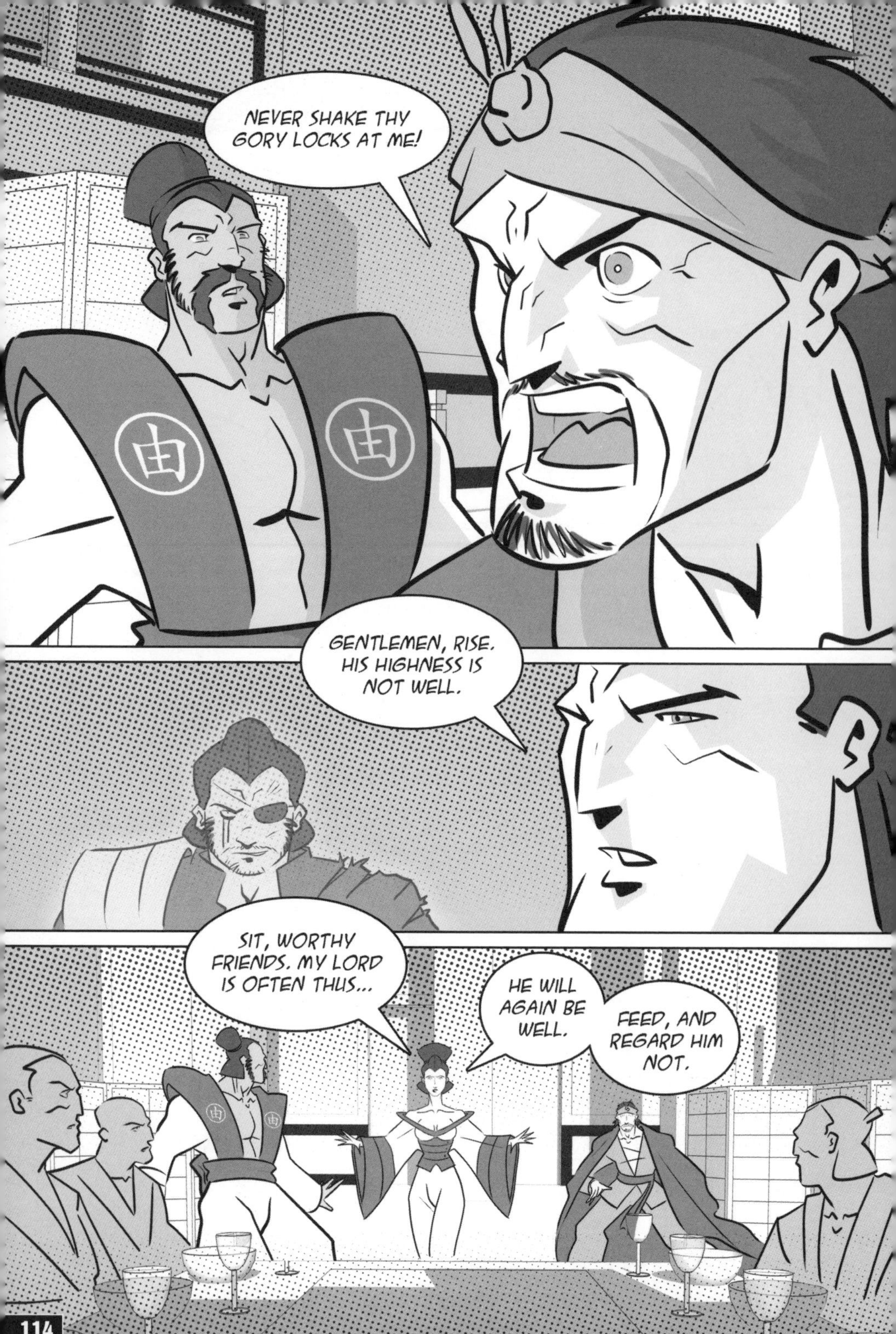
NEVER SHAKE THY GORY LOCKS AT ME!
GENTLEMEN, RISE. HIS HIGHNESS IS NOT WELL.
SIT, WORTHY FRIENDS. MY LORD IS OFTEN THUS...
HE WILL AGAIN BE WELL.
FEED, AND REGARD HIM NOT.

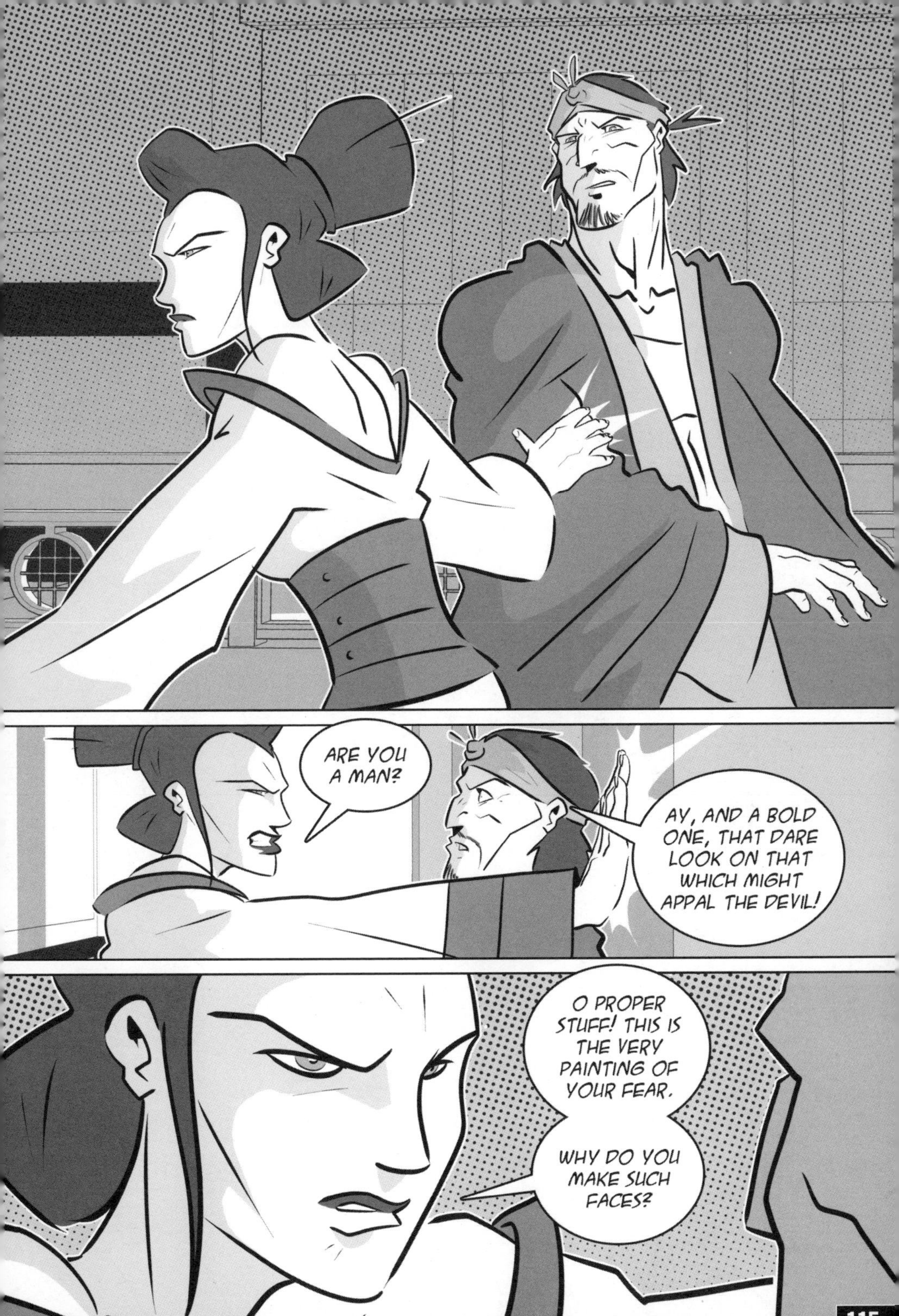

ARE YOU A MAN?
AY, AND A BOLD ONE, THAT DARE LOOK ON THAT WHICH MIGHT APPAL THE DEVIL!
O PROPER STUFF! THIS IS THE VERY PAINTING OF YOUR FEAR.
WHY DO YOU MAKE SUCH FACES?

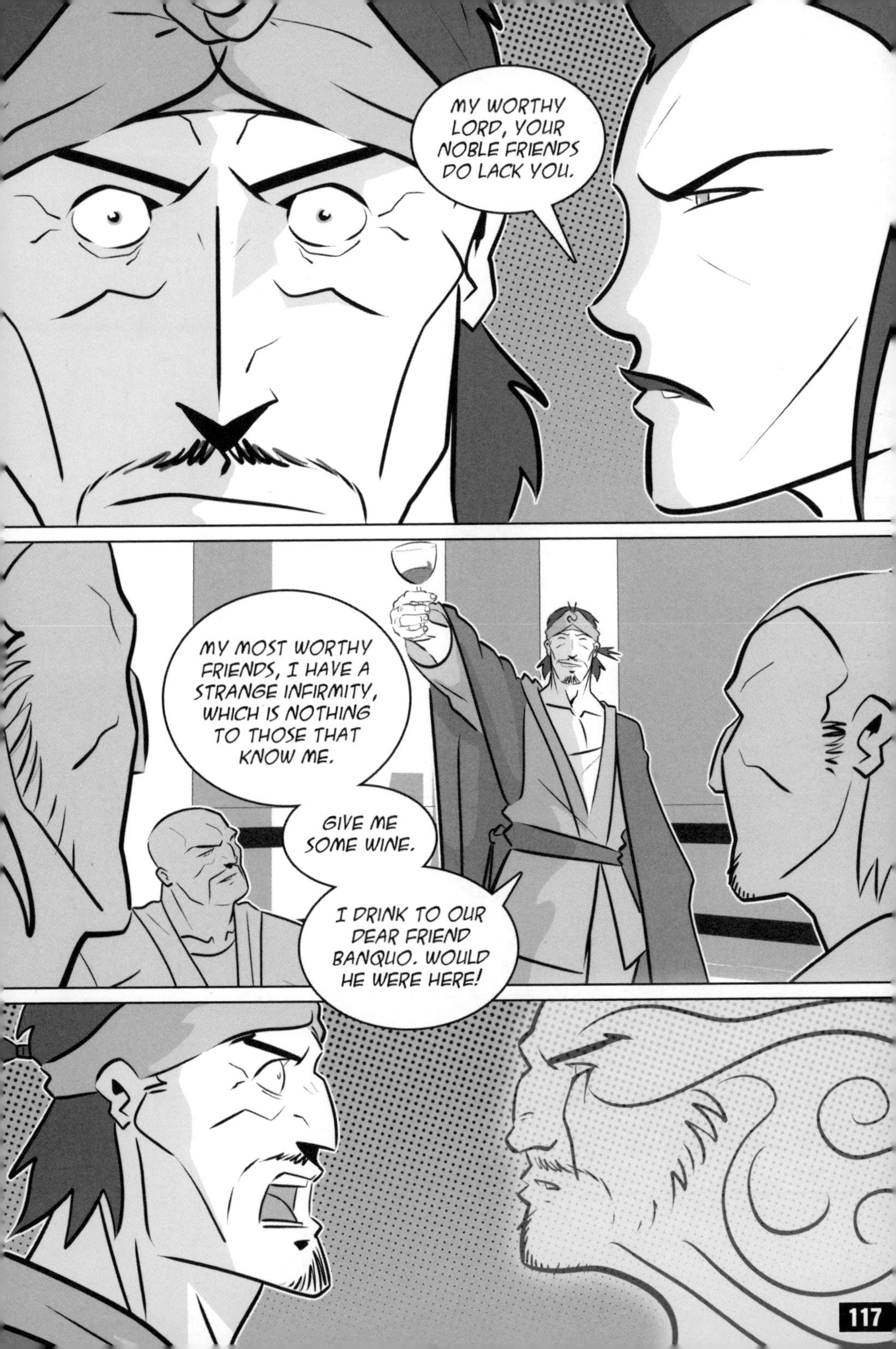
MY WORTHY LORD, YOUR NOBLE FRIENDS DO LACK YOU.
MY MOST WORTHY FRIENDS, I HAVE A STRANGE INFIRMITY, WHICH IS NOTHING TO THOSE THAT KNOW ME.
GIVE ME SOME WINE.
I DRINK TO OUR DEAR FRIEND BANQUO. WOULD HE WERE HERE!

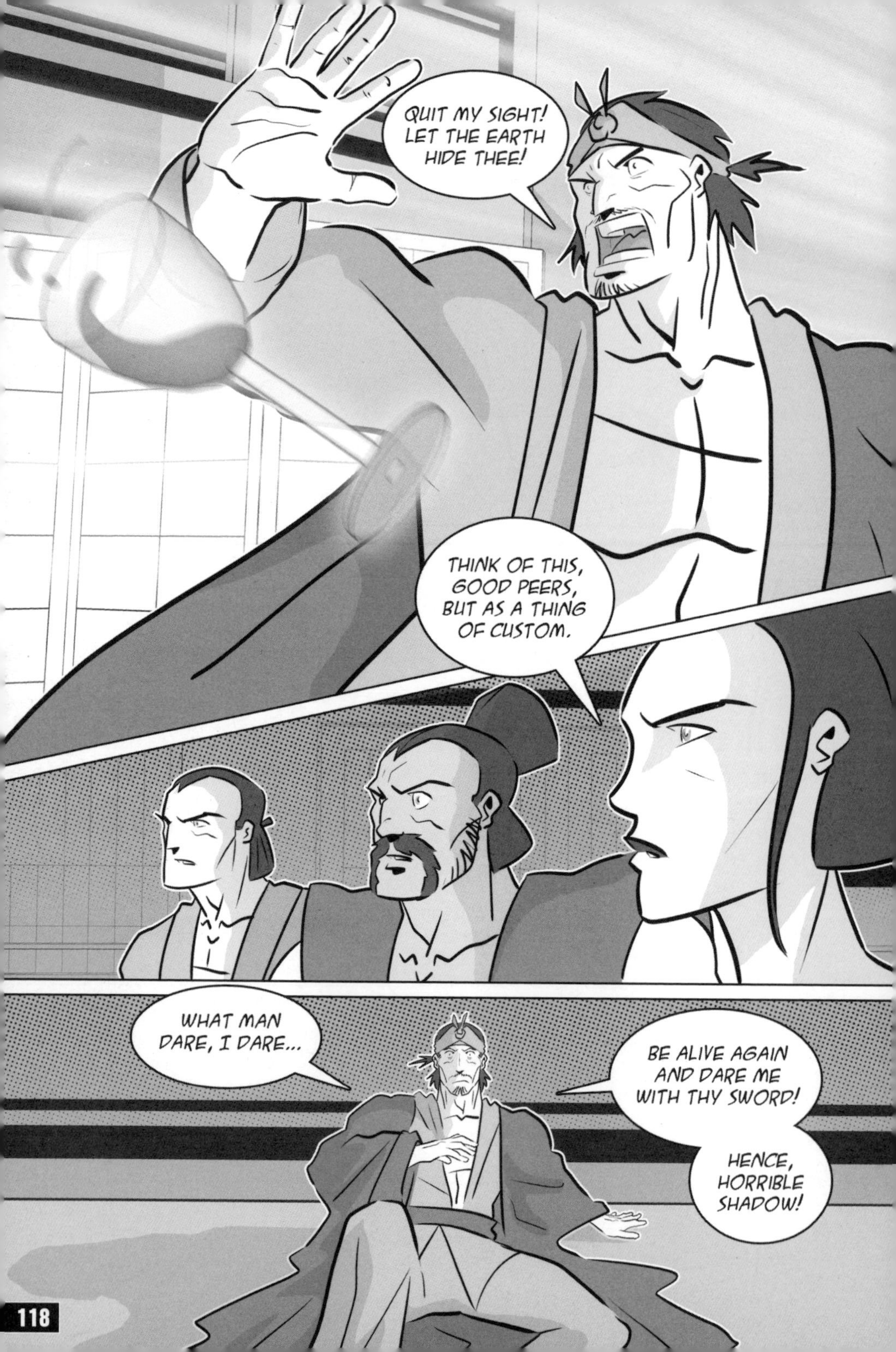
QUIT MY SIGHT! LET THE EARTH HIDE THEE!
THINK OF THIS, GOOD PEERS, BUT AS A THING OF CUSTOM.
WHAT MAN DARE, I DARE...
BE ALIVE AGAIN AND DARE ME WITH THY SWORD!
HENCE, HORRIBLE SHADOW!

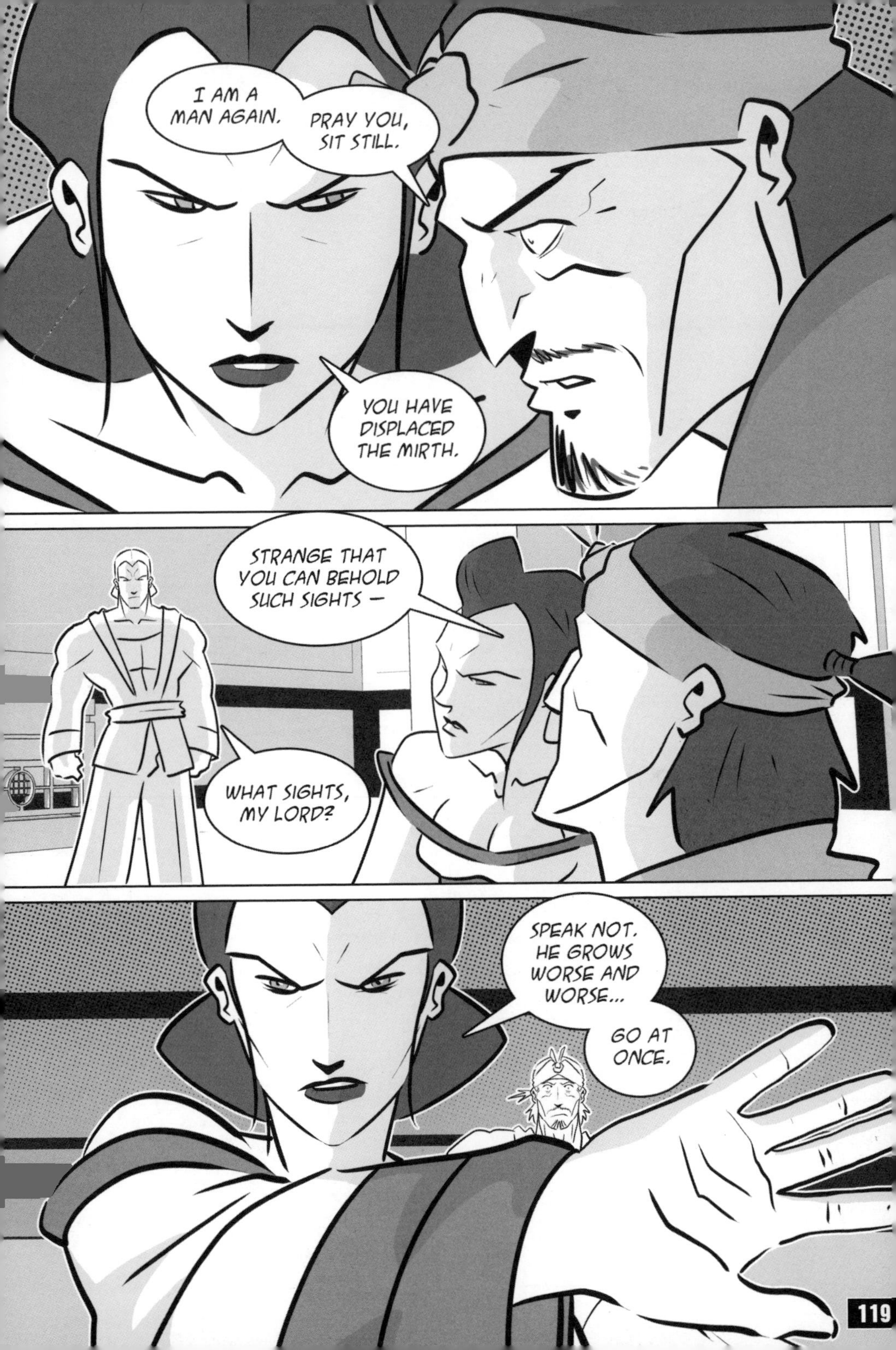
I AM A MAN AGAIN.
PRAY YOU, SIT STILL.
YOU HAVE DISPLACED THE MIRTH.
STRANGE THAT YOU CAN BEHOLD SUCH SIGHTS —
WHAT SIGHTS, MY LORD?
SPEAK NOT. HE GROWS WORSE AND WORSE...
GO AT ONCE.

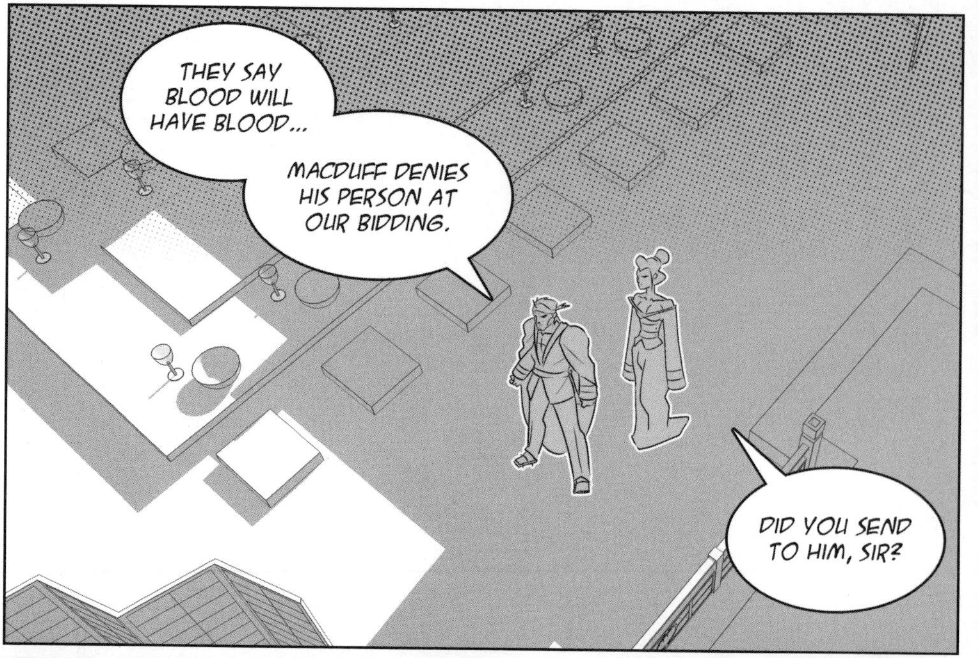
THEY SAY BLOOD WILL HAVE BLOOD...
MACDUFF DENIES HIS PERSON AT OUR BIDDING.
DID YOU SEND TO HIM, SIR?

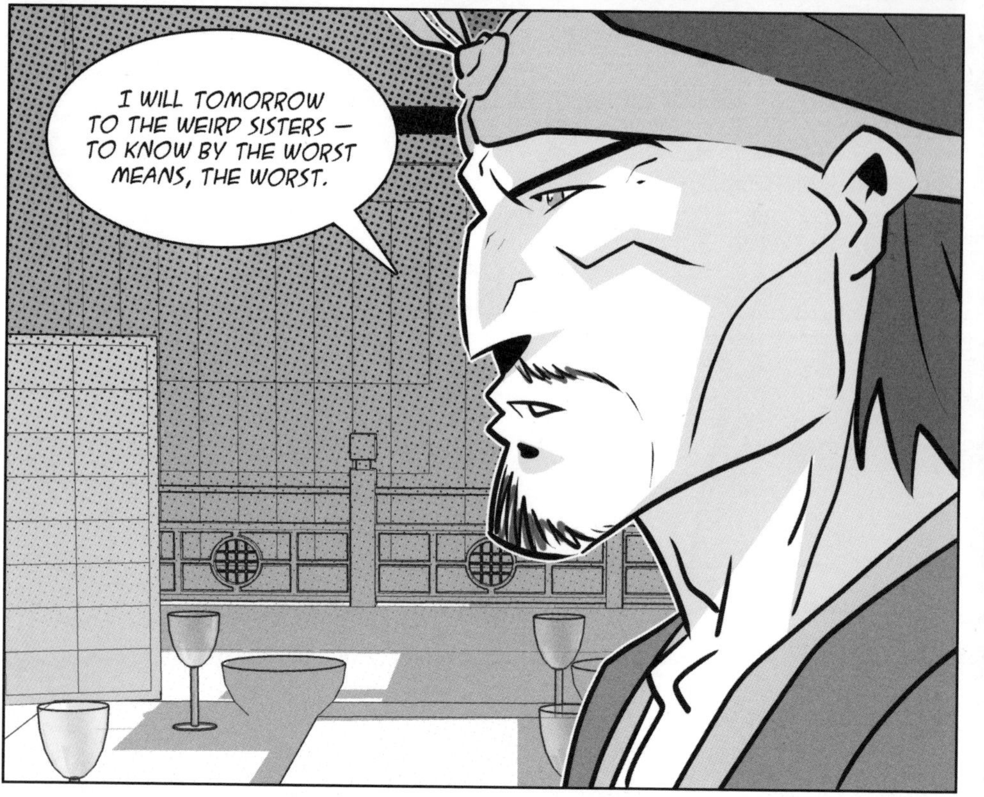
I WILL TOMORROW TO THE WEIRD SISTERS — TO KNOW BY THE WORST MEANS, THE WORST.

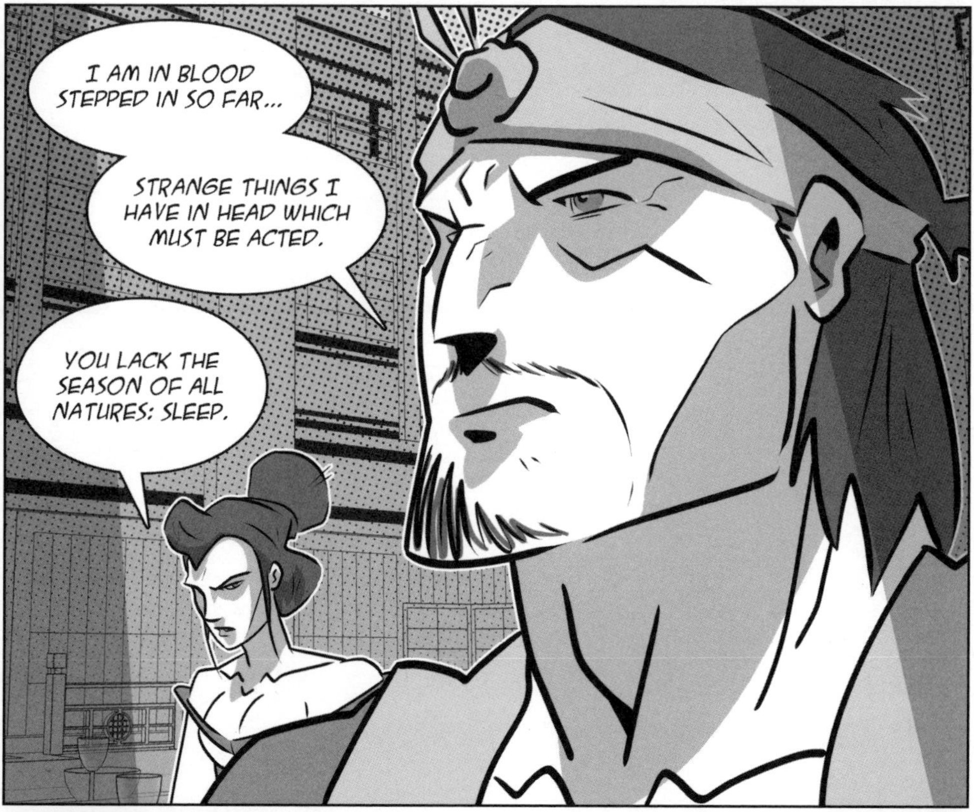
I AM IN BLOOD STEPPED IN SO FAR...
STRANGE THINGS I HAVE IN HEAD WHICH MUST BE ACTED.
YOU LACK THE SEASON OF ALL NATURES: SLEEP.

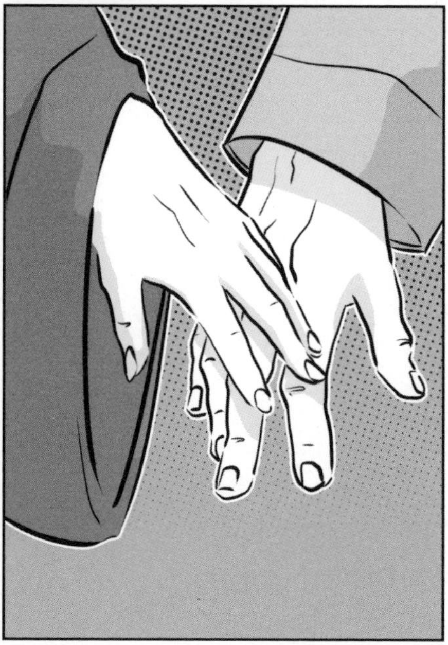

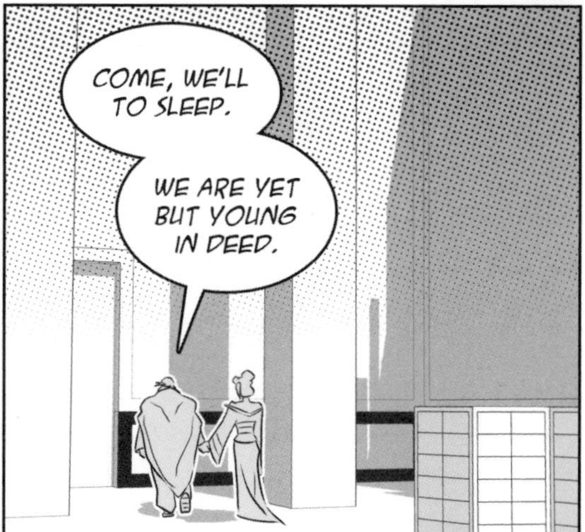
COME, WE'LL TO SLEEP.
WE ARE YET BUT YOUNG IN DEED.

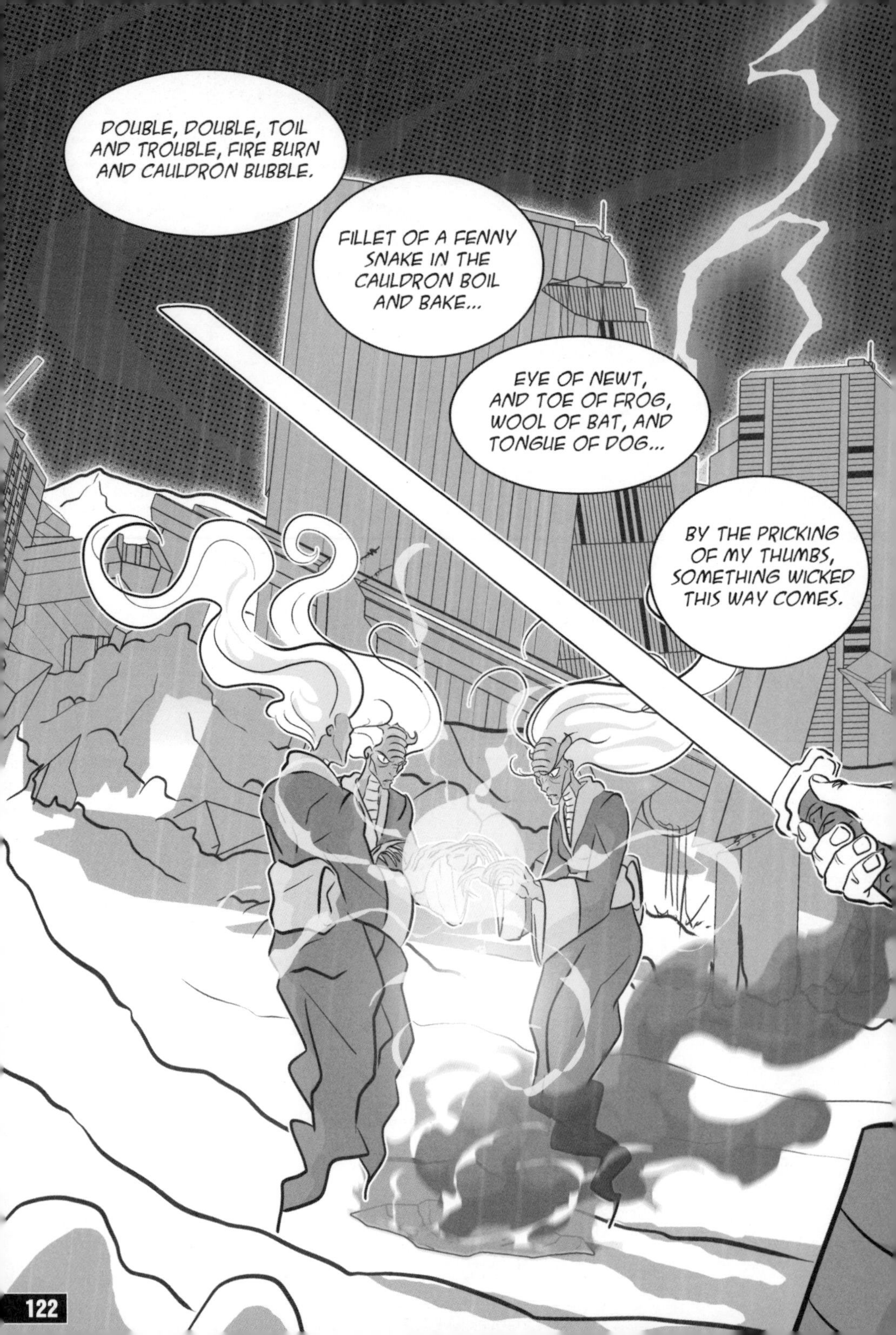
DOUBLE, DOUBLE, TOIL AND TROUBLE, FIRE BURN AND CAULDRON BUBBLE.
FILLET OF A FENNY SNAKE IN THE CAULDRON BOIL AND BAKE...
EYE OF NEWT, AND TOE OF FROG, WOOL OF BAT, AND TONGUE OF DOG...
BY THE PRICKING OF MY THUMBS, SOMETHING WICKED THIS WAY COMES.

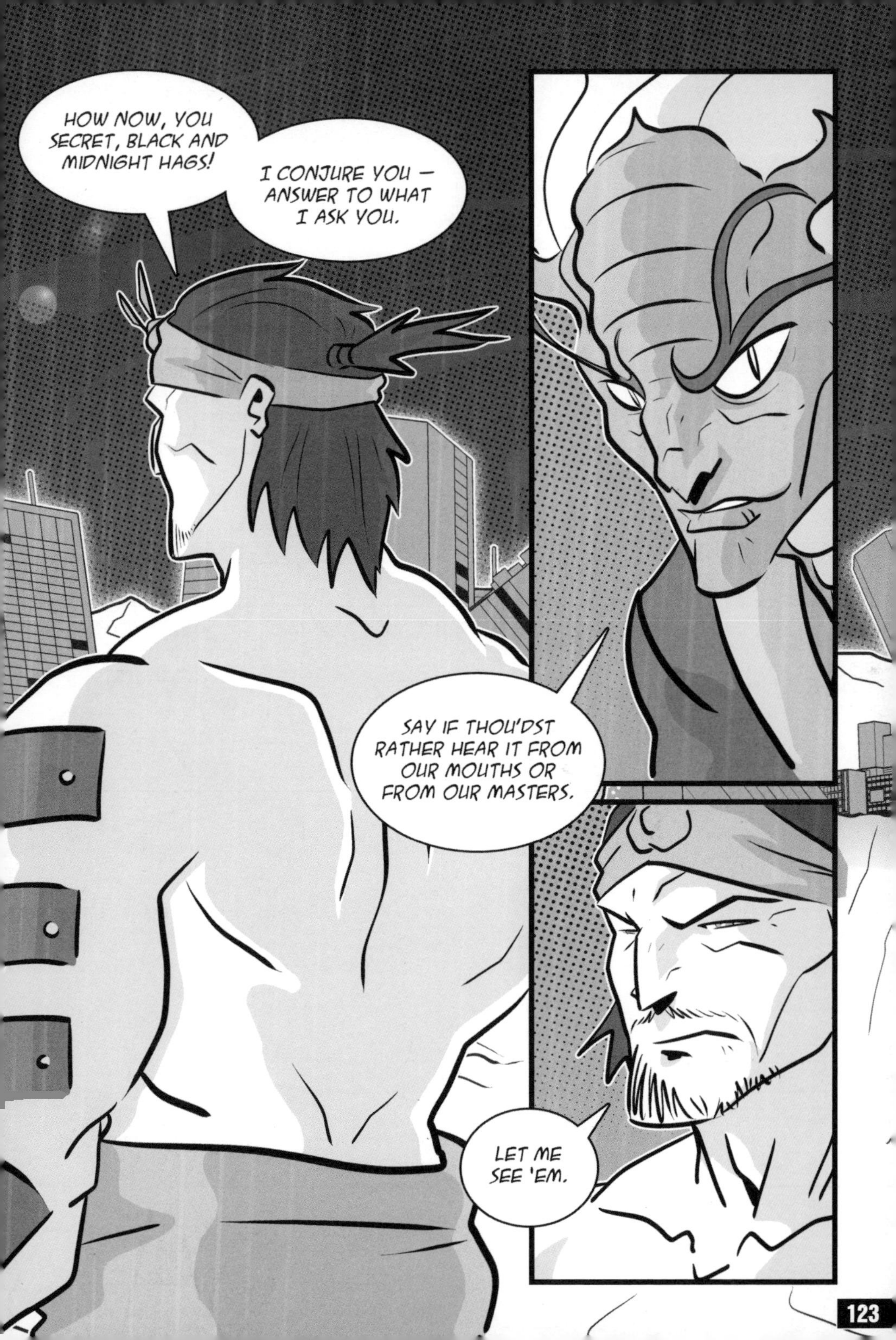
HOW NOW, YOU SECRET, BLACK AND MIDNIGHT HAGS!
I CONJURE YOU — ANSWER TO WHAT I ASK YOU.
SAY IF THOU'DST RATHER HEAR IT FROM OUR MOUTHS OR FROM OUR MASTERS.
LET ME SEE 'EM.

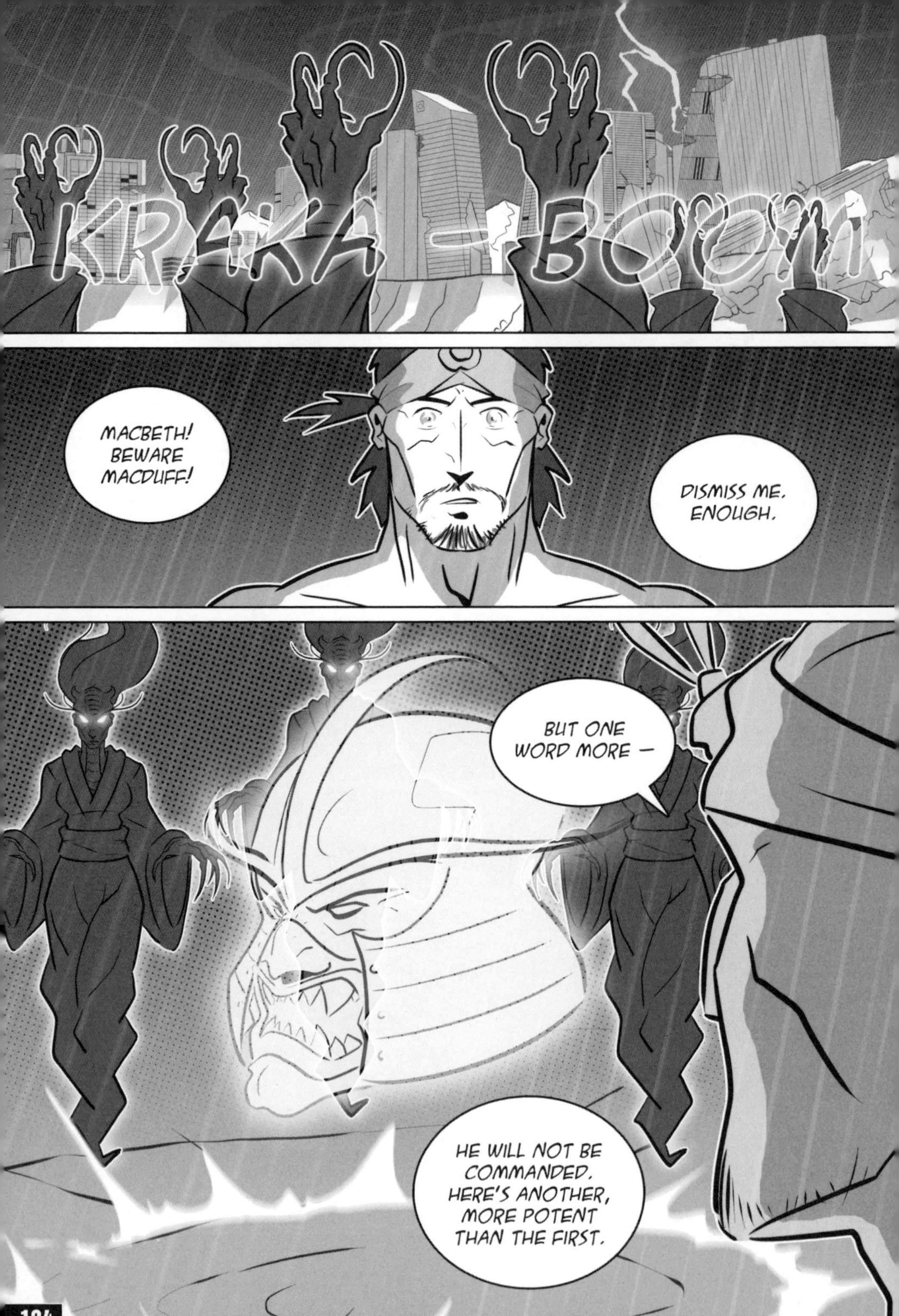
KRAKA-BOOM
MACBETH! BEWARE MACDUFF!
DISMISS ME. ENOUGH.
BUT ONE WORD MORE —
HE WILL NOT BE COMMANDED. HERE'S ANOTHER, MORE POTENT THAN THE FIRST.

KRAKA-BOOM
BE BLOODY, BOLD AND RESOLUTE! NONE OF WOMAN BORN SHALL HARM MACBETH.
THEN LIVE, MACDUFF — WHAT NEED I FEAR OF THEE?
BUT YET I'LL MAKE DOUBLE SURE: THOU SHALT NOT LIVE.

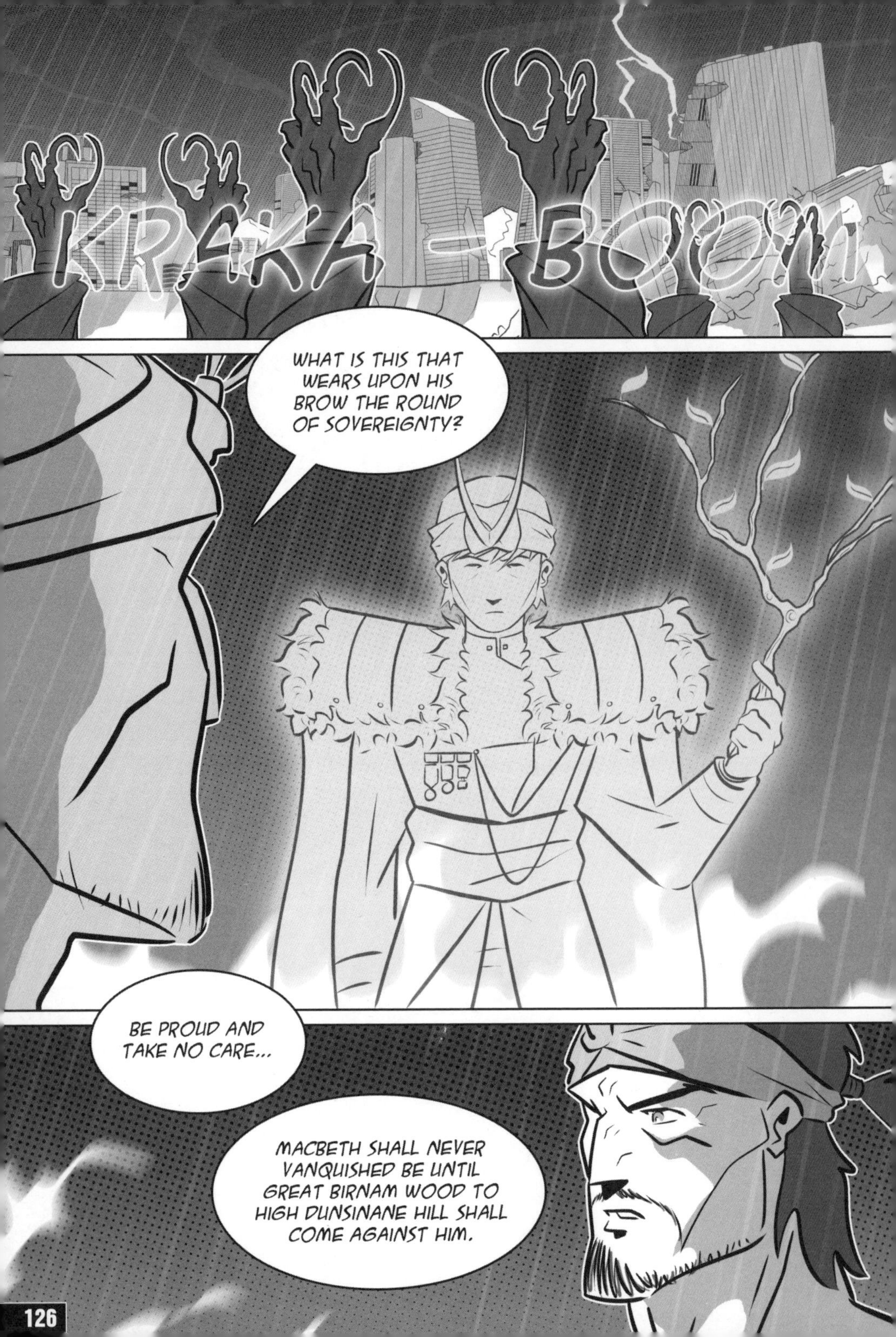
KRAKA-BOOM
WHAT IS THIS THAT WEARS UPON HIS BROW THE ROUND OF SOVEREIGNTY?
BE PROUD AND TAKE NO CARE...
MACBETH SHALL NEVER VANQUISHED BE UNTIL GREAT BIRNAM WOOD TO HIGH DUNSINANE HILL SHALL COME AGAINST HIM.

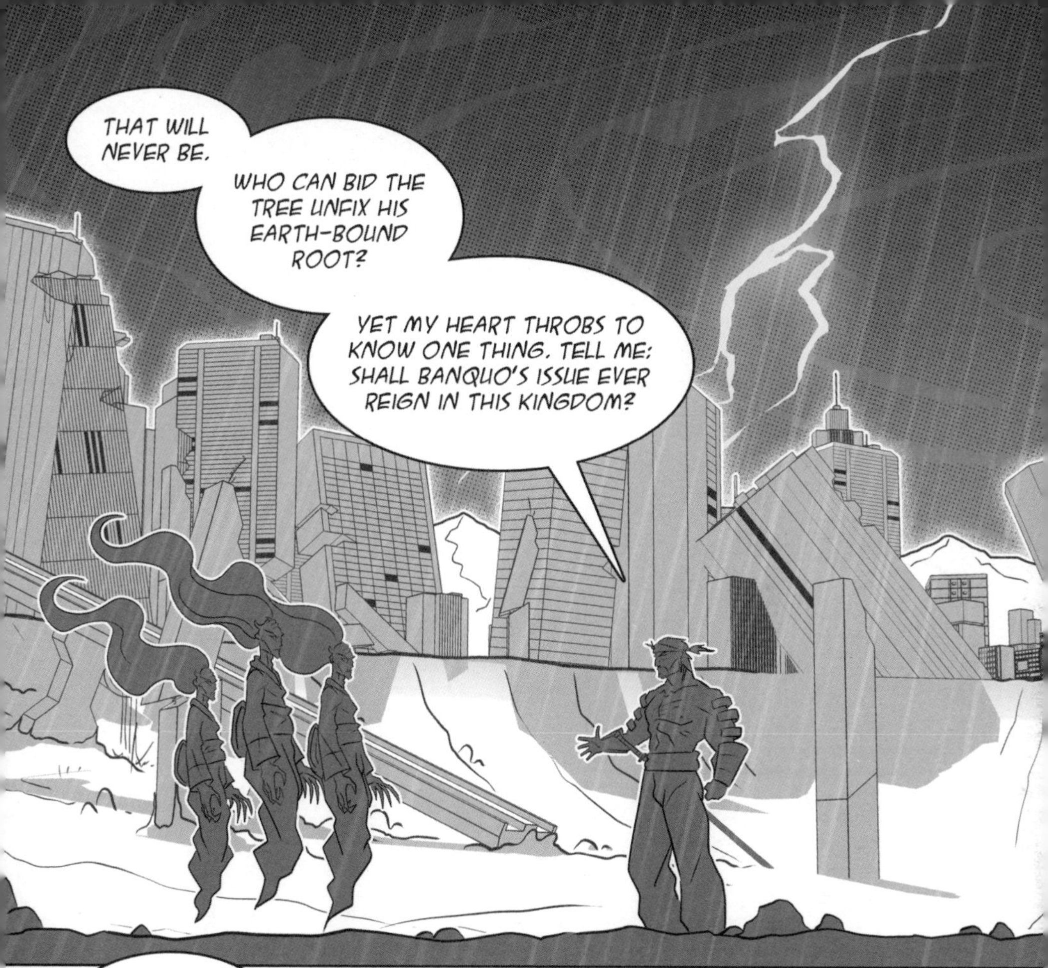
THAT WILL NEVER BE.
WHO CAN BID THE TREE UNFIX HIS EARTH-BOUND ROOT?
YET MY HEART THROBS TO KNOW ONE THING. TELL ME: SHALL BANQUO'S ISSUE EVER REIGN IN THIS KINGDOM?
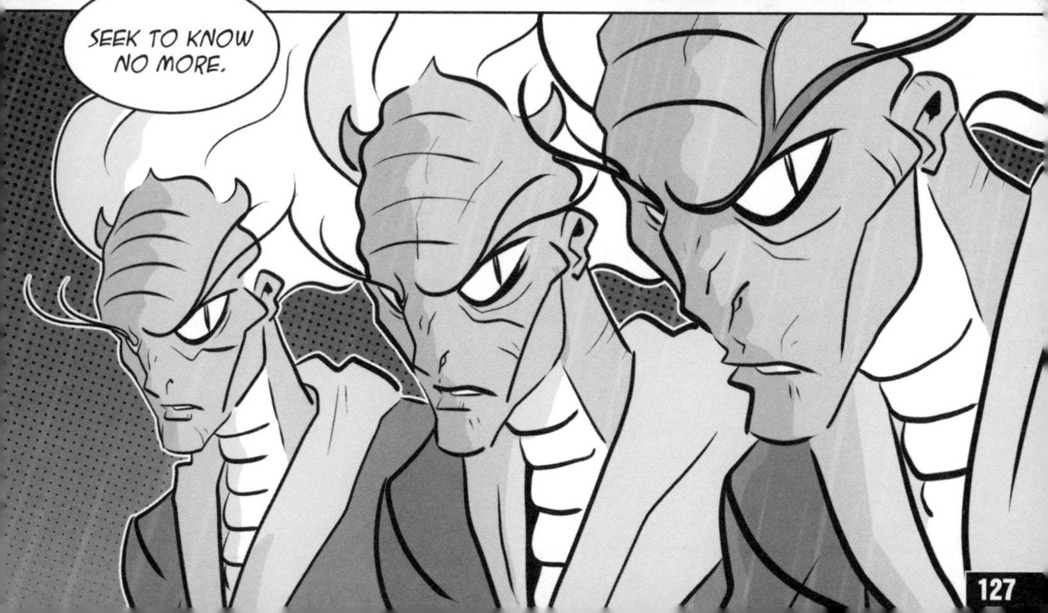
SEEK TO KNOW NO MORE.

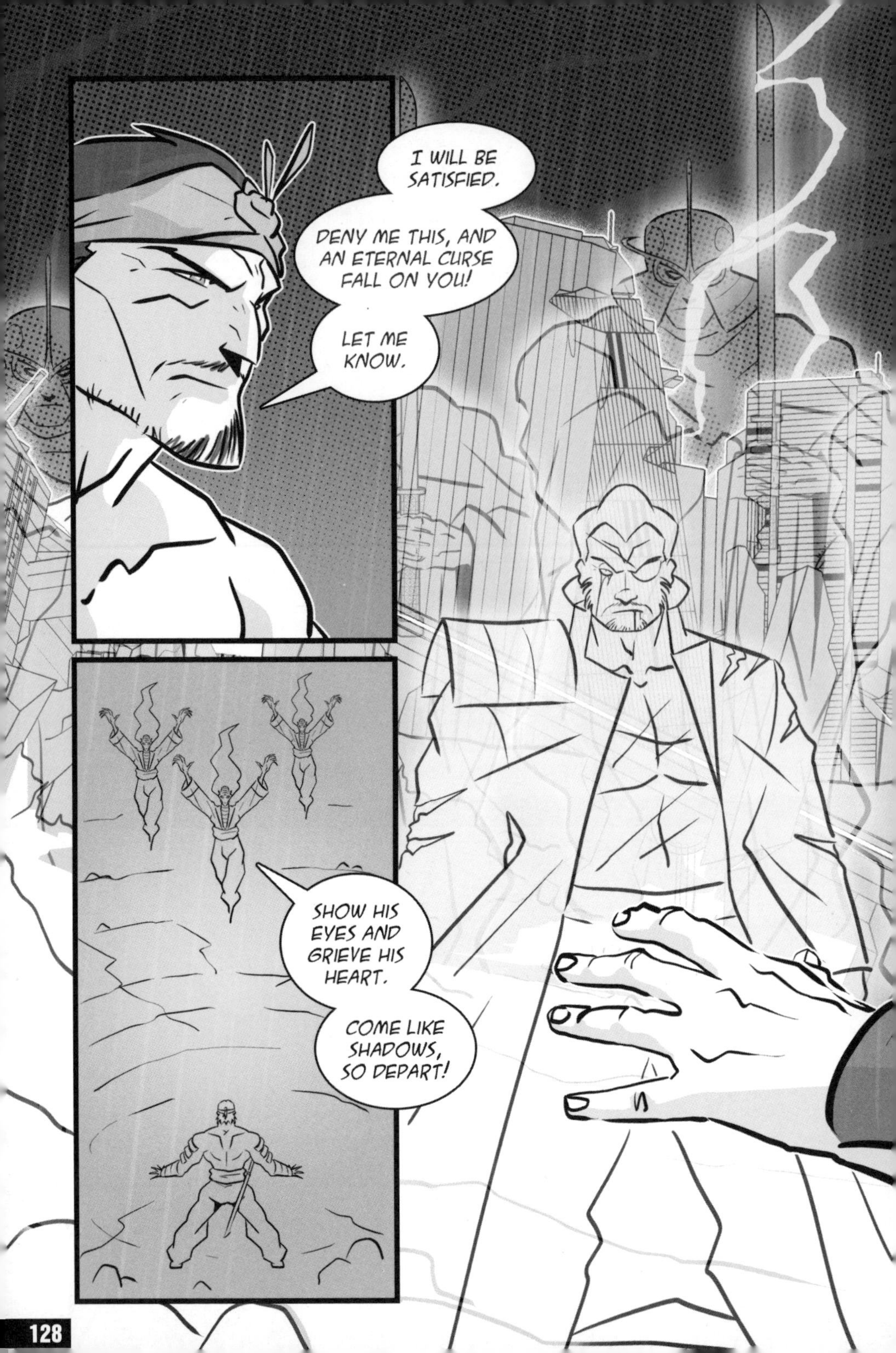
I WILL BE SATISFIED.
DENY ME THIS, AND AN ETERNAL CURSE FALL ON YOU!
LET ME KNOW.
SHOW HIS EYES AND GRIEVE HIS HEART.
COME LIKE SHADOWS, SO DEPART!

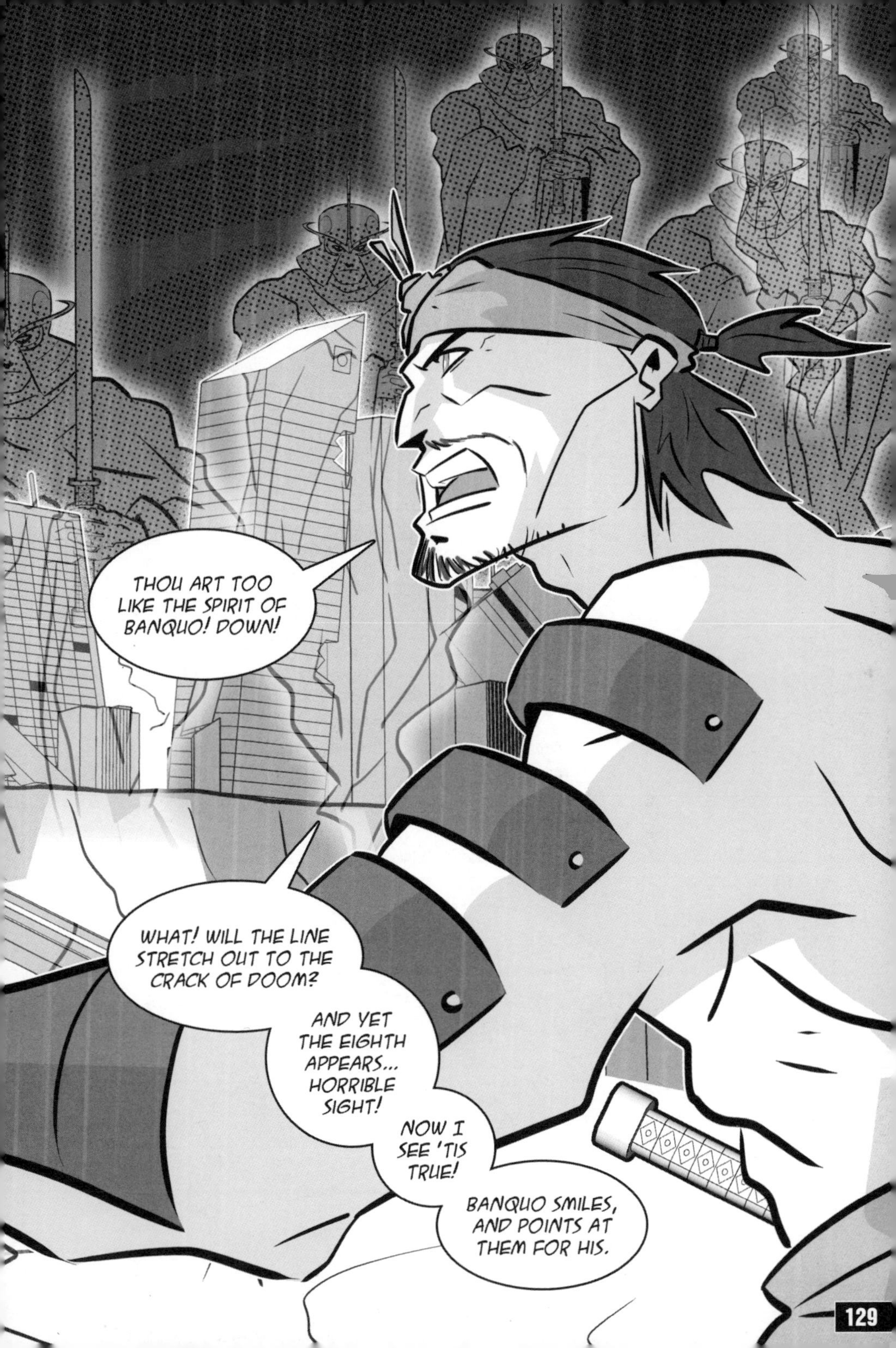
THOU ART TOO LIKE THE SPIRIT OF BANQUO! DOWN!
WHAT! WILL THE LINE STRETCH OUT TO THE CRACK OF DOOM?
AND YET THE EIGHTH APPEARS... HORRIBLE SIGHT!
NOW I SEE 'TIS TRUE!
BANQUO SMILES, AND POINTS AT THEM FOR HIS.

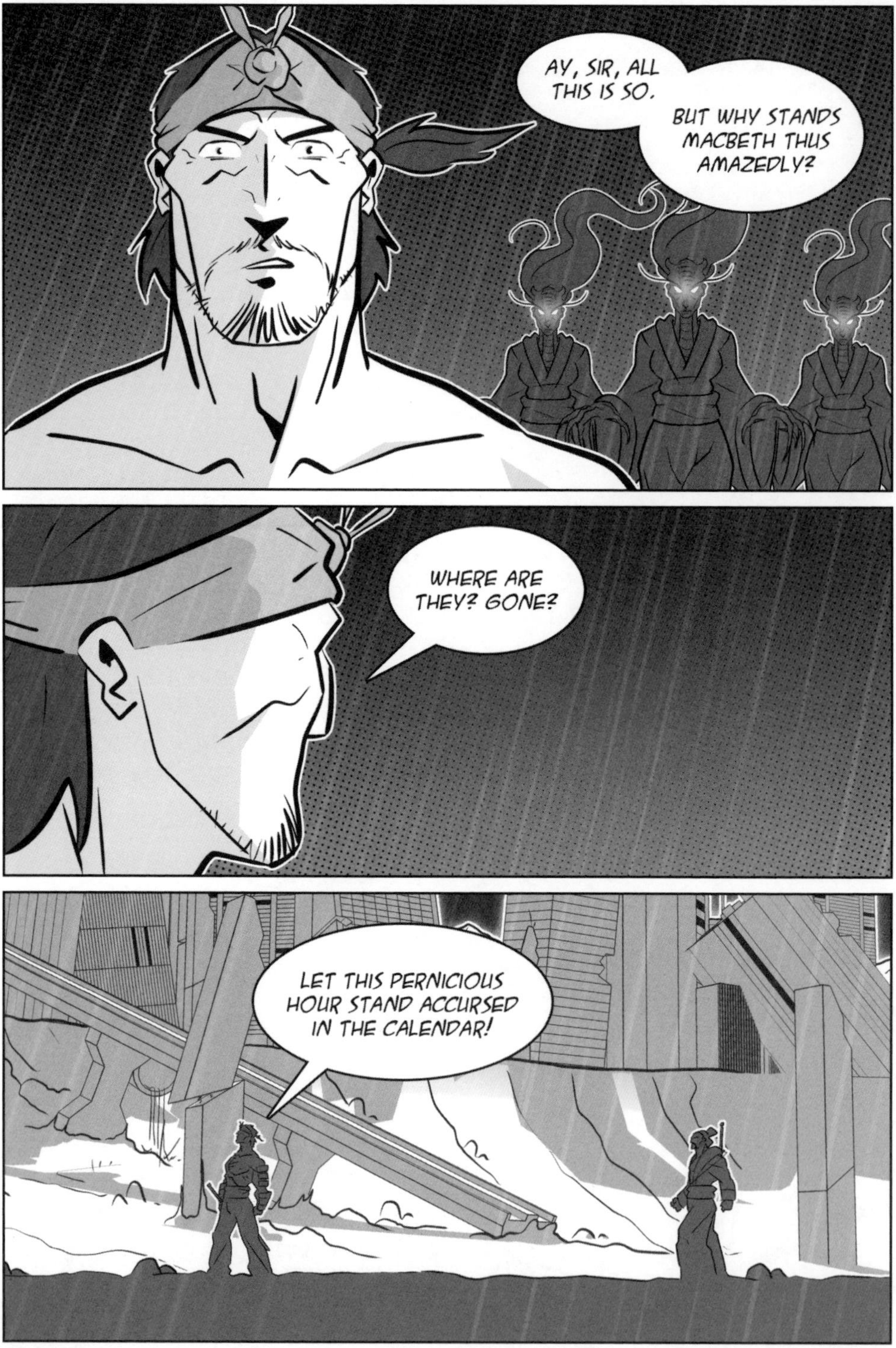
AY, SIR, ALL THIS IS SO.
BUT WHY STANDS MACBETH THUS AMAZEDLY?
WHERE ARE THEY? GONE?
LET THIS PERNICIOUS HOUR STAND ACCURSED IN THE CALENDAR!

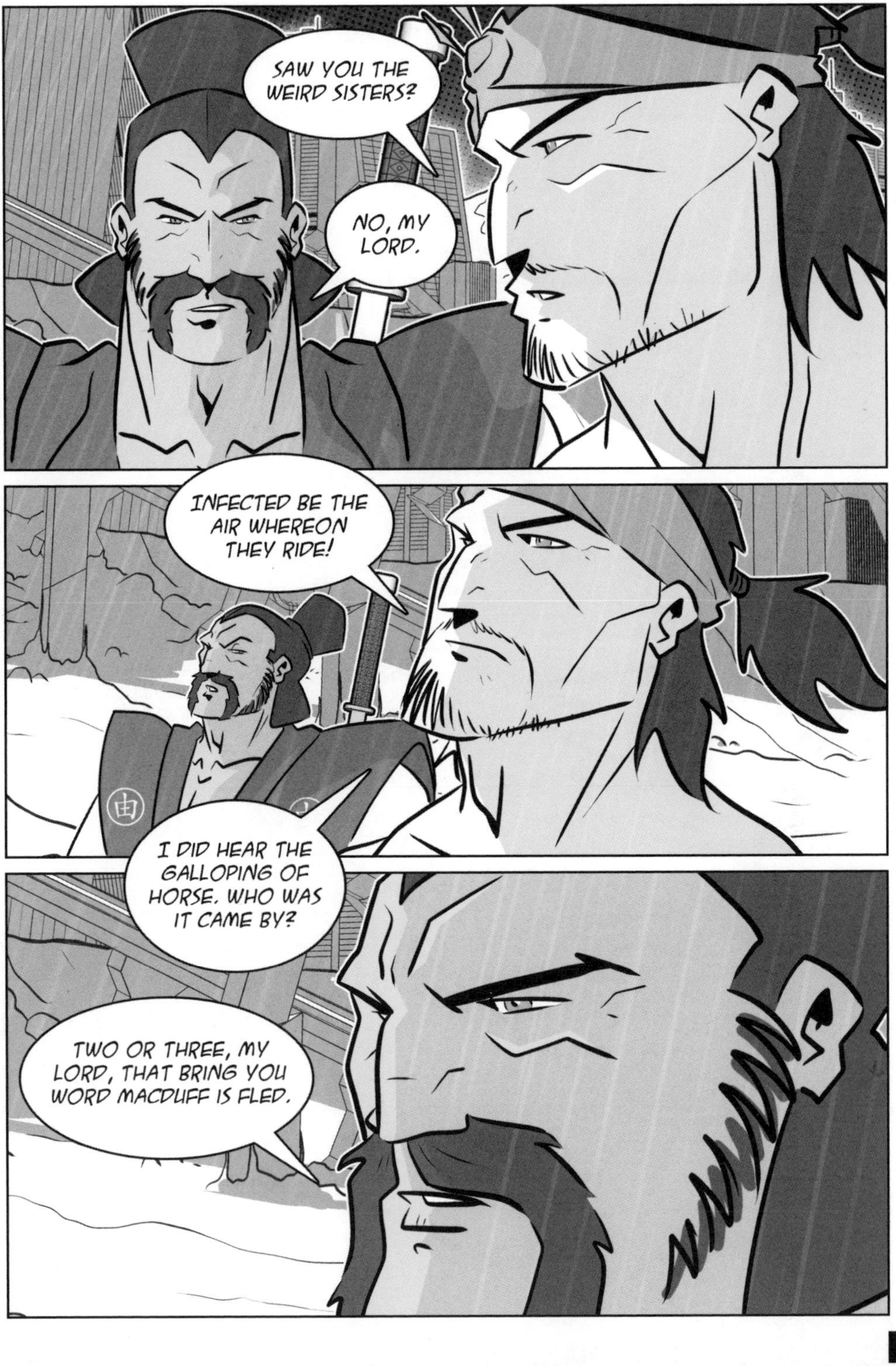
SAW YOU THE WEIRD SISTERS?
NO, MY LORD.
INFECTED BE THE AIR WHEREON THEY RIDE!
I DID HEAR THE GALLOPING OF HORSE. WHO WAS IT CAME BY?
TWO OR THREE, MY LORD, THAT BRING YOU WORD MACDUFF IS FLED.

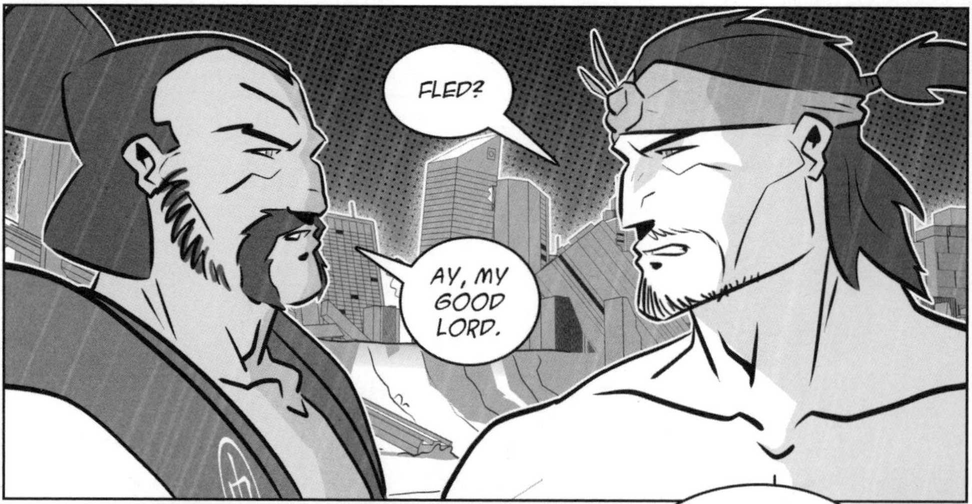
FLED?
AY, MY GOOD LORD.

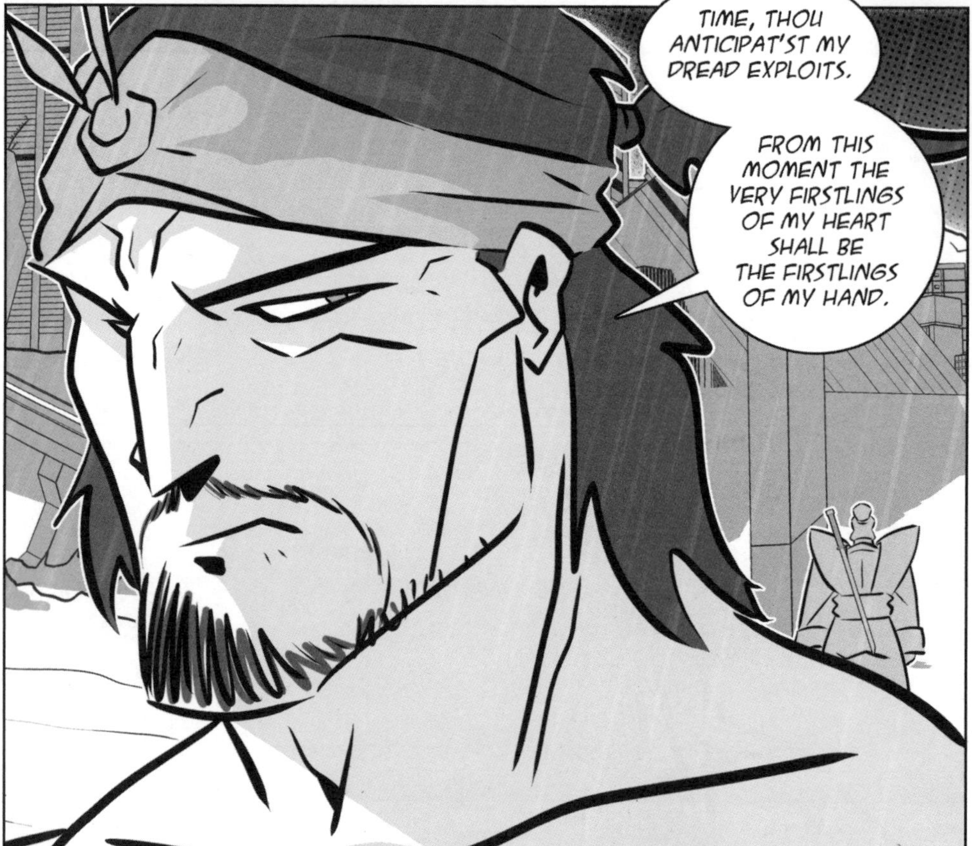
TIME, THOU ANTICIPAT'ST MY DREAD EXPLOITS.
FROM THIS MOMENT THE VERY FIRSTLINGS OF MY HEART SHALL BE THE FIRSTLINGS OF MY HAND.

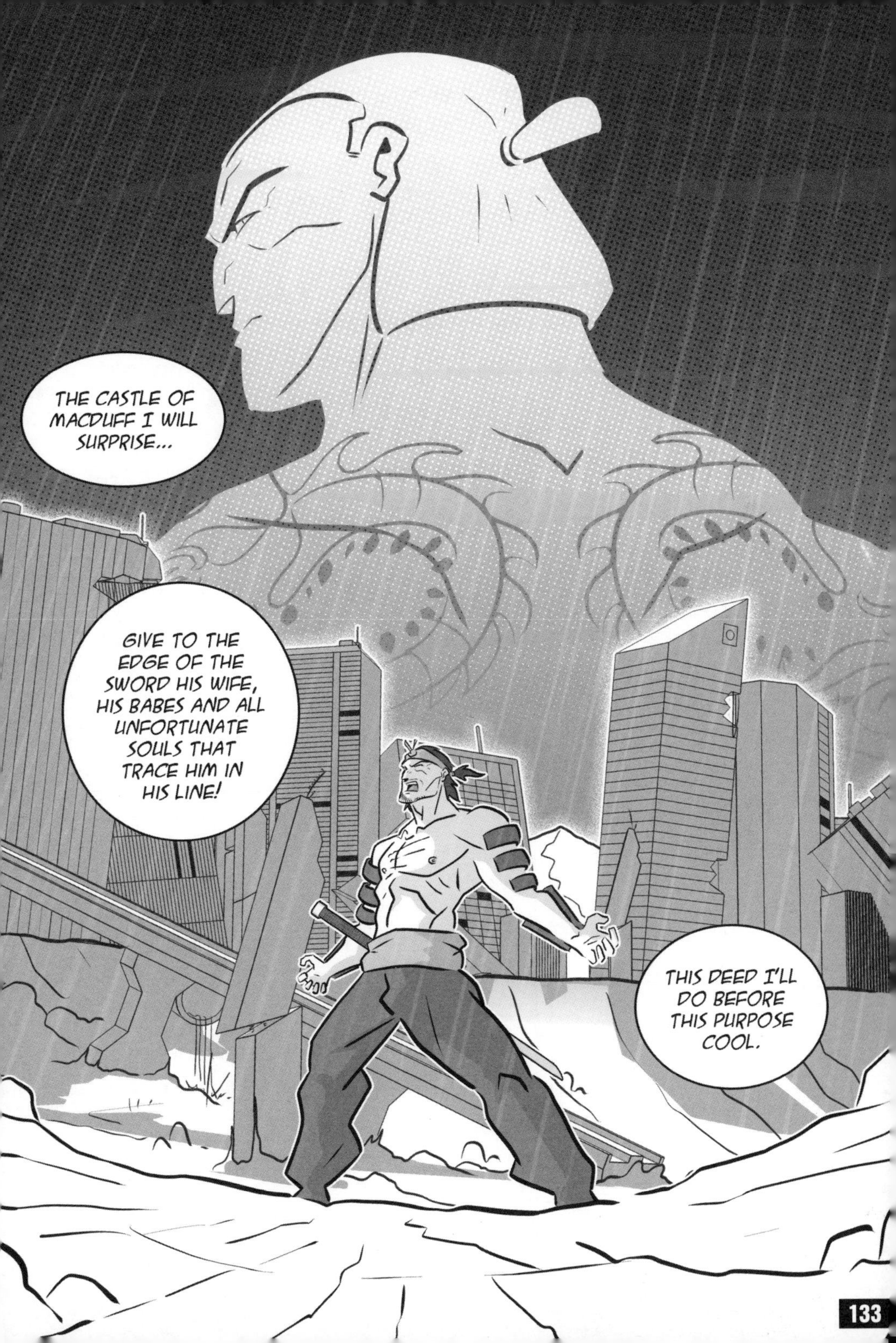
THE CASTLE OF MACDUFF I WILL SURPRISE...
GIVE TO THE EDGE OF THE SWORD HIS WIFE, HIS BABES AND ALL UNFORTUNATE SOULS THAT TRACE HIM IN HIS LINE!
THIS DEED I'LL DO BEFORE THIS PURPOSE COOL.

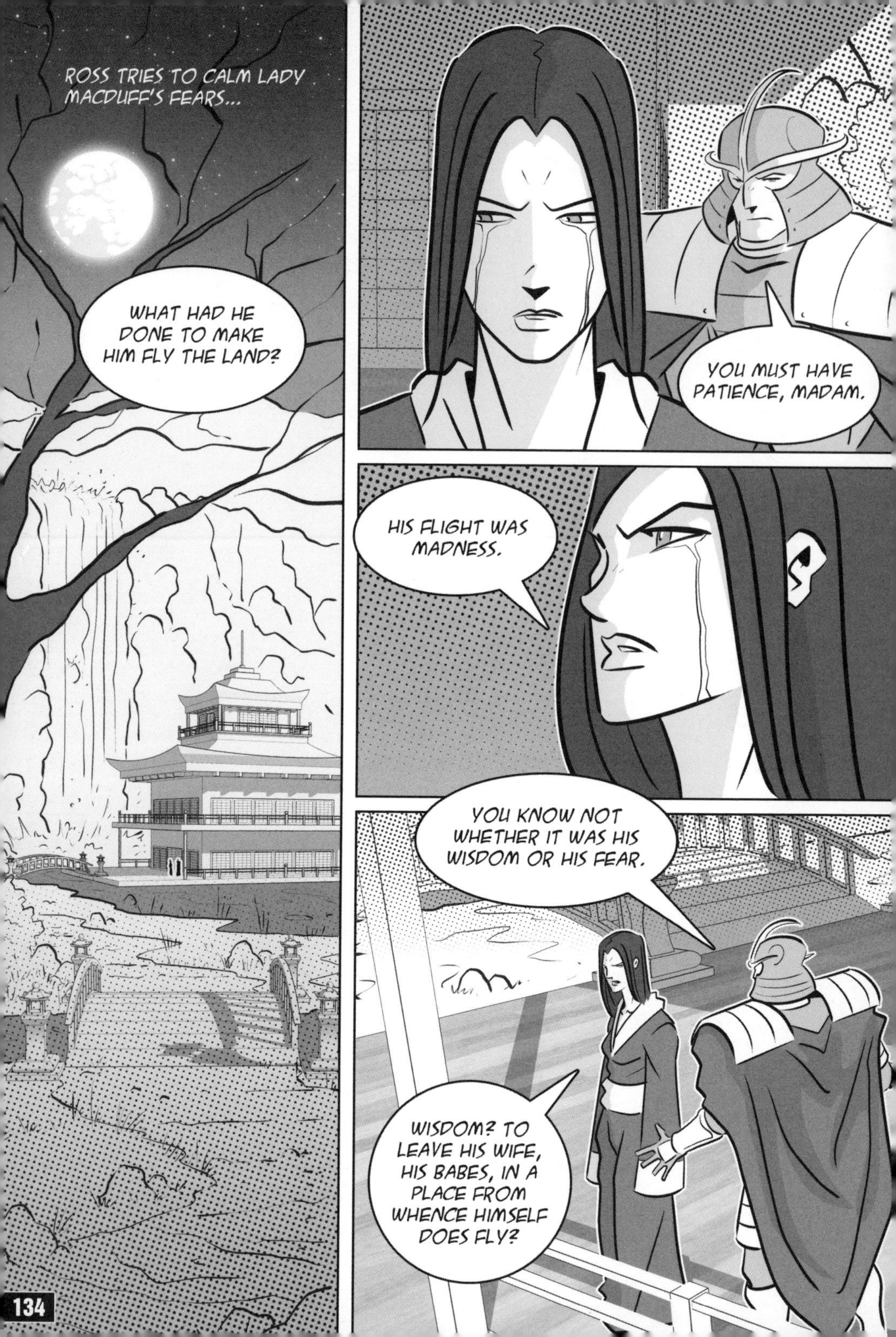
ROSS TRIES TO CALM LADY MACDUFF'S FEARS...
WHAT HAD HE DONE TO MAKE HIM FLY THE LAND?
YOU MUST HAVE PATIENCE, MADAM.
HIS FLIGHT WAS MADNESS.
YOU KNOW NOT WHETHER IT WAS HIS WISDOM OR HIS FEAR.
WISDOM? TO LEAVE HIS WIFE, HIS BABES, IN A PLACE FROM WHENCE HIMSELF DOES FLY?

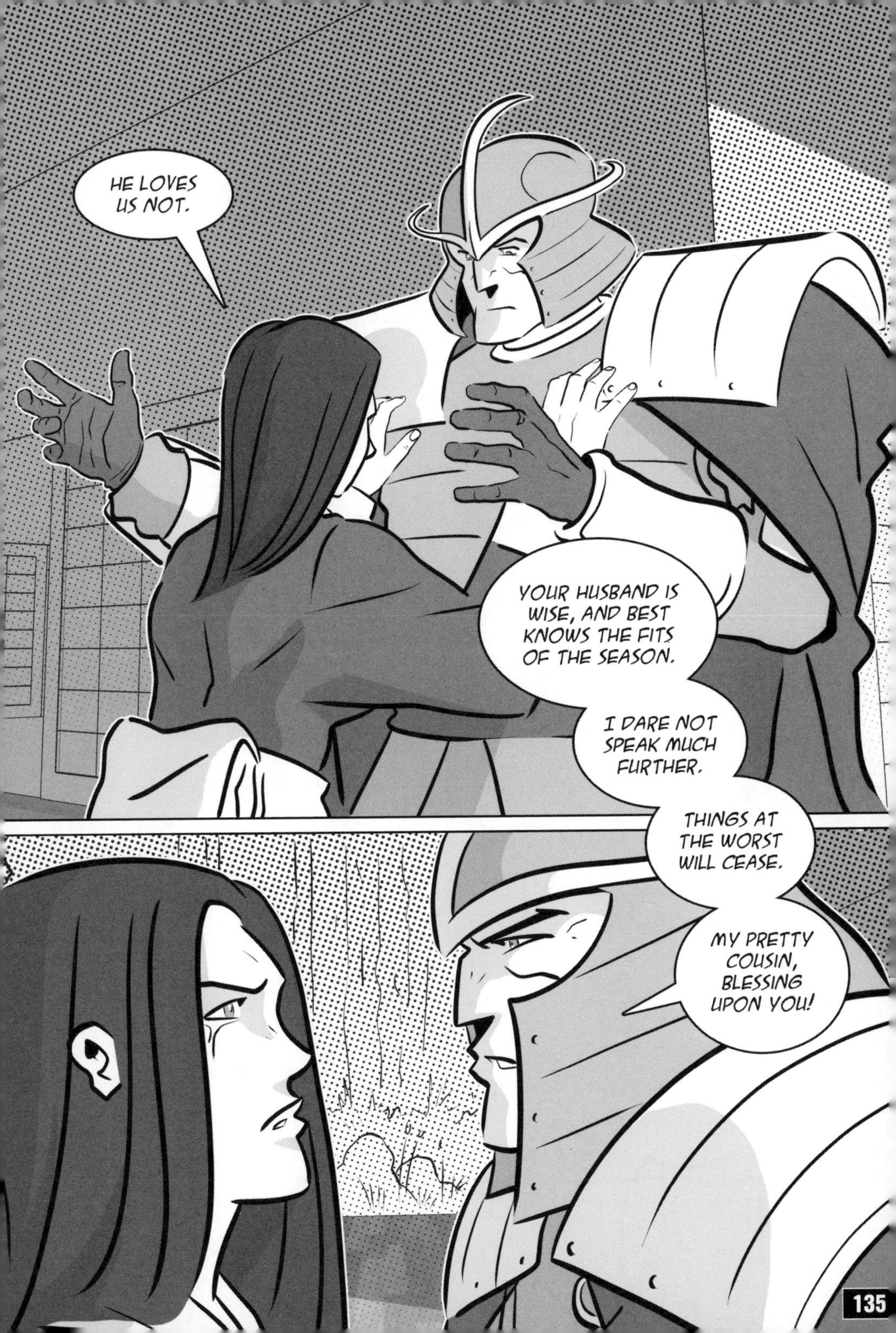
HE LOVES US NOT.
YOUR HUSBAND IS WISE, AND BEST KNOWS THE FITS OF THE SEASON.
I DARE NOT SPEAK MUCH FURTHER.
THINGS AT THE WORST WILL CEASE.
MY PRETTY COUSIN, BLESSING UPON YOU!

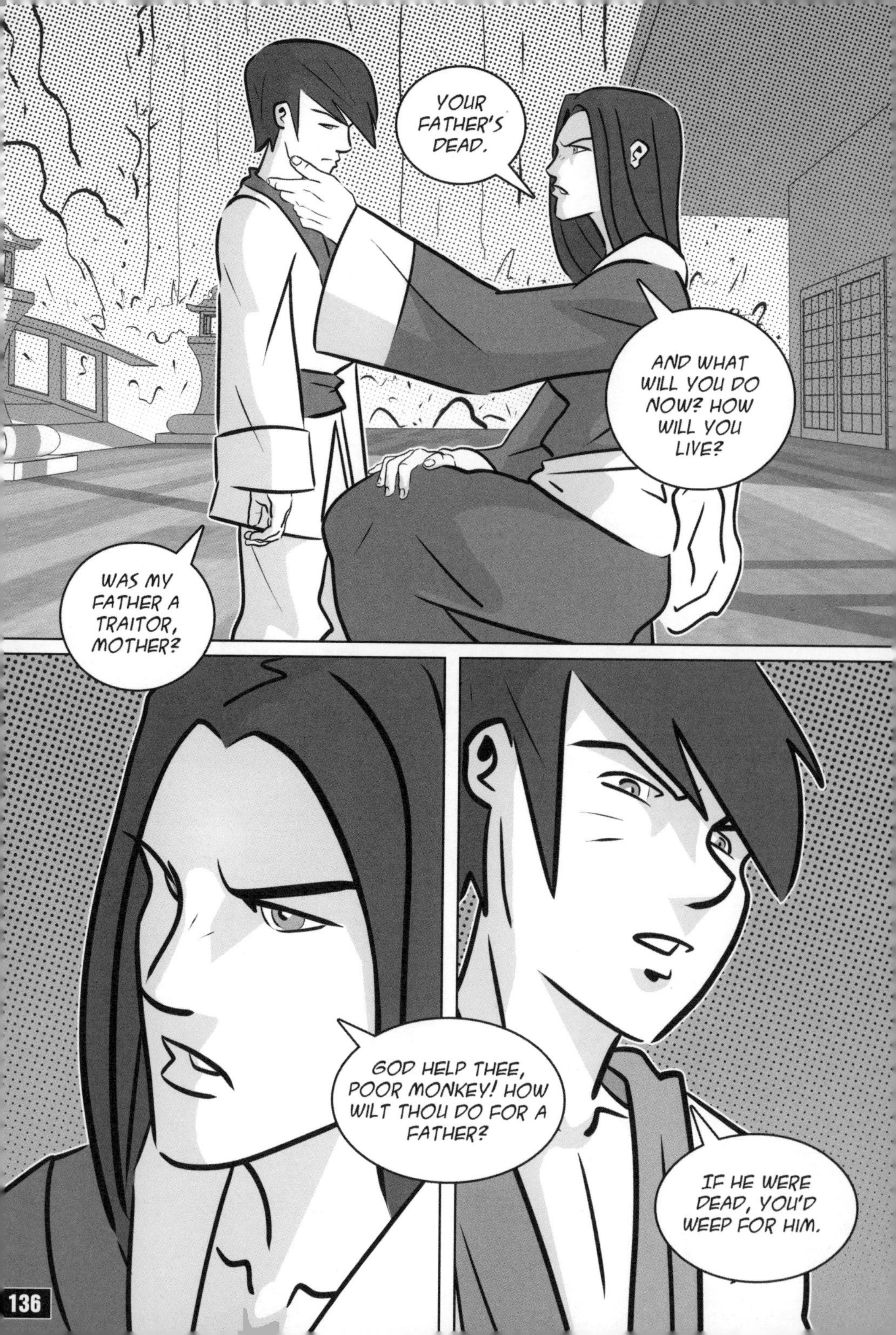
YOUR FATHER'S DEAD.
WAS MY FATHER A TRAITOR, MOTHER?
AND WHAT WILL YOU DO NOW? HOW WILL YOU LIVE?
GOD HELP THEE, POOR MONKEY! HOW WILT THOU DO FOR A FATHER?
IF HE WERE DEAD, YOU'D WEEP FOR HIM.

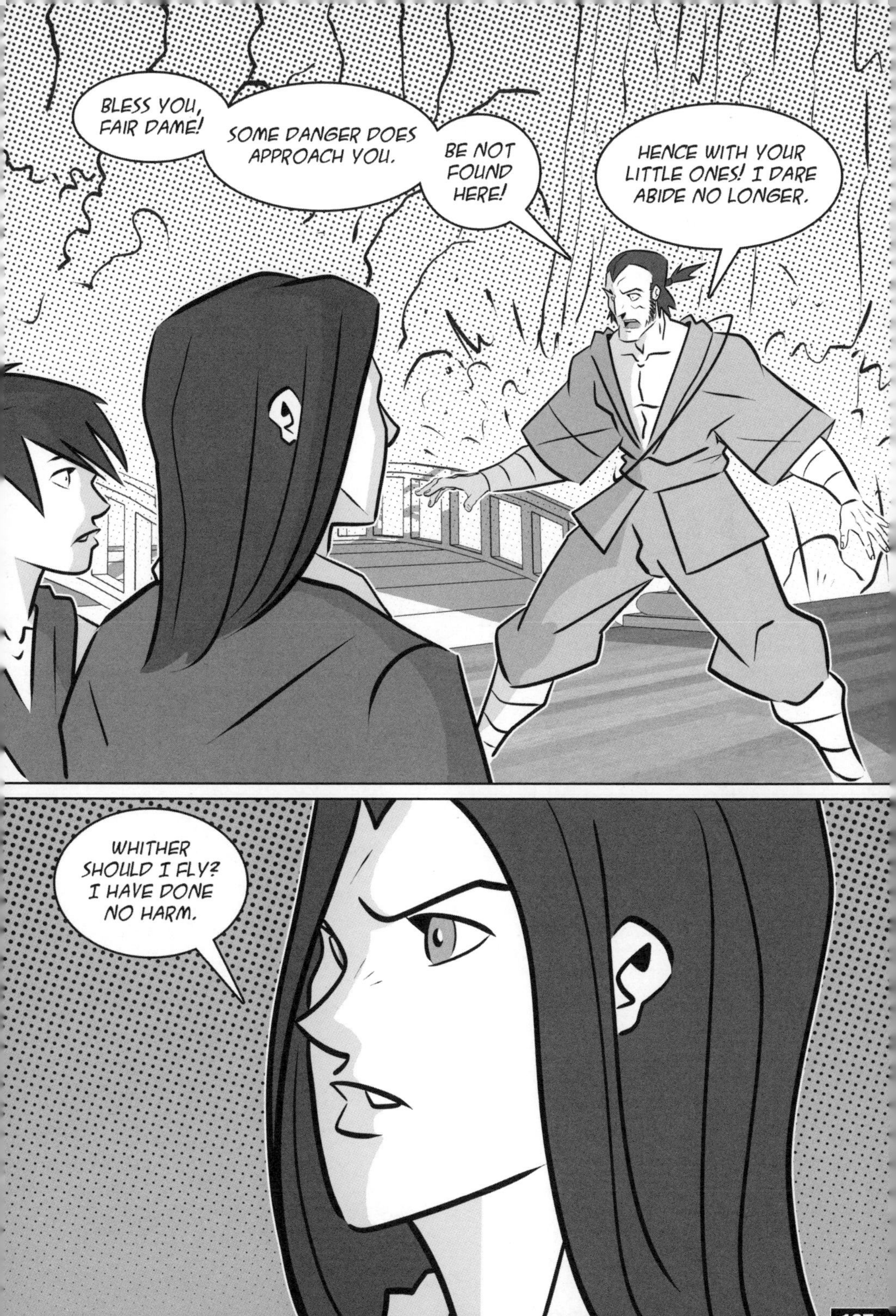
BLESS YOU, FAIR DAME!
SOME DANGER DOES APPROACH YOU.
BE NOT FOUND HERE!
HENCE WITH YOUR LITTLE ONES! I DARE ABIDE NO LONGER.
WHITHER SHOULD I FLY? I HAVE DONE NO HARM.

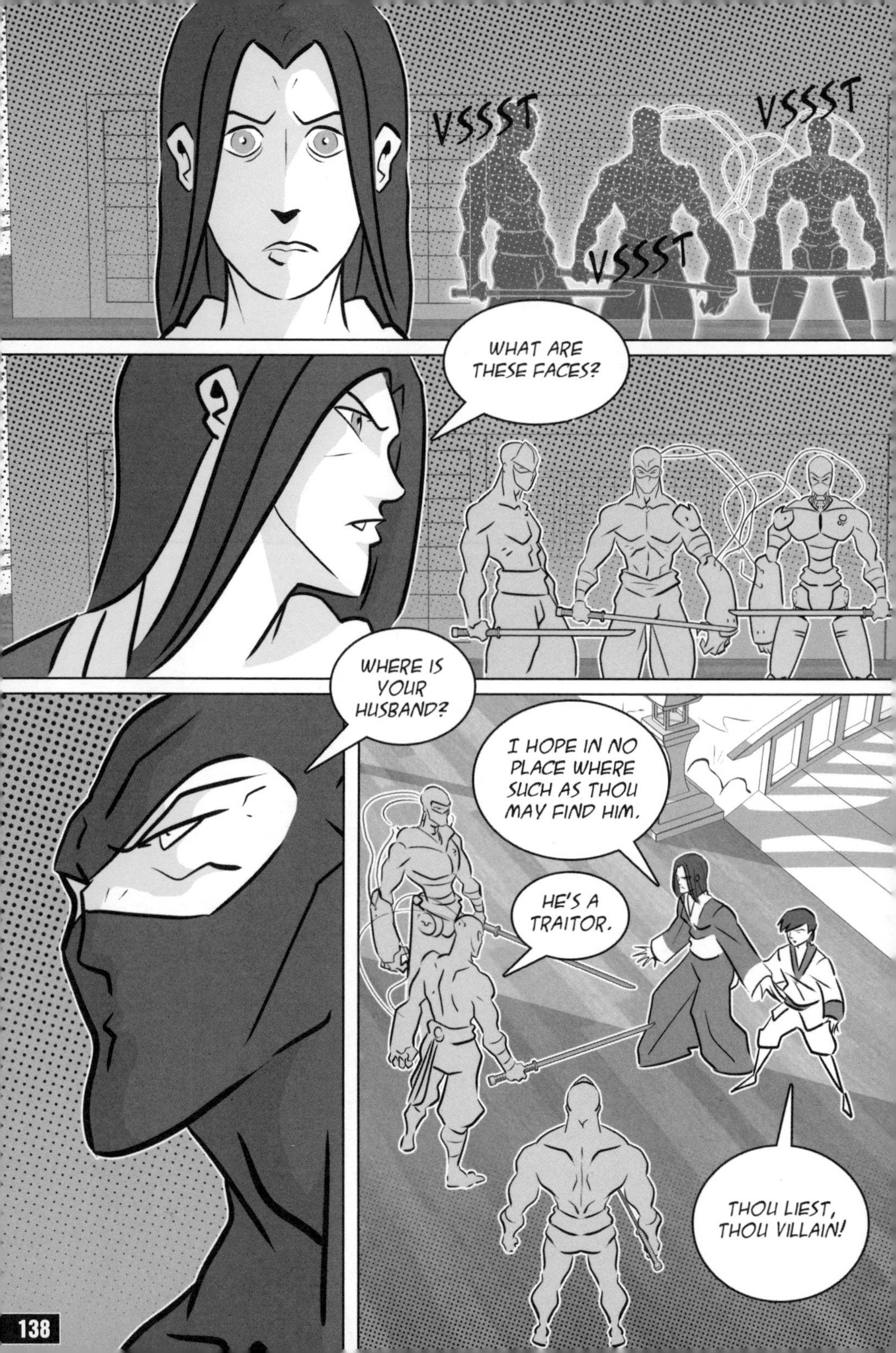
VSSST
VSSST
VSSST
WHAT ARE THESE FACES?
WHERE IS YOUR HUSBAND?
I HOPE IN NO PLACE WHERE SUCH AS THOU MAY FIND HIM.
HE'S A TRAITOR.
THOU LIEST, THOU VILLAIN!

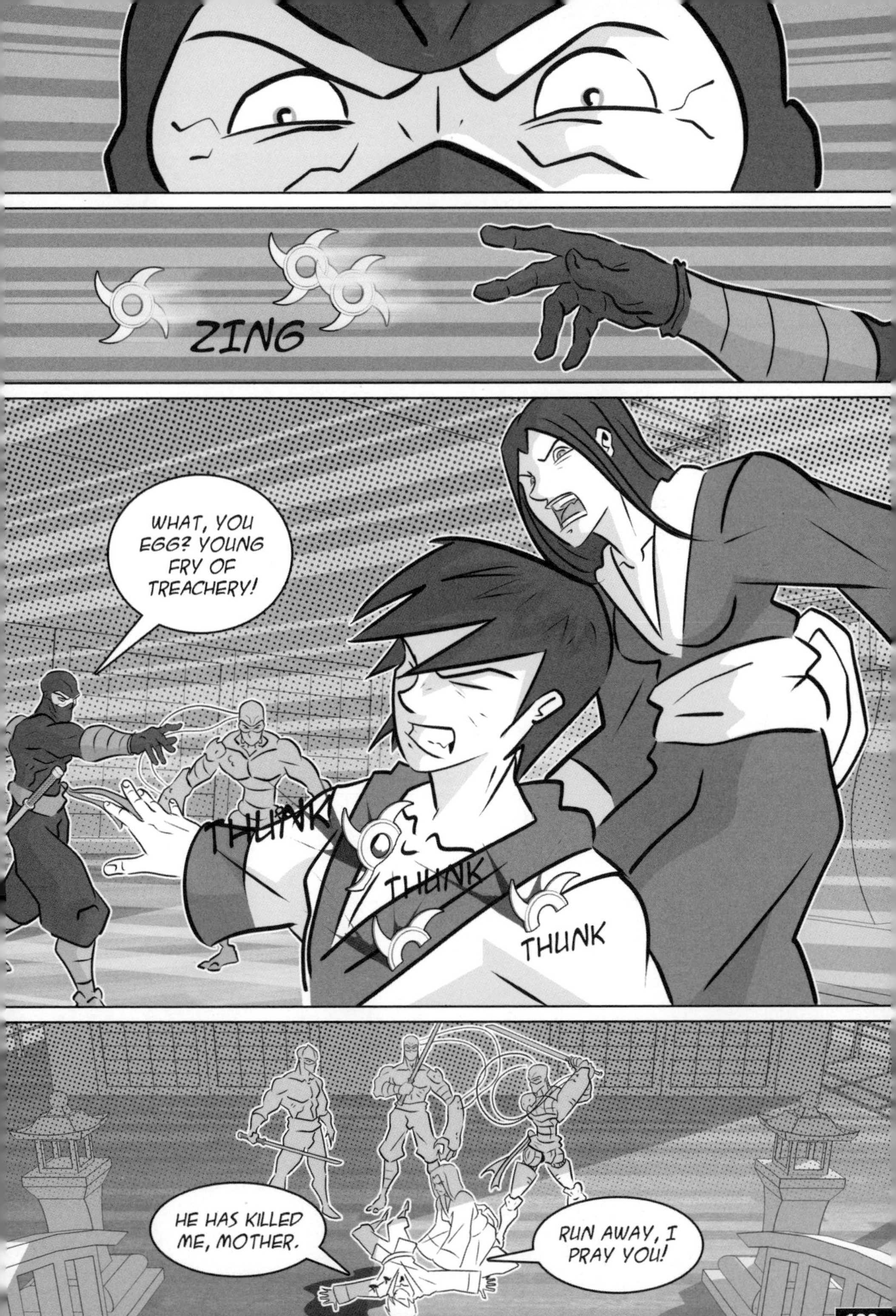

ZING
WHAT, YOU EGG? YOUNG FRY OF TREACHERY!
THUNK
THUNK
THUNK
HE HAS KILLED ME, MOTHER.
RUN AWAY, I PRAY YOU!

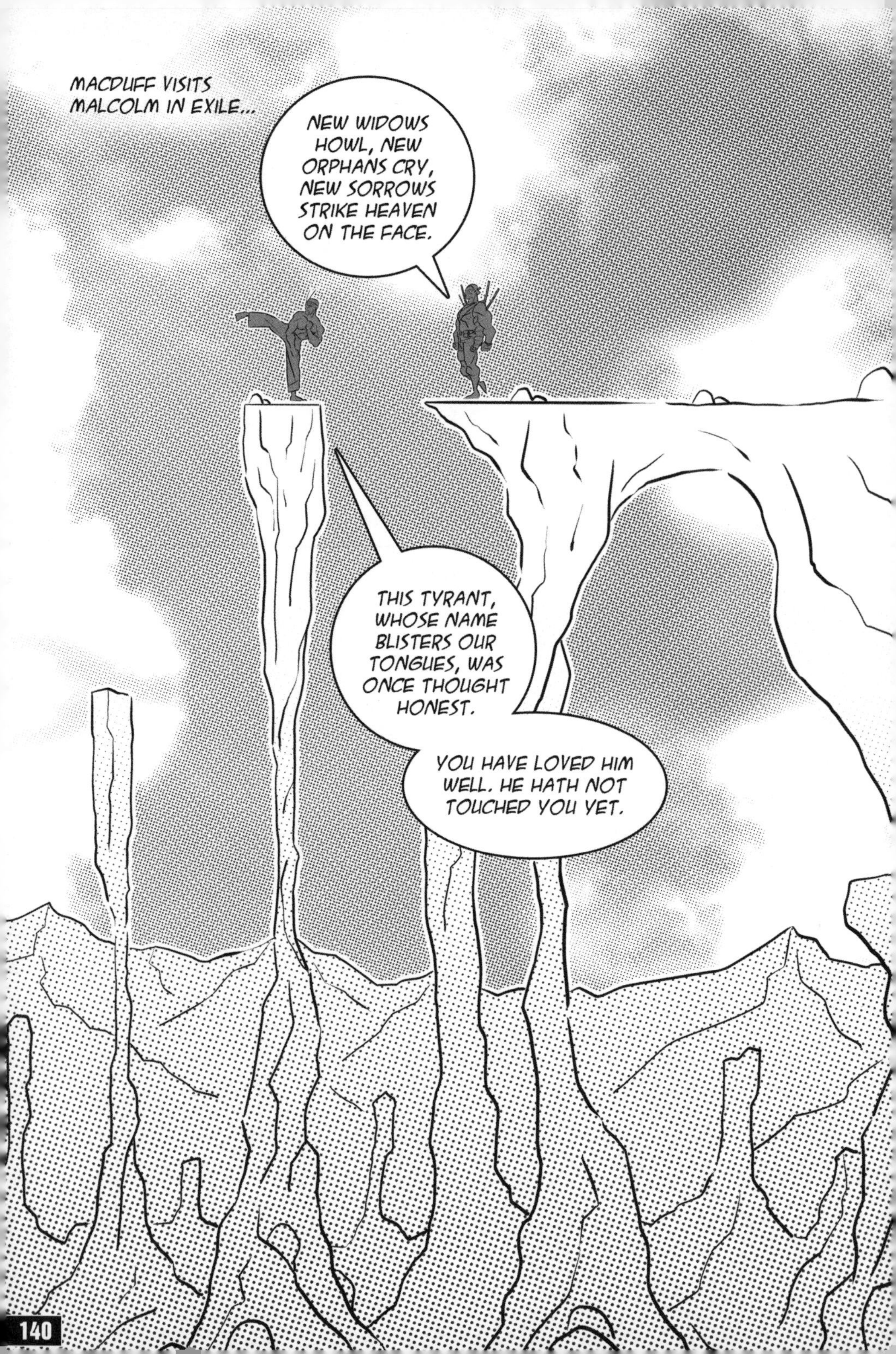
MACDUFF VISITS MALCOLM IN EXILE...
NEW WIDOWS HOWL, NEW ORPHANS CRY, NEW SORROWS STRIKE HEAVEN ON THE FACE.
THIS TYRANT, WHOSE NAME BLISTERS OUR TONGUES, WAS ONCE THOUGHT HONEST.
YOU HAVE LOVED HIM WELL. HE HATH NOT TOUCHED YOU YET.

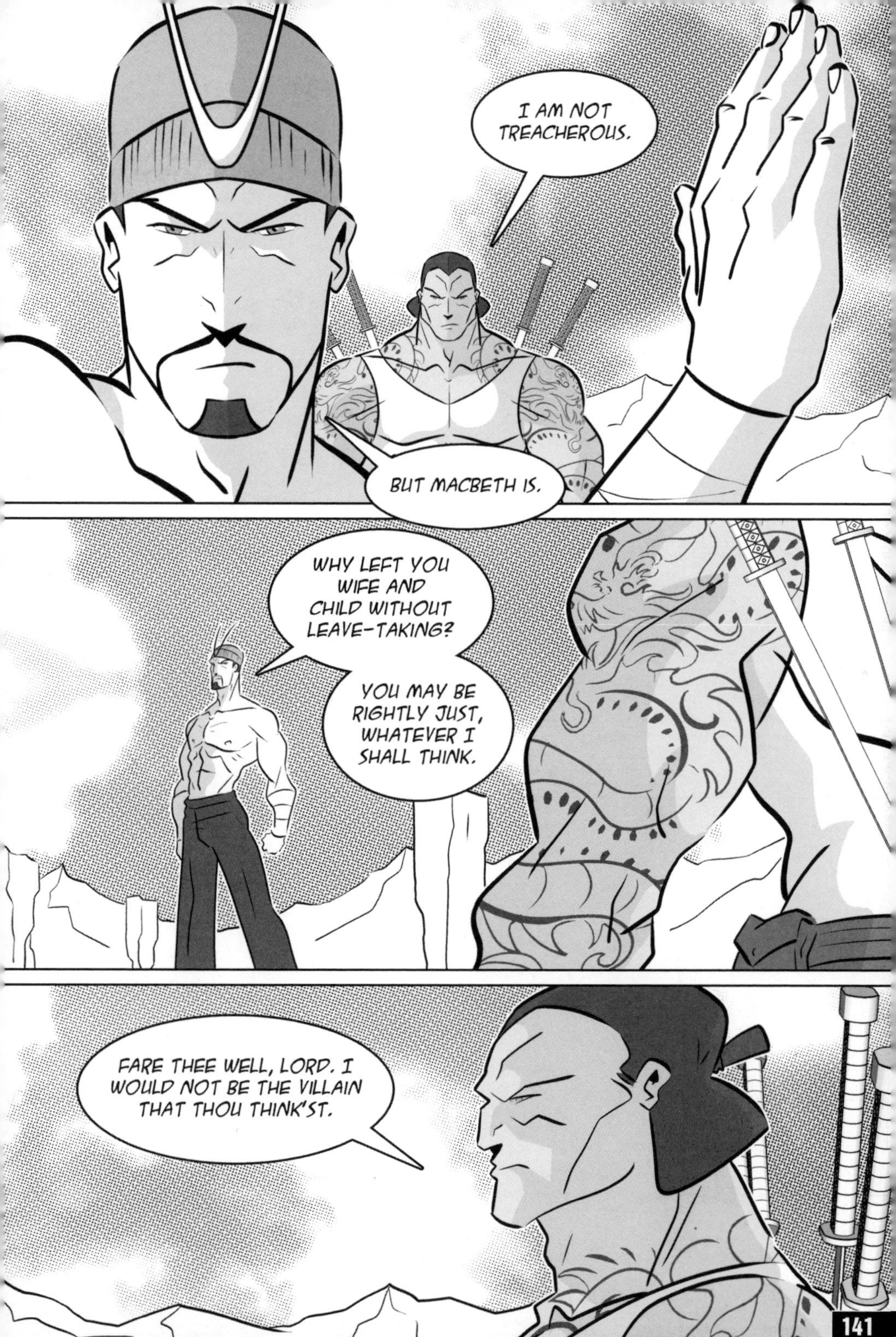
I AM NOT TREACHEROUS.
BUT MACBETH IS.
WHY LEFT YOU WIFE AND CHILD WITHOUT LEAVE-TAKING?
YOU MAY BE RIGHTLY JUST, WHATEVER I SHALL THINK.
FARE THEE WELL, LORD. I WOULD NOT BE THE VILLAIN THAT THOU THINK'ST.

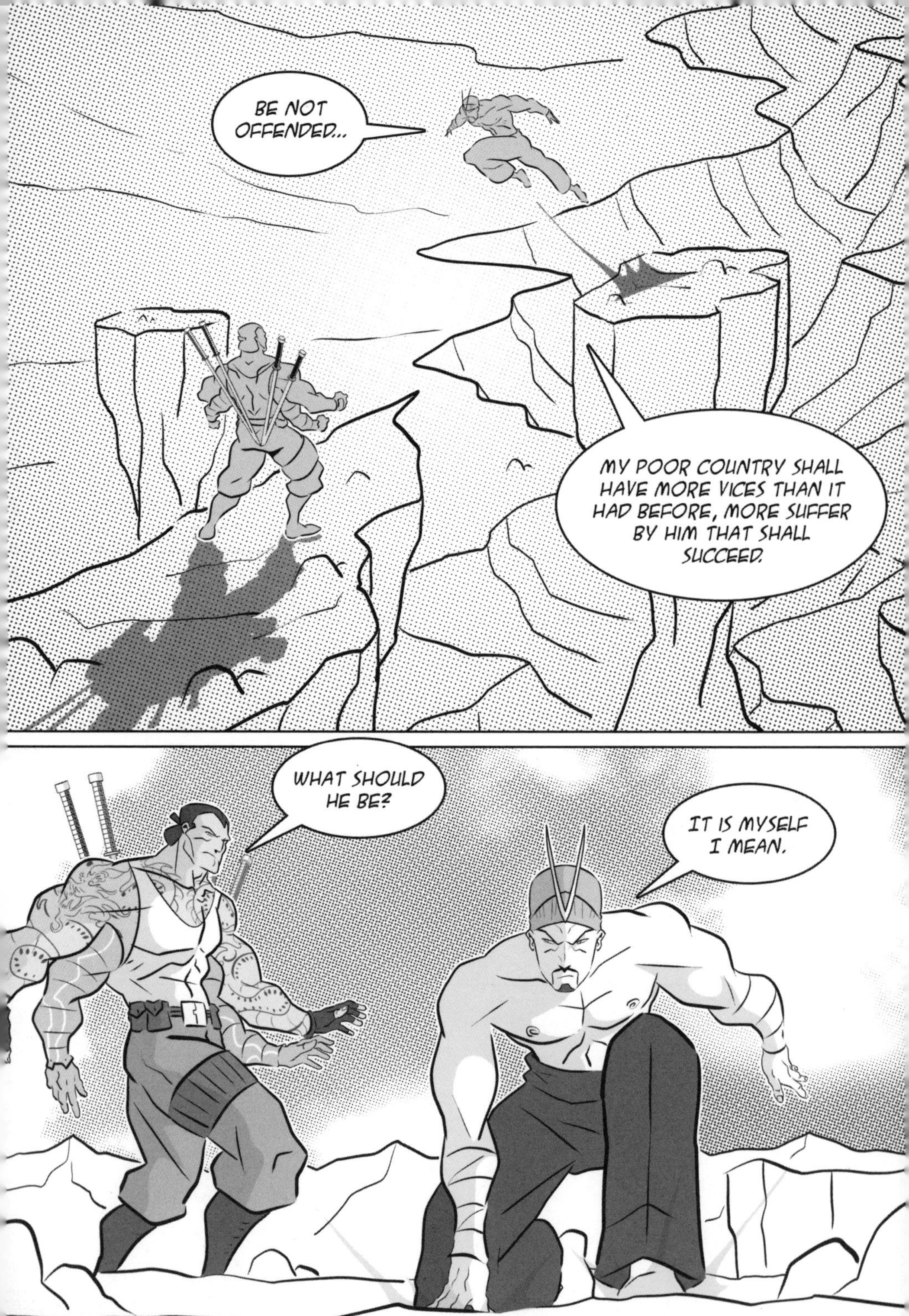
BE NOT OFFENDED...
MY POOR COUNTRY SHALL HAVE MORE VICES THAN IT HAD BEFORE, MORE SUFFER BY HIM THAT SHALL SUCCEED.
WHAT SHOULD HE BE?
IT IS MYSELF I MEAN.

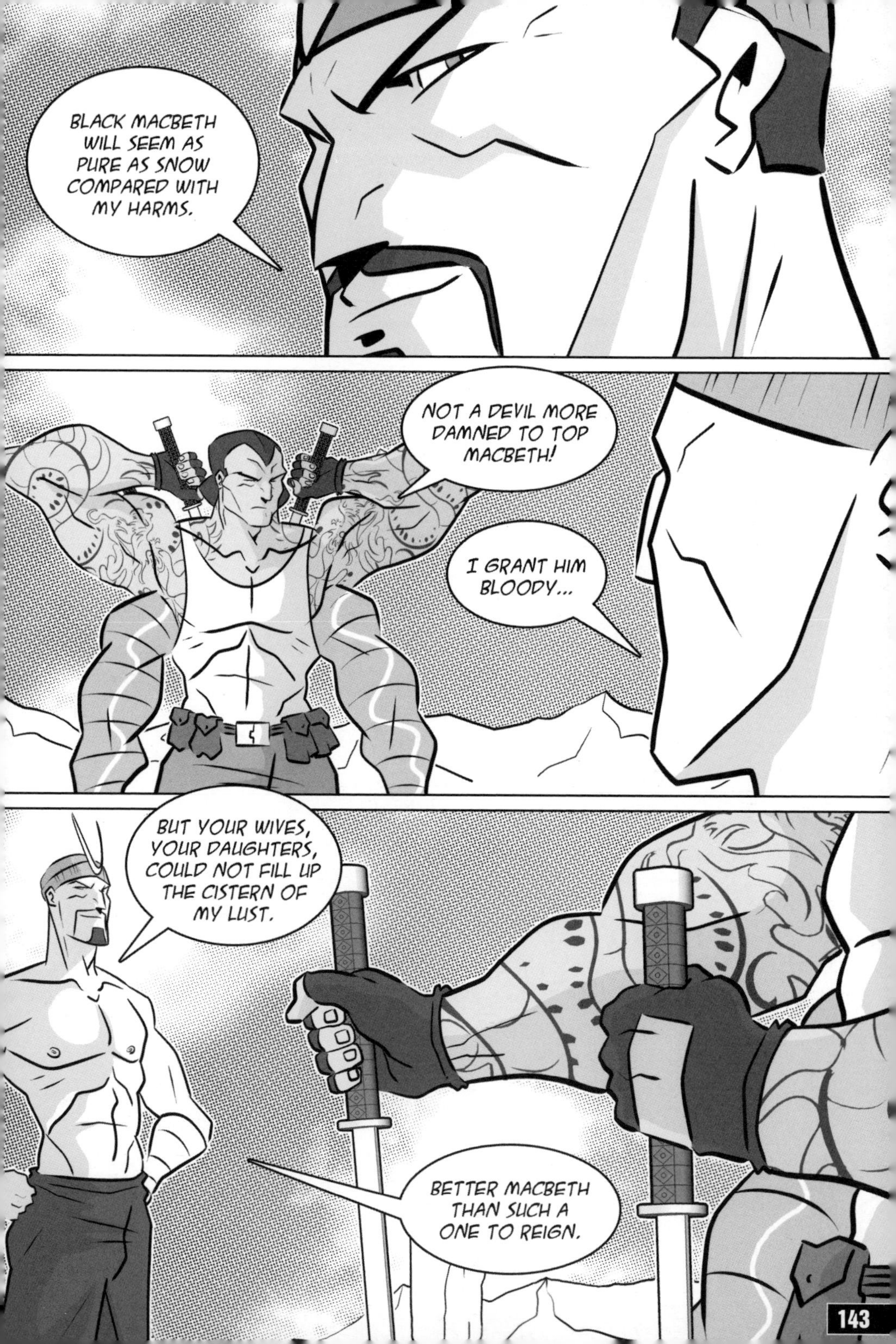
BLACK MACBETH WILL SEEM AS PURE AS SNOW COMPARED WITH MY HARMS.
NOT A DEVIL MORE DAMNED TO TOP MACBETH!
I GRANT HIM BLOODY...
BUT YOUR WIVES, YOUR DAUGHTERS, COULD NOT FILL UP THE CISTERN OF MY LUST.
BETTER MACBETH THAN SUCH A ONE TO REIGN.

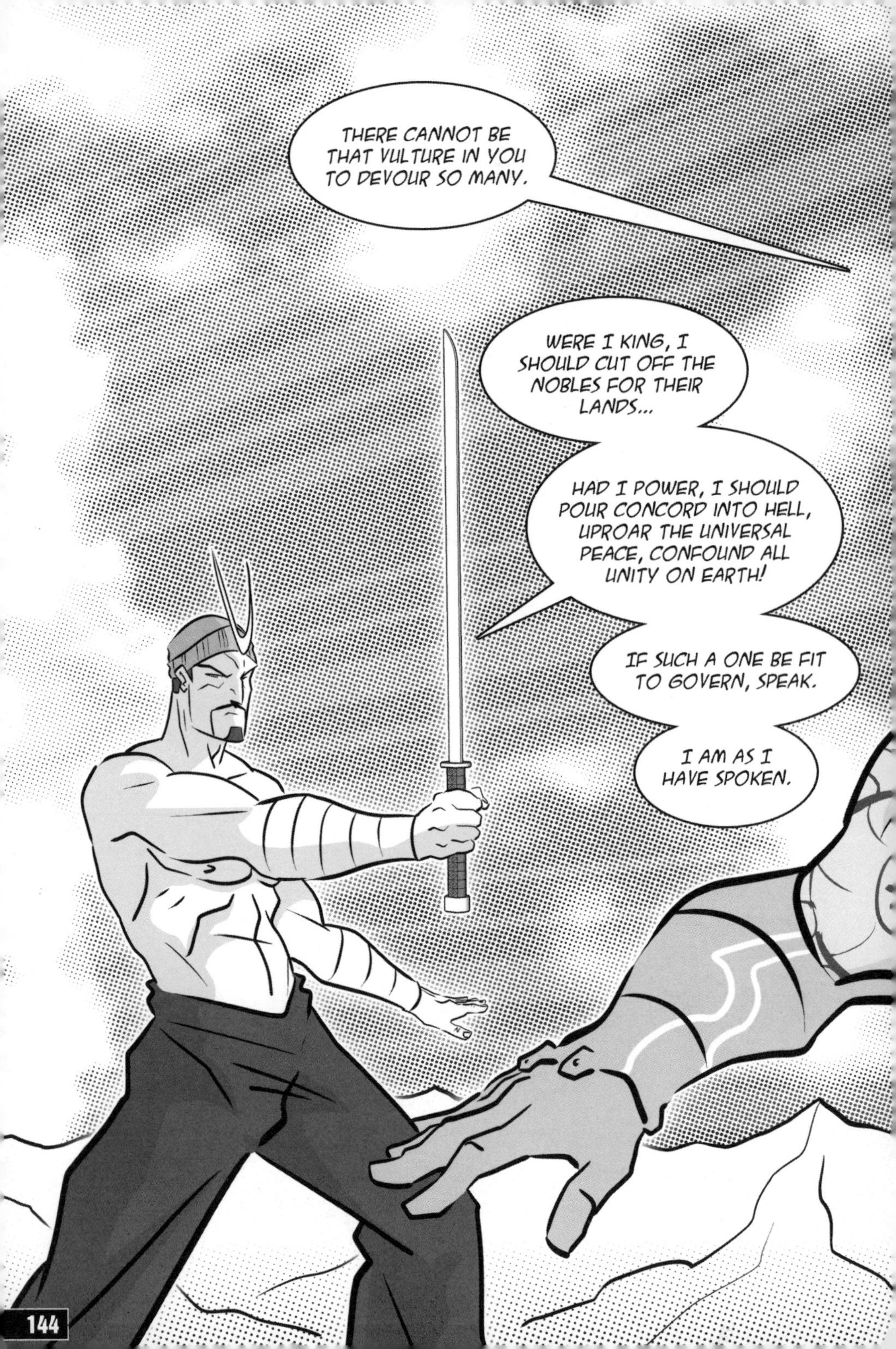
THERE CANNOT BE THAT VULTURE IN YOU TO DEVOUR SO MANY.
WERE I KING, I SHOULD CUT OFF THE NOBLES FOR THEIR LANDS...
HAD I POWER, I SHOULD POUR CONCORD INTO HELL, UPROAR THE UNIVERSAL PEACE, CONFOUND ALL UNITY ON EARTH!
IF SUCH A ONE BE FIT TO GOVERN, SPEAK.
I AM AS I HAVE SPOKEN.

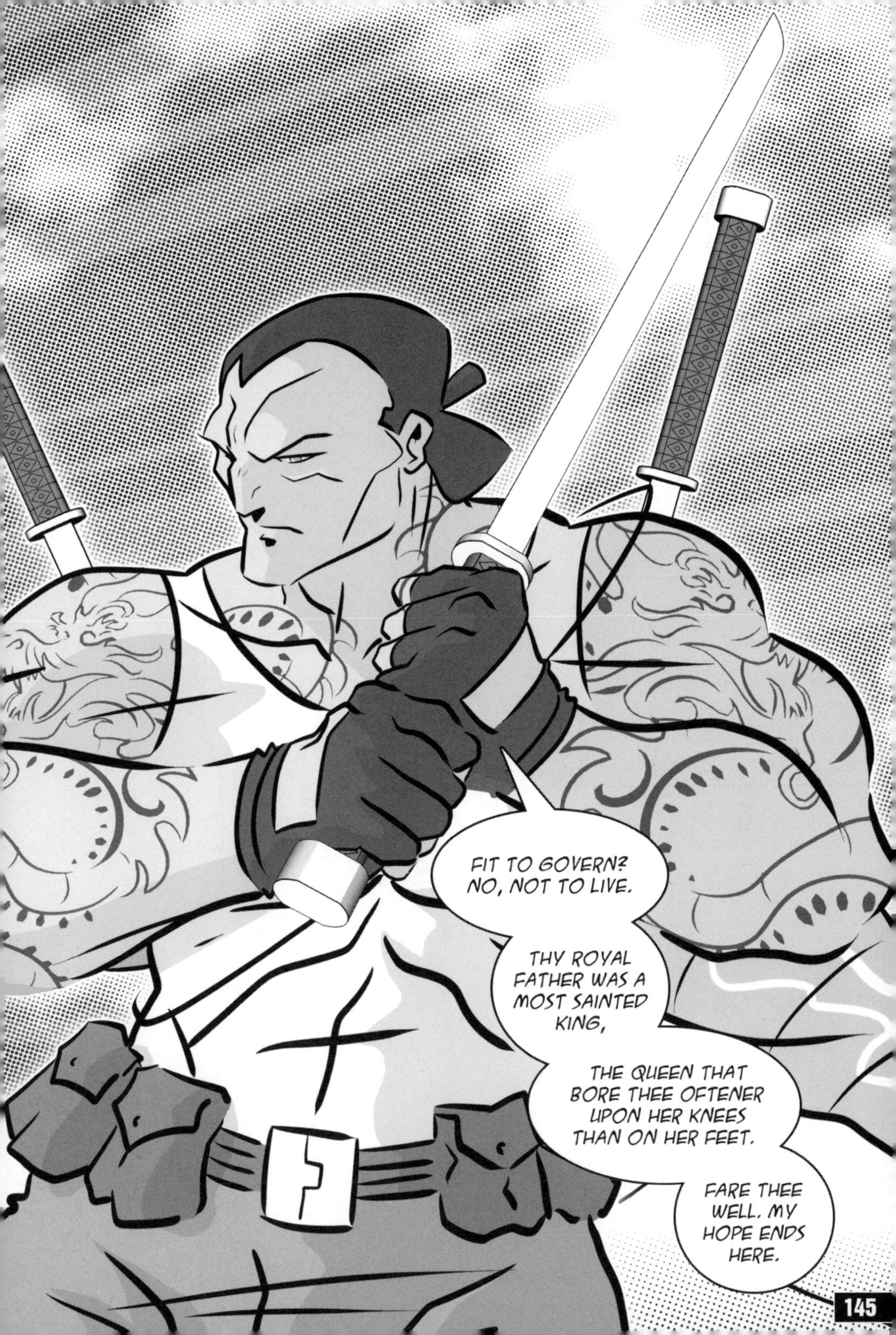
FIT TO GOVERN? NO, NOT TO LIVE.
THY ROYAL FATHER WAS A MOST SAINTED KING,
THE QUEEN THAT BORE THEE OFTENER UPON HER KNEES THAN ON HER FEET.
FARE THEE WELL. MY HOPE ENDS HERE.

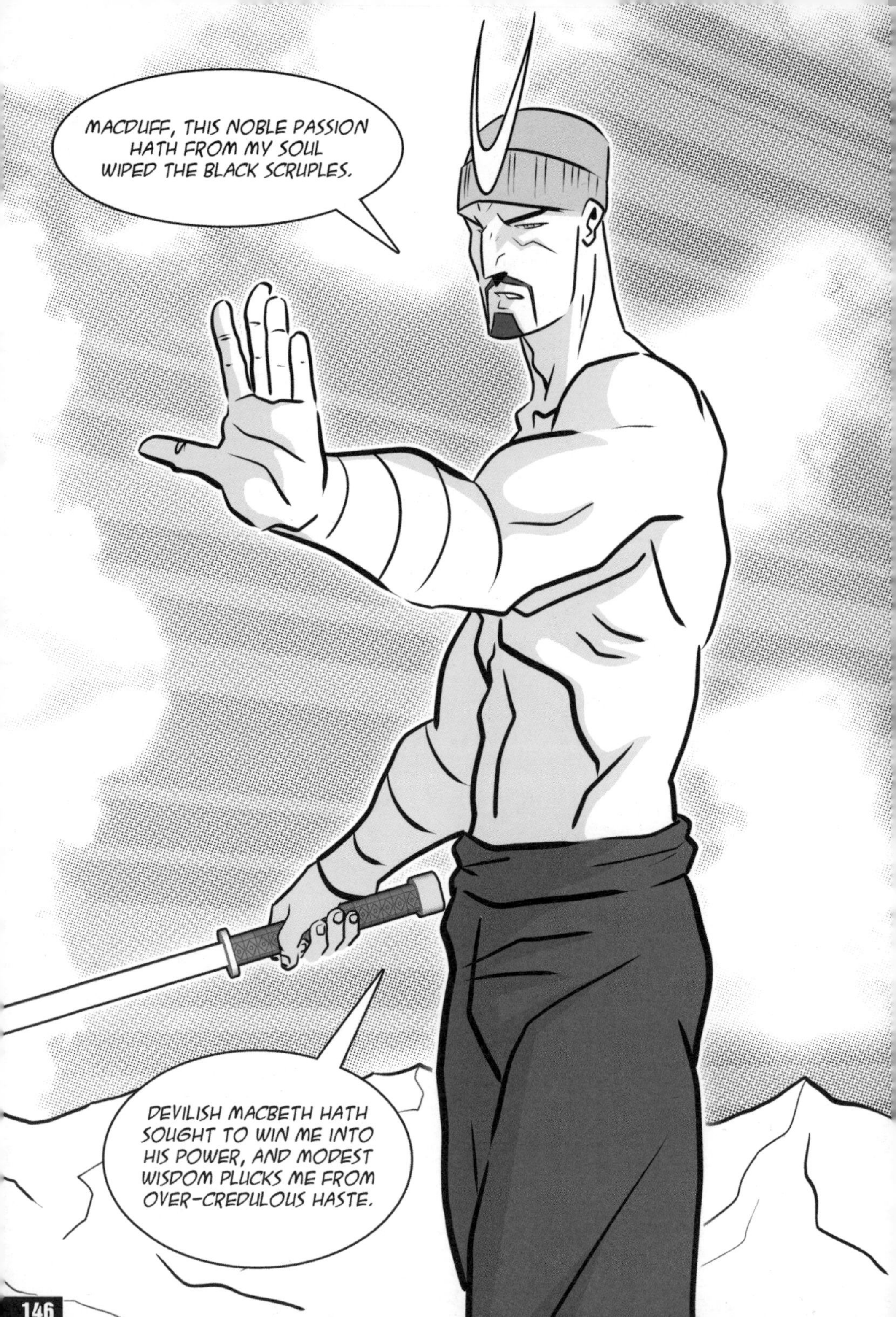
MACDUFF, THIS NOBLE PASSION HATH FROM MY SOUL WIPED THE BLACK SCRUPLES.
DEVILISH MACBETH HATH SOUGHT TO WIN ME INTO HIS POWER, AND MODEST WISDOM PLUCKS ME FROM OVER-CREDULOUS HASTE.

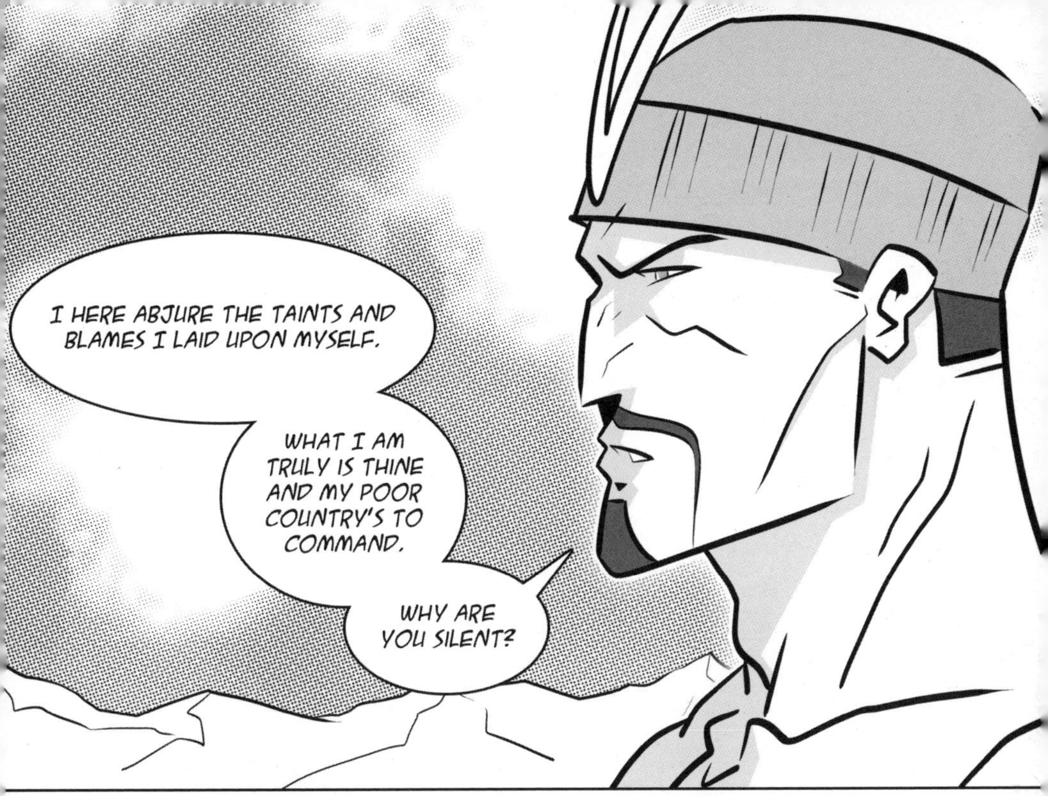
I HERE ABJURE THE TAINTS AND BLAMES I LAID UPON MYSELF.
WHAT I AM TRULY IS THINE AND MY POOR COUNTRY'S TO COMMAND.
WHY ARE YOU SILENT?

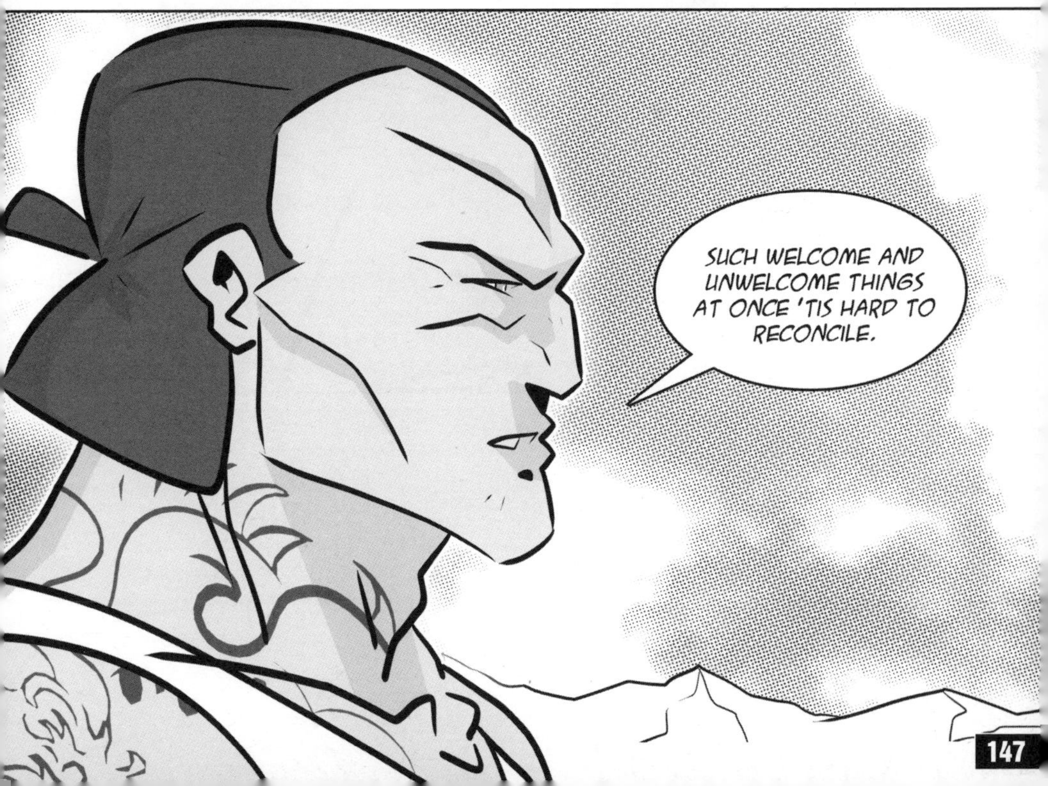
SUCH WELCOME AND UNWELCOME THINGS AT ONCE 'TIS HARD TO RECONCILE.

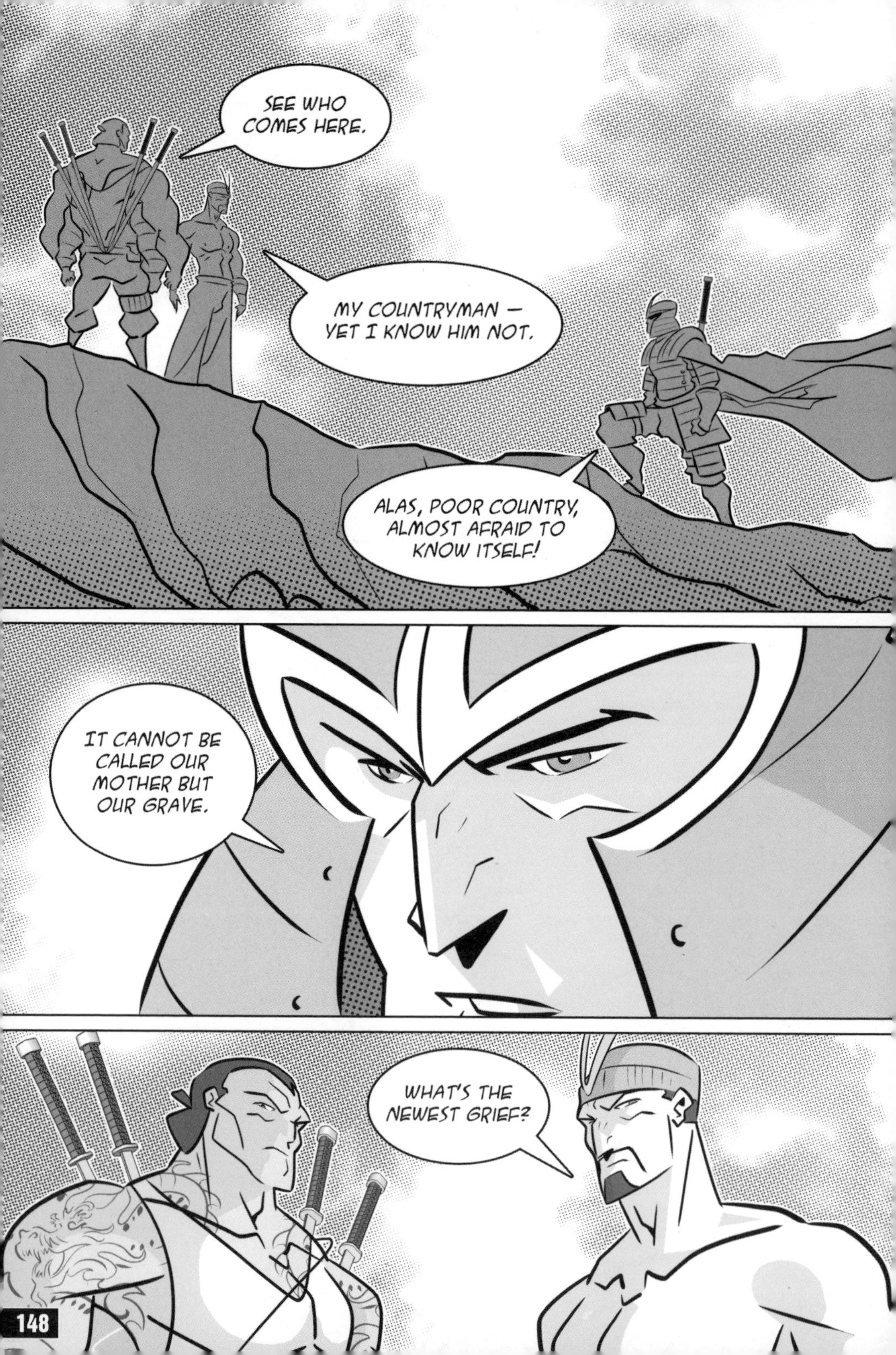
SEE WHO COMES HERE.
MY COUNTRYMAN — YET I KNOW HIM NOT.
ALAS, POOR COUNTRY, ALMOST AFRAID TO KNOW ITSELF!
IT CANNOT BE CALLED OUR MOTHER BUT OUR GRAVE.
WHAT'S THE NEWEST GRIEF?

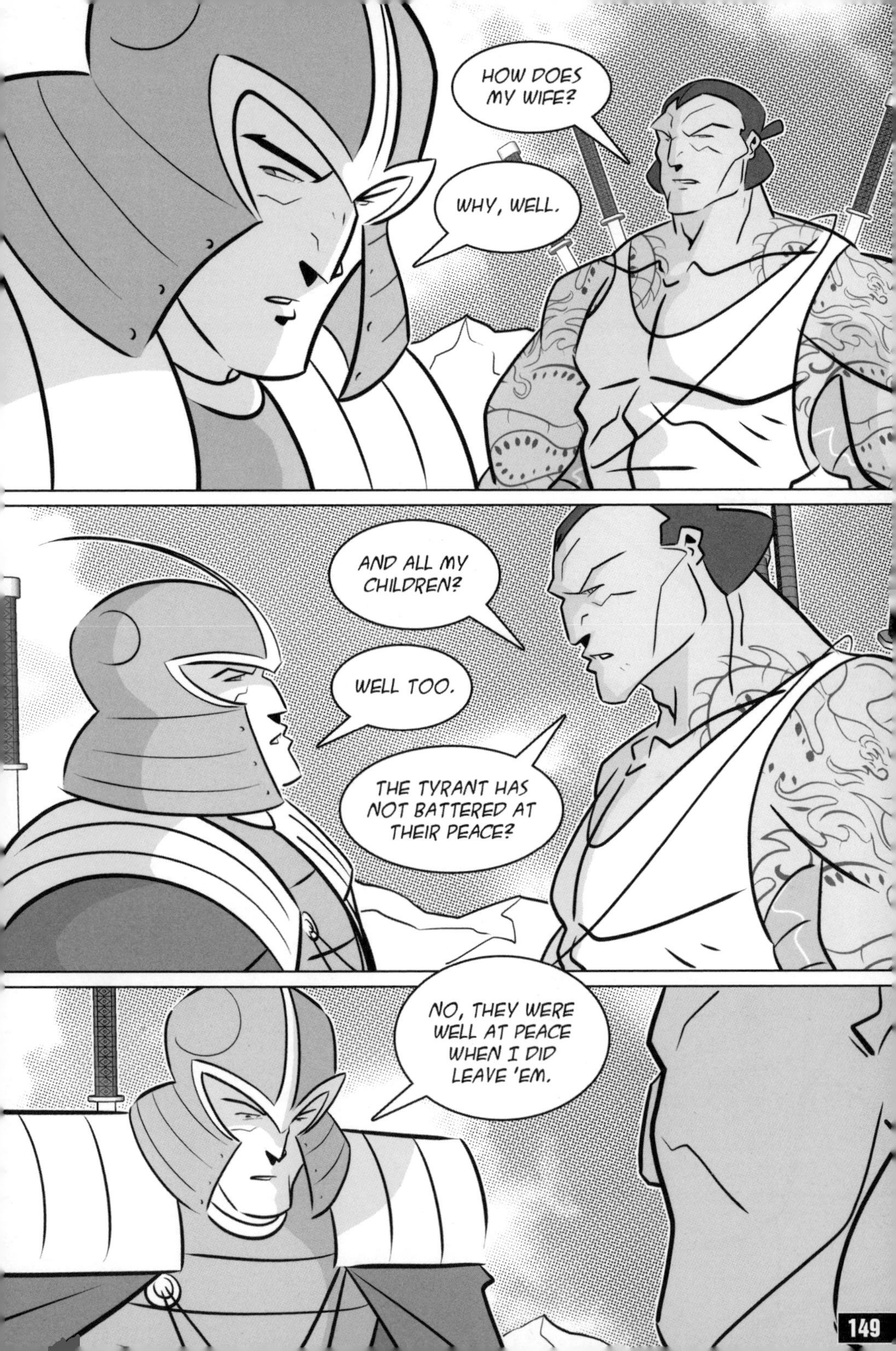
HOW DOES MY WIFE?
WHY, WELL.
AND ALL MY CHILDREN?
WELL TOO.
THE TYRANT HAS NOT BATTERED AT THEIR PEACE?
NO, THEY WERE WELL AT PEACE WHEN I DID LEAVE 'EM.

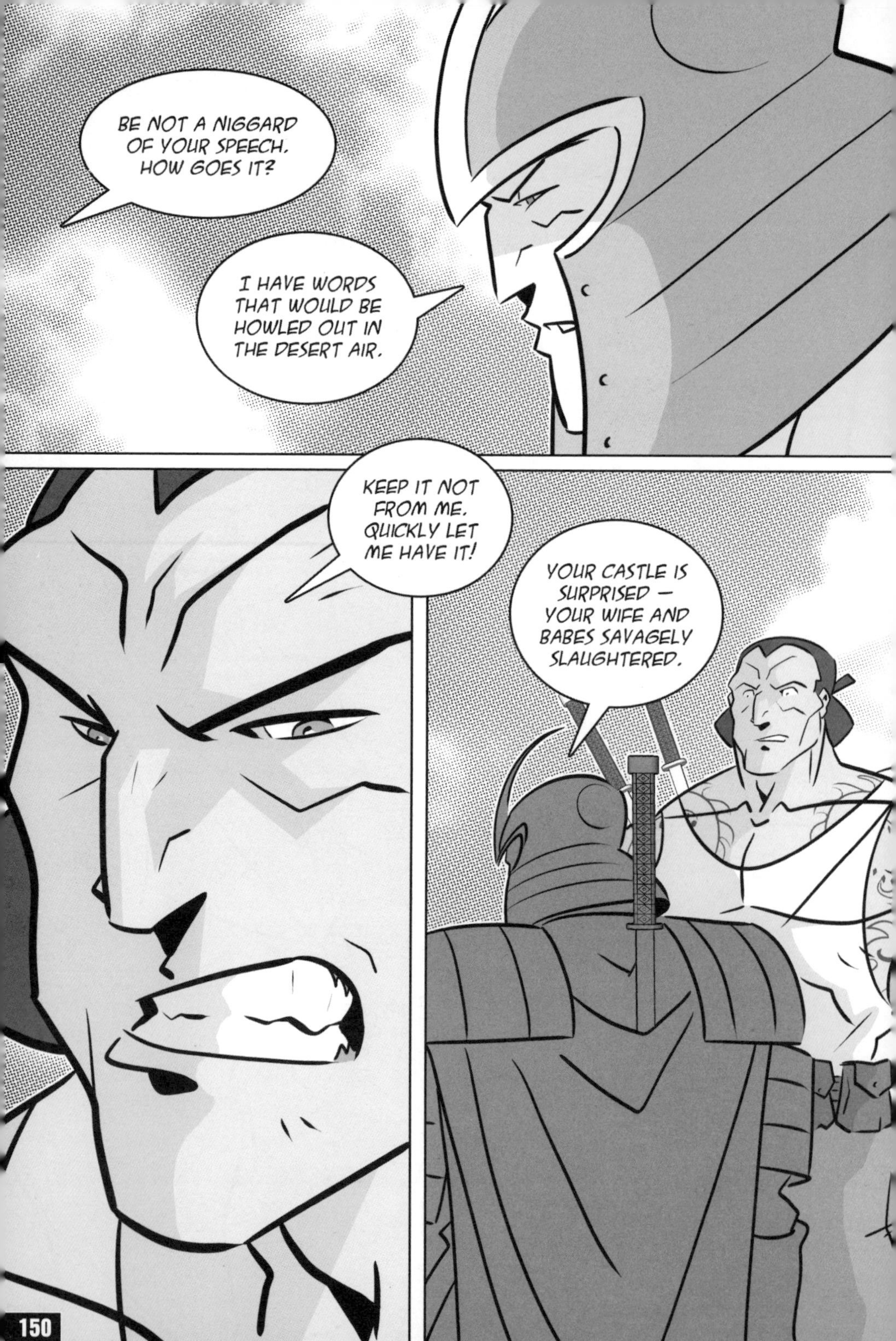

BE NOT A NIGGARD OF YOUR SPEECH. HOW GOES IT?
I HAVE WORDS THAT WOULD BE HOWLED OUT IN THE DESERT AIR.
KEEP IT NOT FROM ME. QUICKLY LET ME HAVE IT!
YOUR CASTLE IS SURPRISED — YOUR WIFE AND BABES SAVAGELY SLAUGHTERED.

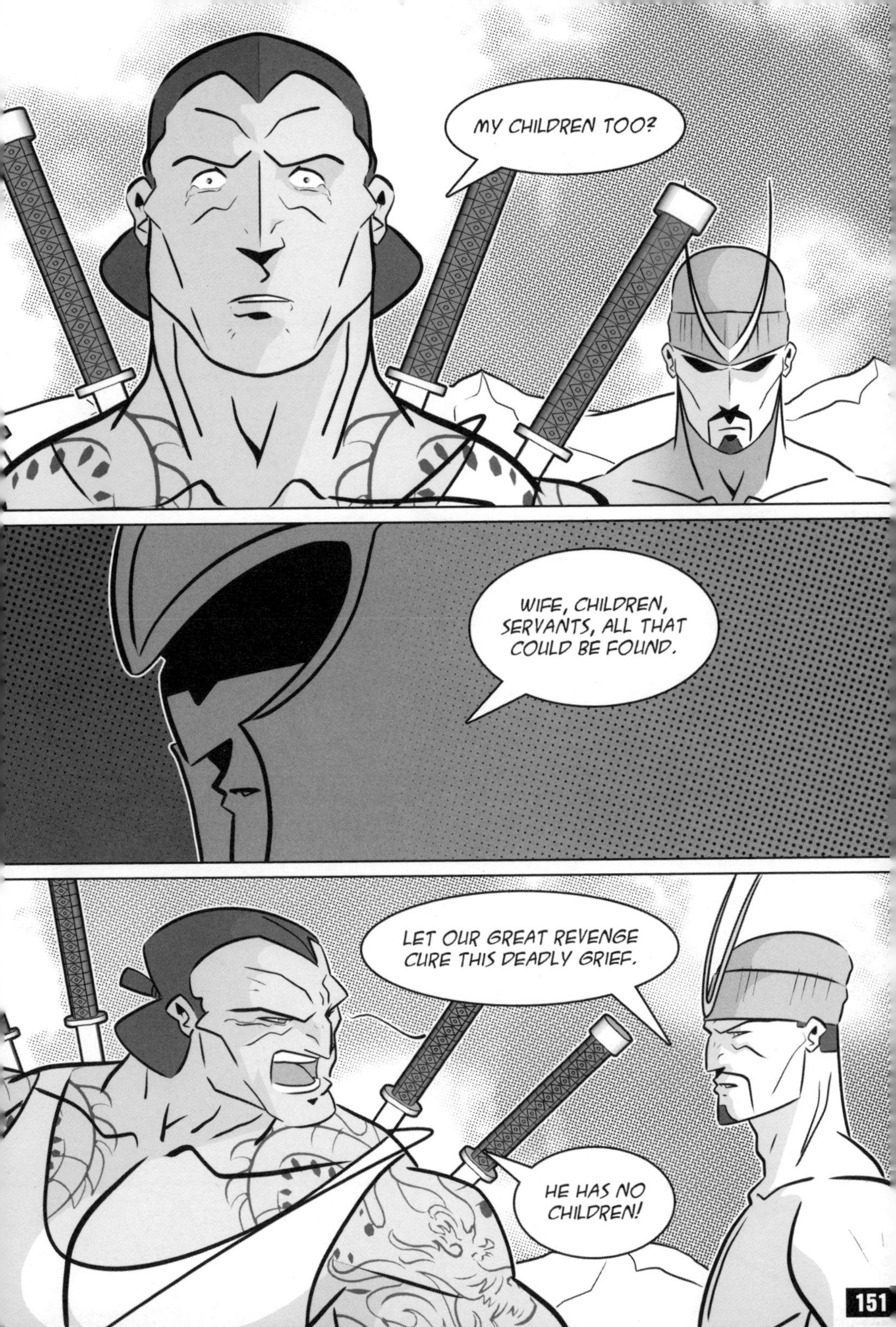
MY CHILDREN TOO?
WIFE, CHILDREN, SERVANTS, ALL THAT COULD BE FOUND.
LET OUR GREAT REVENGE CURE THIS DEADLY GRIEF.
HE HAS NO CHILDREN!

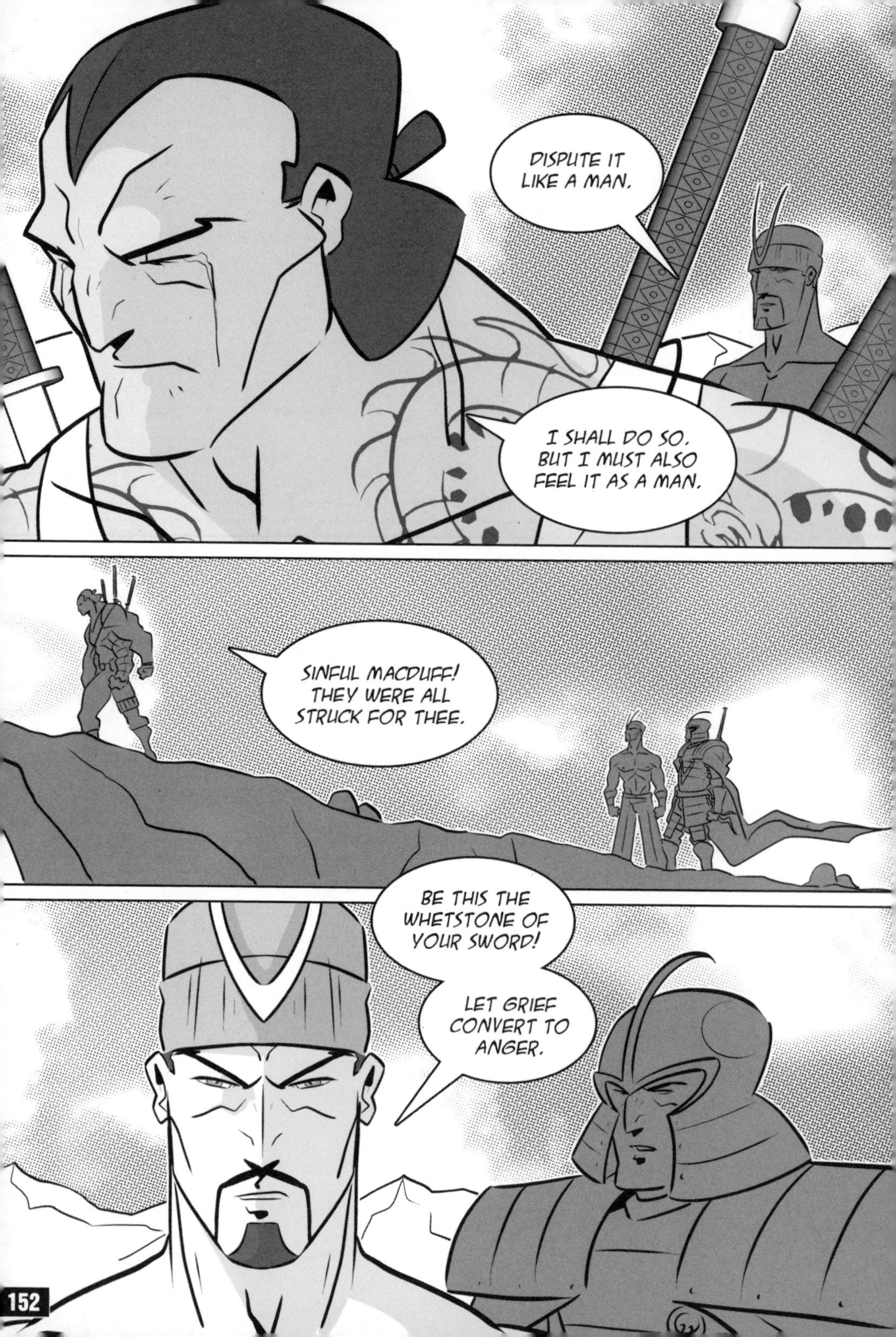
DISPUTE IT LIKE A MAN.
I SHALL DO SO. BUT I MUST ALSO FEEL IT AS A MAN.
SINFUL MACDUFF! THEY WERE ALL STRUCK FOR THEE.
BE THIS THE WHETSTONE OF YOUR SWORD!
LET GRIEF CONVERT TO ANGER.

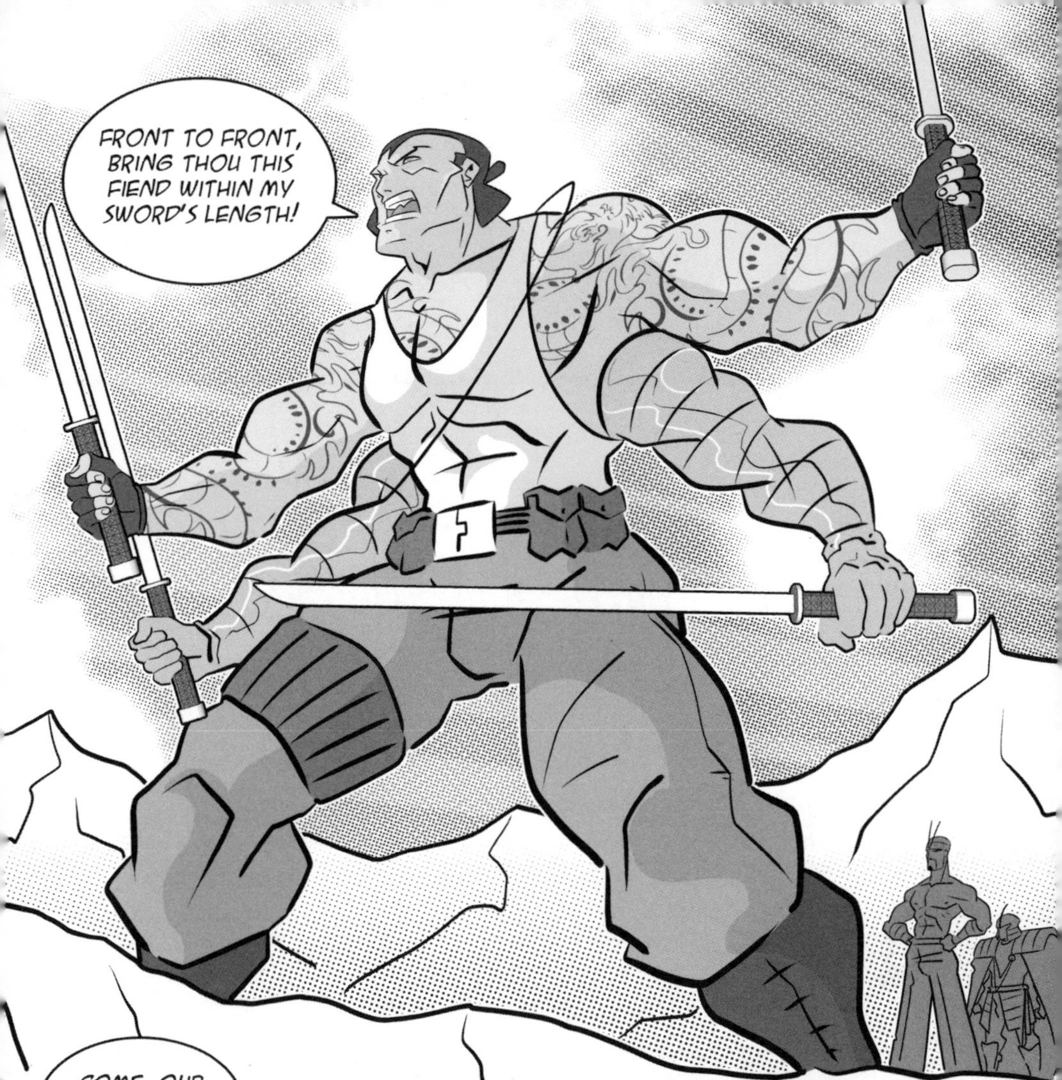
FRONT TO FRONT, BRING THOU THIS FIEND WITHIN MY SWORD'S LENGTH!

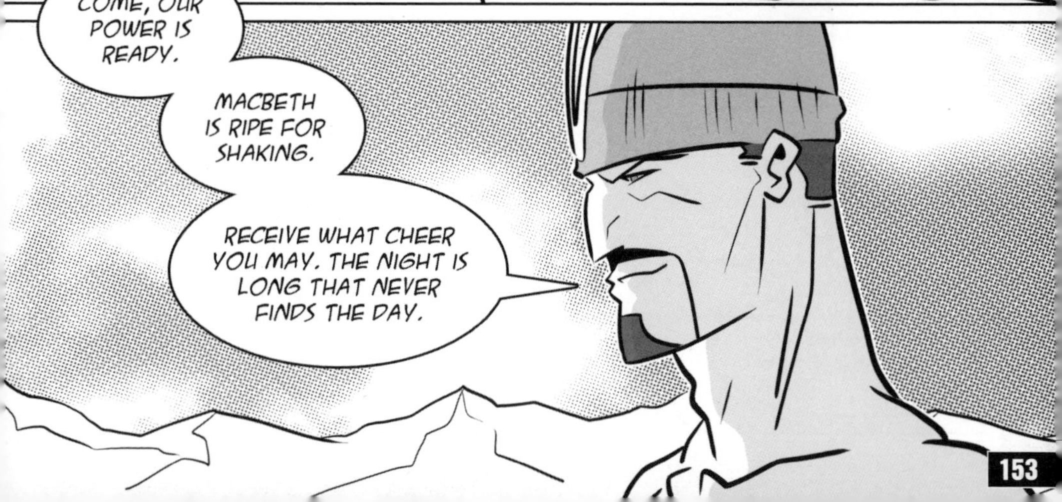
COME, OUR POWER IS READY.
MACBETH IS RIPE FOR SHAKING.
RECEIVE WHAT CHEER YOU MAY. THE NIGHT IS LONG THAT NEVER FINDS THE DAY.

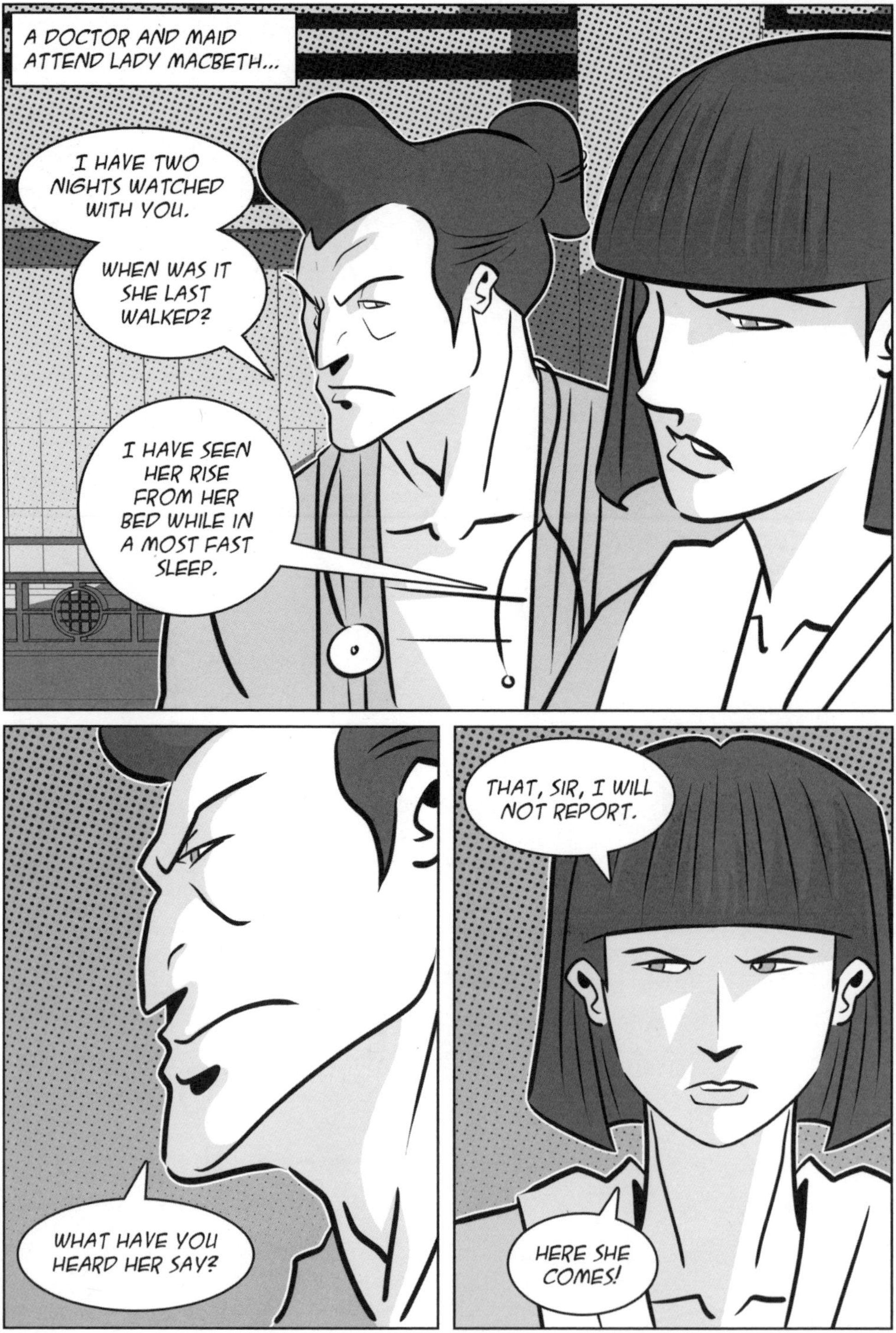
A DOCTOR AND MAID ATTEND LADY MACBETH...
I HAVE TWO NIGHTS WATCHED WITH YOU.
WHEN WAS IT SHE LAST WALKED?
I HAVE SEEN HER RISE FROM HER BED WHILE IN A MOST FAST SLEEP.
WHAT HAVE YOU HEARD HER SAY?
THAT, SIR, I WILL NOT REPORT.
HERE SHE COMES!

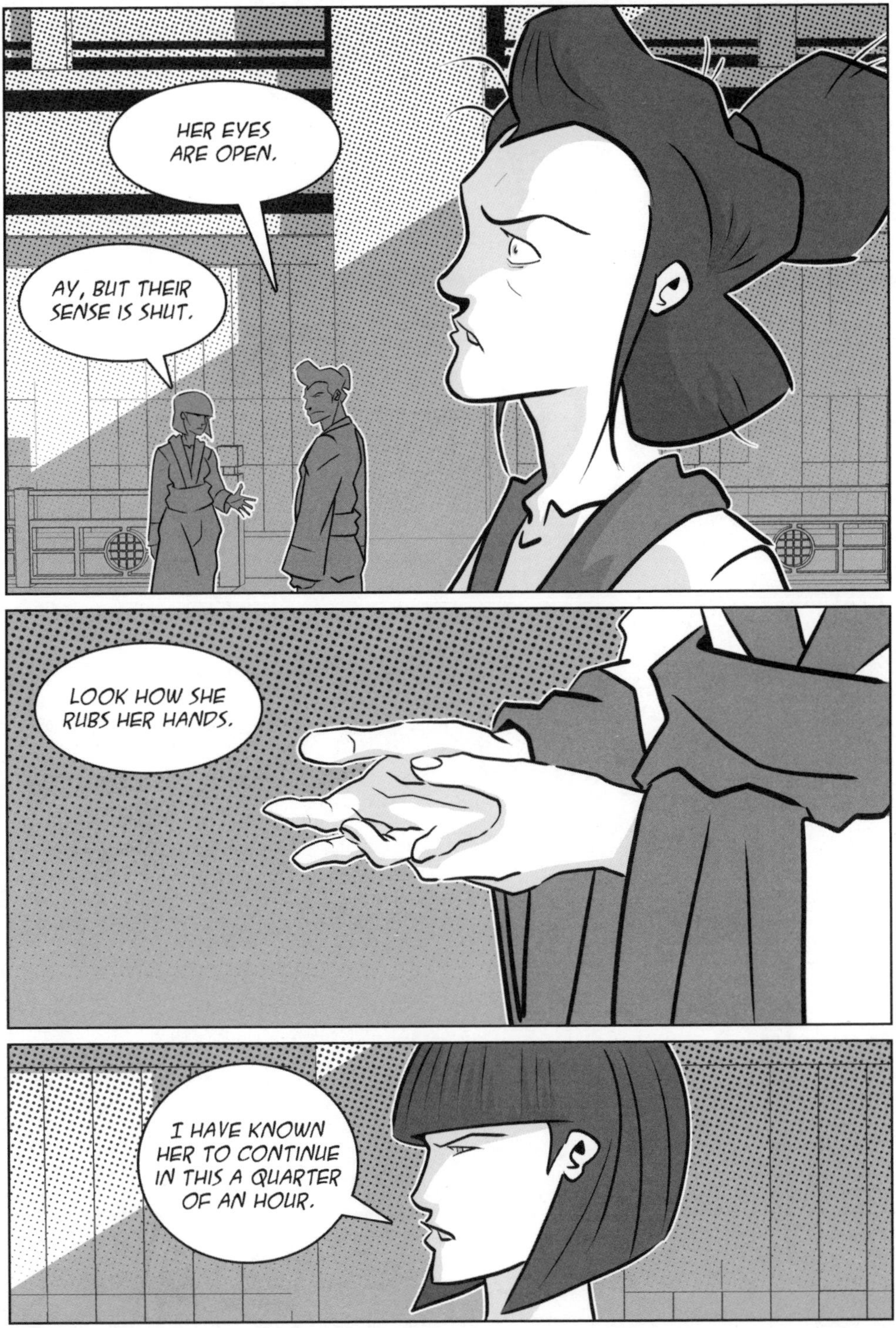
HER EYES ARE OPEN.
AY, BUT THEIR SENSE IS SHUT.
LOOK HOW SHE RUBS HER HANDS.
I HAVE KNOWN HER TO CONTINUE IN THIS A QUARTER OF AN HOUR.

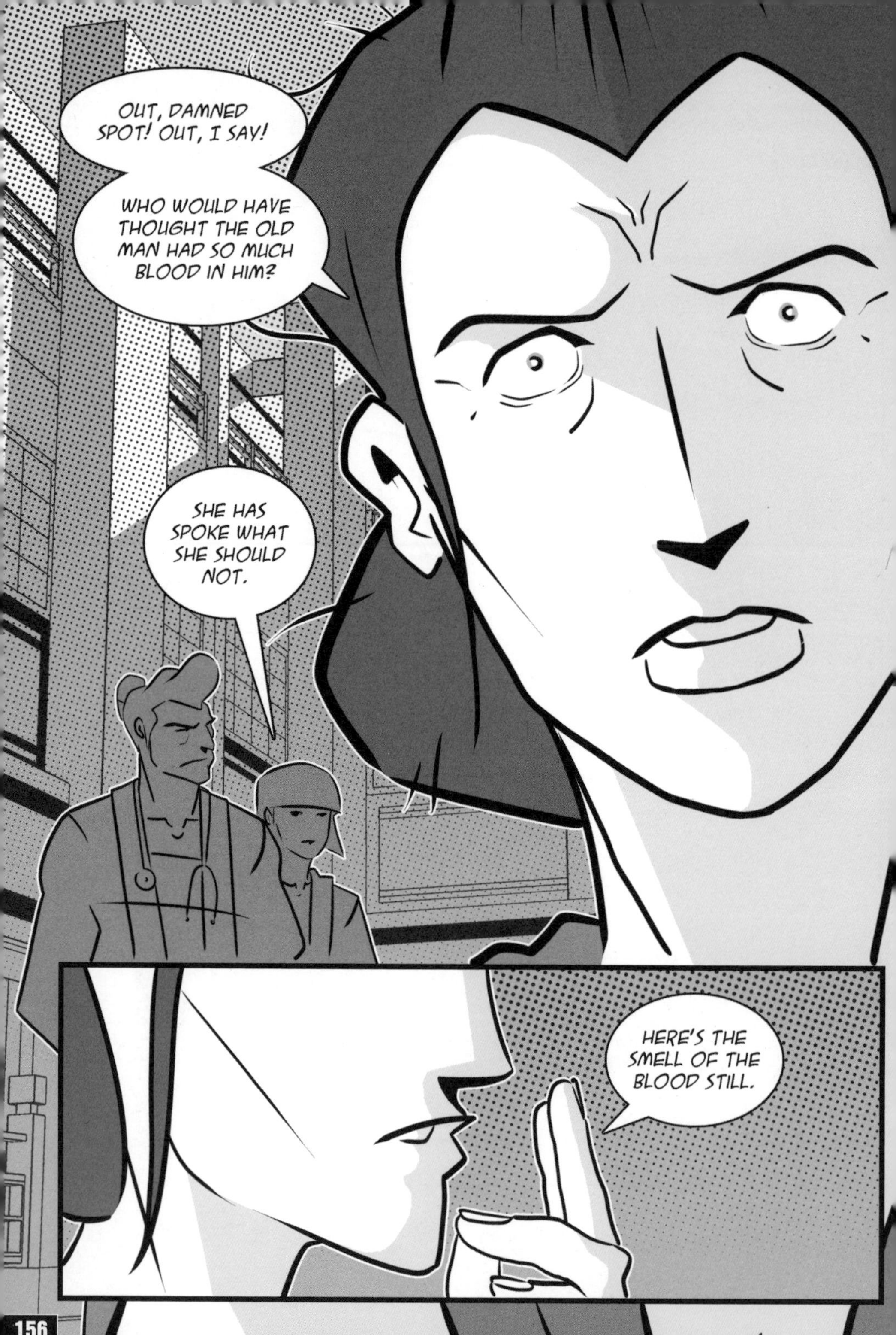
OUT, DAMNED SPOT! OUT, I SAY!
WHO WOULD HAVE THOUGHT THE OLD MAN HAD SO MUCH BLOOD IN HIM?
SHE HAS SPOKE WHAT SHE SHOULD NOT.
HERE'S THE SMELL OF THE BLOOD STILL.

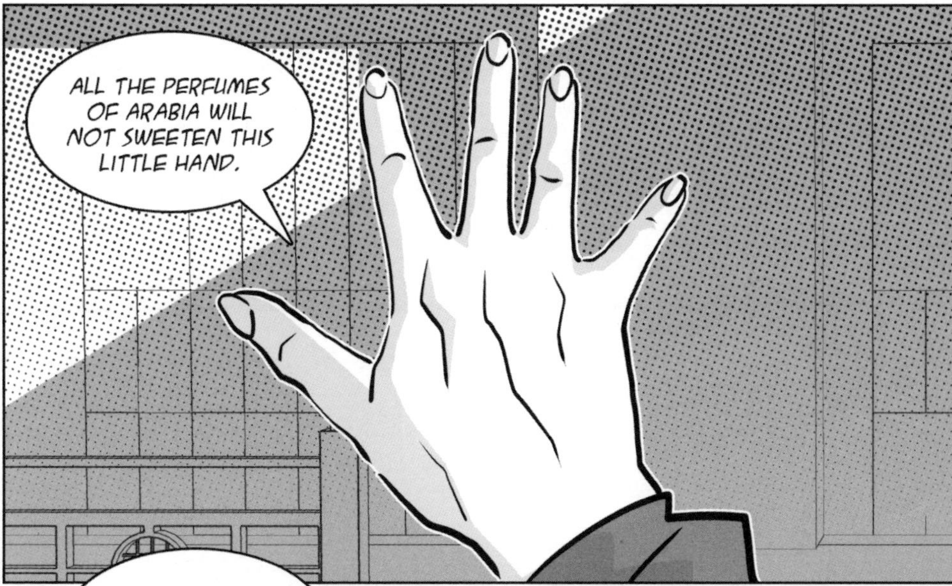
ALL THE PERFUMES OF ARABIA WILL NOT SWEETEN THIS LITTLE HAND.

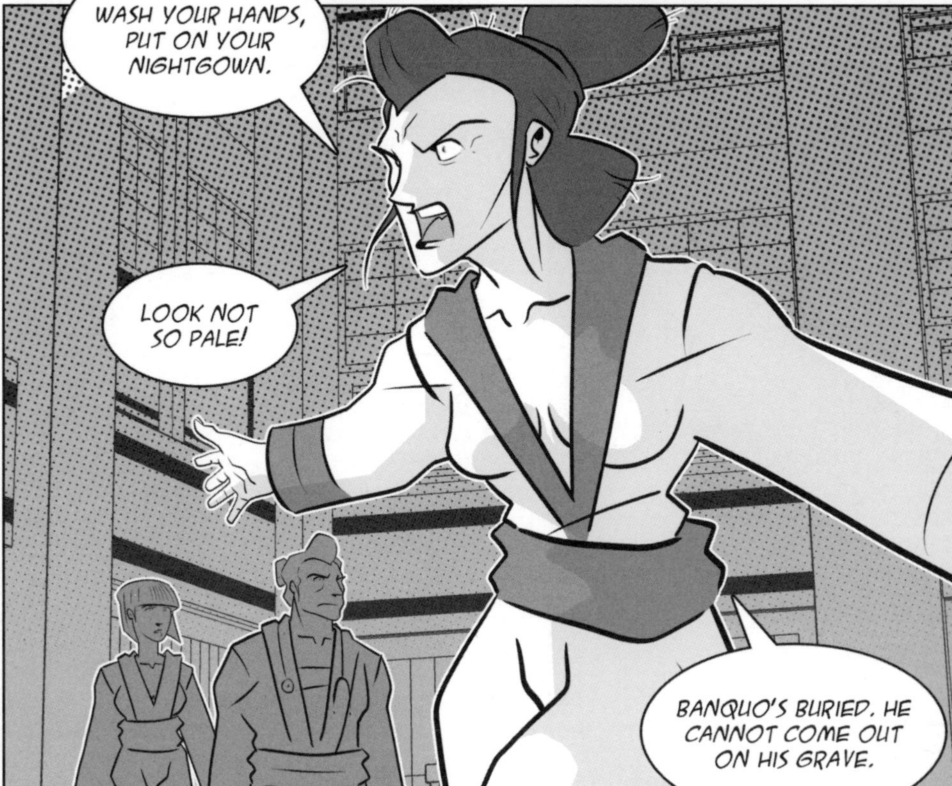
WASH YOUR HANDS, PUT ON YOUR NIGHTGOWN.
LOOK NOT SO PALE!
BANQUO'S BURIED. HE CANNOT COME OUT ON HIS GRAVE.

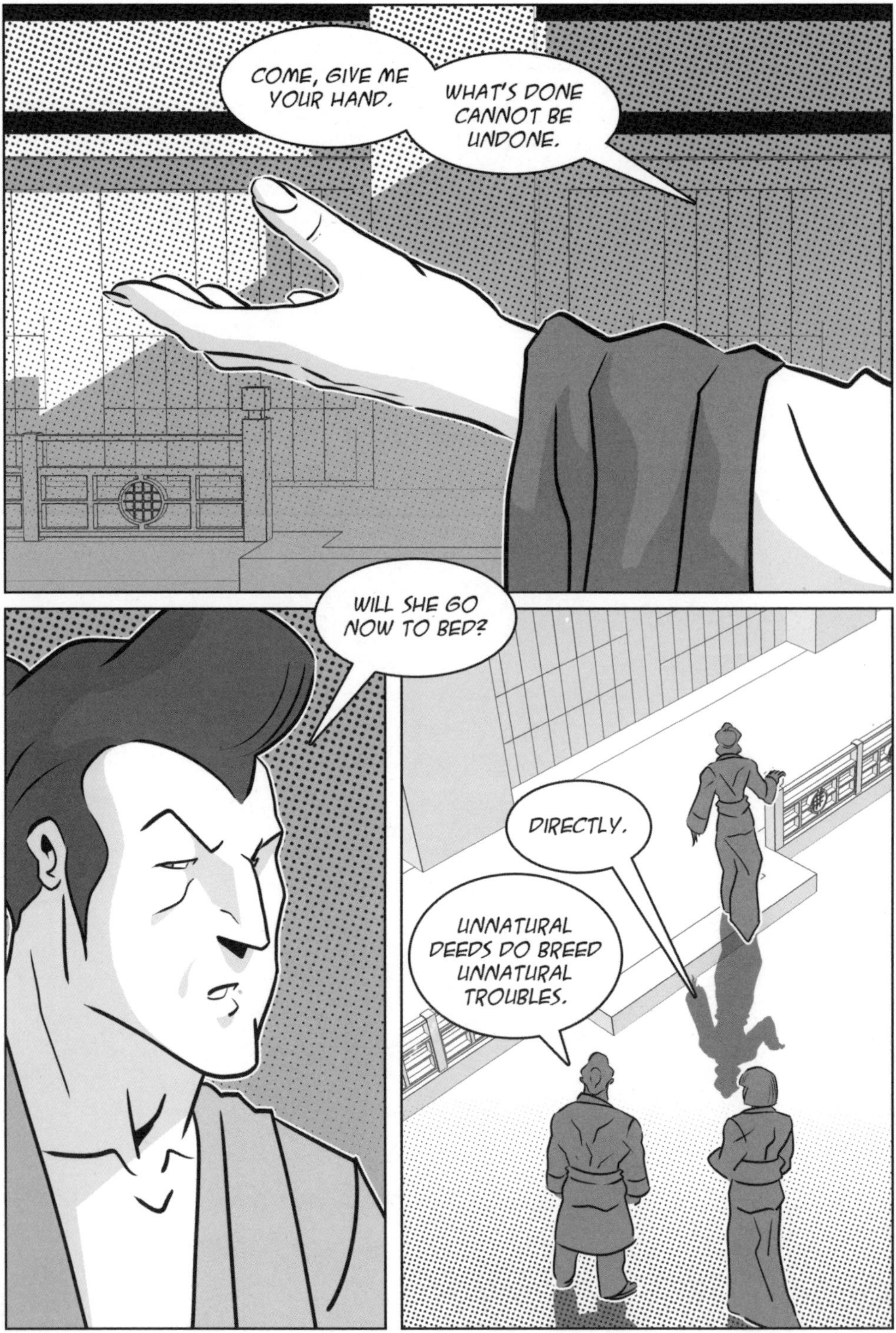
COME, GIVE ME YOUR HAND.
WHAT'S DONE CANNOT BE UNDONE.
WILL SHE GO NOW TO BED?
DIRECTLY.
UNNATURAL DEEDS DO BREED UNNATURAL TROUBLES.

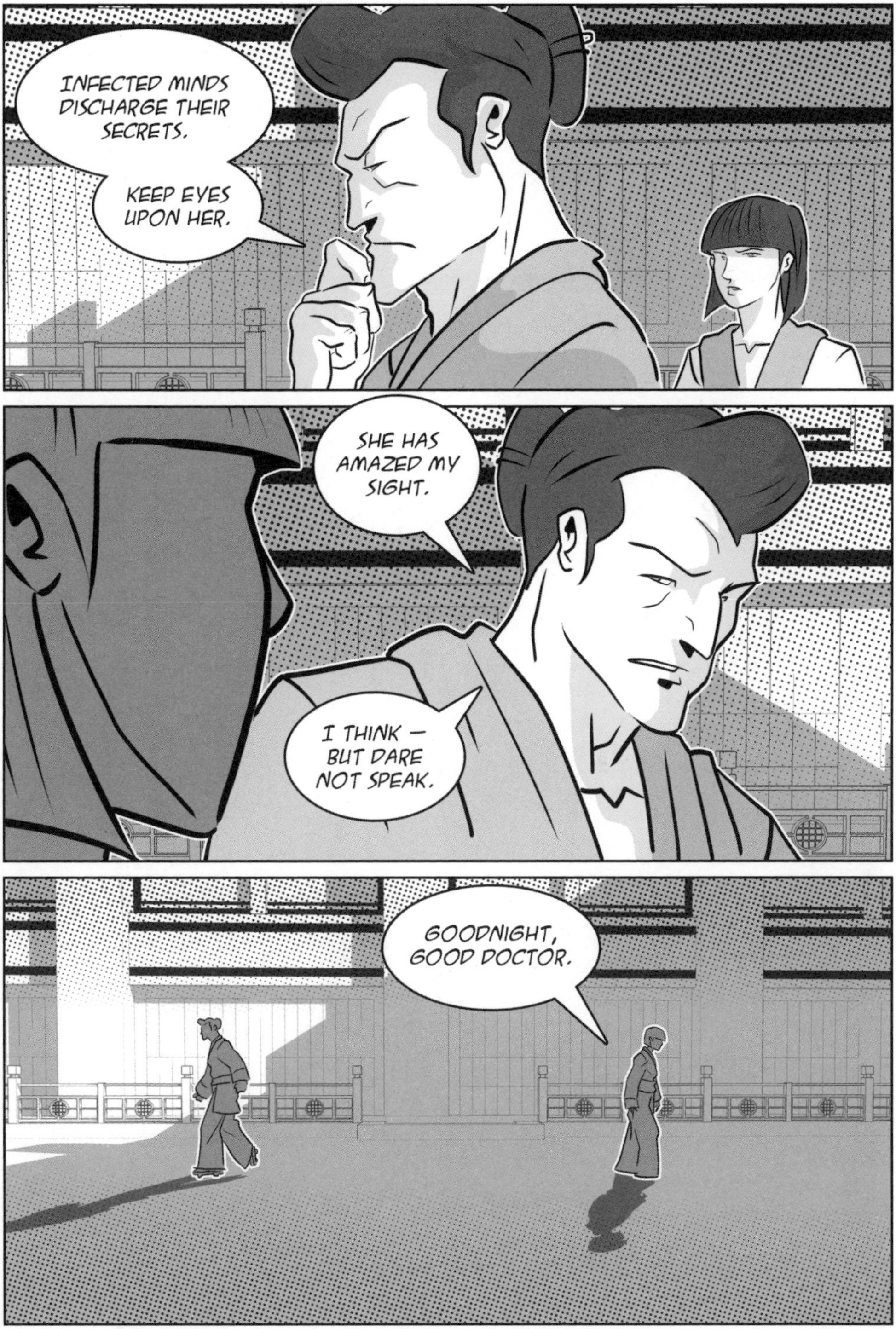
INFECTED MINDS DISCHARGE THEIR SECRETS.
KEEP EYES UPON HER.
SHE HAS AMAZED MY SIGHT.
I THINK — BUT DARE NOT SPEAK.
GOODNIGHT, GOOD DOCTOR.

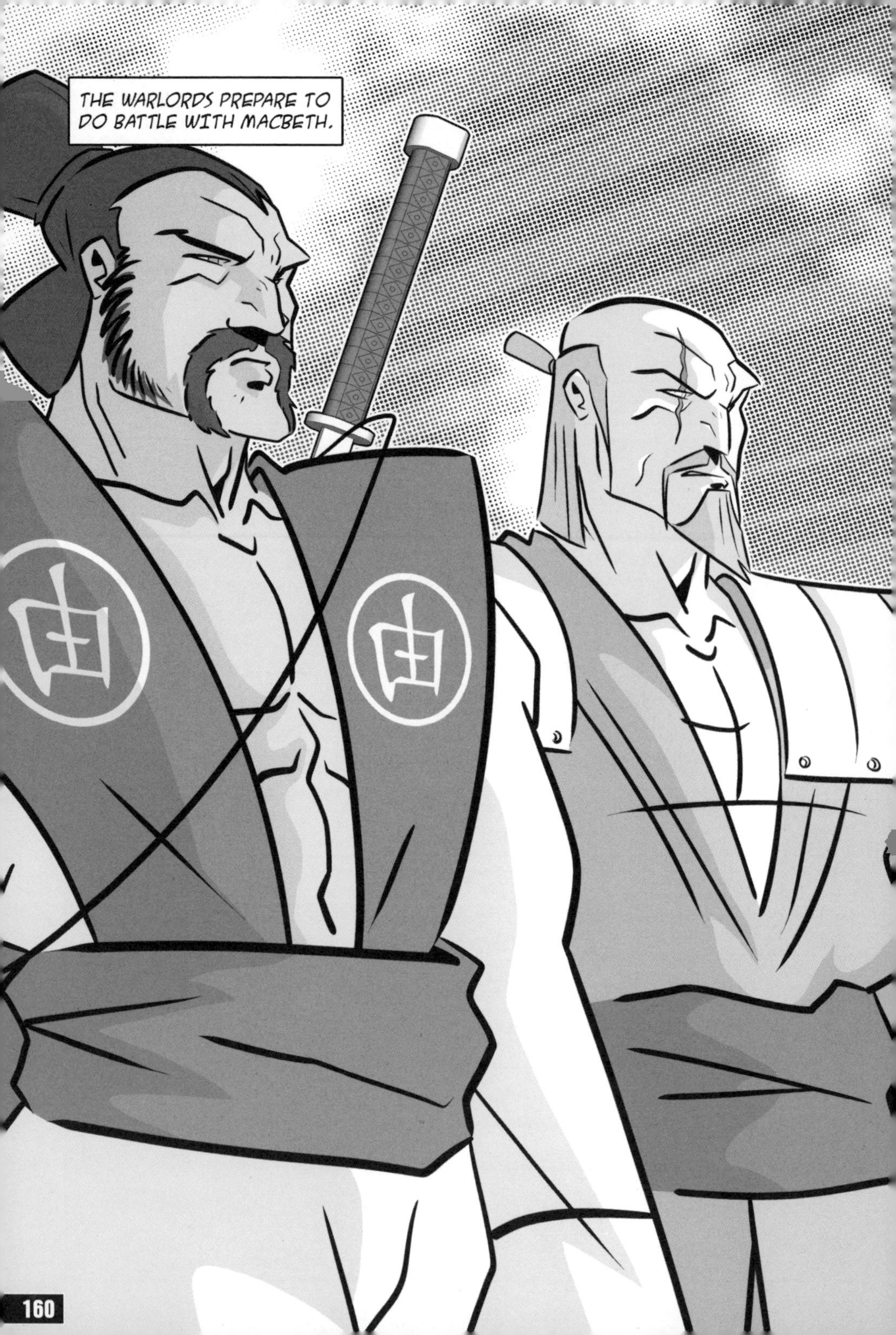
THE WARLORDS PREPARE TO DO BATTLE WITH MACBETH.

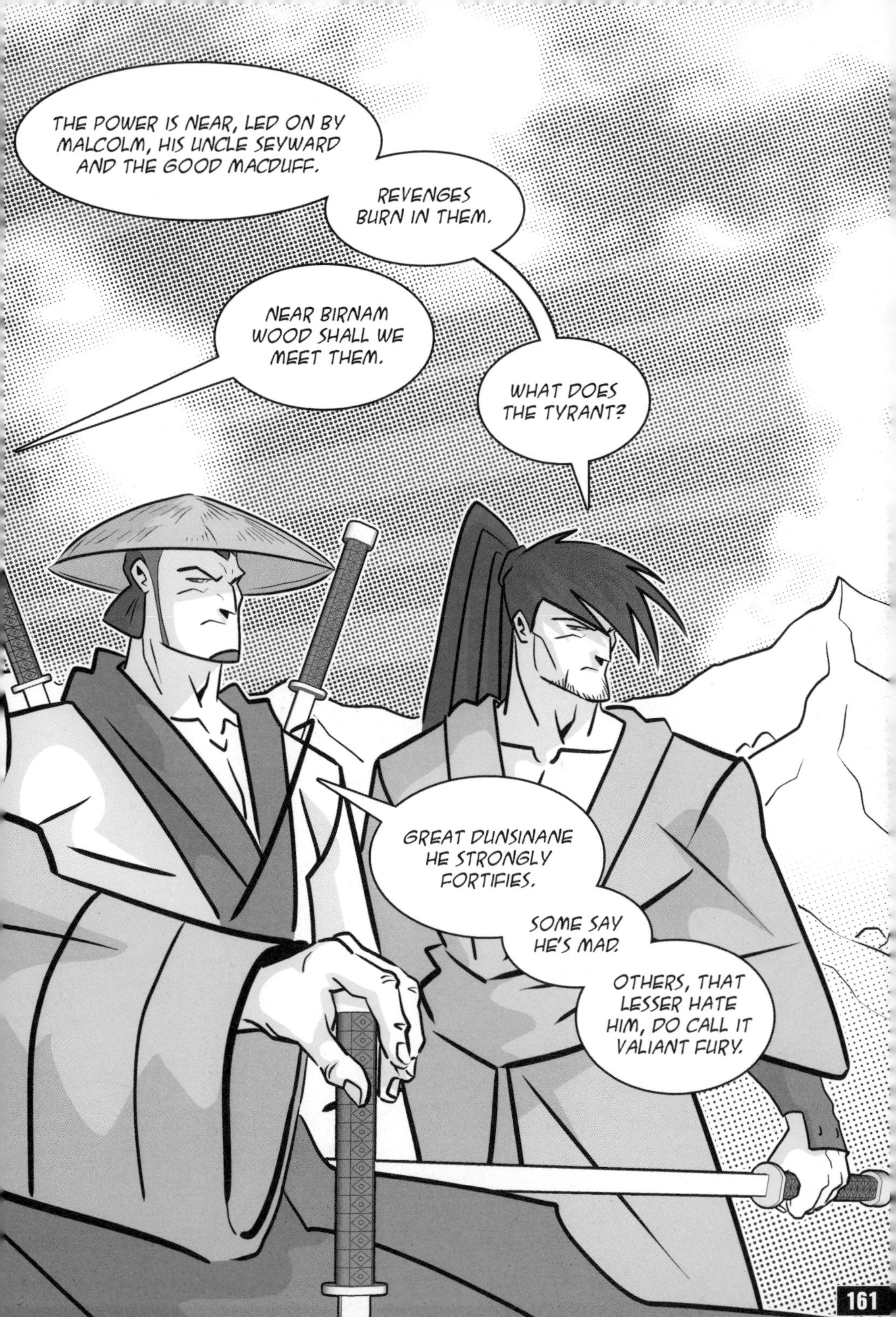
THE POWER IS NEAR, LED ON BY MALCOLM, HIS UNCLE SEYWARD AND THE GOOD MACDUFF.
REVENGES BURN IN THEM.
NEAR BIRNAM WOOD SHALL WE MEET THEM.
WHAT DOES THE TYRANT?
GREAT DUNSINANE HE STRONGLY FORTIFIES.
SOME SAY HE'S MAD.
OTHERS, THAT LESSER HATE HIM, DO CALL IT VALIANT FURY.

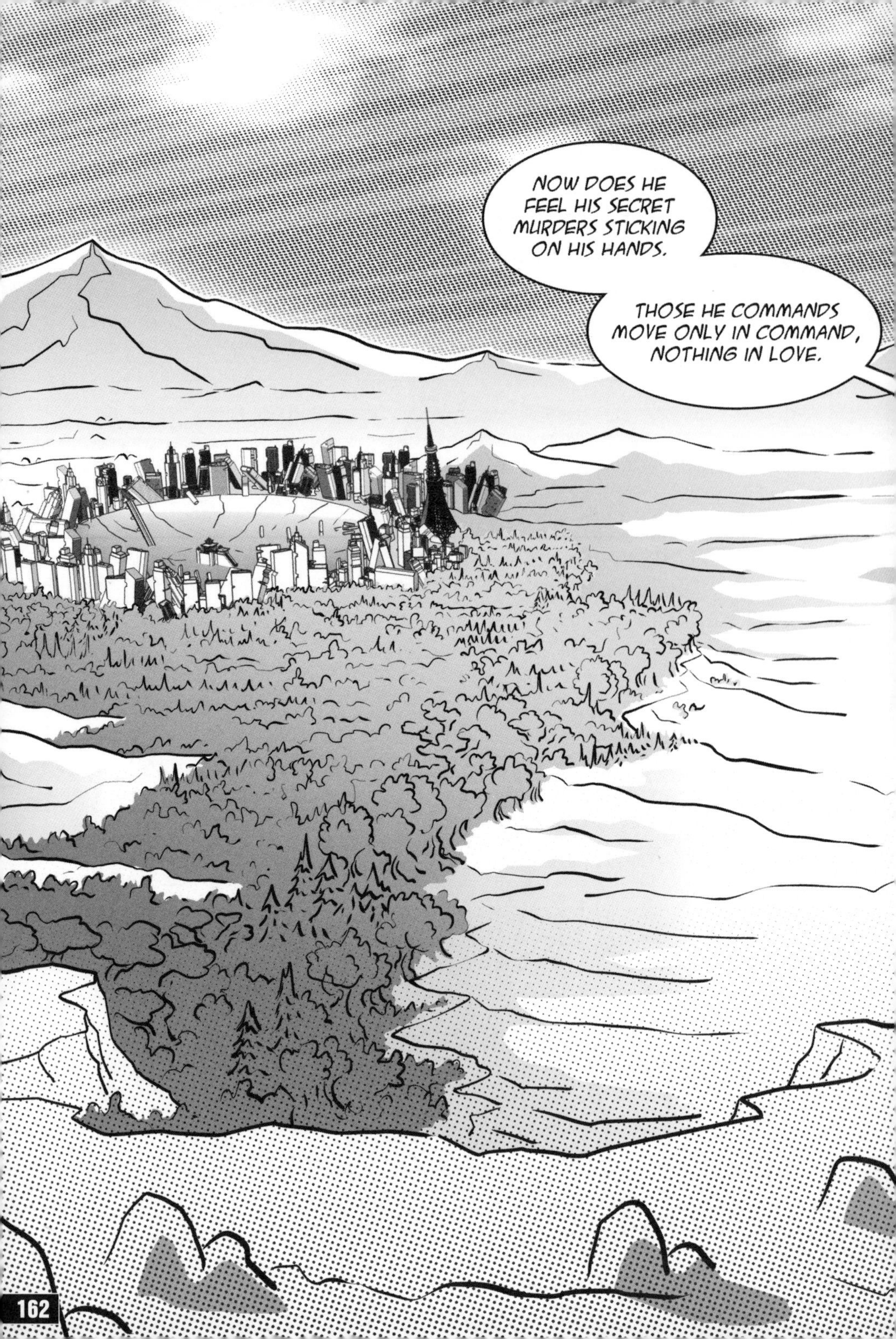
NOW DOES HE FEEL HIS SECRET MURDERS STICKING ON HIS HANDS.
THOSE HE COMMANDS MOVE ONLY IN COMMAND, NOTHING IN LOVE.

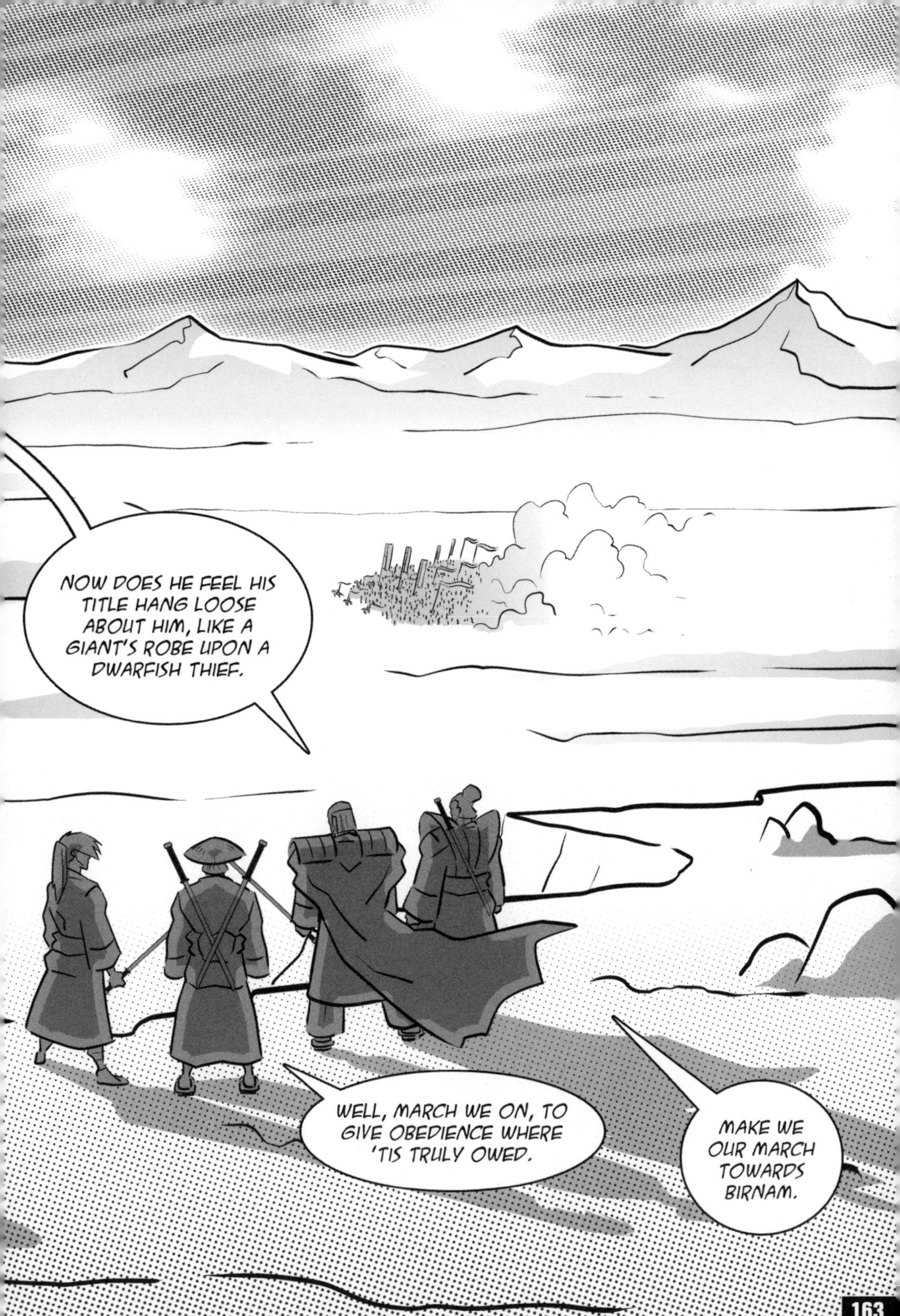
NOW DOES HE FEEL HIS TITLE HANG LOOSE ABOUT HIM, LIKE A GIANT'S ROBE UPON A DWARFISH THIEF.
WELL, MARCH WE ON, TO GIVE OBEDIENCE WHERE 'TIS TRULY OWED.
MAKE WE OUR MARCH TOWARDS BIRNAM.

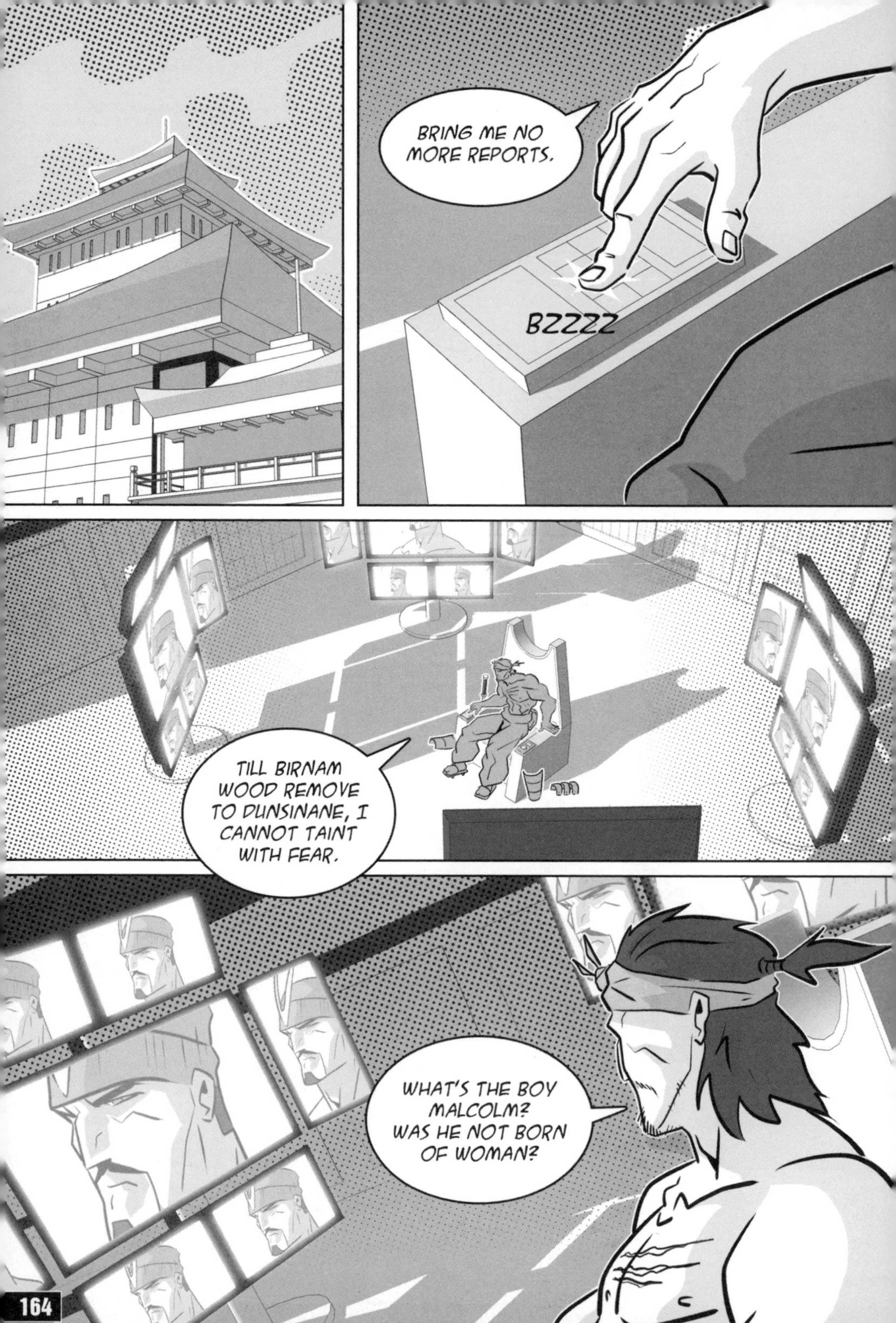
BRING ME NO MORE REPORTS.
BZZZZ
TILL BIRNAM WOOD REMOVE TO DUNSINANE, I CANNOT TAINT WITH FEAR.
WHAT'S THE BOY MALCOLM? WAS HE NOT BORN OF WOMAN?

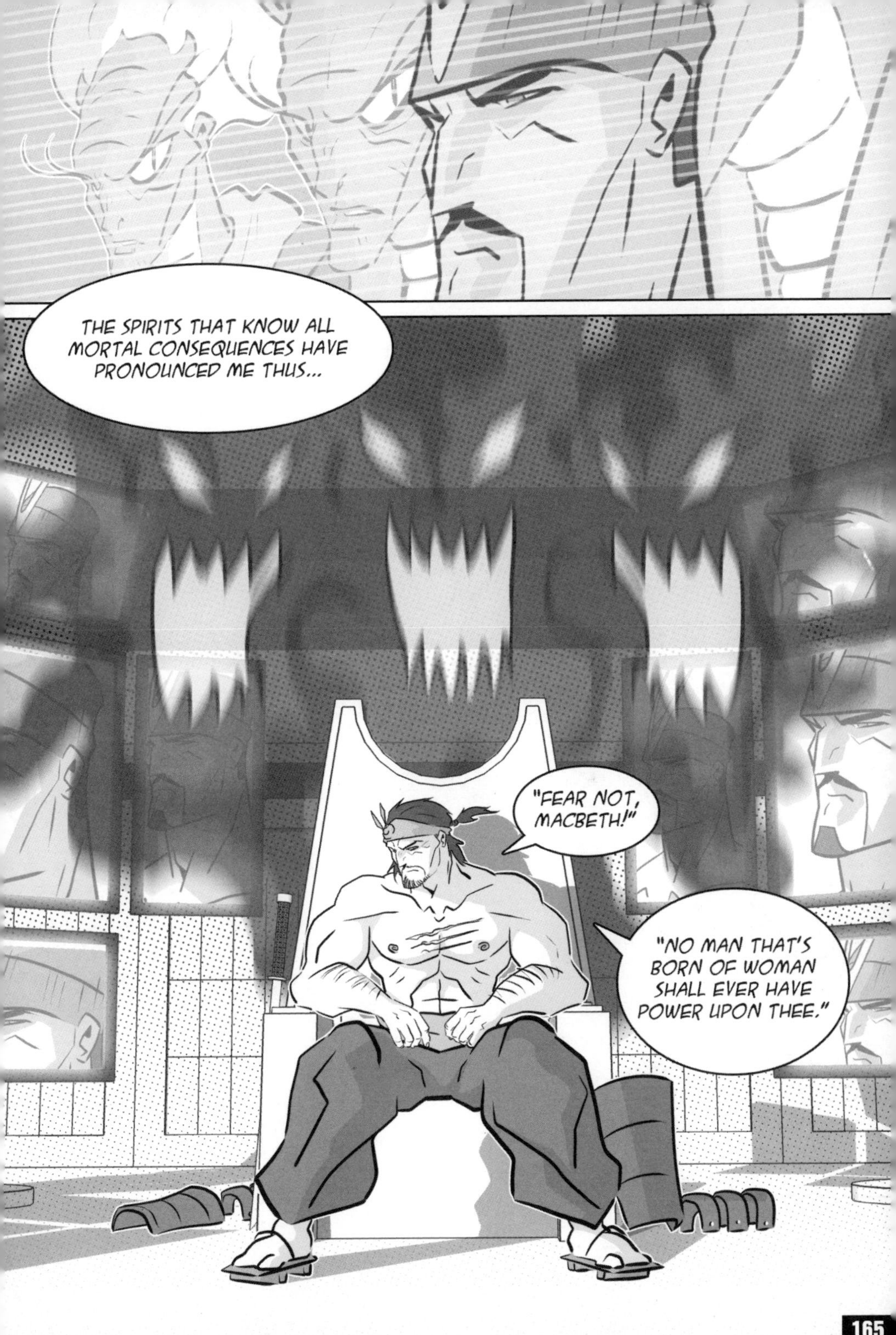
THE SPIRITS THAT KNOW ALL MORTAL CONSEQUENCES HAVE PRONOUNCED ME THUS...
"FEAR NOT, MACBETH!"
"NO MAN THAT'S BORN OF WOMAN SHALL EVER HAVE POWER UPON THEE."

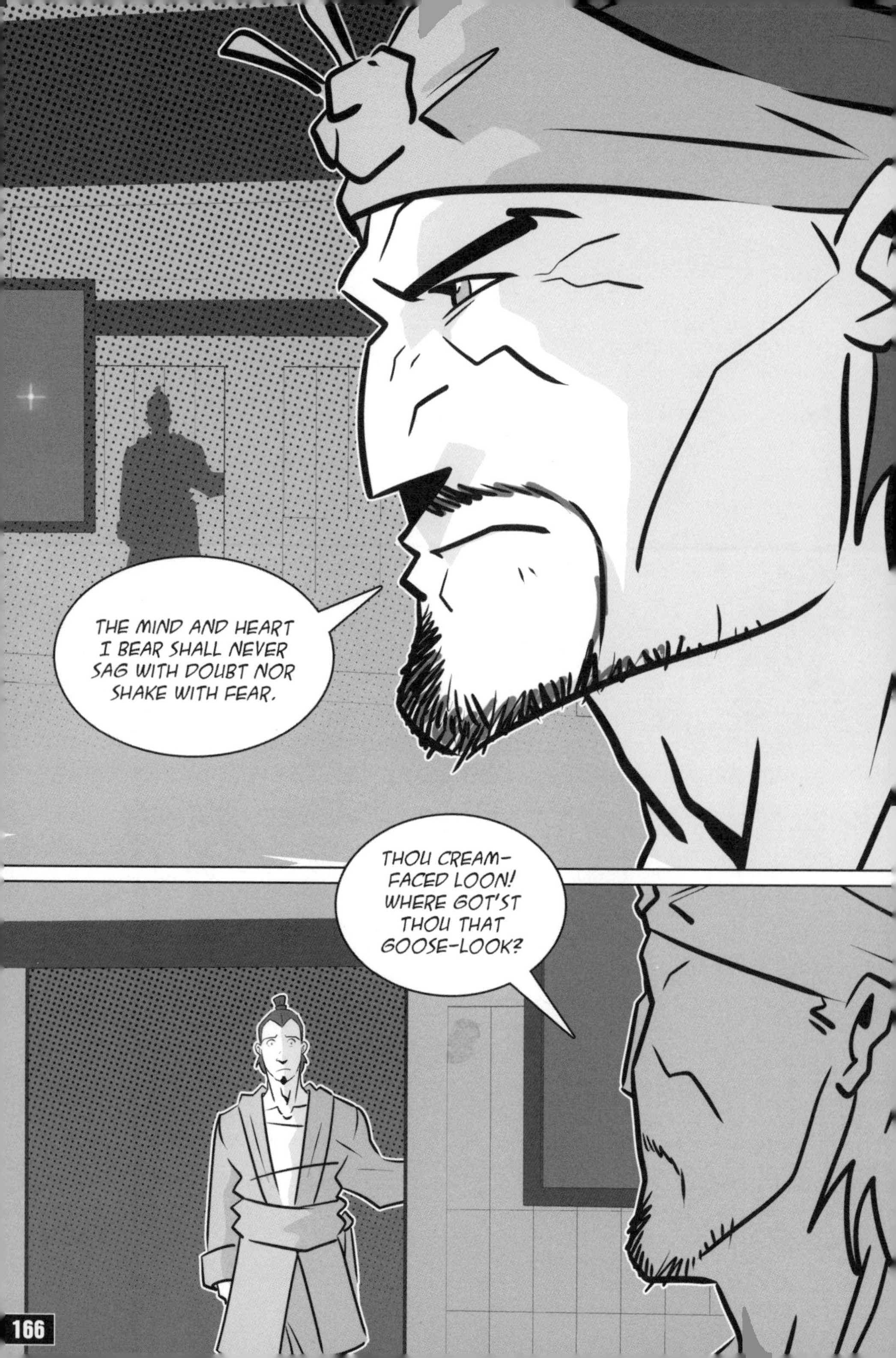
THE MIND AND HEART I BEAR SHALL NEVER SAG WITH DOUBT NOR SHAKE WITH FEAR.
THOU CREAM-FACED LOON! WHERE GOT'ST THOU THAT GOOSE-LOOK?

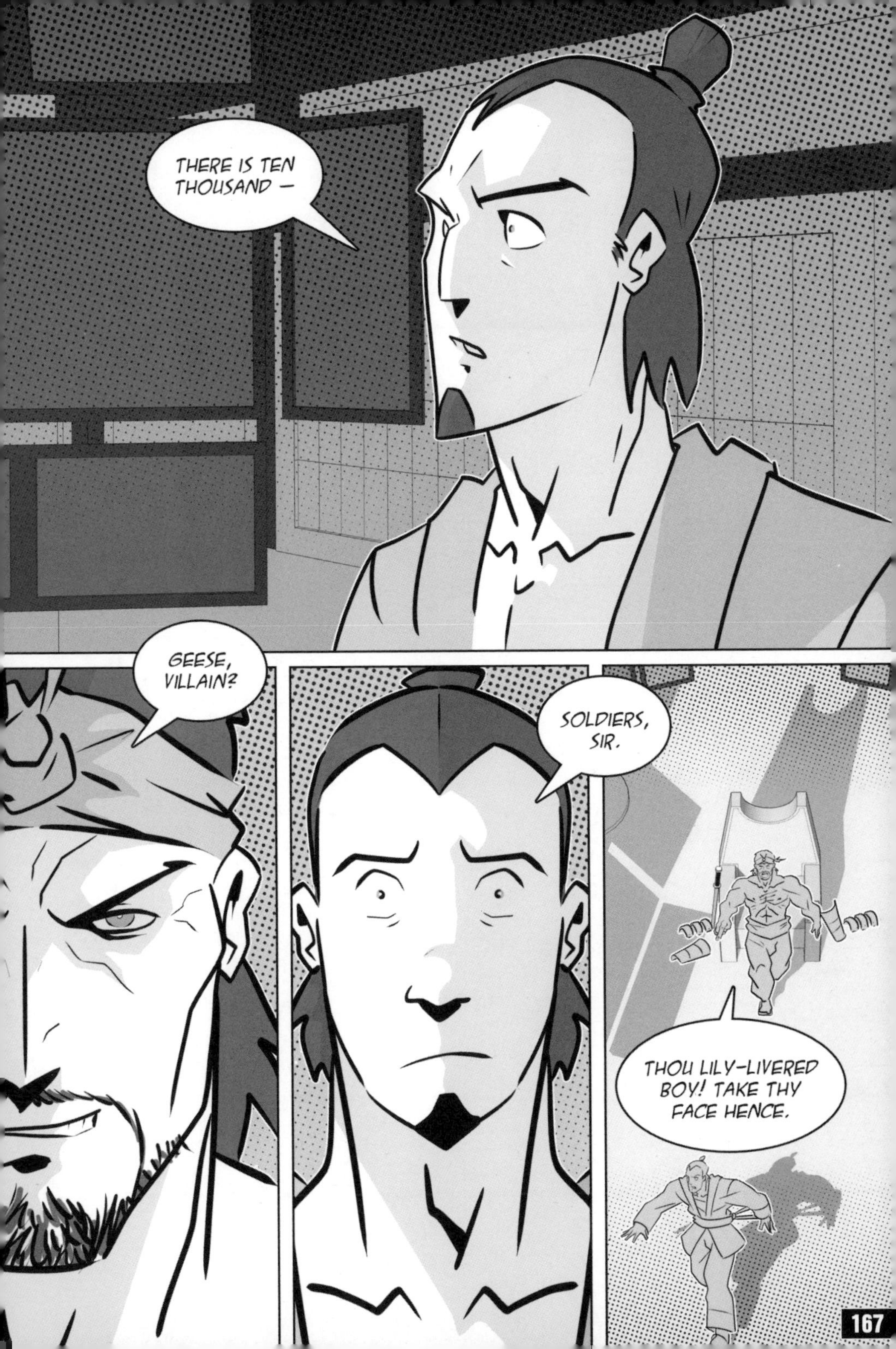

THERE IS TEN THOUSAND —
GEESE, VILLAIN?
SOLDIERS, SIR.
THOU LILY-LIVERED BOY! TAKE THY FACE HENCE.

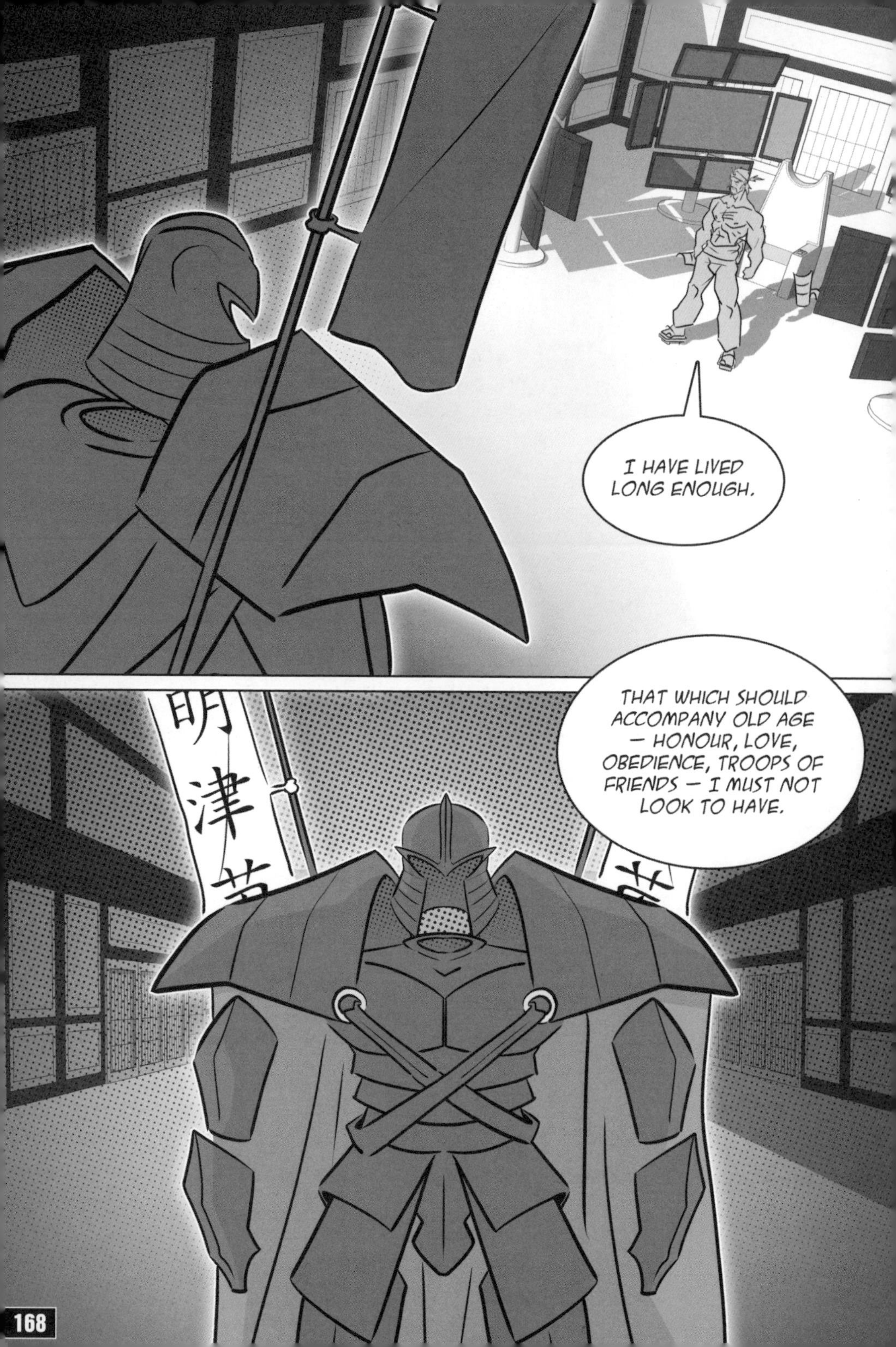
I HAVE LIVED LONG ENOUGH.
THAT WHICH SHOULD ACCOMPANY OLD AGE — HONOUR, LOVE, OBEDIENCE, TROOPS OF FRIENDS — I MUST NOT LOOK TO HAVE.
明津

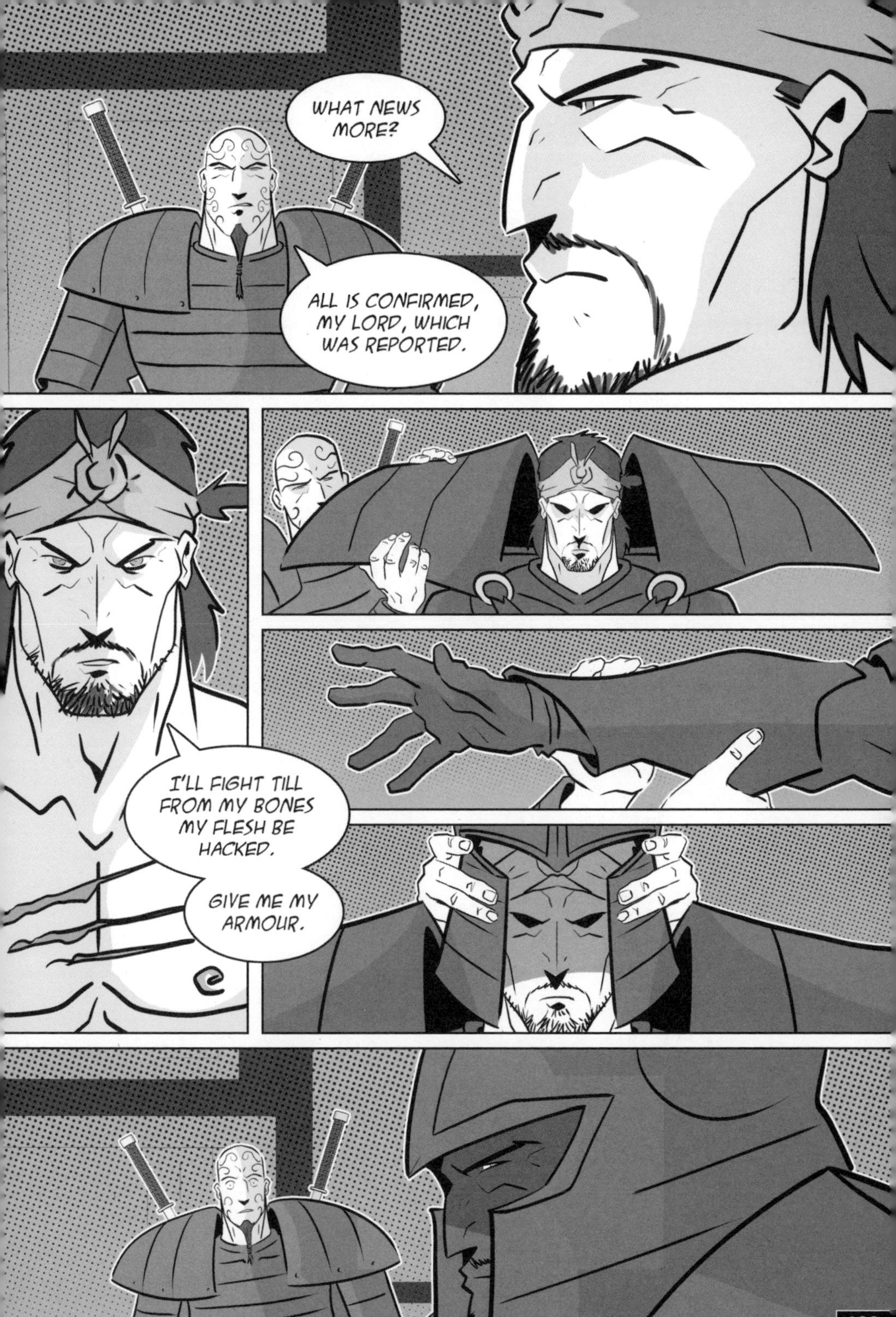
WHAT NEWS MORE?
ALL IS CONFIRMED, MY LORD, WHICH WAS REPORTED.
I'LL FIGHT TILL FROM MY BONES MY FLESH BE HACKED.
GIVE ME MY ARMOUR.

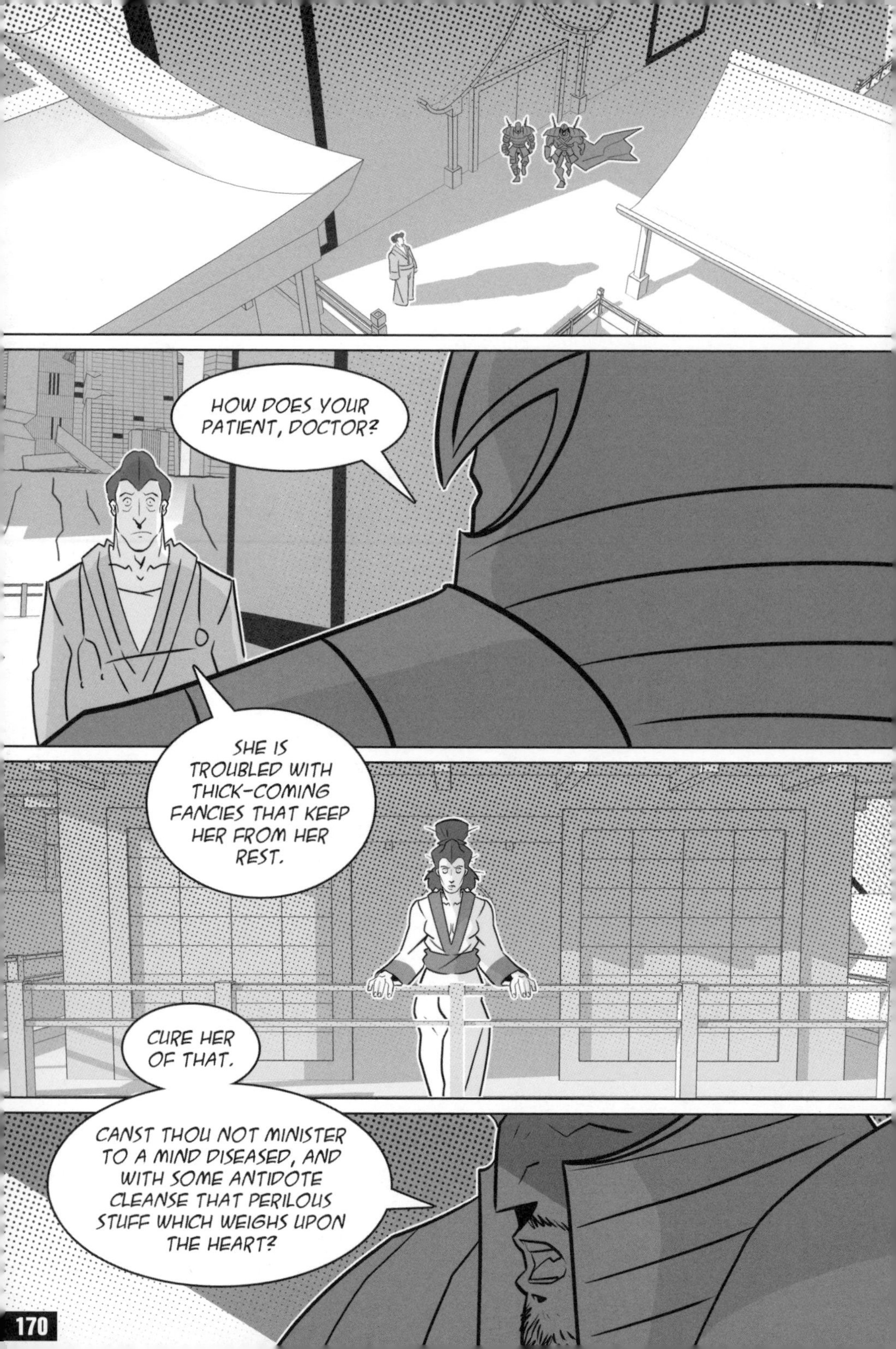
HOW DOES YOUR PATIENT, DOCTOR?
SHE IS TROUBLED WITH THICK-COMING FANCIES THAT KEEP HER FROM HER REST.
CURE HER OF THAT.
CANST THOU NOT MINISTER TO A MIND DISEASED, AND WITH SOME ANTIDOTE CLEANSE THAT PERILOUS STUFF WHICH WEIGHS UPON THE HEART?

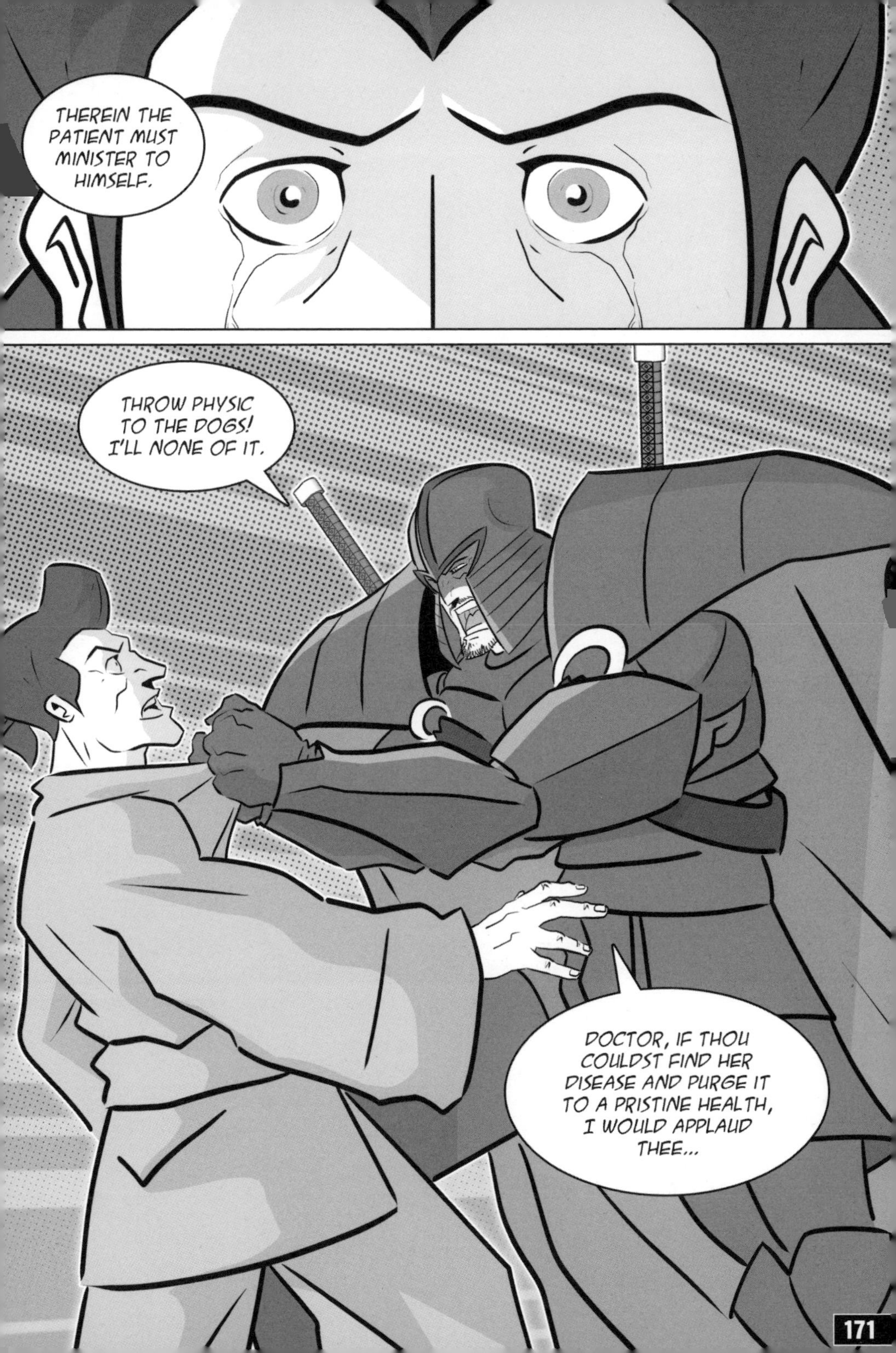
THEREIN THE PATIENT MUST MINISTER TO HIMSELF.
THROW PHYSIC TO THE DOGS! I'LL NONE OF IT.
DOCTOR, IF THOU COULDST FIND HER DISEASE AND PURGE IT TO A PRISTINE HEALTH, I WOULD APPLAUD THEE...

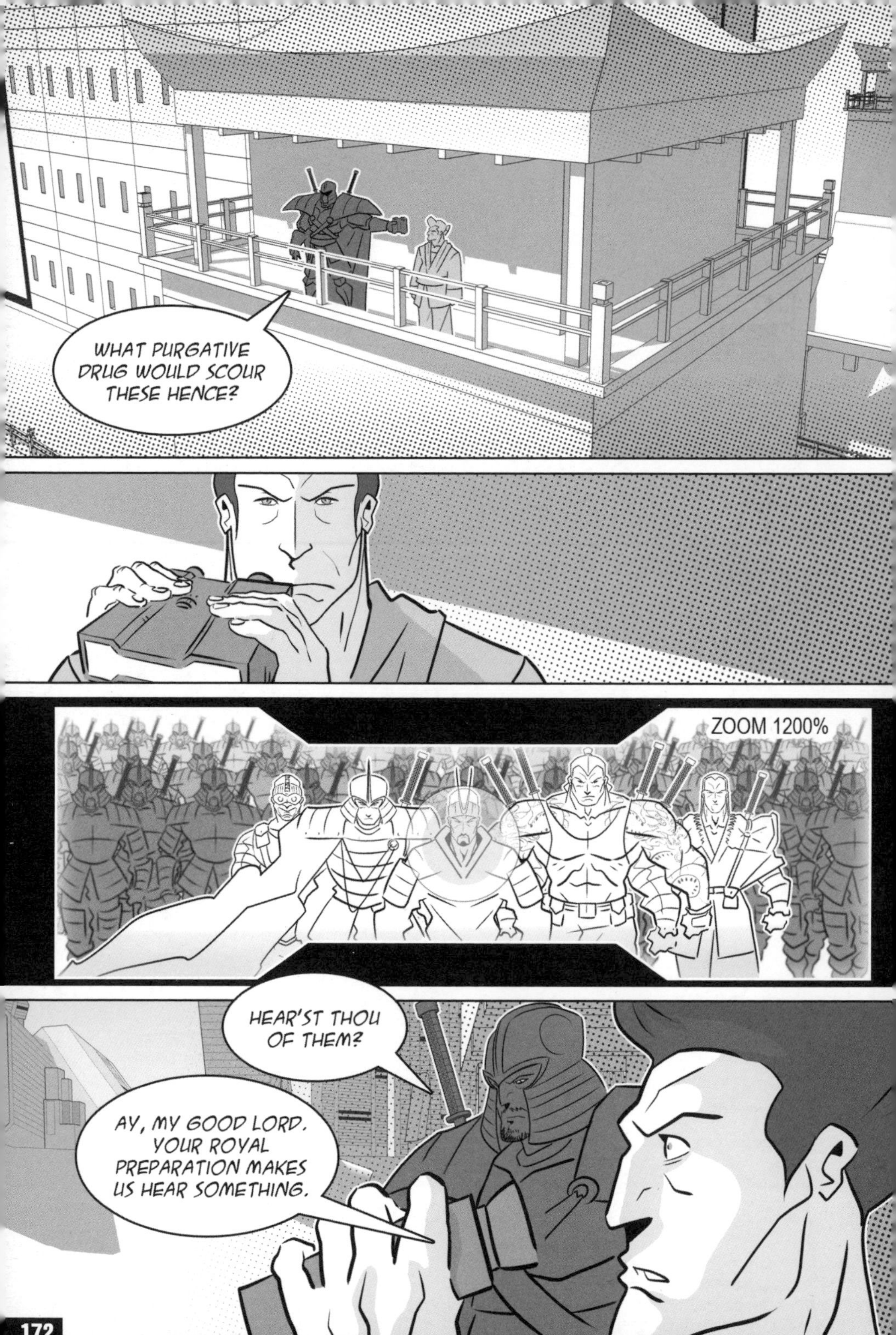
WHAT PURGATIVE DRUG WOULD SCOUR THESE HENCE?
ZOOM 1200%
HEAR'ST THOU OF THEM?
AY, MY GOOD LORD. YOUR ROYAL PREPARATION MAKES US HEAR SOMETHING.

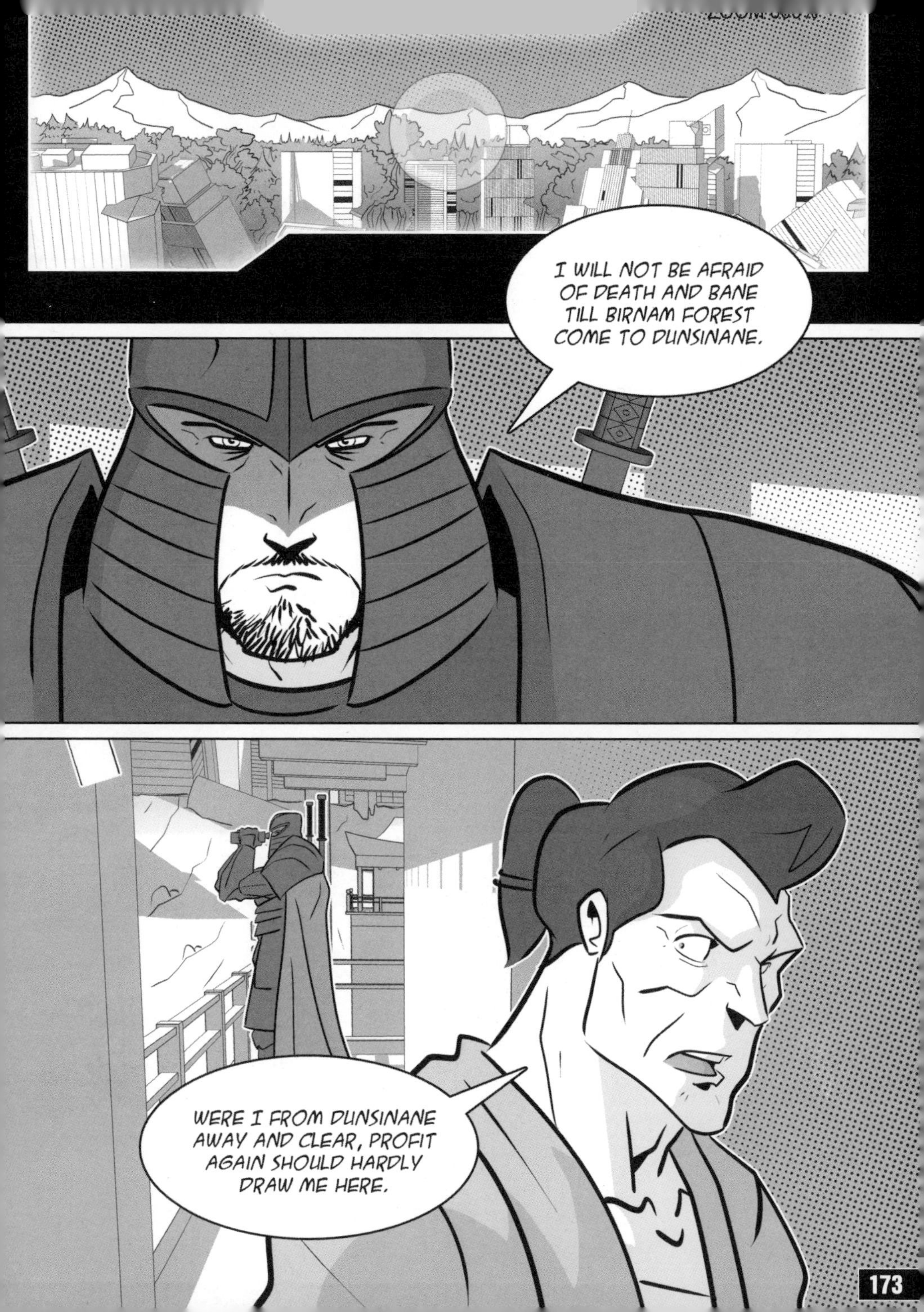
I WILL NOT BE AFRAID OF DEATH AND BANE TILL BIRNAM FOREST COME TO DUNSINANE.
WERE I FROM DUNSINANE AWAY AND CLEAR, PROFIT AGAIN SHOULD HARDLY DRAW ME HERE.

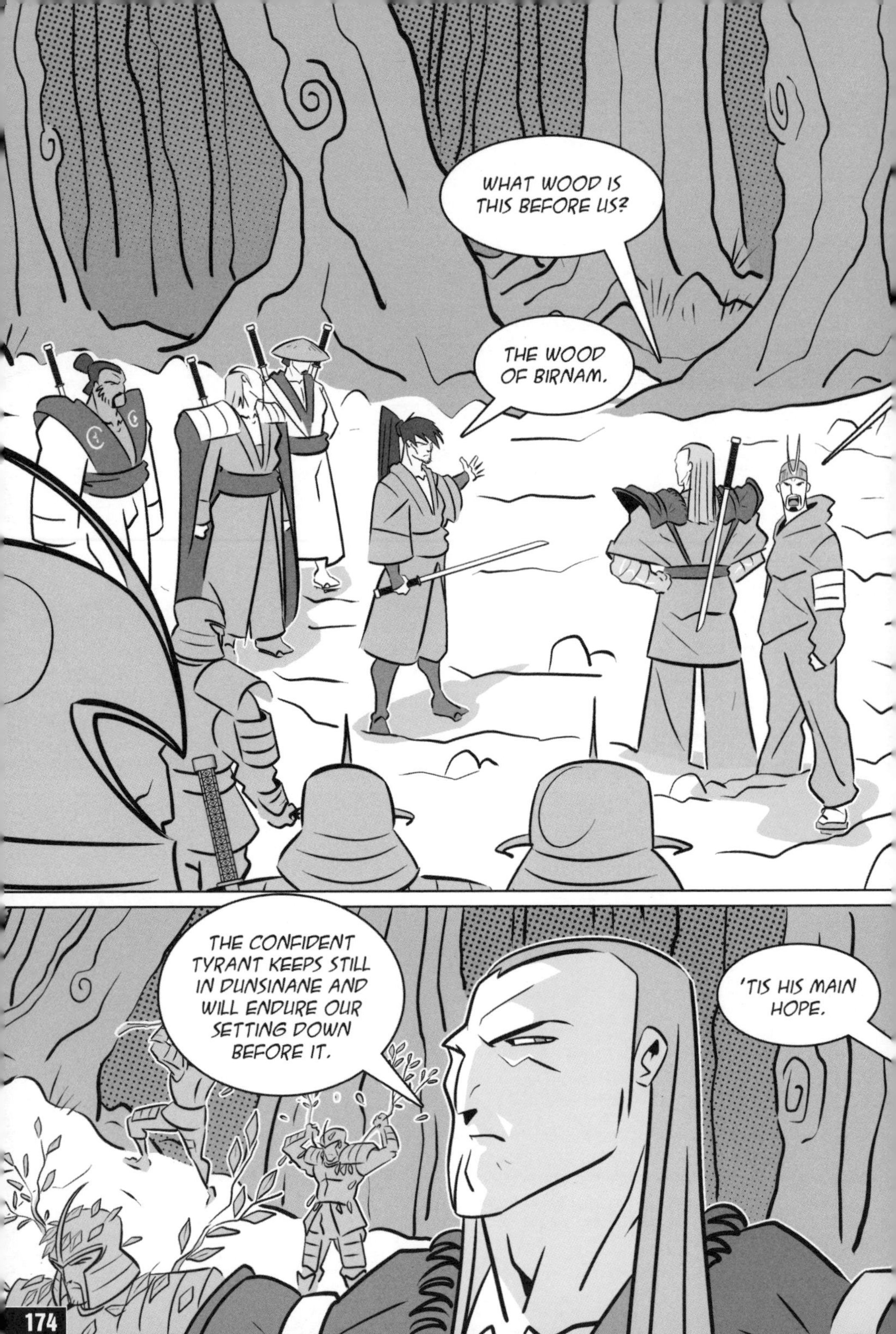
WHAT WOOD IS THIS BEFORE US?
THE WOOD OF BIRNAM.
THE CONFIDENT TYRANT KEEPS STILL IN DUNSINANE AND WILL ENDURE OUR SETTING DOWN BEFORE IT.
'TIS HIS MAIN HOPE.

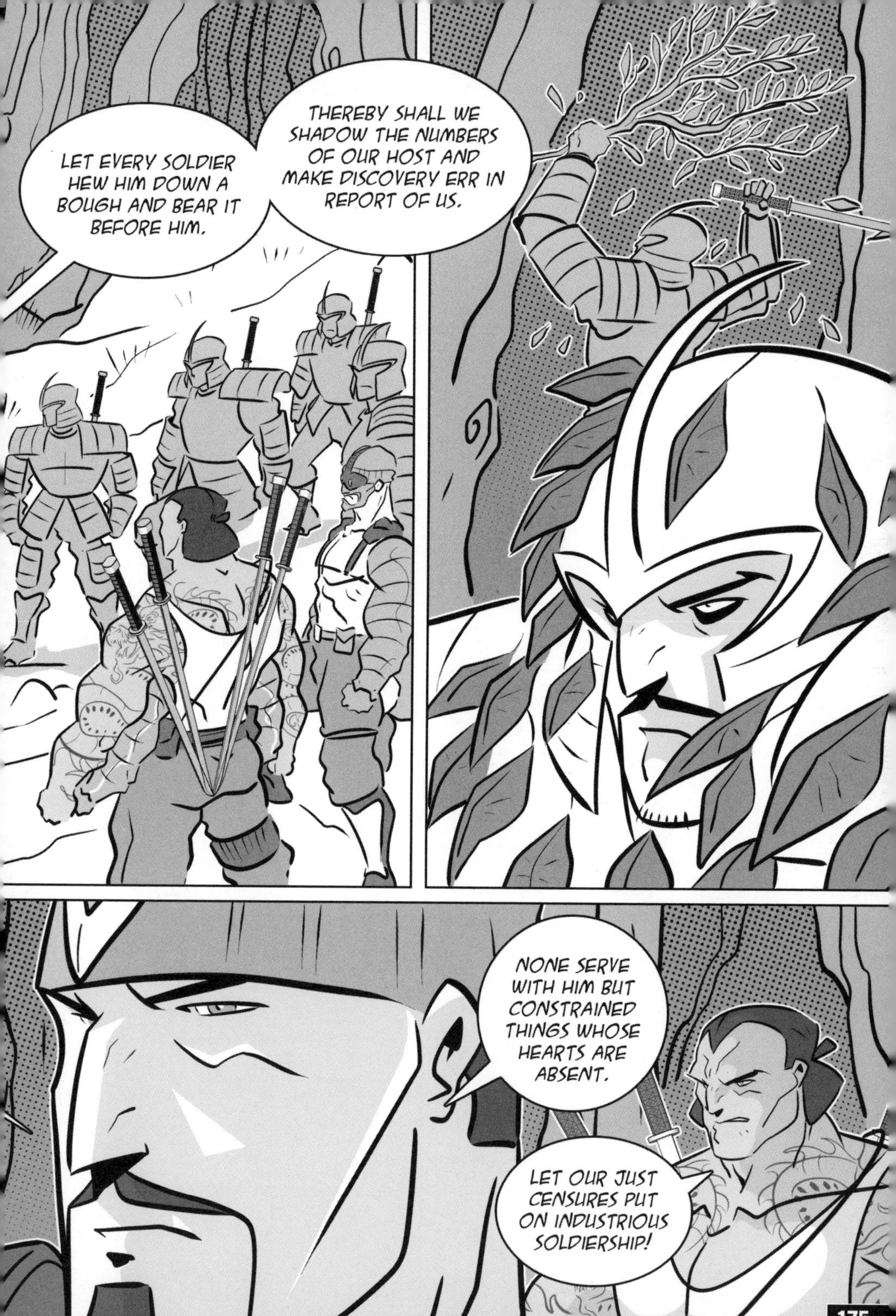
LET EVERY SOLDIER HEW HIM DOWN A BOUGH AND BEAR IT BEFORE HIM.
THEREBY SHALL WE SHADOW THE NUMBERS OF OUR HOST AND MAKE DISCOVERY ERR IN REPORT OF US.
NONE SERVE WITH HIM BUT CONSTRAINED THINGS WHOSE HEARTS ARE ABSENT.
LET OUR JUST CENSURES PUT ON INDUSTRIOUS SOLDIERSHIP!

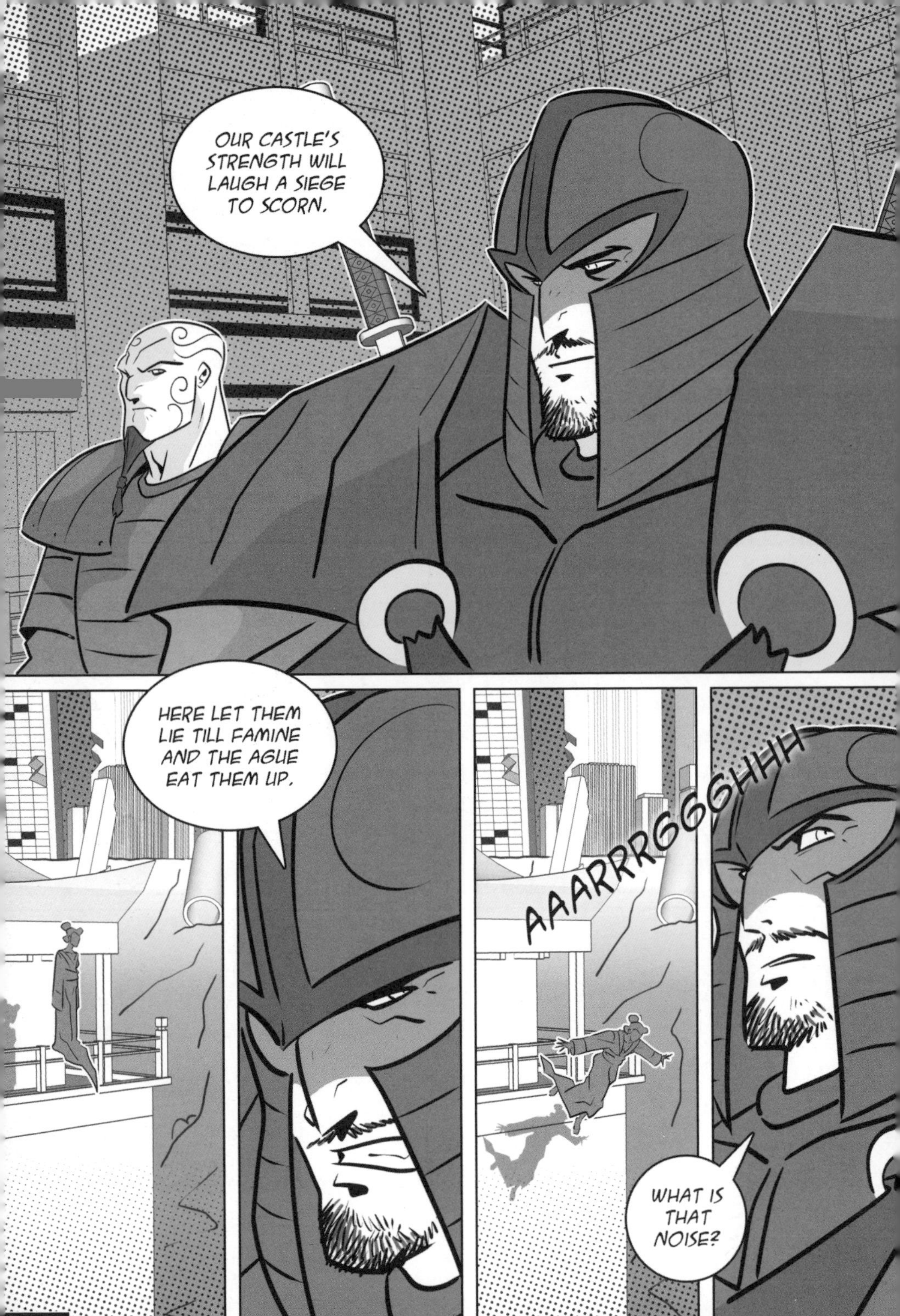

OUR CASTLE'S STRENGTH WILL LAUGH A SIEGE TO SCORN.
HERE LET THEM LIE TILL FAMINE AND THE AGUE EAT THEM UP.
AAARRRGGGHHH
WHAT IS THAT NOISE?

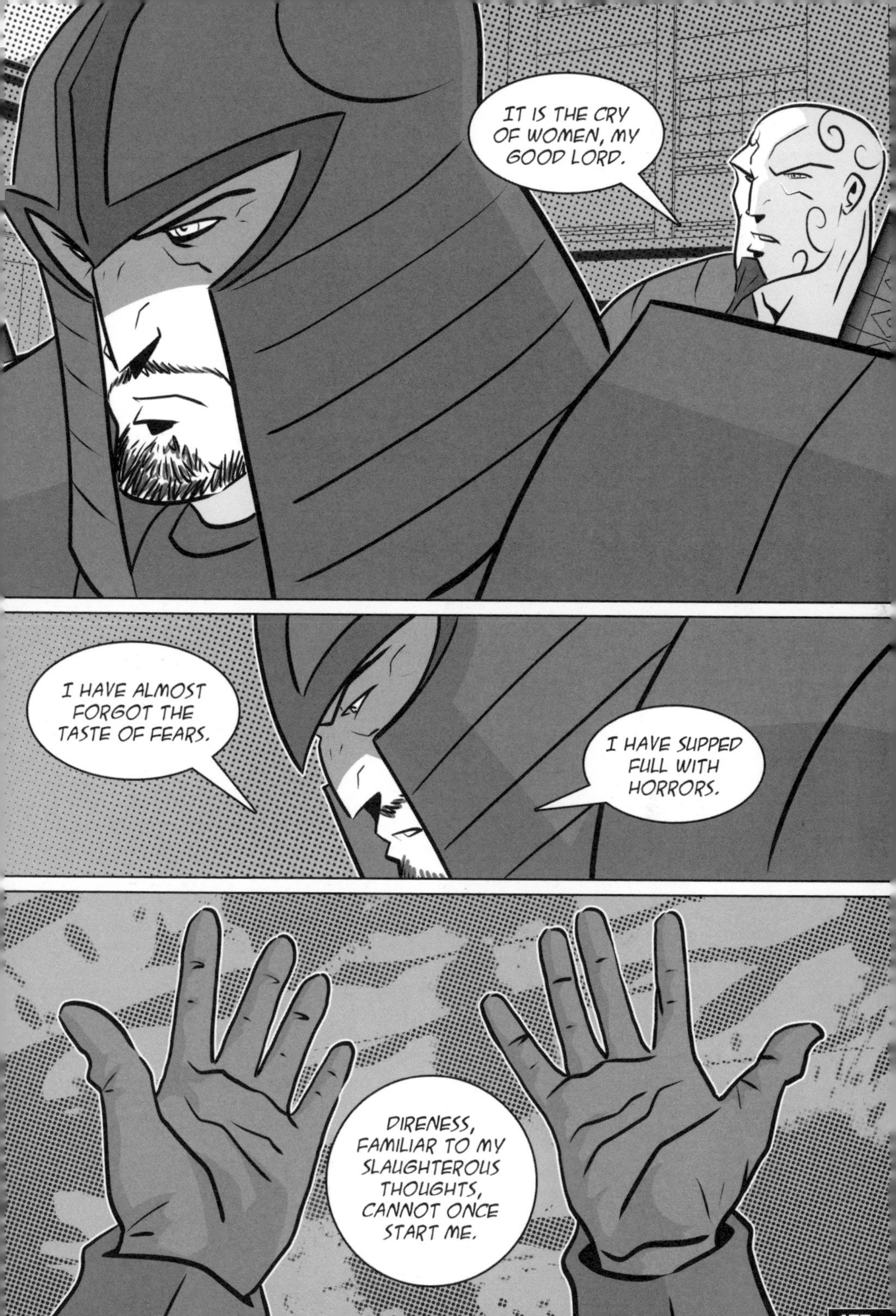
IT IS THE CRY OF WOMEN, MY GOOD LORD.
I HAVE ALMOST FORGOT THE TASTE OF FEARS.
I HAVE SUPPED FULL WITH HORRORS.
DIRENESS, FAMILIAR TO MY SLAUGHTEROUS THOUGHTS, CANNOT ONCE START ME.

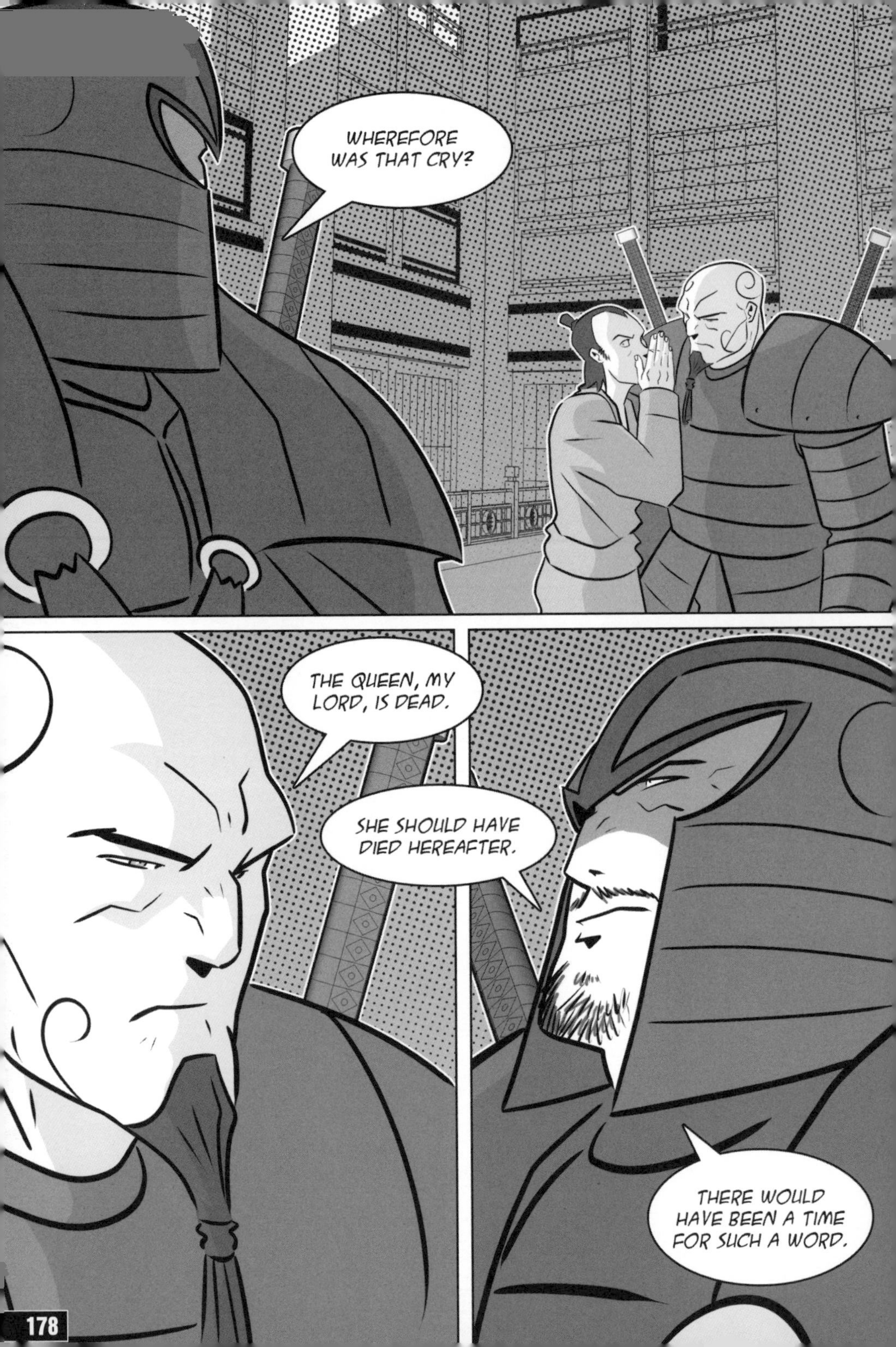
WHEREFORE WAS THAT CRY?
THE QUEEN, MY LORD, IS DEAD.
SHE SHOULD HAVE DIED HEREAFTER.
THERE WOULD HAVE BEEN A TIME FOR SUCH A WORD.

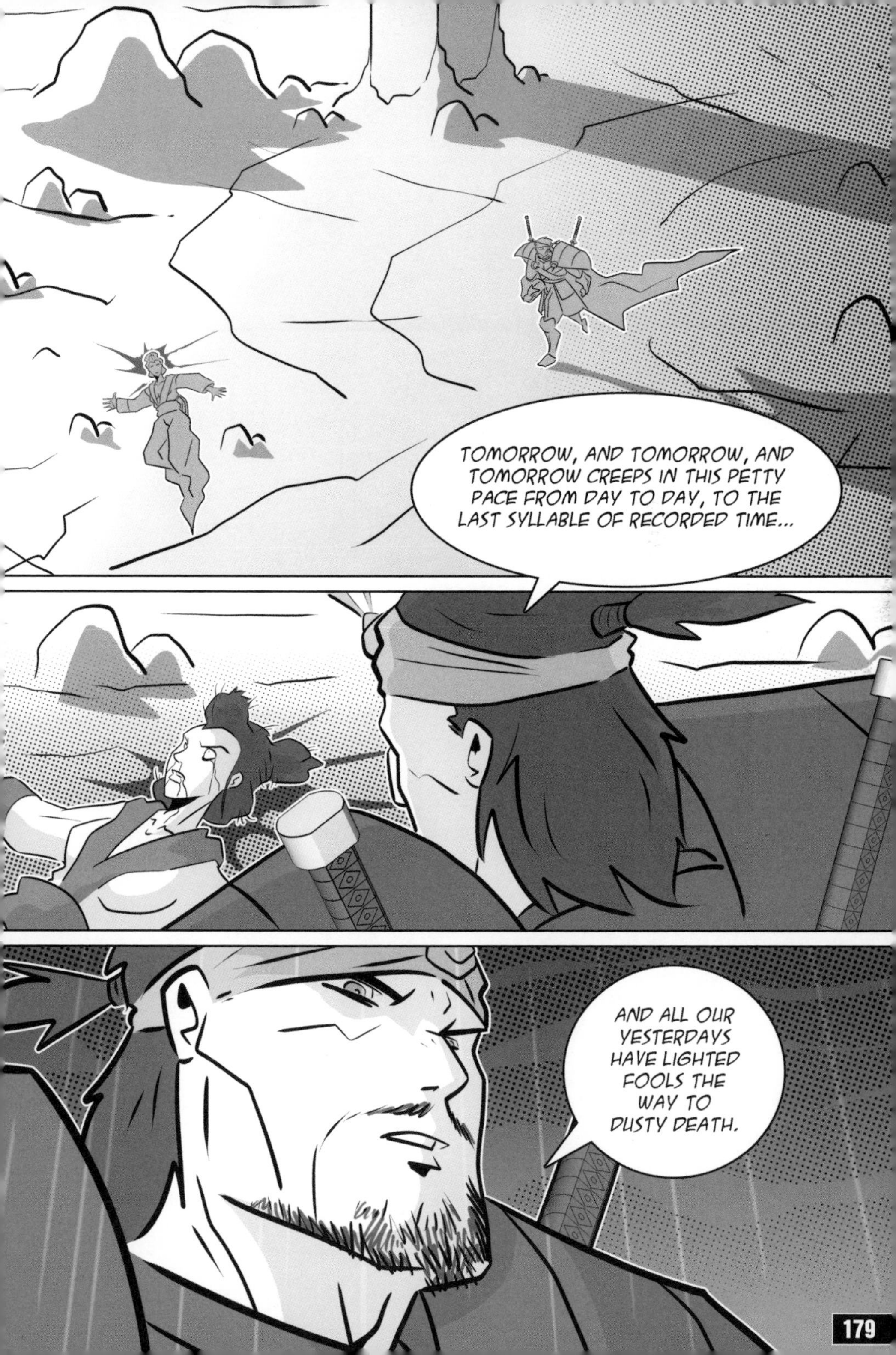
TOMORROW, AND TOMORROW, AND TOMORROW CREEPS IN THIS PETTY PACE FROM DAY TO DAY, TO THE LAST SYLLABLE OF RECORDED TIME...
AND ALL OUR YESTERDAYS HAVE LIGHTED FOOLS THE WAY TO DUSTY DEATH.

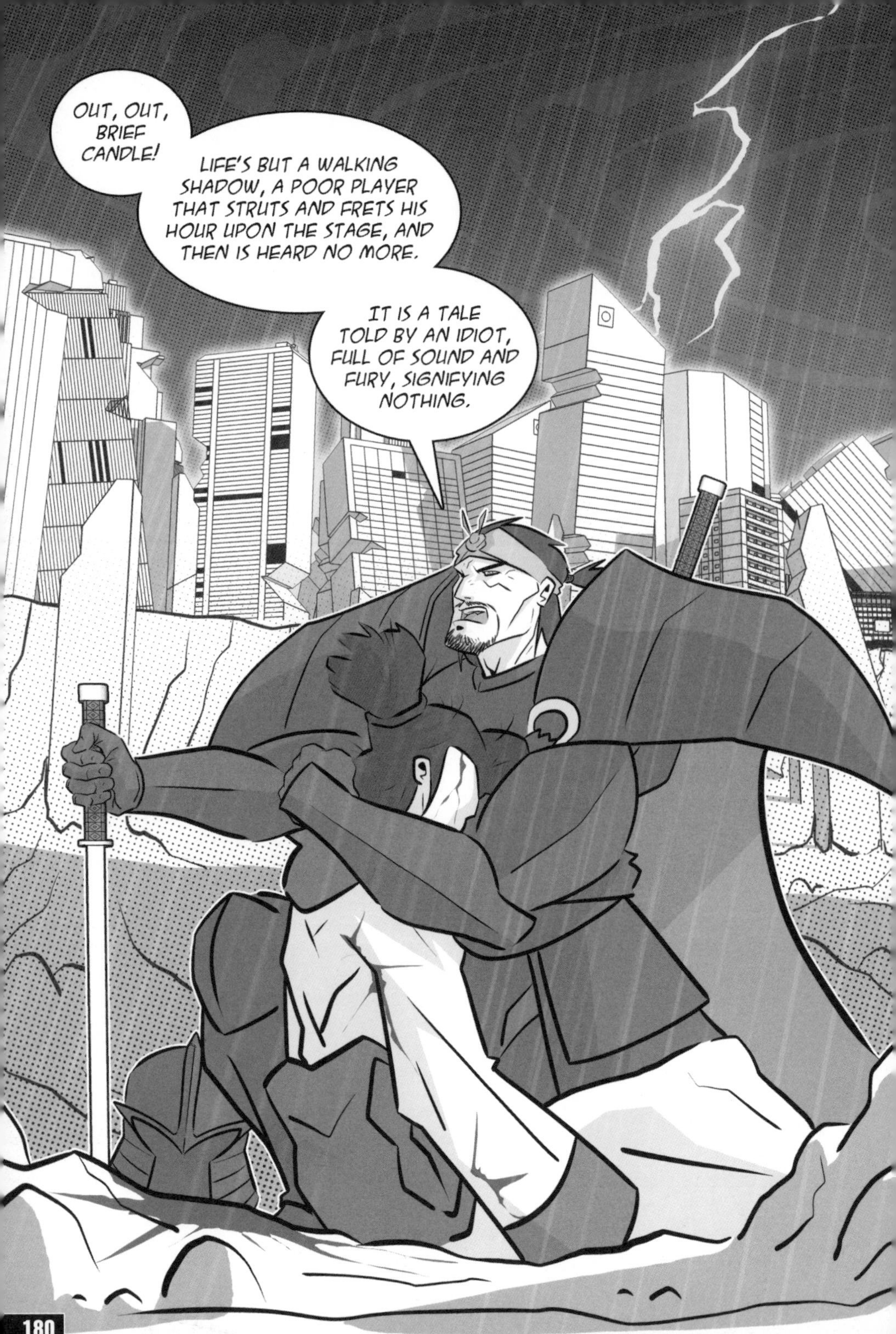
OUT, OUT, BRIEF CANDLE!
LIFE'S BUT A WALKING SHADOW, A POOR PLAYER THAT STRUTS AND FRETS HIS HOUR UPON THE STAGE, AND THEN IS HEARD NO MORE.
IT IS A TALE TOLD BY AN IDIOT, FULL OF SOUND AND FURY, SIGNIFYING NOTHING.

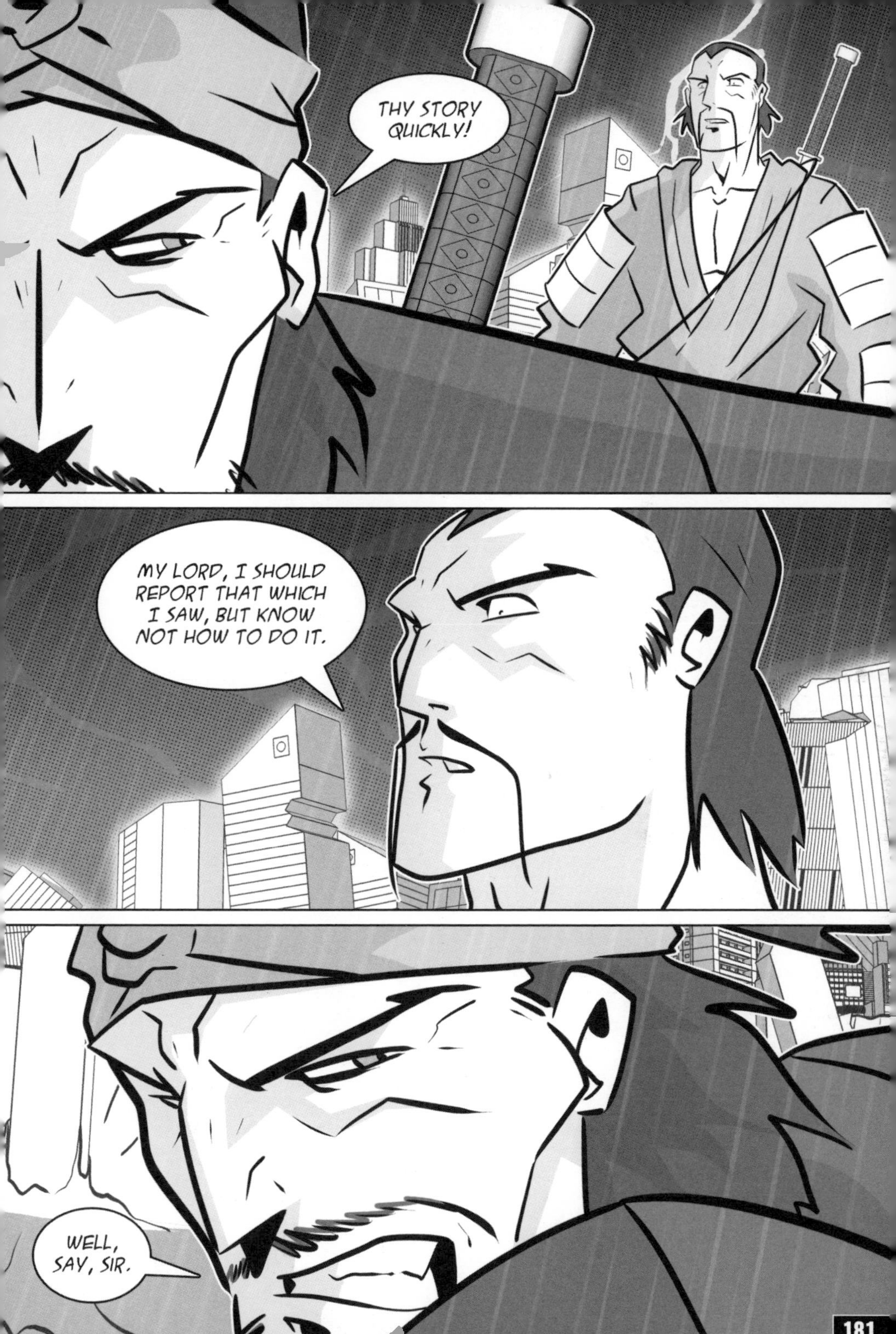
THY STORY QUICKLY!
MY LORD, I SHOULD REPORT THAT WHICH I SAW, BUT KNOW NOT HOW TO DO IT.
WELL, SAY, SIR.

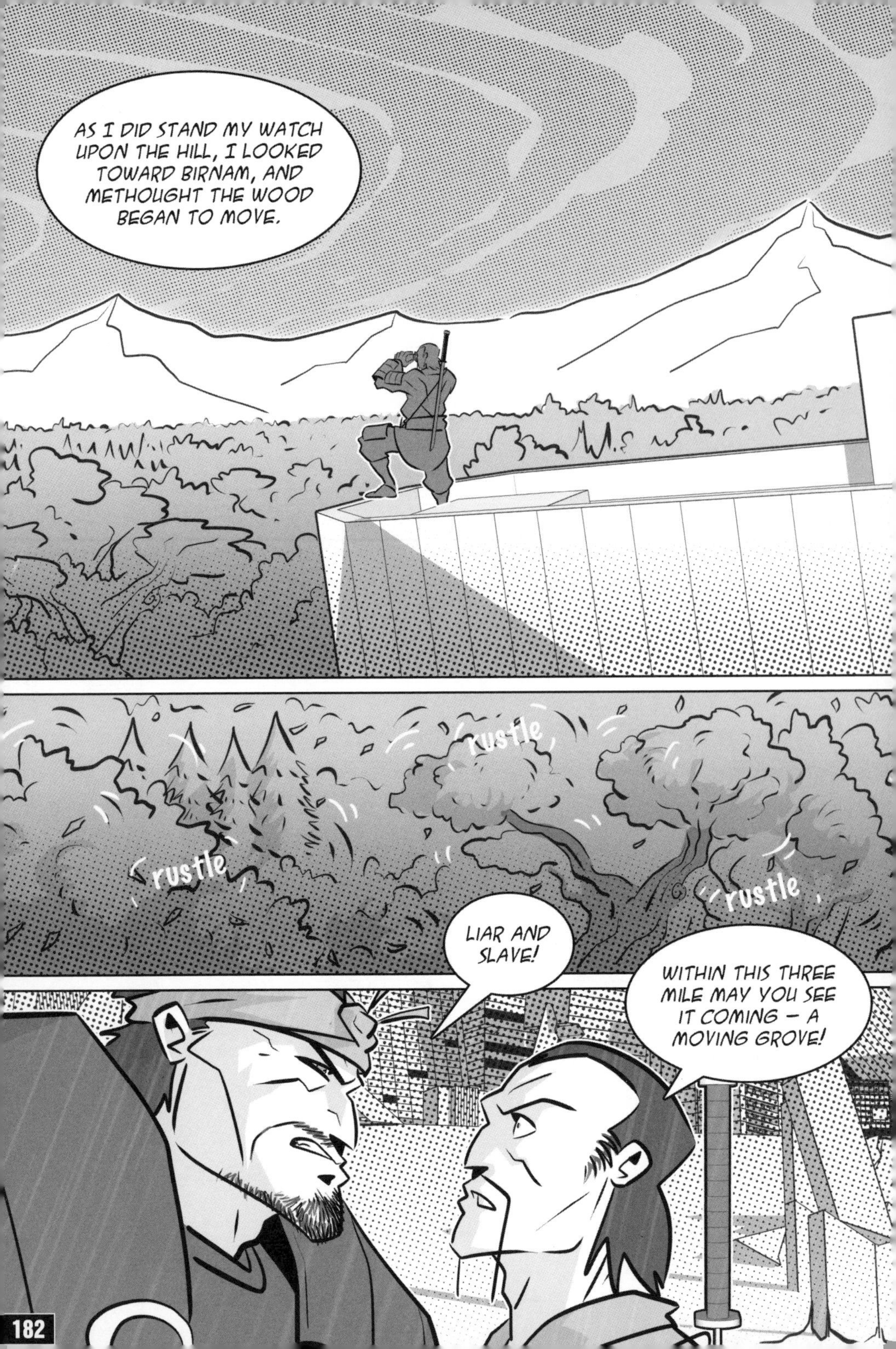
AS I DID STAND MY WATCH UPON THE HILL, I LOOKED TOWARD BIRNAM, AND METHOUGHT THE WOOD BEGAN TO MOVE.
rustle
rustle
rustle
LIAR AND SLAVE!
WITHIN THIS THREE MILE MAY YOU SEE IT COMING – A MOVING GROVE!

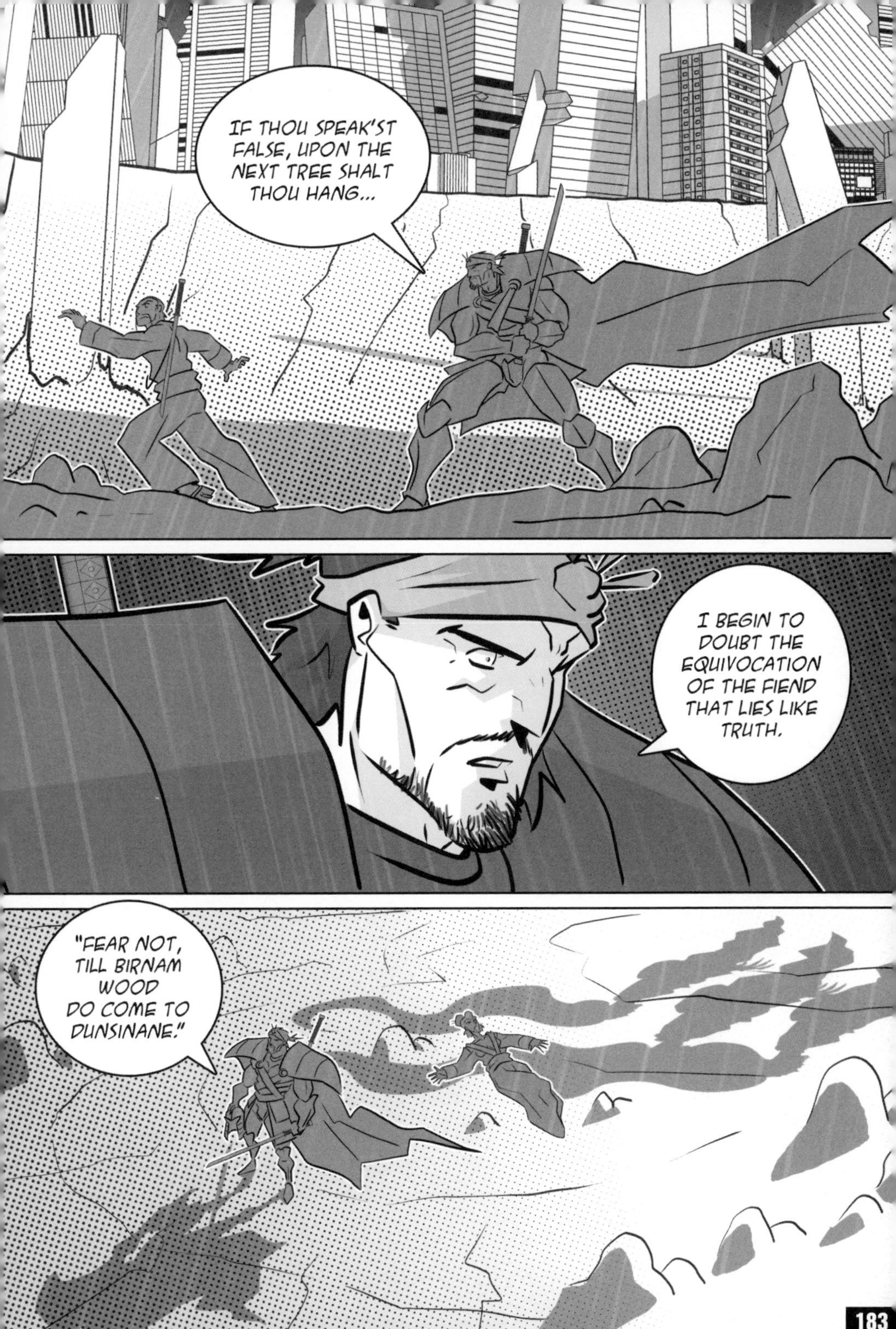
IF THOU SPEAK'ST FALSE, UPON THE NEXT TREE SHALT THOU HANG...
I BEGIN TO DOUBT THE EQUIVOCATION OF THE FIEND THAT LIES LIKE TRUTH.
"FEAR NOT, TILL BIRNAM WOOD DO COME TO DUNSINANE."

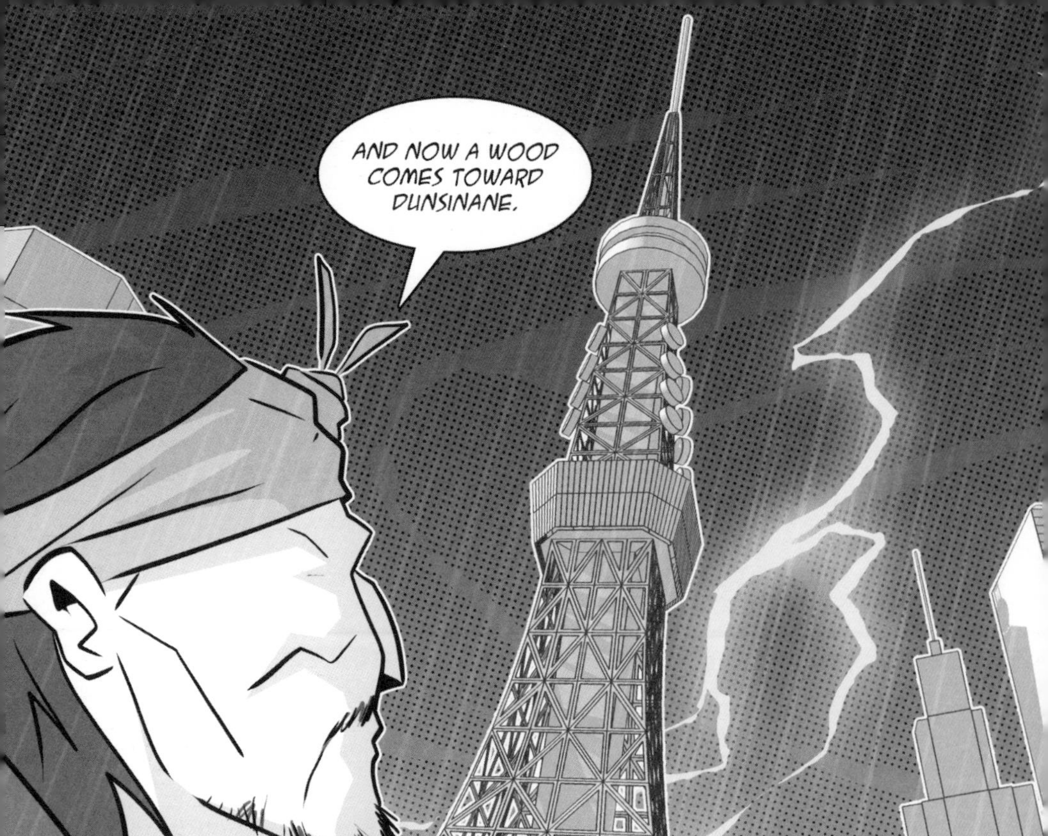
AND NOW A WOOD COMES TOWARD DUNSINANE.

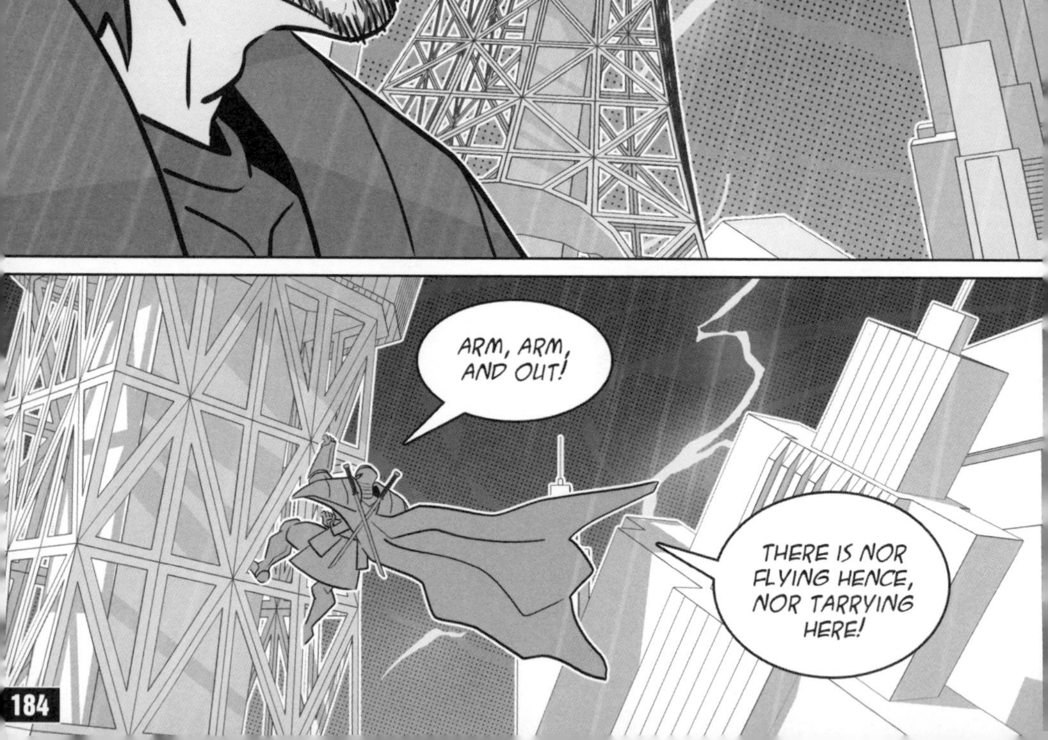
ARM, ARM, AND OUT!
THERE IS NOR FLYING HENCE, NOR TARRYING HERE!

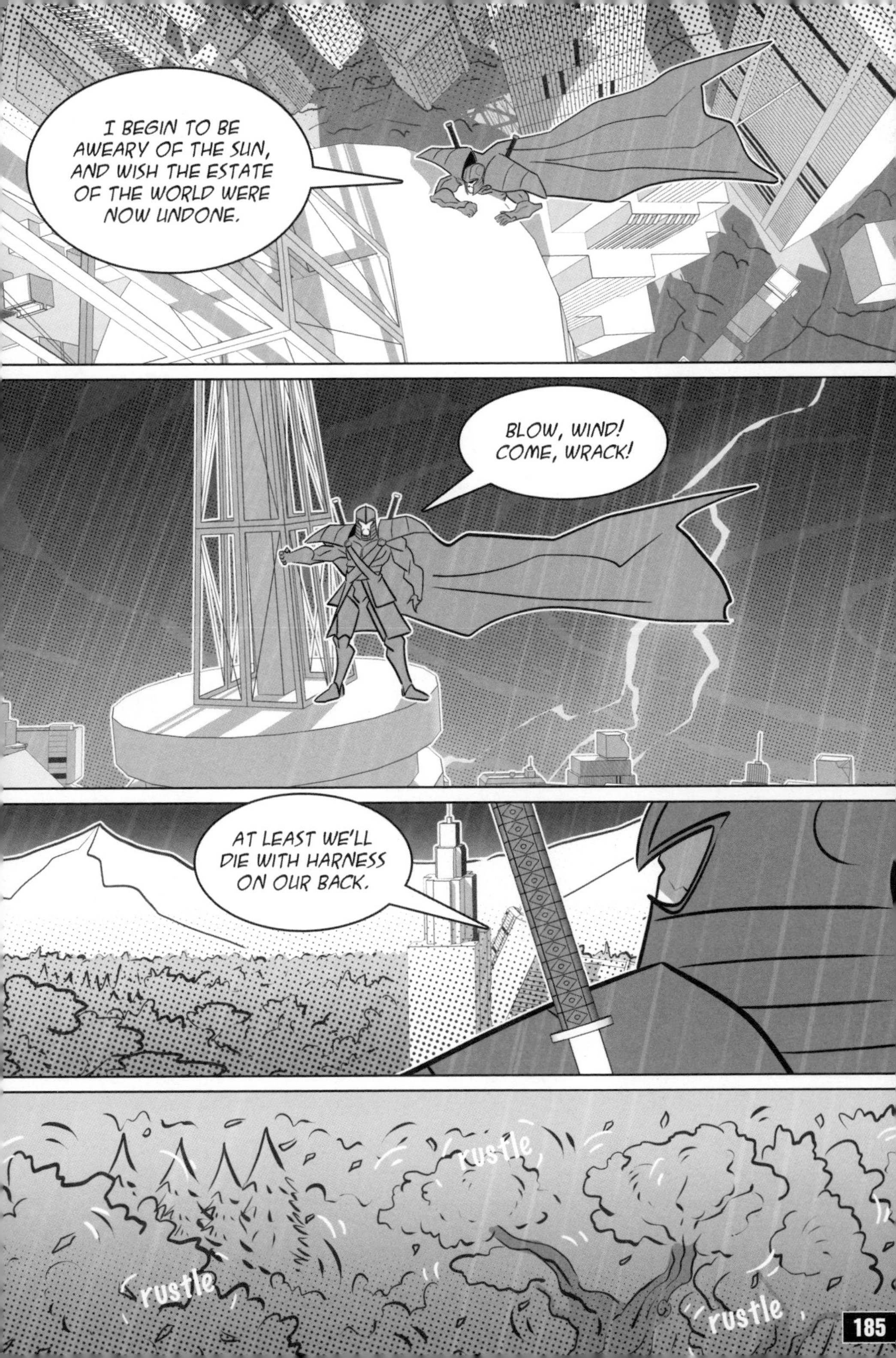
I BEGIN TO BE AWEARY OF THE SUN, AND WISH THE ESTATE OF THE WORLD WERE NOW UNDONE.
BLOW, WIND! COME, WRACK!
AT LEAST WE'LL DIE WITH HARNESS ON OUR BACK.
rustle
rustle
rustle

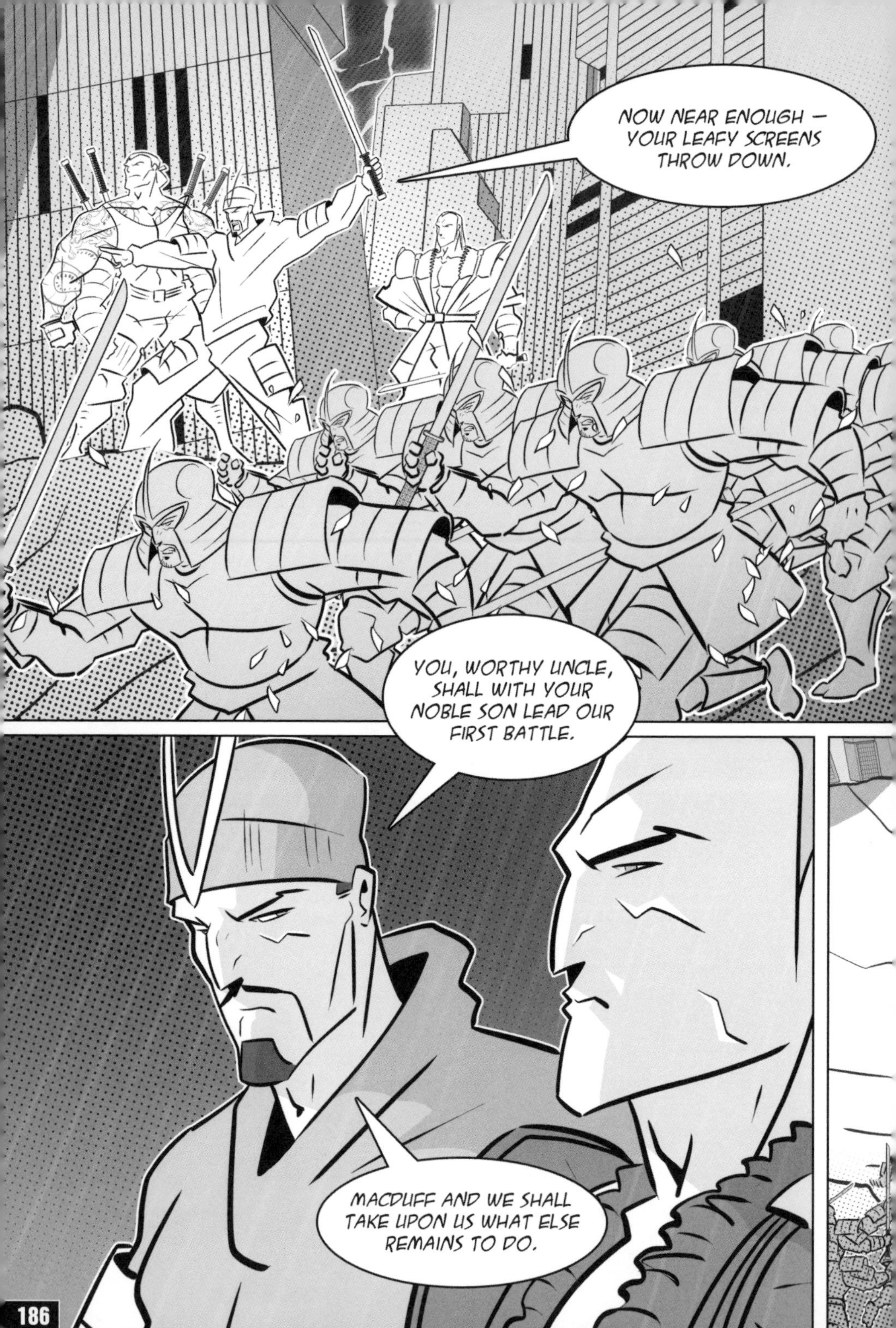
NOW NEAR ENOUGH — YOUR LEAFY SCREENS THROW DOWN.
YOU, WORTHY UNCLE, SHALL WITH YOUR NOBLE SON LEAD OUR FIRST BATTLE.
MACDUFF AND WE SHALL TAKE UPON US WHAT ELSE REMAINS TO DO.

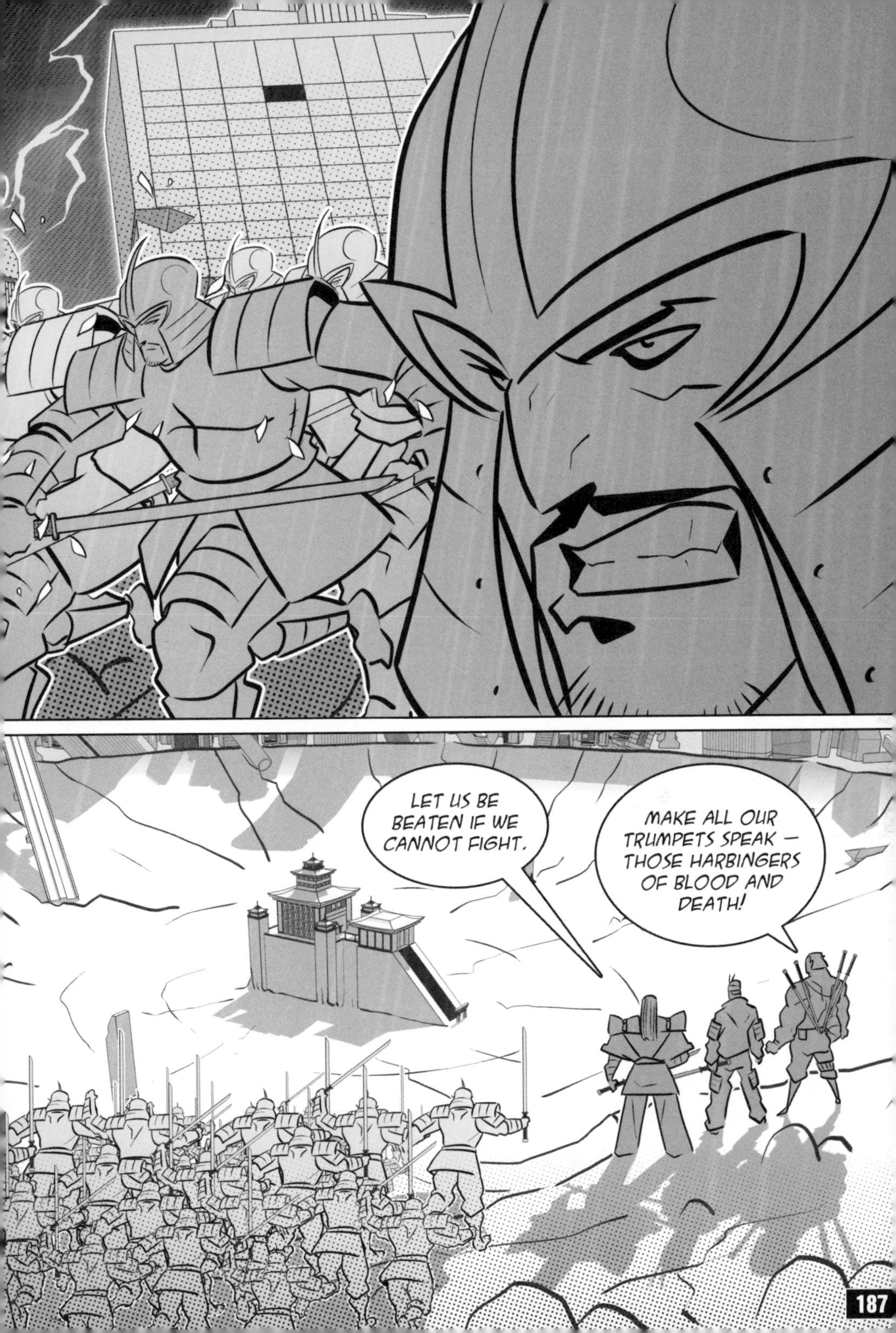
LET US BE BEATEN IF WE CANNOT FIGHT.
MAKE ALL OUR TRUMPETS SPEAK — THOSE HARBINGERS OF BLOOD AND DEATH!

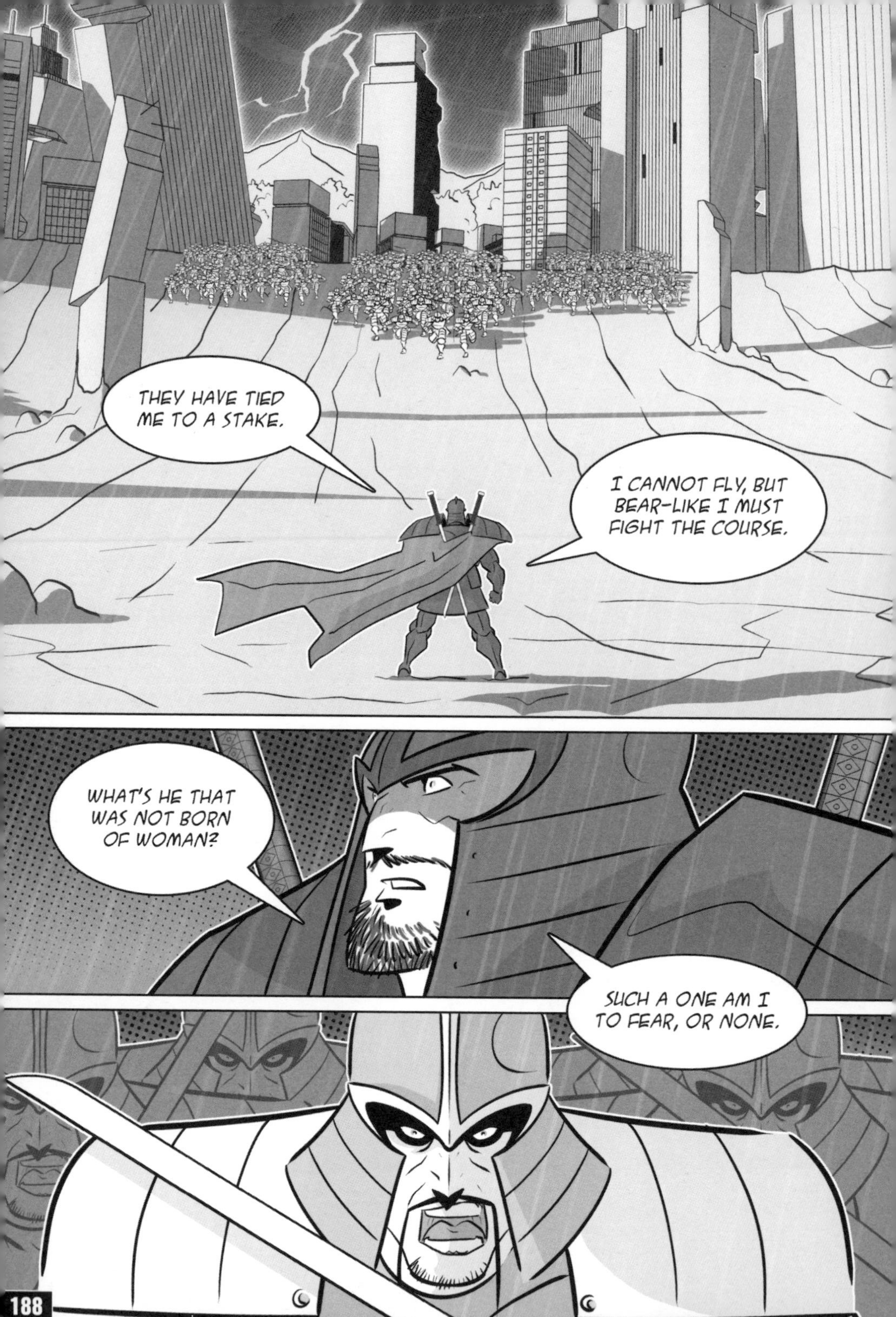

THEY HAVE TIED ME TO A STAKE.
I CANNOT FLY, BUT BEAR-LIKE I MUST FIGHT THE COURSE.
WHAT'S HE THAT WAS NOT BORN OF WOMAN?
SUCH A ONE AM I TO FEAR, OR NONE.

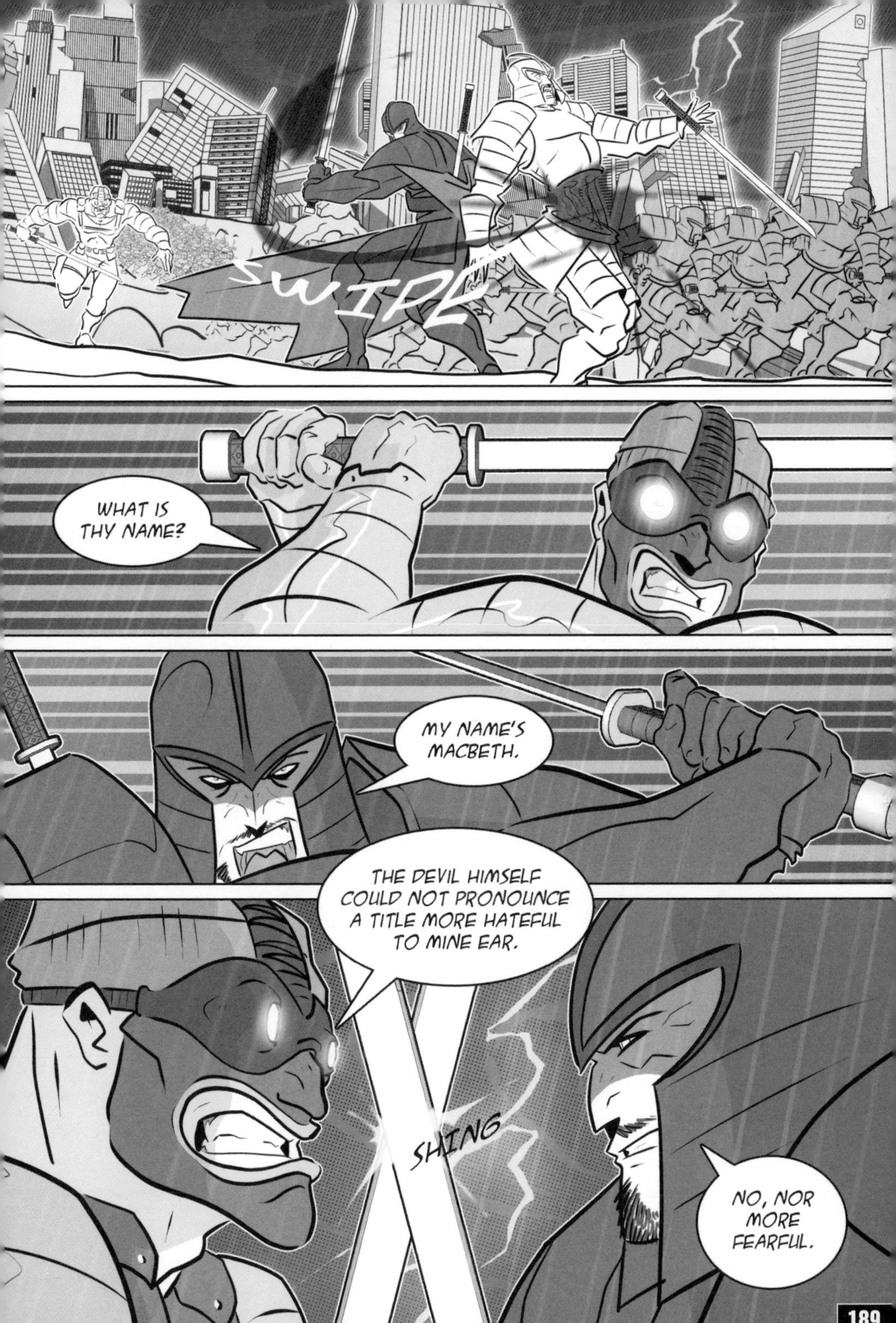
SWIPE
WHAT IS THY NAME?
MY NAME'S MACBETH.
THE DEVIL HIMSELF COULD NOT PRONOUNCE A TITLE MORE HATEFUL TO MINE EAR.
SHING
NO, NOR MORE FEARFUL.

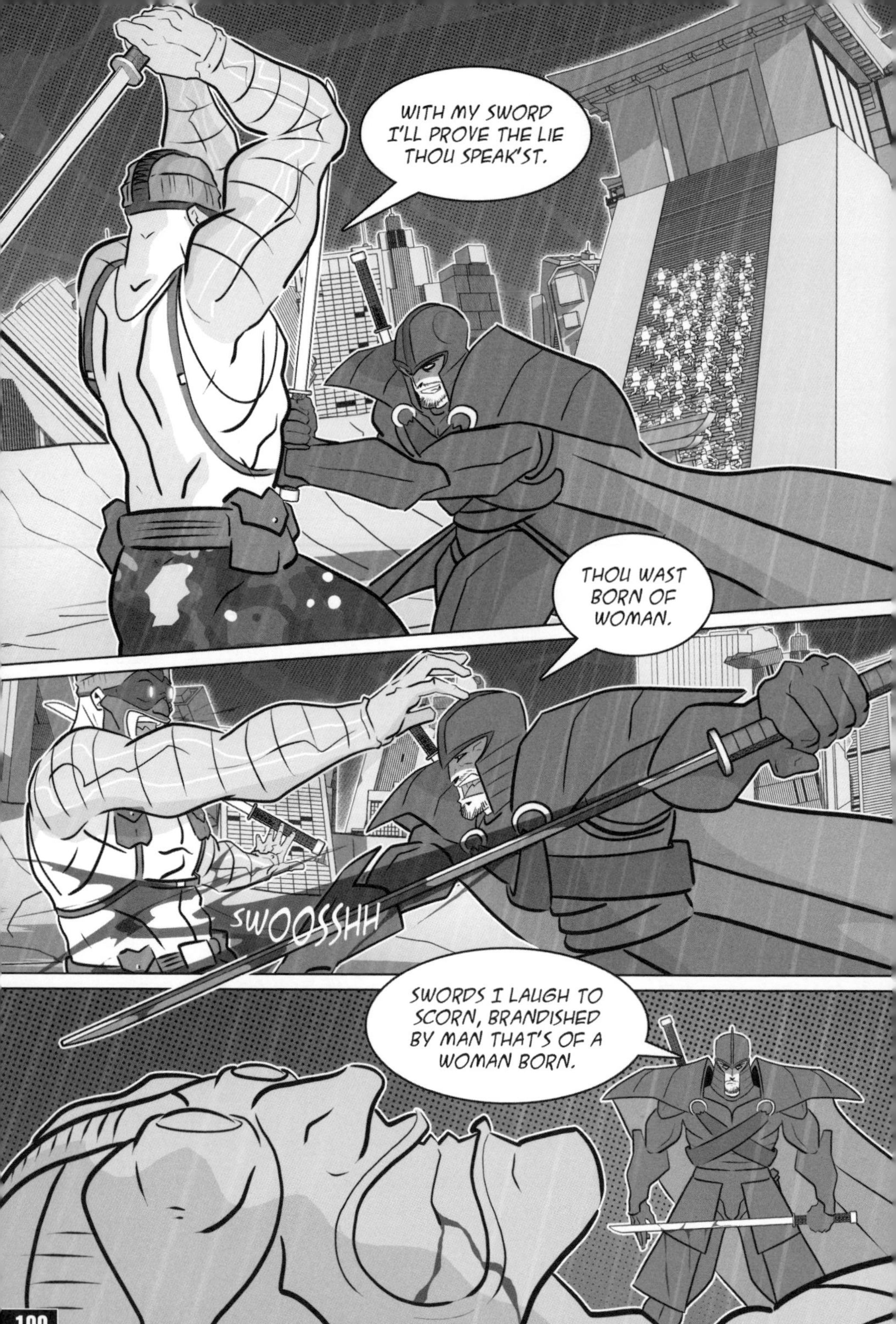
WITH MY SWORD I'LL PROVE THE LIE THOU SPEAK'ST.
THOU WAST BORN OF WOMAN.
SWOOSSHH
SWORDS I LAUGH TO SCORN, BRANDISHED BY MAN THAT'S OF A WOMAN BORN.

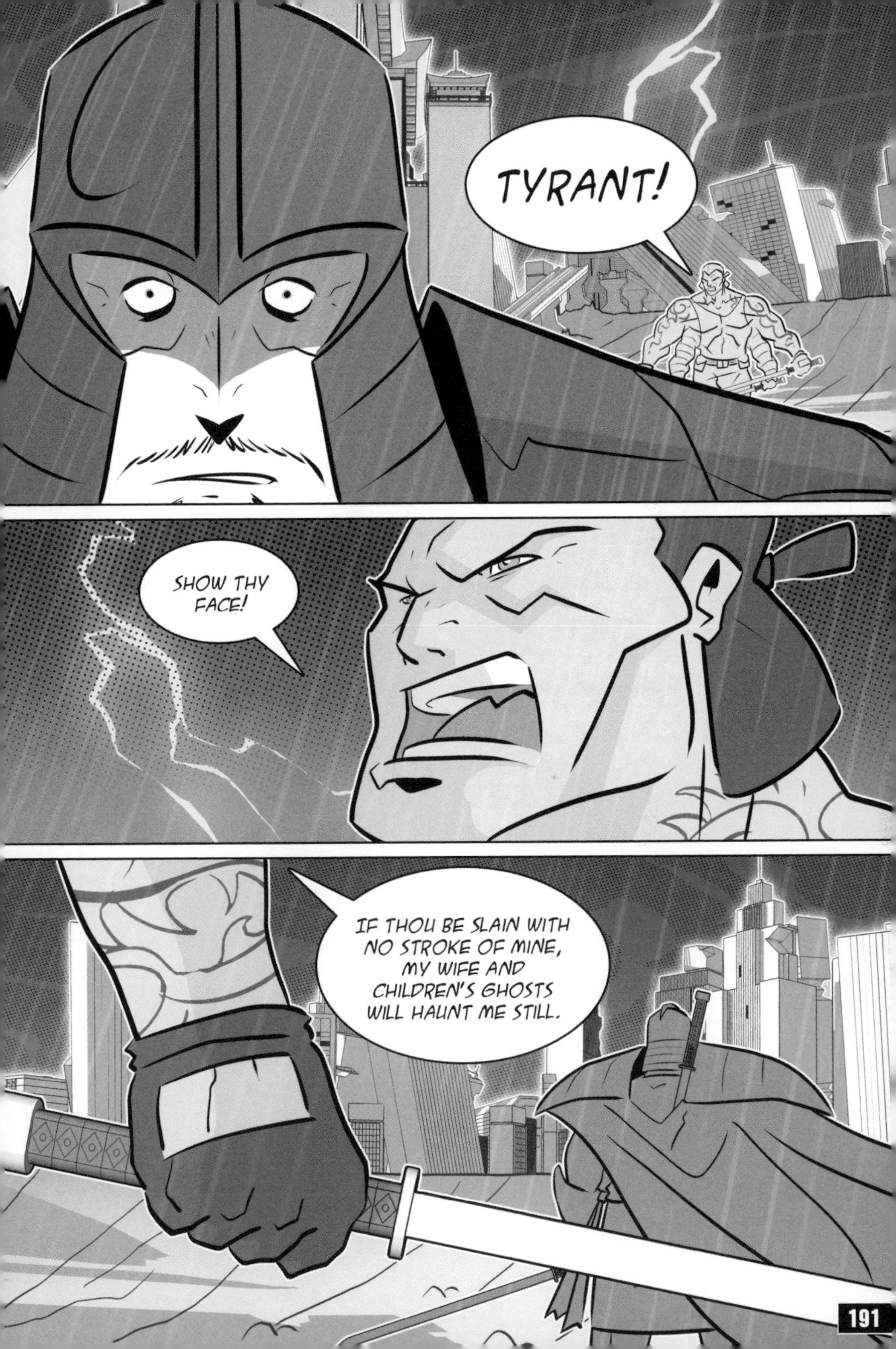
TYRANT!
SHOW THY FACE!
IF THOU BE SLAIN WITH NO STROKE OF MINE, MY WIFE AND CHILDREN'S GHOSTS WILL HAUNT ME STILL.

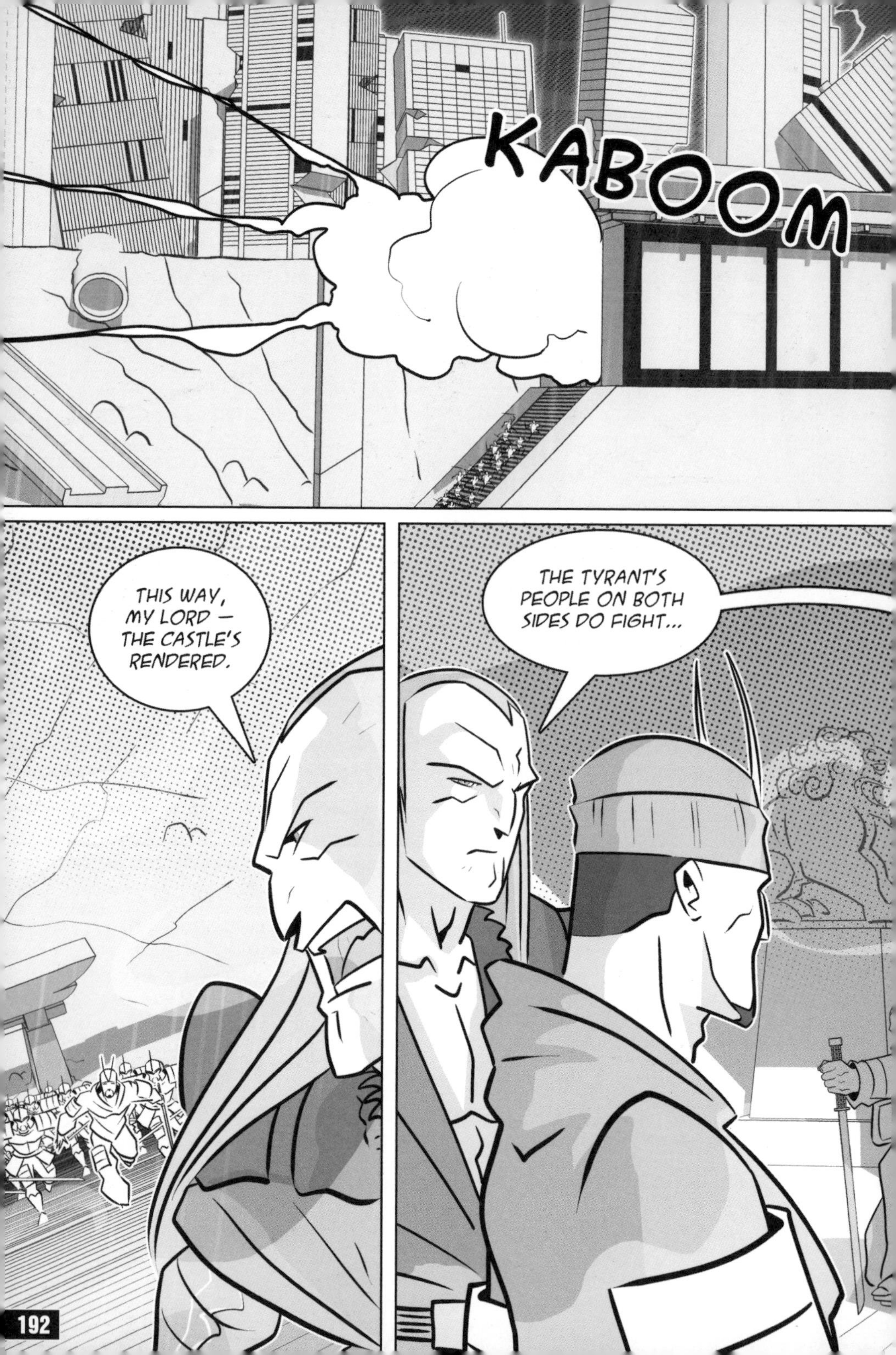
KABOOM
THIS WAY, MY LORD — THE CASTLE'S RENDERED.
THE TYRANT'S PEOPLE ON BOTH SIDES DO FIGHT...

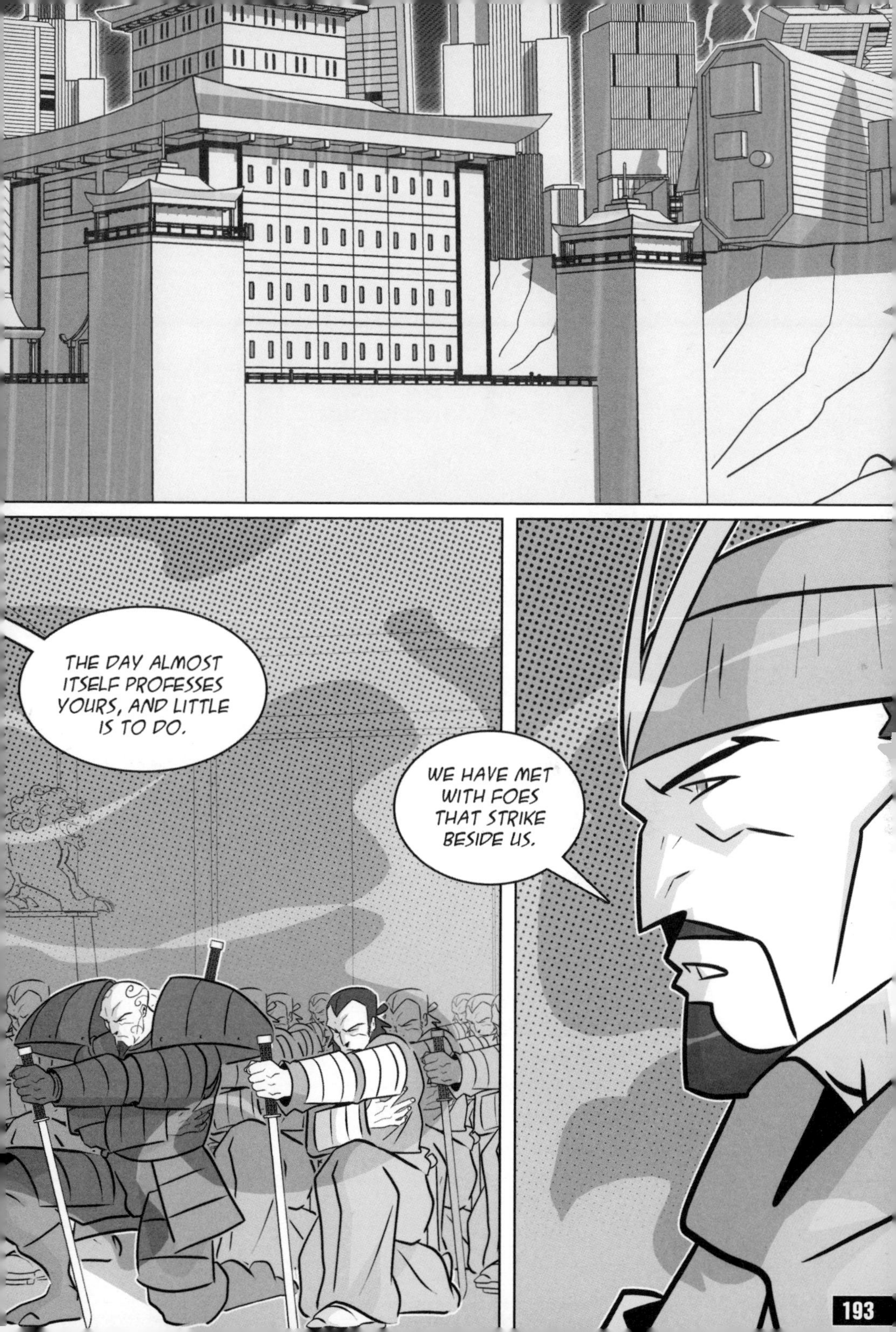
THE DAY ALMOST ITSELF PROFESSES YOURS, AND LITTLE IS TO DO.
WE HAVE MET WITH FOES THAT STRIKE BESIDE US.

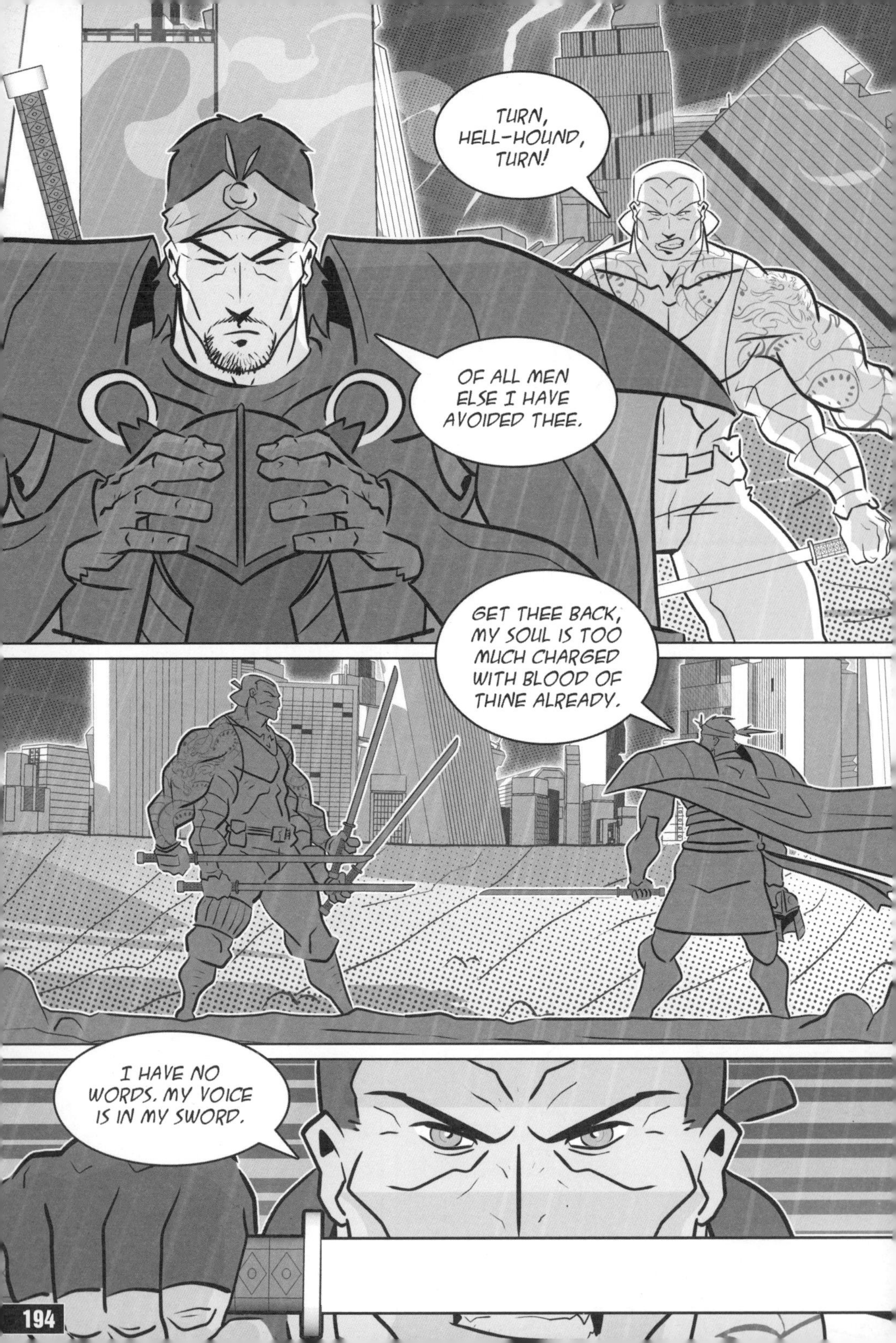
TURN, HELL-HOUND, TURN!
OF ALL MEN ELSE I HAVE AVOIDED THEE.
GET THEE BACK, MY SOUL IS TOO MUCH CHARGED WITH BLOOD OF THINE ALREADY.
I HAVE NO WORDS. MY VOICE IS IN MY SWORD.

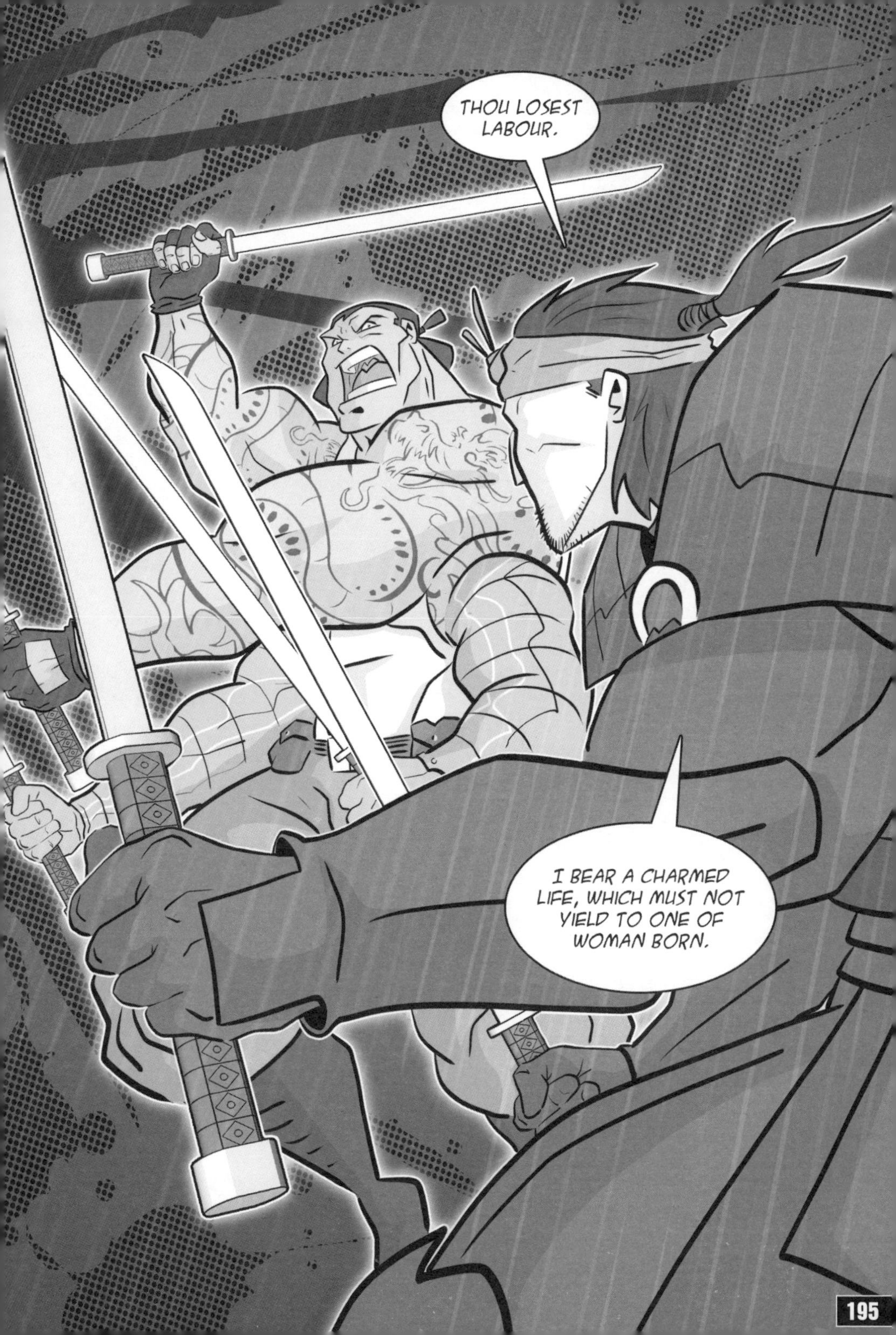
THOU LOSEST LABOUR.
I BEAR A CHARMED LIFE, WHICH MUST NOT YIELD TO ONE OF WOMAN BORN.

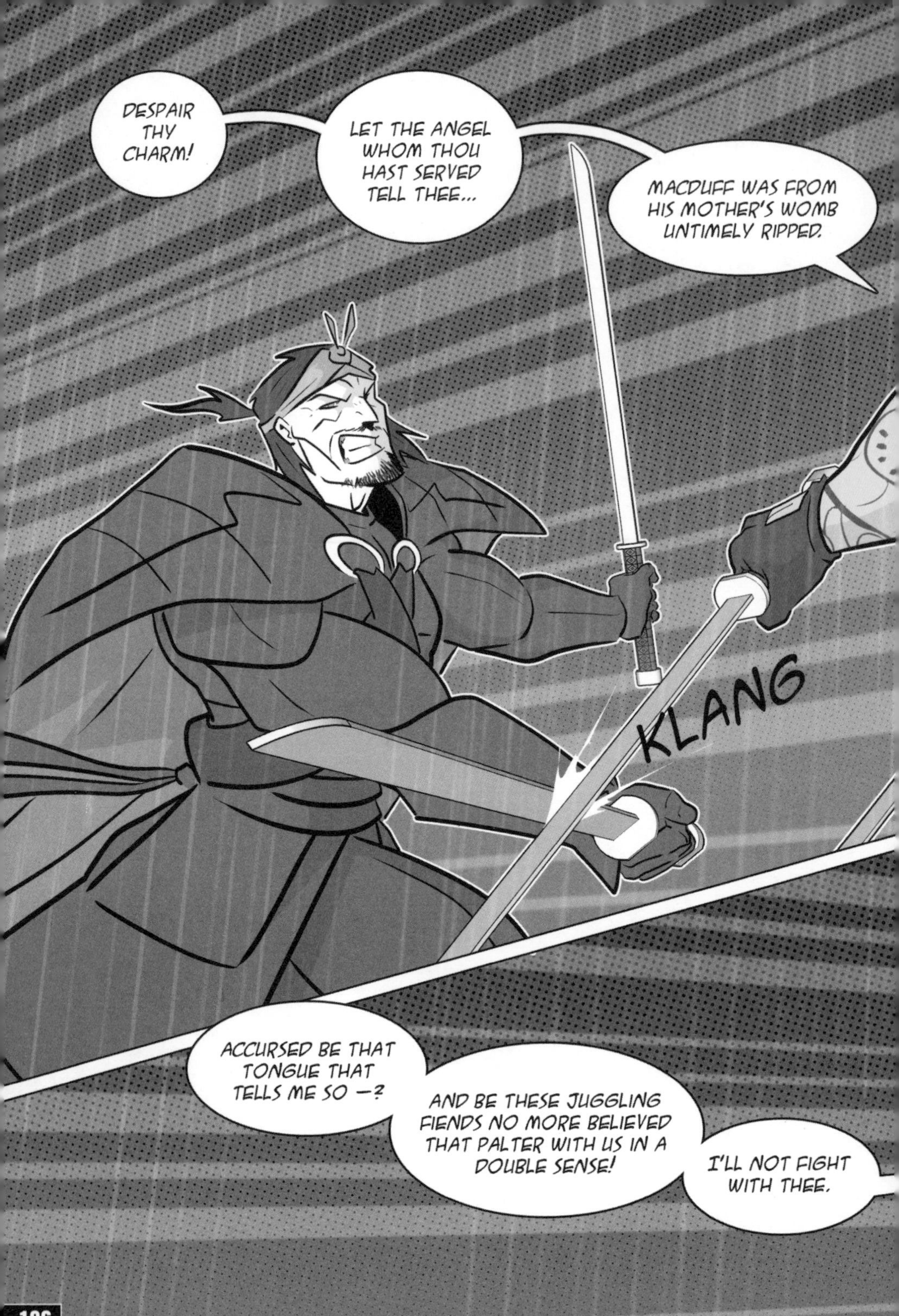

DESPAIR THY CHARM!
LET THE ANGEL WHOM THOU HAST SERVED TELL THEE...
MACDUFF WAS FROM HIS MOTHER'S WOMB UNTIMELY RIPPED.
KLANG
ACCURSED BE THAT TONGUE THAT TELLS ME SO —?
AND BE THESE JUGGLING FIENDS NO MORE BELIEVED THAT PALTER WITH US IN A DOUBLE SENSE!
I'LL NOT FIGHT WITH THEE.

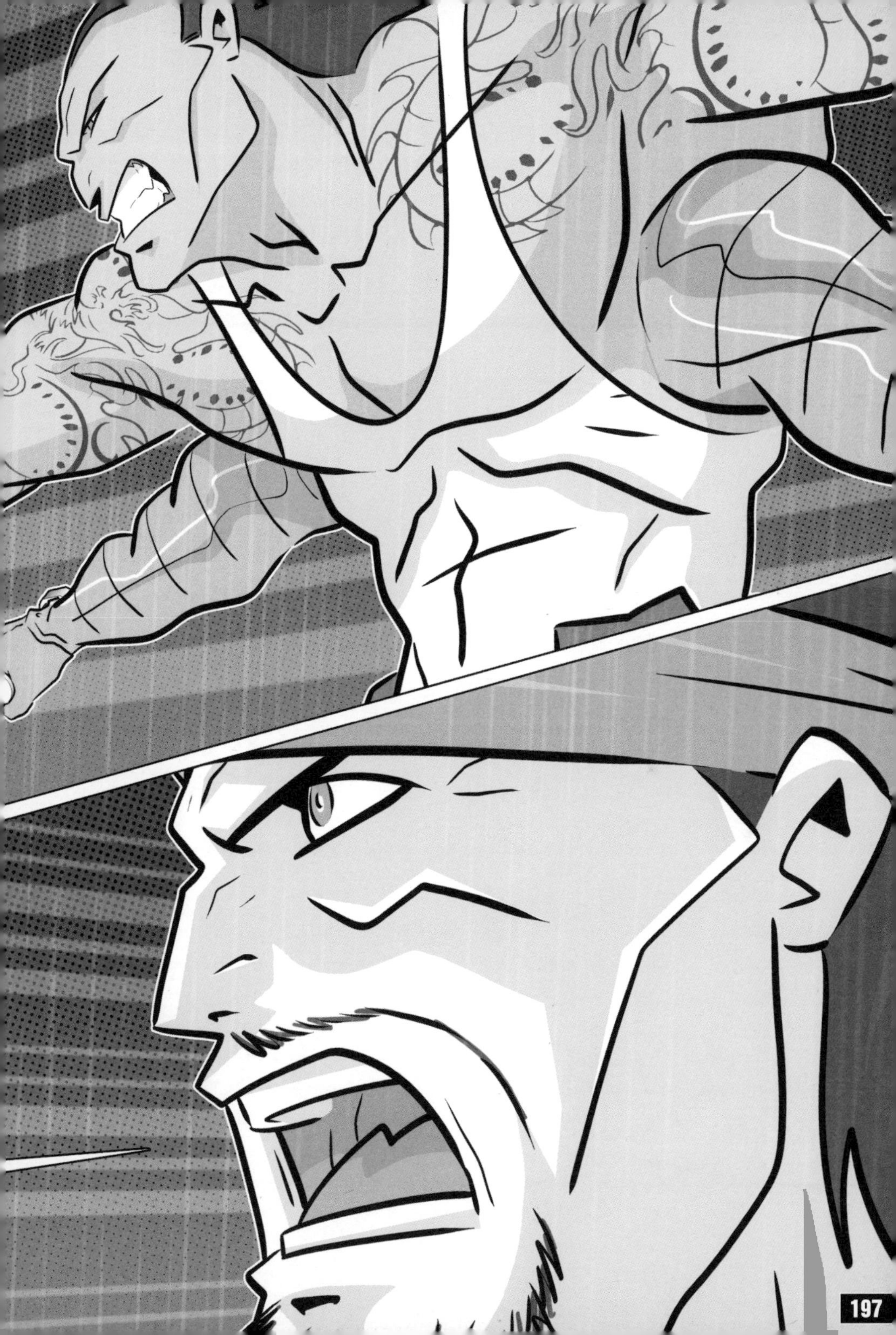

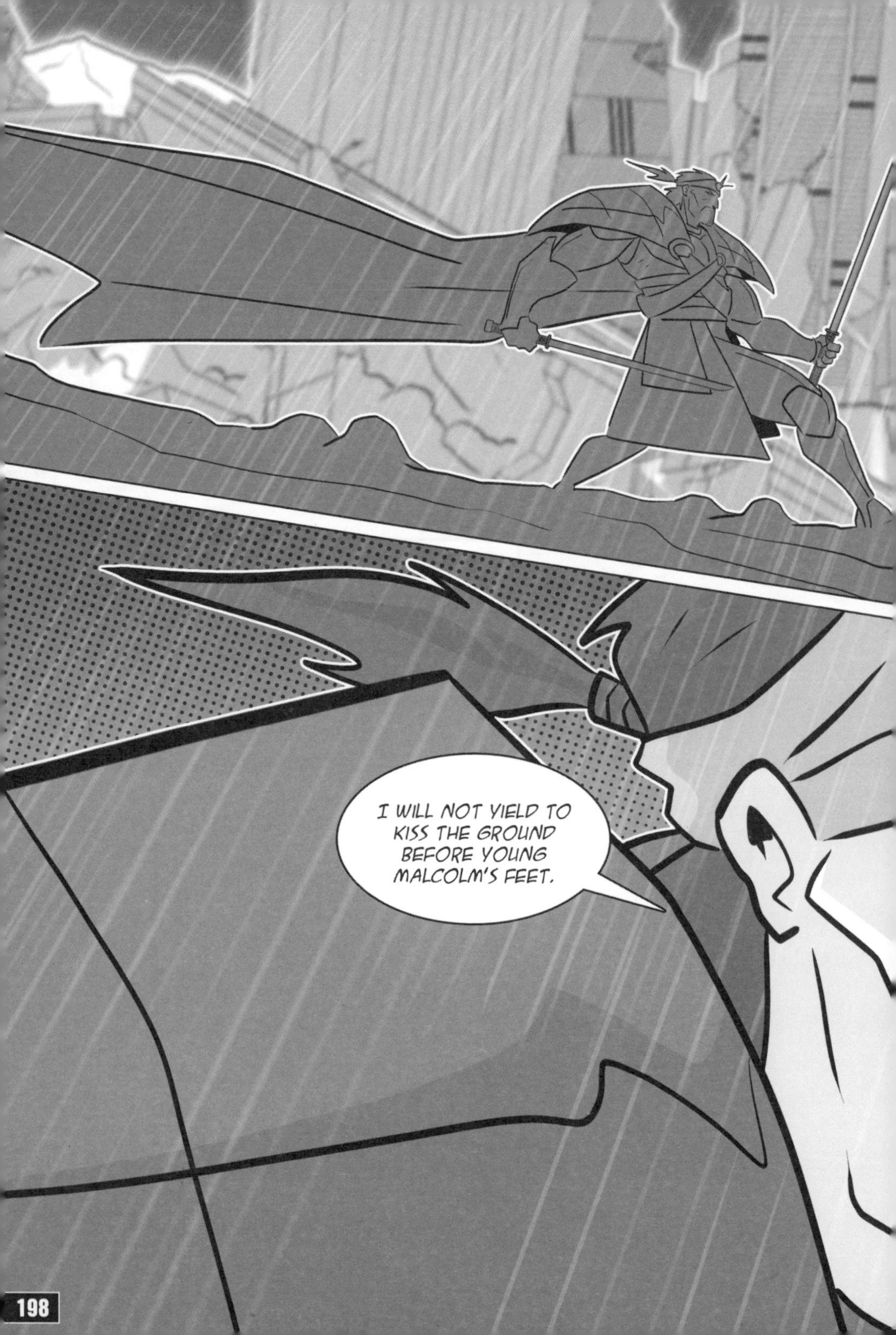
I WILL NOT YIELD TO KISS THE GROUND BEFORE YOUNG MALCOLM'S FEET.

THEN YIELD THEE, COWARD, AND LIVE TO BE THE SHOW AND GAZE OF THE TIME.
WE'LL HAVE THEE, AS OUR RARER MONSTERS ARE, ON A POLE — AND UNDERWRIT, "HERE MAY YOU SEE THE TYRANT."
THOUGH BIRNAM WOOD BE COME TO DUNSINANE, AND THOU BEING OF NO WOMAN BORN, YET I WILL TRY THE LAST.
LAY ON, MACDUFF, AND DAMNED BE HIM THAT FIRST CRIES, "HOLD, ENOUGH!"

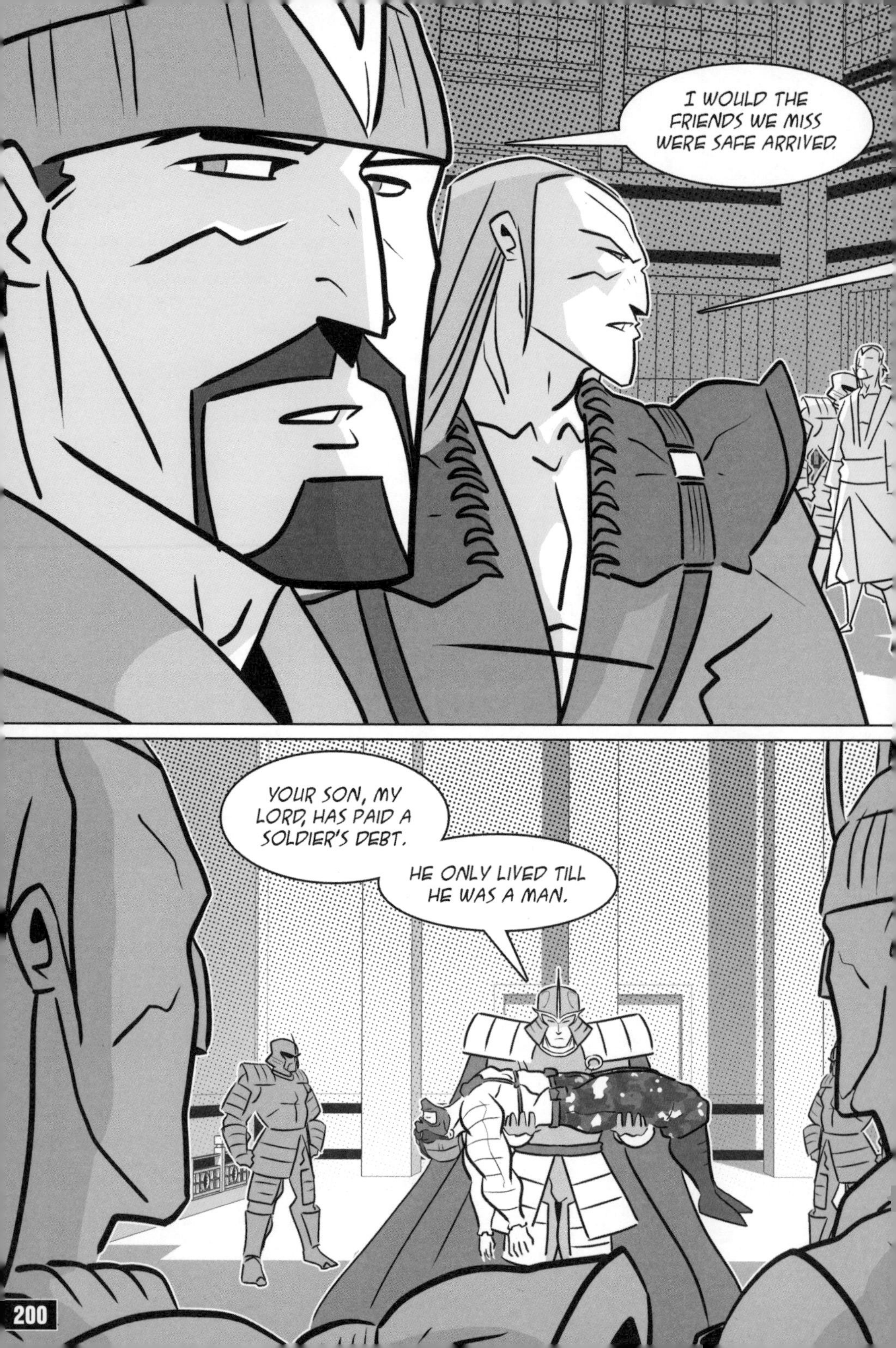
I WOULD THE FRIENDS WE MISS WERE SAFE ARRIVED.
YOUR SON, MY LORD, HAS PAID A SOLDIER'S DEBT.
HE ONLY LIVED TILL HE WAS A MAN.

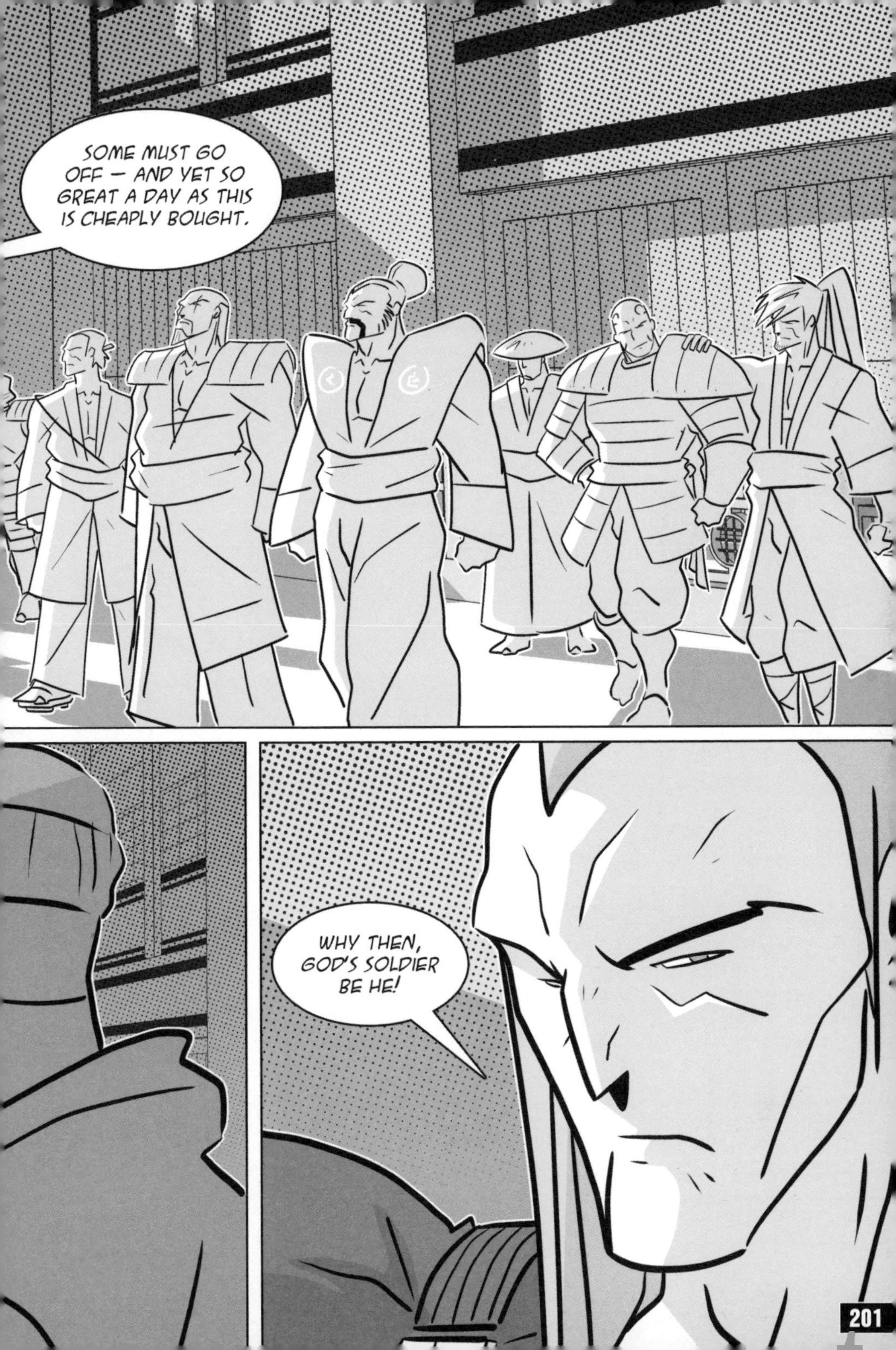
SOME MUST GO OFF — AND YET SO GREAT A DAY AS THIS IS CHEAPLY BOUGHT.
WHY THEN, GOD'S SOLDIER BE HE!

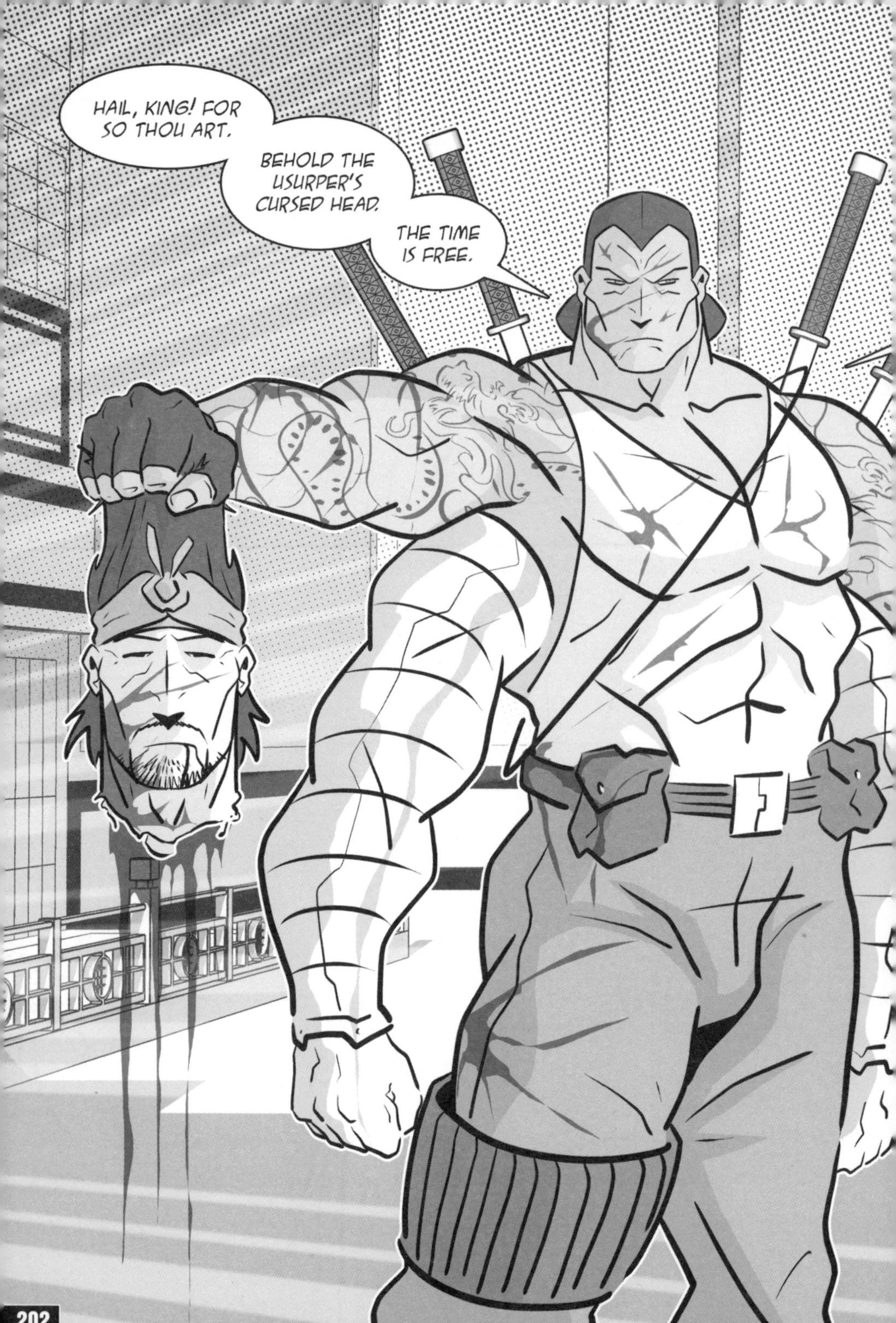
HAIL, KING! FOR SO THOU ART.
BEHOLD THE USURPER'S CURSED HEAD.
THE TIME IS FREE.

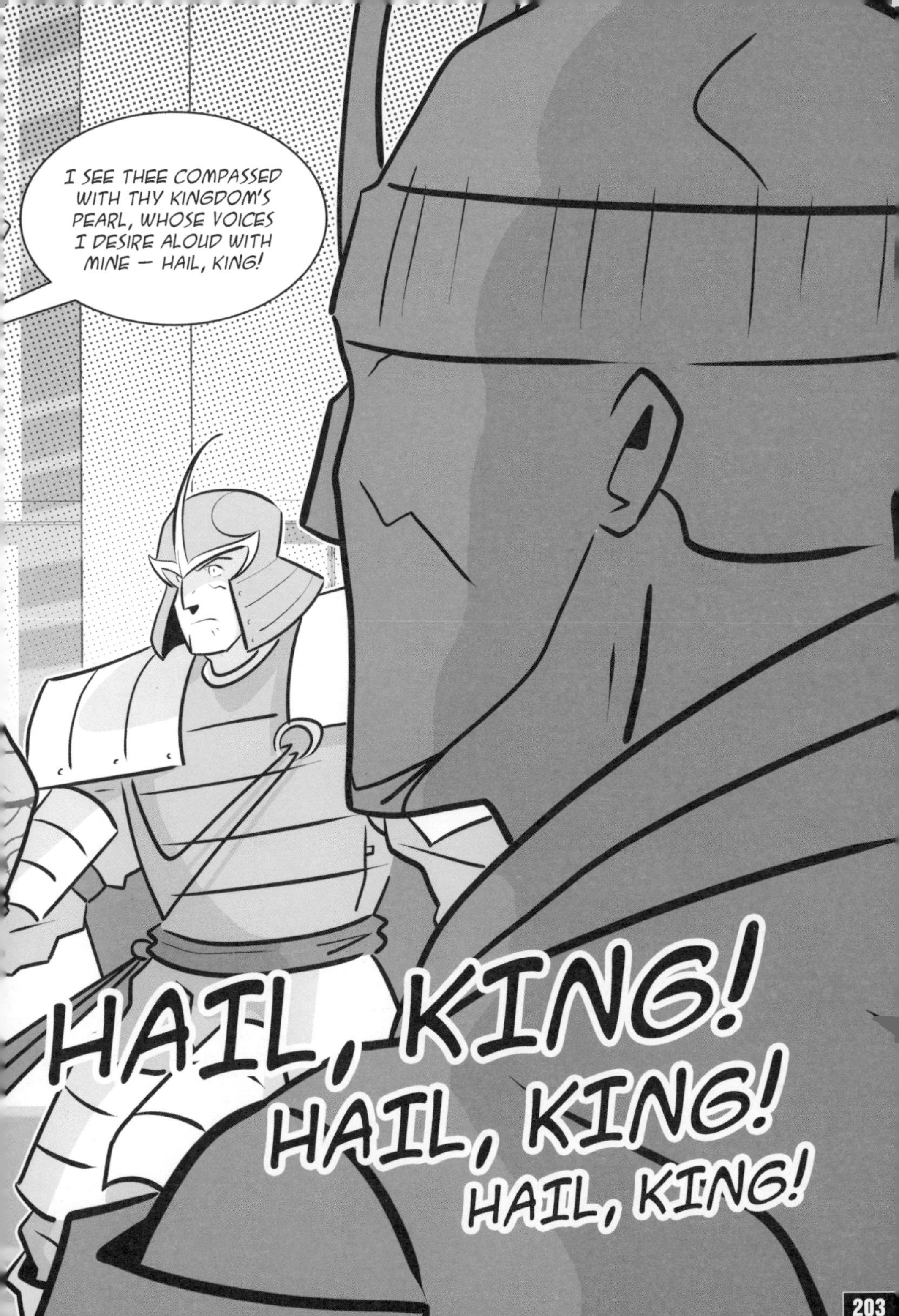

I SEE THEE COMPASSED WITH THY KINGDOM'S PEARL, WHOSE VOICES I DESIRE ALOUD WITH MINE — HAIL, KING!
HAIL, KING!
HAIL, KING!
HAIL, KING!

WE SHALL NOT SPEND A LARGE EXPENSE OF TIME BEFORE WE MAKE US EVEN WITH YOU.
MY KINSMEN, HENCEFORTH BE EARLS, THE FIRST EVER IN SUCH AN HONOUR NAMED, WHOM WE INVITE TO SEE US CROWNED.
WHAT'S MORE TO DO, AS CALLING HOME OUR EXILED FRIENDS THAT FLED THE SNARES OF THIS DEAD BUTCHER AND HIS FIEND-LIKE QUEEN, WHO BY SELF-VIOLENT HANDS TOOK OFF HER LIFE...

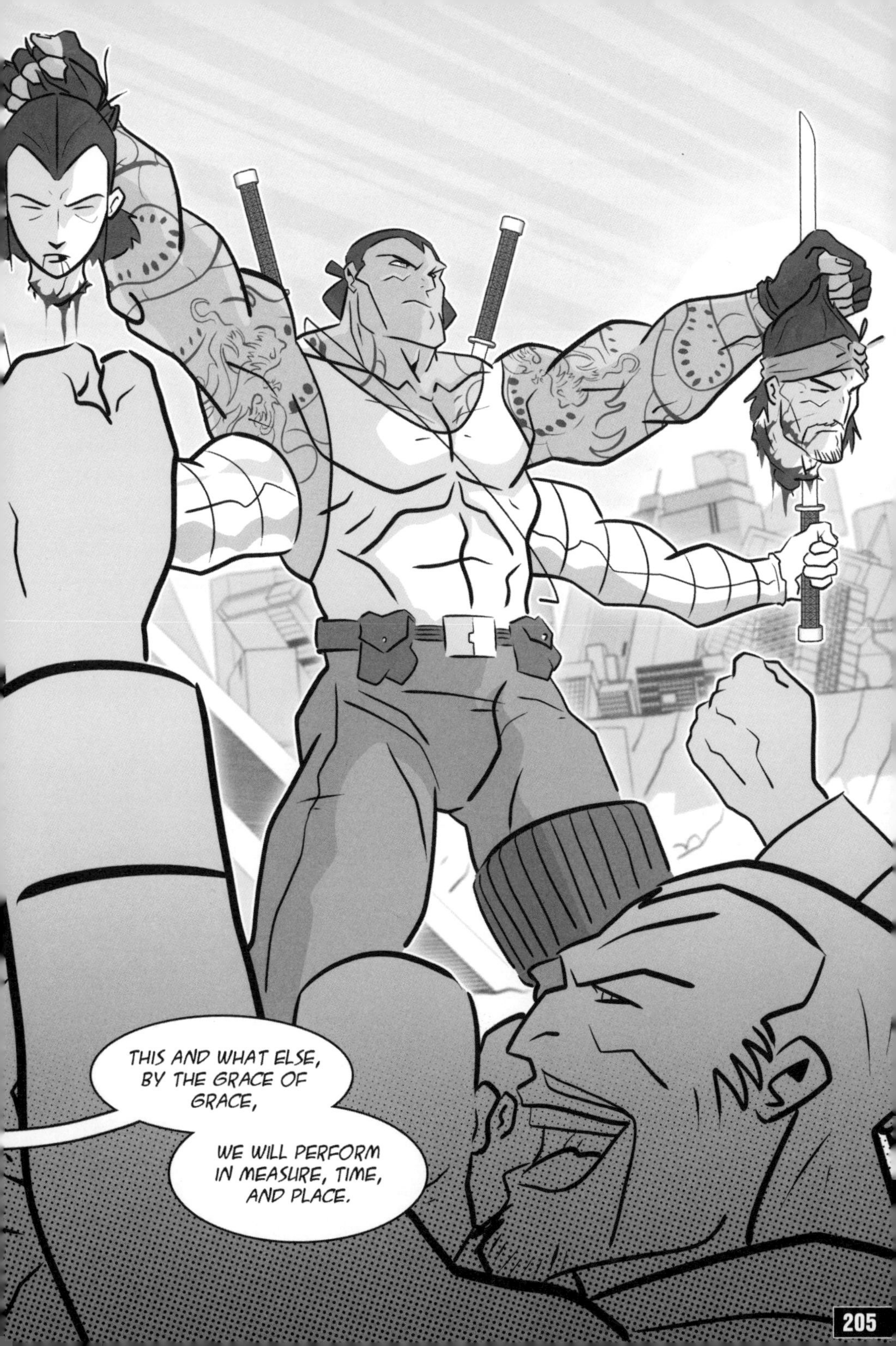
THIS AND WHAT ELSE, BY THE GRACE OF GRACE,
WE WILL PERFORM IN MEASURE, TIME, AND PLACE.

PLOT SUMMARY OF MACBETH

The rule of good King Duncan has been saved from rebel forces: his loyal warlords, Macbeth and Banquo, have triumphed in battle over an invading army, and the traitorous Thane of Cawdor is among the prisoners. Returning home, Macbeth and Banquo encounter three witches, who deliver a series of prophecies: Macbeth will inherit the Thane of Cawdor's title and will become king; Banquo will father a dynasty of kings, though will never himself be king.

Duncan orders the execution of the captured Thane of Cawdor, bestowing that title on Macbeth – and this fulfilment of the first of the witches' prophecies stirs Macbeth's ambition. He confides in his wife, Lady Macbeth, who persuades him to murder Duncan as he sleeps.

When Duncan's body is discovered, Macbeth kills the dead king's bodyguards, and Duncan's sons, Malcolm and Donalbain, flee in fear of their lives. Now crowned king, Macbeth acts to prevent Banquo's descendants becoming kings. Banquo is brutally killed in an ambush – but his son, Fleance, escapes.

Tormented by a vision of Banquo's bloody ghost, Macbeth seeks out the three witches, who seem to offer reassurance: Macbeth, they say, cannot be harmed by anyone "of woman born", and can rest secure until the great forest of Birnam Wood "come to Dunsinane". Feeling himself immune, Macbeth dispatches assassins to murder the family of Macduff (one of Duncan's warlords), who has fled to join forces with Malcolm.

News of his family's slaughter is brought to Macduff during an interview with Malcolm. United in their grief, they march with their armies to overthrow Macbeth. Meanwhile, Lady Macbeth's guilt has driven her to insanity and suicide. Macbeth staves off despair by remembering the witches' prophecy... until the impossible news arrives that Birnam Wood is approaching Dunsinane: Malcolm's armies have camouflaged themselves with its branches.

In the ensuing battle, Macbeth fights valiantly – until he encounters Macduff, who declares that he is not "of woman born": his birth was by Caesarean section.

Macbeth has been misled by the witches. He is slain and beheaded by Macduff. Malcolm is proclaimed king. And, as Shakespeare's first audiences would have known, Fleance's descendants included their own royal family. And our own.

A BRIEF LIFE OF WILLIAM SHAKESPEARE

Shakespeare's birthday is traditionally said to be the 23rd of April – St George's Day, patron saint of England. A good start for England's greatest writer. But that date and even his name are uncertain. He signed his own name in different ways. "Shakespeare" is now the accepted one out of dozens of different versions.

He was born at Stratford-upon-Avon in 1564, and baptized on 26th April. His mother, Mary Arden, was the daughter of a prosperous farmer. His father, John Shakespeare, a glove-maker, was a respected civic figure – and probably also a Catholic. In 1570, just as Will began school, his father was accused of illegal dealings. The family fell into debt and disrepute.

Will attended a local school for eight years. He did not go to university. The next ten years are a blank filled by suppositions. Was he briefly a Latin teacher, a soldier, a sea-faring explorer? Was he prosecuted and whipped for poaching deer?

We do know that in 1582 he married Anne Hathaway, eight years his senior, and three months pregnant. Two more children – twins – were born three years later but, by around 1590, Will had left Stratford to pursue a theatre career in London. Shakespeare's apprenticeship began as an actor and "pen for hire". He learned his craft the hard way. He soon won fame as a playwright with often-staged popular hits.

He and his colleagues formed a stage company, the Lord Chamberlain's Men, which built the famous Globe Theatre. It opened in 1599 but was destroyed by fire in 1613 during a performance of *Henry VIII* which used gunpowder special effects. It was rebuilt in brick the following year.

Shakespeare was a financially successful writer who invested his money wisely in property. In 1597, he bought an enormous house in Stratford, and in 1608 became a shareholder in London's Blackfriars Theatre. He also redeemed the family's honour by acquiring a personal coat of arms.

Shakespeare wrote over 40 works, including poems, "lost" plays and collaborations, in a career spanning nearly 25 years. He retired to Stratford in 1613, where he died on 23rd April 1616, aged 52, apparently of a fever after a "merry meeting" of drinks with friends. Shakespeare did in fact die on St George's Day! He was buried "full 17 foot deep" in Holy Trinity Church, Stratford, and left an epitaph cursing anyone who dared disturb his bones.

There have been preposterous theories disputing Shakespeare's authorship. Some claim that Sir Francis Bacon (1561–1626), philosopher and Lord Chancellor, was the real author of Shakespeare's plays. Others propose Edward de Vere, Earl of Oxford (1550–1604), or, even more weirdly, Queen Elizabeth I. The implication is that the "real" Shakespeare had to be a university graduate or an aristocrat. Nothing less would do for the world's greatest writer.

Shakespeare is mysteriously hidden behind his work. His life will not tell us what inspired his genius.

MANGA SHAKESPEARE

Praise for
Manga Shakespeare:

ALA Quick Pick
ALA Best Books for Young Adults
New York Public Library Best Book
for the Teen Age

978-0-8109-4222-6
$10.95 paperback

978-0-8109-4323-0
$10.95 paperback

978-0-8109-8351-9
$10.95 paperback

978-0-8109-8350-2
$10.95 paperback

978-0-8109-9324-2
$10.95 paperback

978-0-8109-7072-4
$10.95 paperback

978-0-8109-7073-1
$10.95 paperback

978-0-8109-9475-1
$10.95 paperback

978-0-8109-9325-9
$10.95 paperback

978-0-8109-9476-8
$10.95 paperback